hatsu haru

13

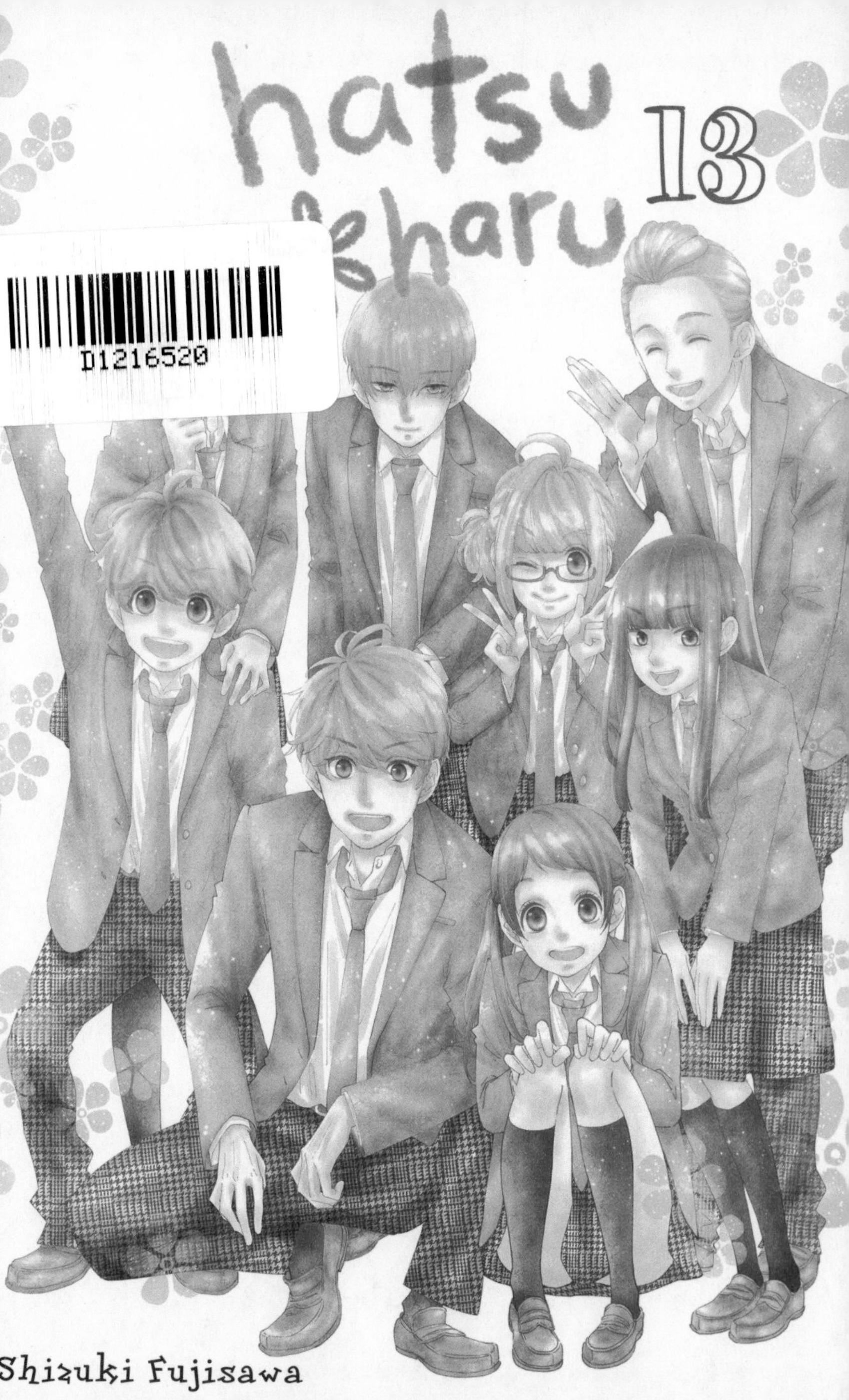

Shizuki Fujisawa

CONTENTS

hatsu ✳ haru

13

Thank you so much for picking up the last volume of HATSU ✳ HARU!

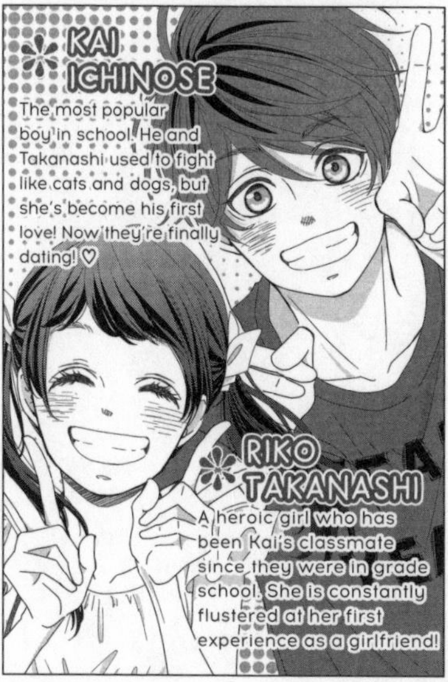
KAI ICHINOSE
The most popular boy in school. He and Takanashi used to fight like cats and dogs, but she's become his first love! Now they're finally dating! ♡
RIKO TAKANASHI
A heroic girl who has been Kai's classmate since they were in grade school. She is constantly flustered at her first experience as a girlfriend!

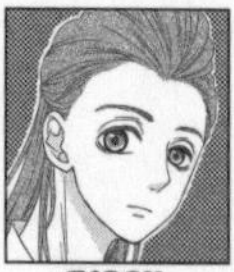

TAROU TORAMARU

The heir to a Buddhist temple and the heiress to a Shinto shrine. Childhood friends. Kagura has an instinctual disdain for playboy Tora, but...!?

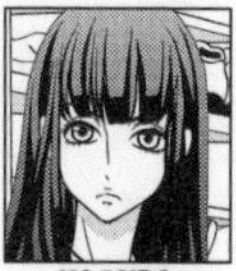

KAGURA TATSUNAMI

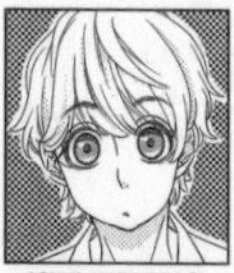

MIKI KIRITANI

A pure and innocent couple whose love level is always rising. ♡ Their height difference doesn't bother them one bit. ♡

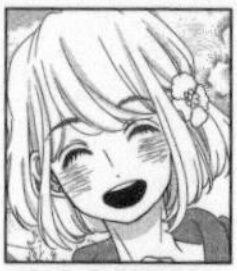

KIYO OOSHIMA

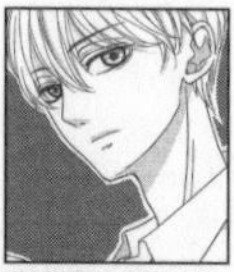

TAKAYA MISAKI

They became a fake couple to help Kai and Riko get together, but...?

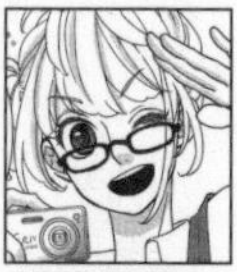

AYUMI SHIMURA

STORY

● Kai, the school's most popular playboy, falls in love for the first time with his combative and short-tempered childhood friend, Riko Takanashi! After some time struggling with their feelings for each other, they have finally started dating! ♡ Despite an awkward start, they gradually grow closer.

● While on the class trip Kagura confesses to Tora that she has been in love with him. Tora doesn't understand what it means to be in love with someone, and it takes some help from Kai and Father John before he realizes that he loves Kagura back, and they become a couple.

● Meanwhile, Taka and Ayumi's relationship is discovered by her father, and mayhem ensues!? But Taka's efforts are rewarded, Ayumi's father approves of their relationship, and their bond grows even stronger...♡

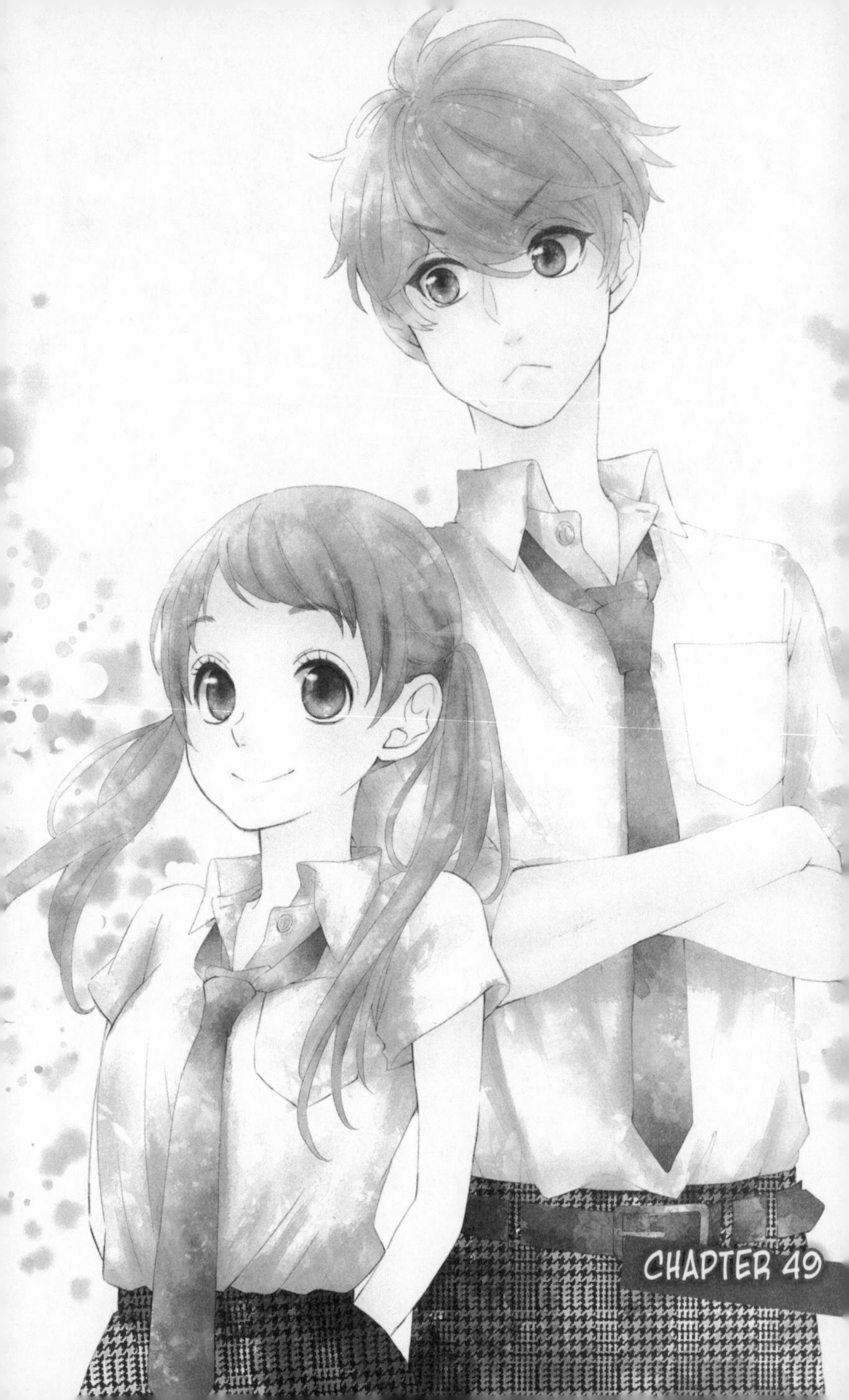
CHAPTER 49

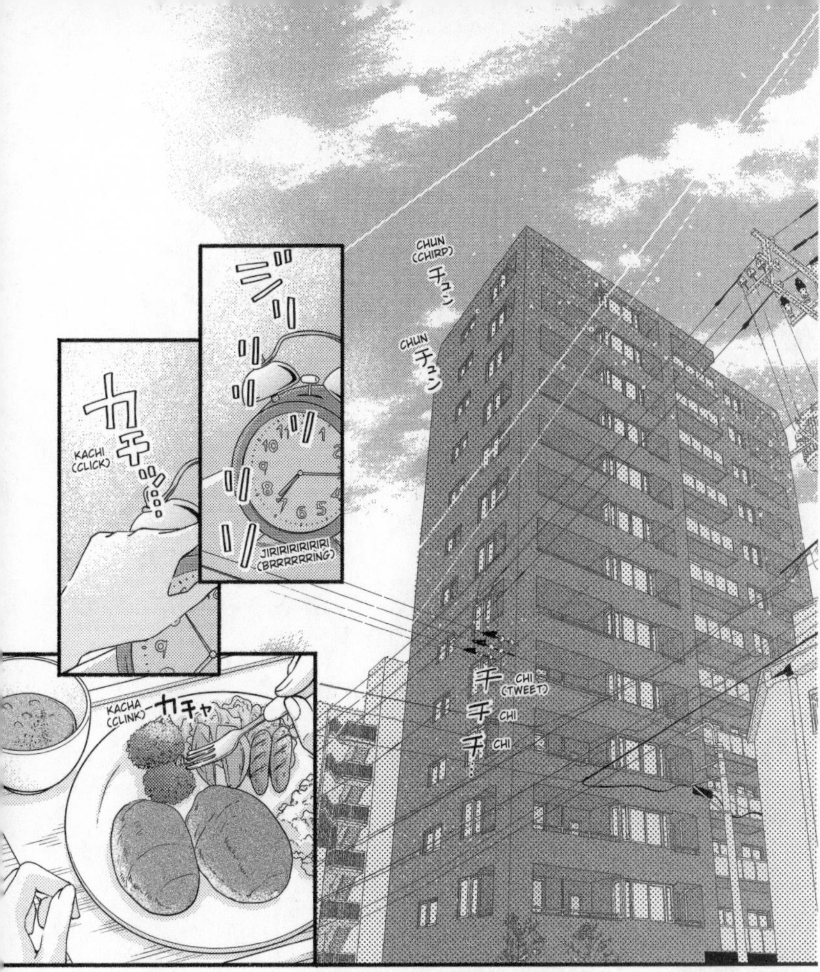
CHUN (CHIRP) チュン
CHUN チュン
CHI (TWEET) チ
CHI チ
CHI チ
ジリリリリリリ
JIRIRIRIRIRIRI (BRRRRRRING)
カチ
KACHI (CLICK)
KACHA (CLINK) カチャ

hatsu haru

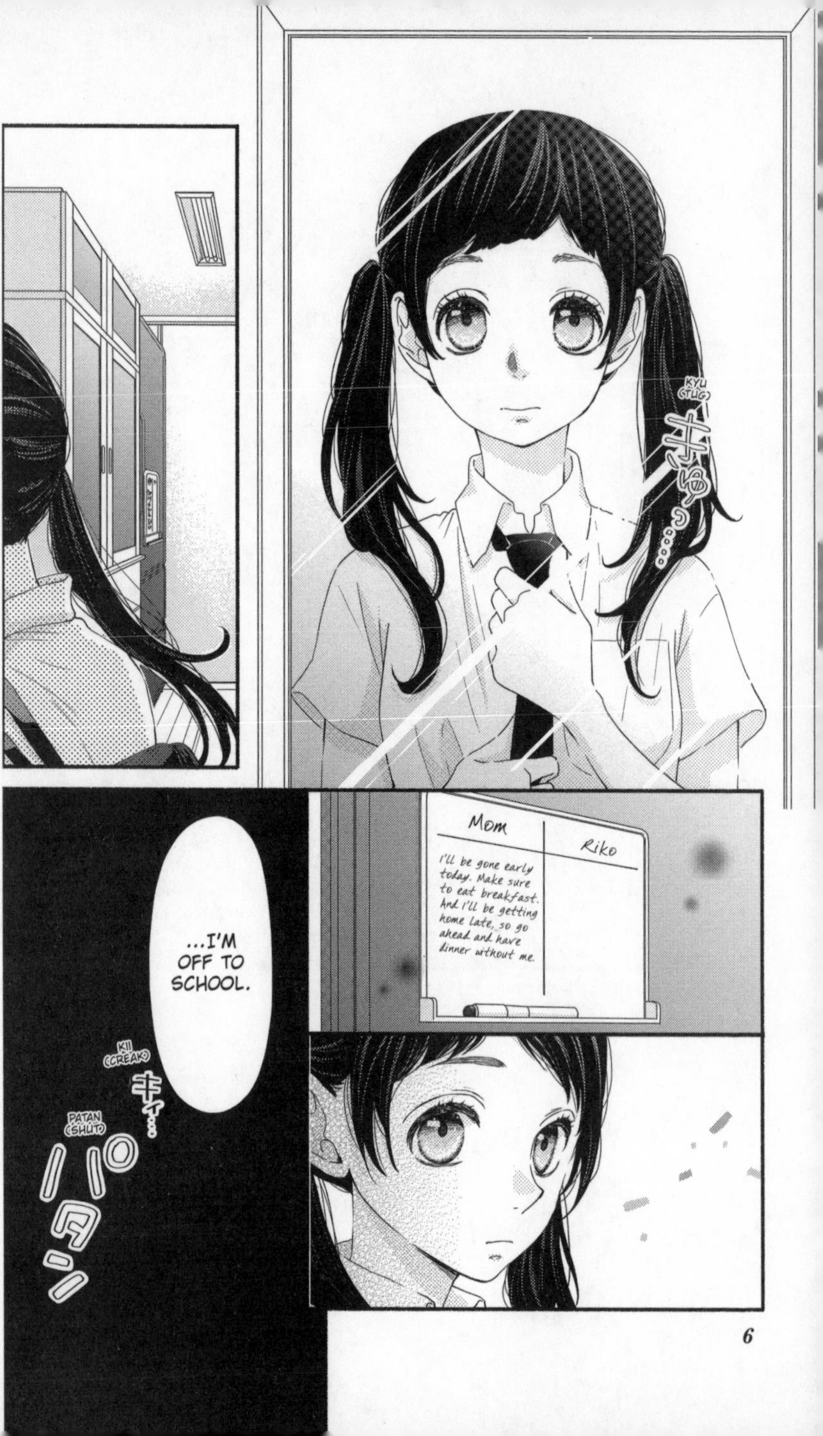
KYU (TUG)
きゅっ…
Mom
Riko
I'll be gone early today. Make sure to eat breakfast. And I'll be getting home late, so go ahead and have dinner without me.
...I'M OFF TO SCHOOL.
KII (CREAK)
キィ…
PATAN (SHUT)
パタン

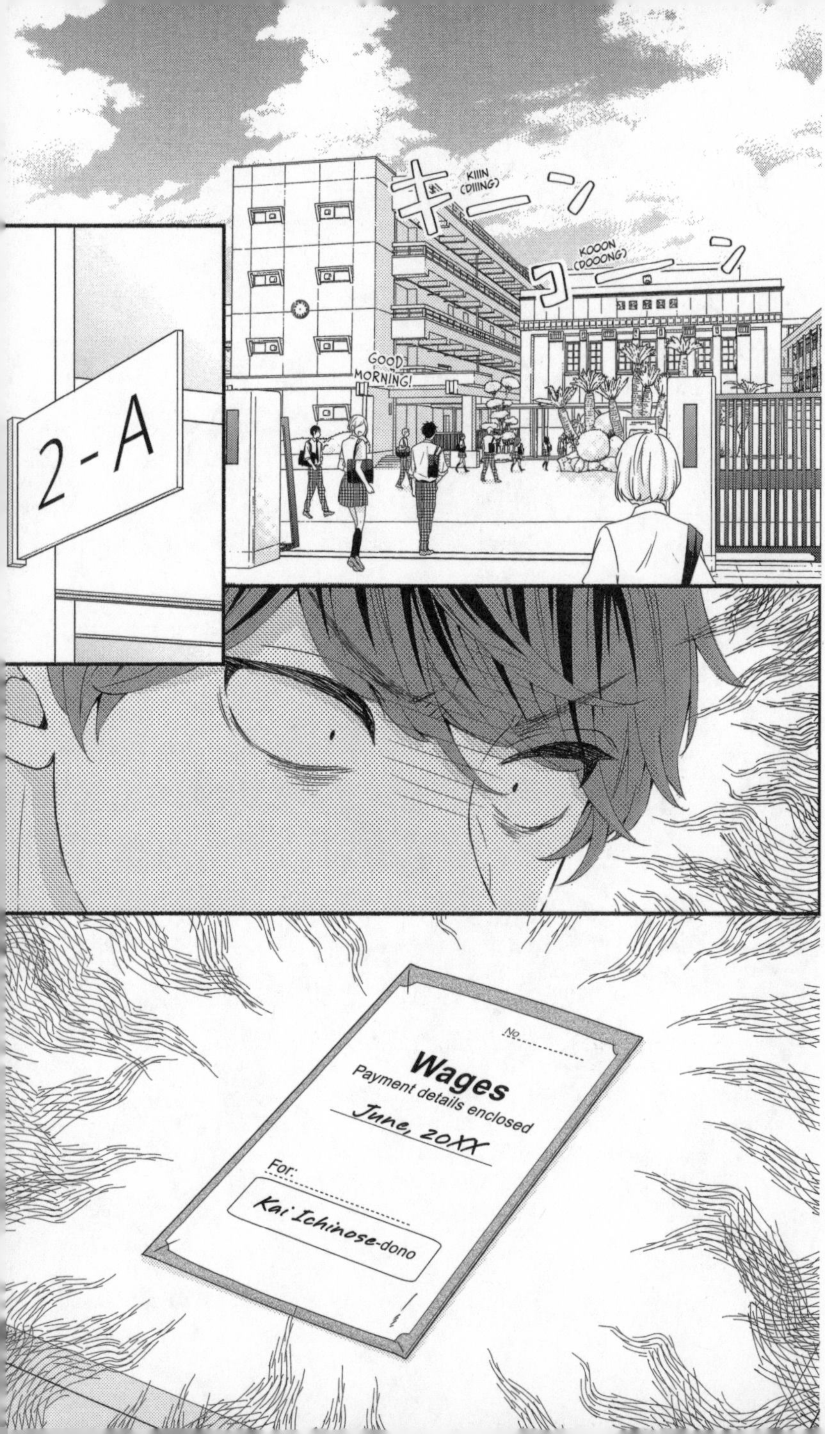
KIIIN (DIIING)
KOOON (DOOONG)
GOOD MORNING!
2-A
No.
Wages
Payment details enclosed
June, 20XX
For:
Kai Ichinose-dono

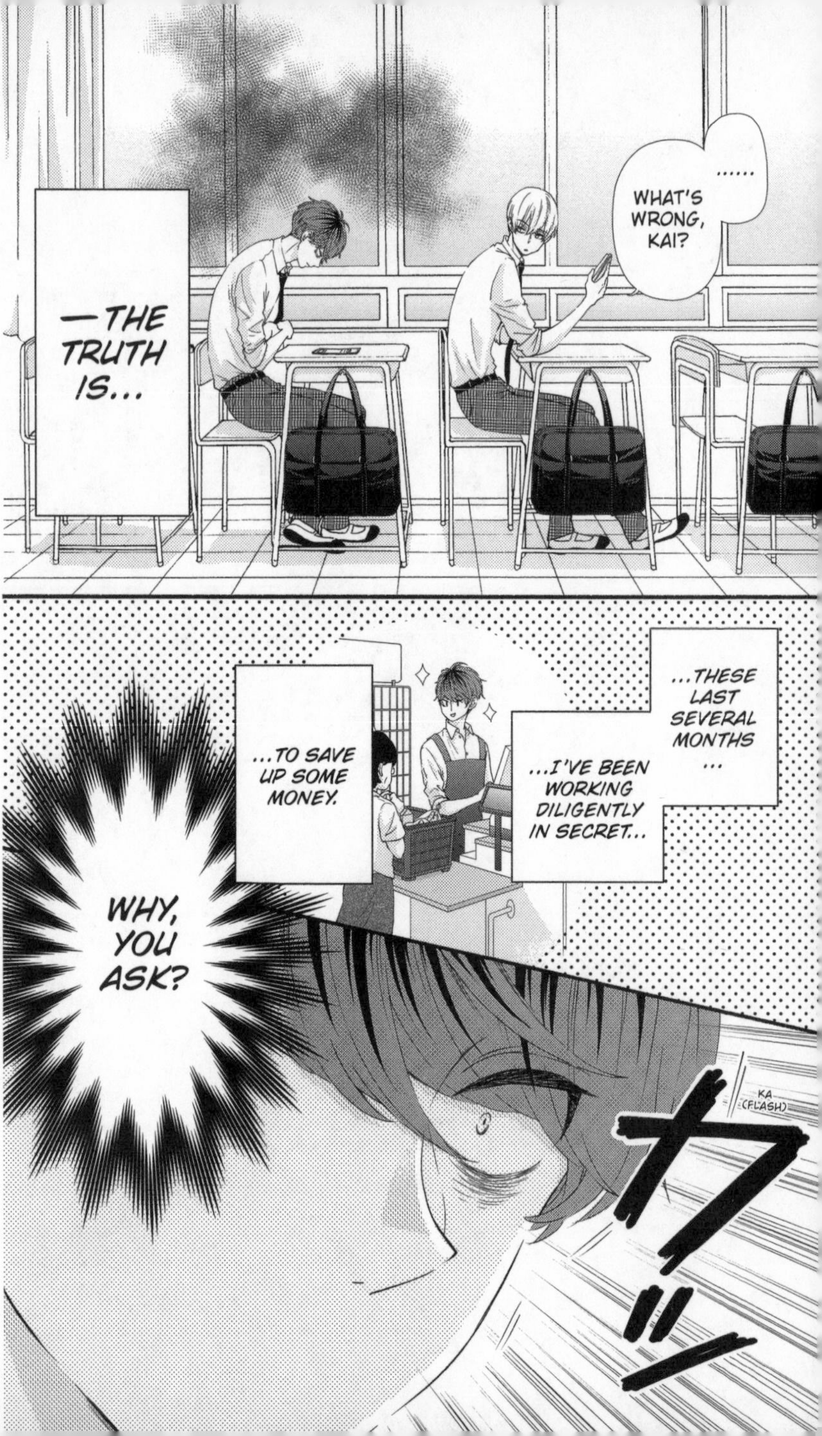
......
WHAT'S WRONG, KAI?
—THE TRUTH IS...
...THESE LAST SEVERAL MONTHS ...
...I'VE BEEN WORKING DILIGENTLY IN SECRET...
...TO SAVE UP SOME MONEY.
WHY, YOU ASK?
KA (FLASH)

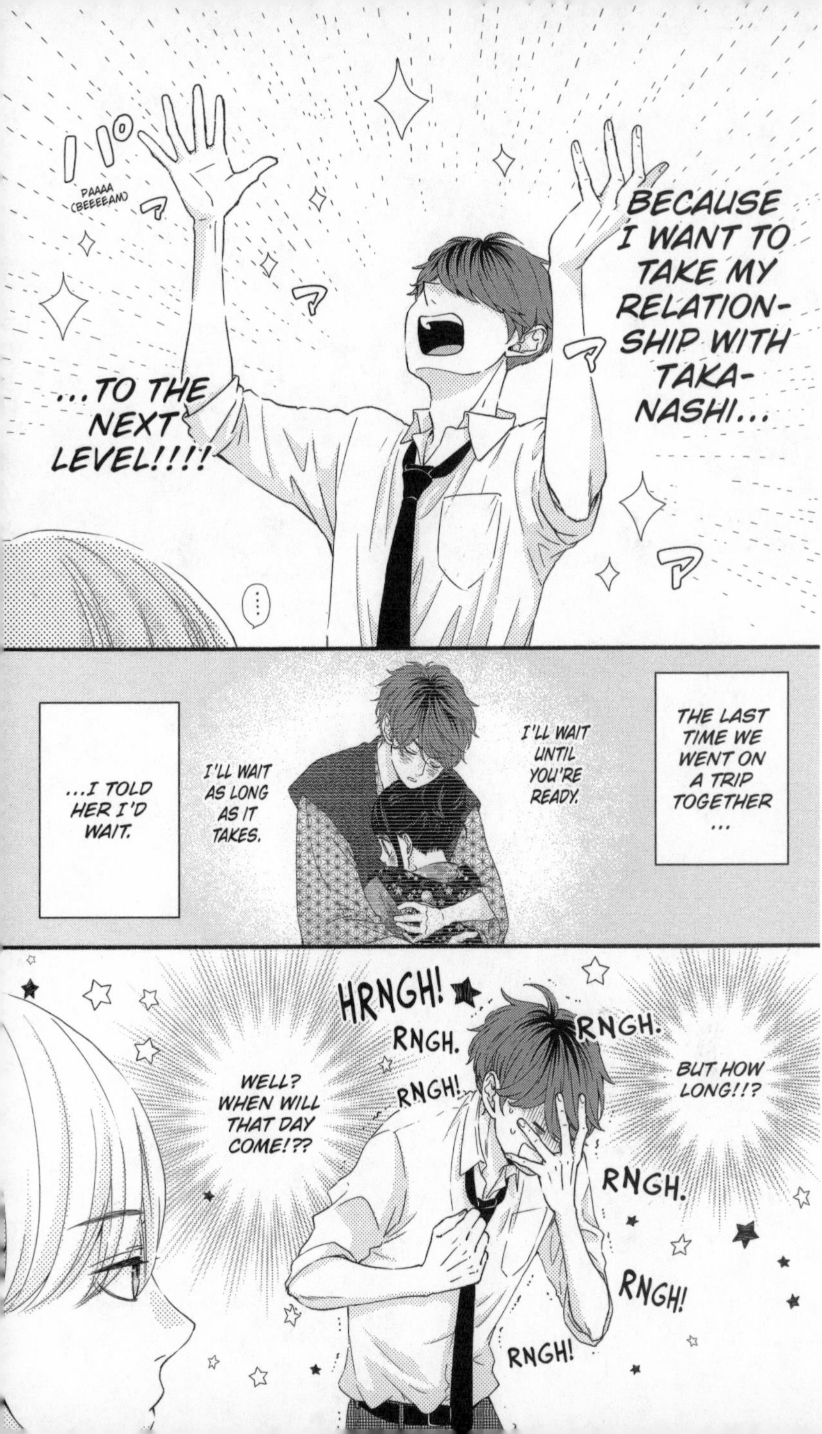
BECAUSE I WANT TO TAKE MY RELATION-SHIP WITH TAKA-NASHI...
...TO THE NEXT LEVEL!!!!
PAAAA (BEEEEAM)
......
THE LAST TIME WE WENT ON A TRIP TOGETHER...
I'LL WAIT UNTIL YOU'RE READY.
I'LL WAIT AS LONG AS IT TAKES.
...I TOLD HER I'D WAIT.
BUT HOW LONG!!?
RNGH.
HRNGH!
RNGH.
RNGH!
WELL? WHEN WILL THAT DAY COME!??
RNGH.
RNGH!
RNGH!

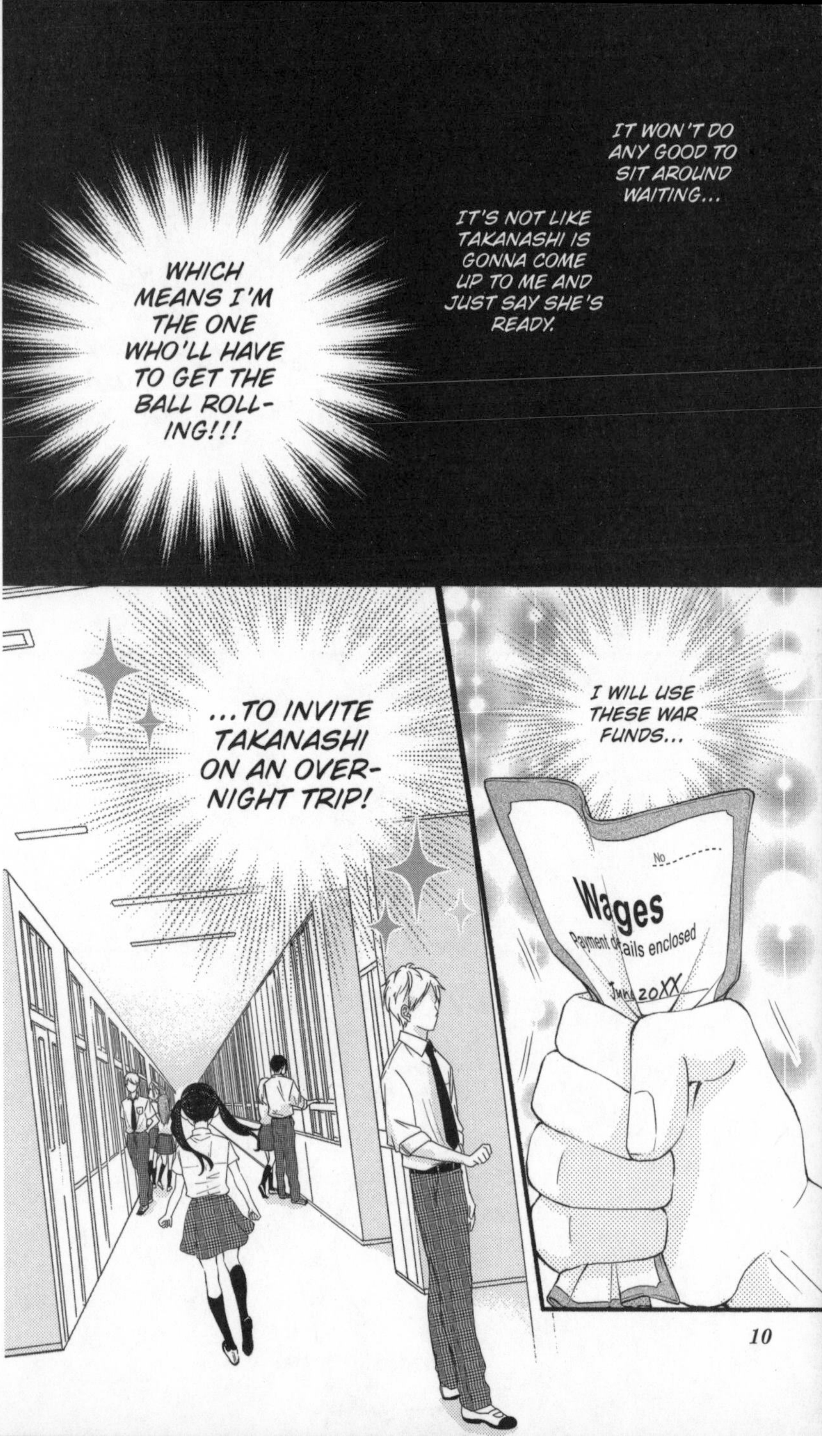
IT WON'T DO ANY GOOD TO SIT AROUND WAITING...
IT'S NOT LIKE TAKANASHI IS GONNA COME UP TO ME AND JUST SAY SHE'S READY.
WHICH MEANS I'M THE ONE WHO'LL HAVE TO GET THE BALL ROLL-ING!!!
I WILL USE THESE WAR FUNDS...
No
Wages
...TO INVITE TAKANASHI ON AN OVER-NIGHT TRIP!

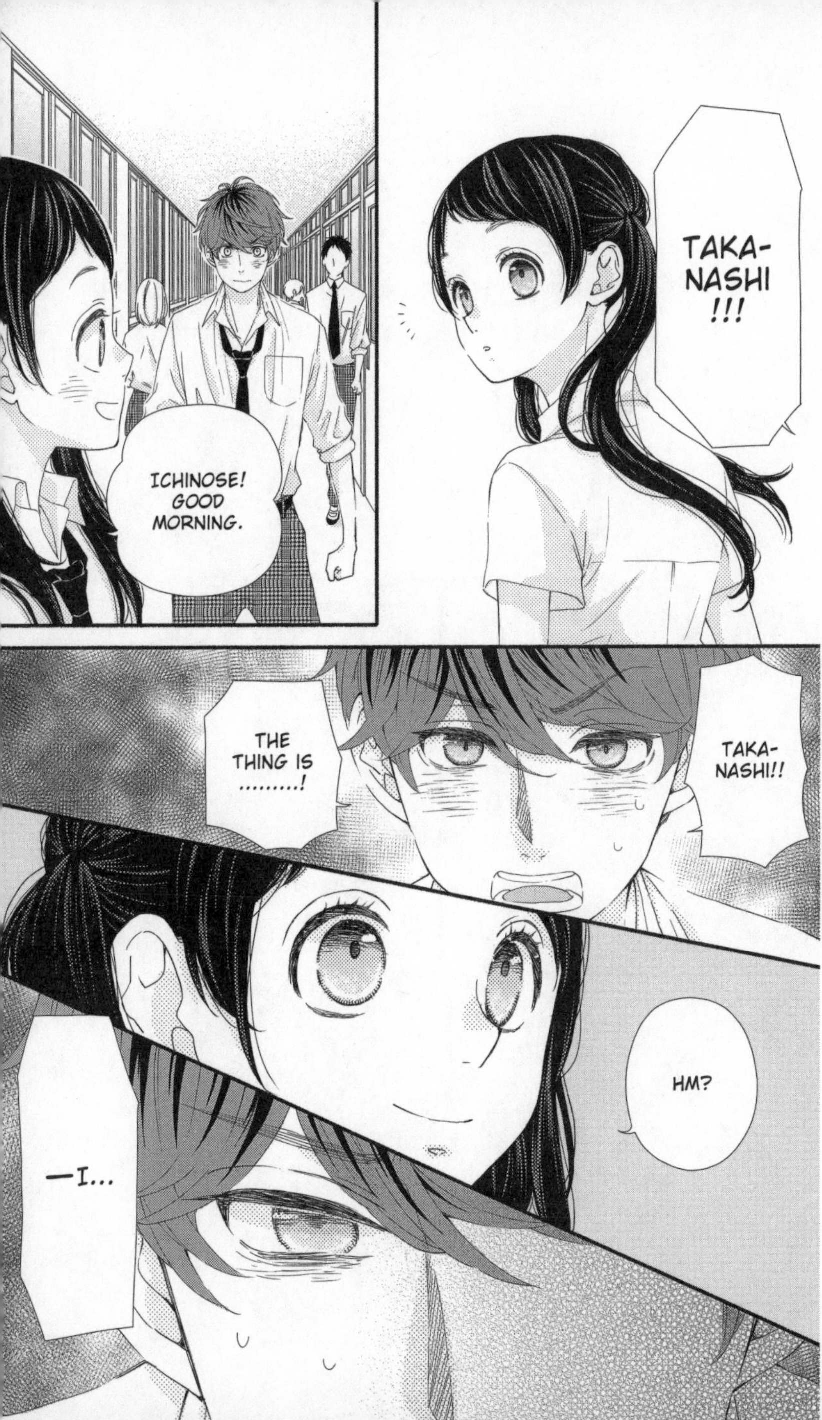
TAKA-NASHI!!!
ICHINOSE! GOOD MORNING.
TAKA-NASHI!!
THE THING IS ....!
HM?
—I...

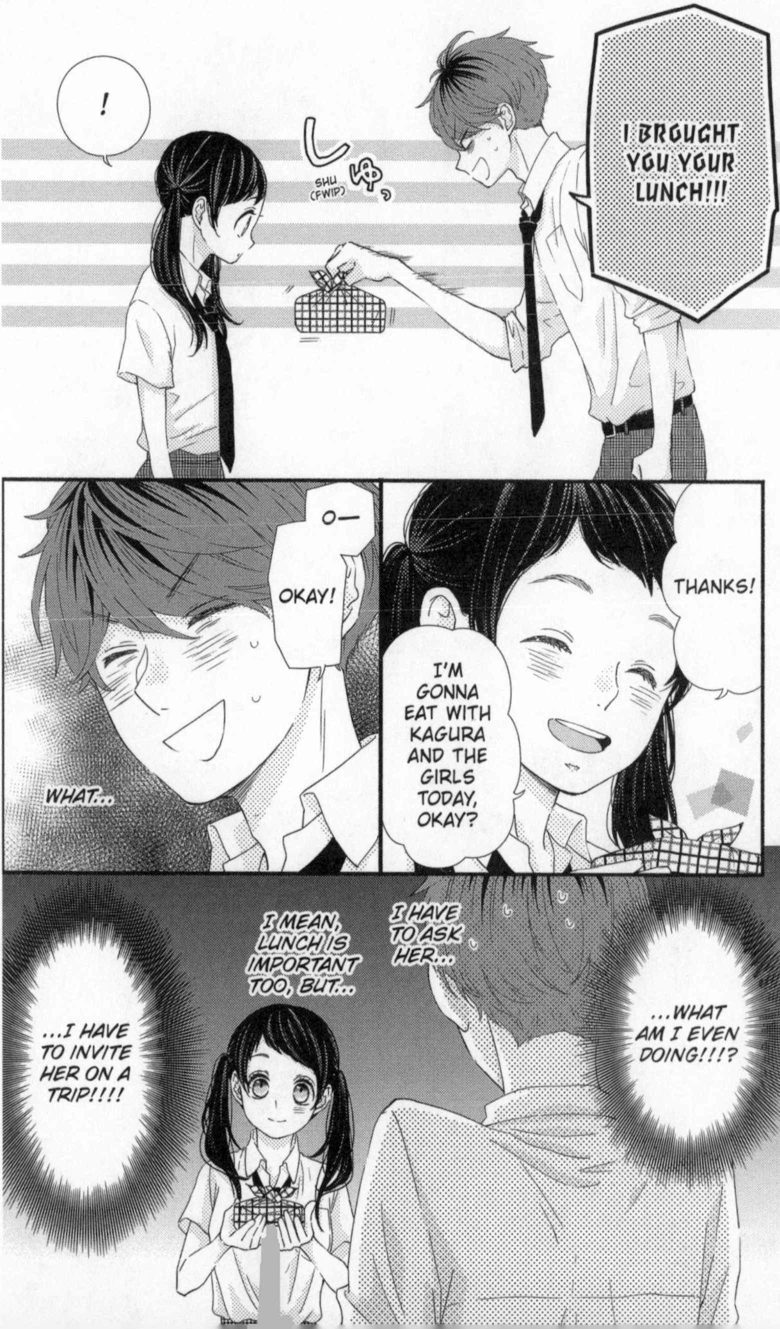
I BROUGHT YOU YOUR LUNCH!!!
しゅっ
SHU (FWIP)
!
THANKS!
I'M GONNA EAT WITH KAGURA AND THE GIRLS TODAY, OKAY?
O—
OKAY!
WHAT...
...WHAT AM I EVEN DOING!!!?
I HAVE TO ASK HER...
I MEAN, LUNCH IS IMPORTANT TOO, BUT...
...I HAVE TO INVITE HER ON A TRIP!!!!

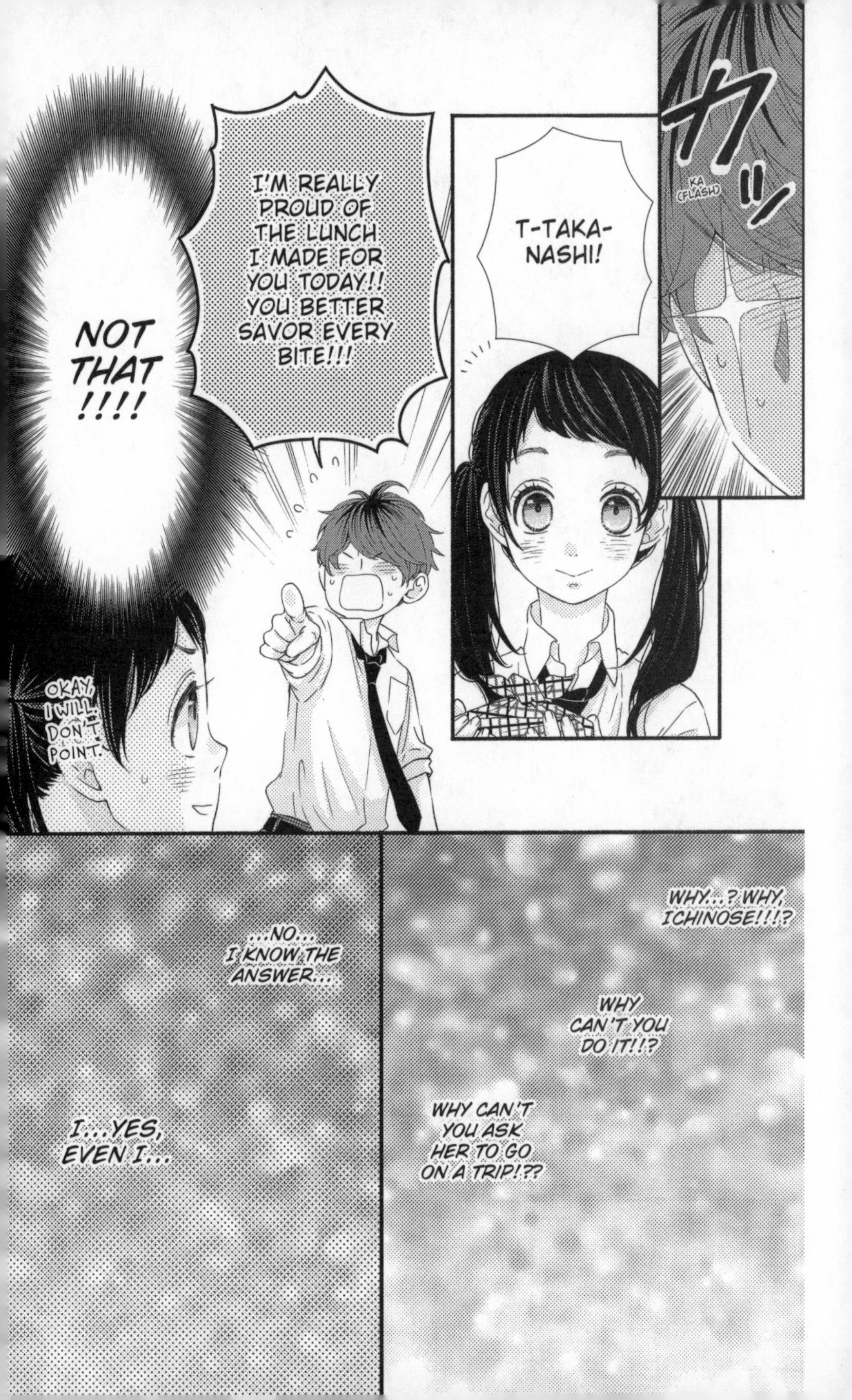
KA (FLASH)
T-TAKA-NASHI!
I'M REALLY PROUD OF THE LUNCH I MADE FOR YOU TODAY!! YOU BETTER SAVOR EVERY BITE!!!
NOT THAT!!!!
OKAY, I WILL. DON'T POINT.
WHY...? WHY, ICHINOSE!!!?
WHY CAN'T YOU DO IT!!?
WHY CAN'T YOU ASK HER TO GO ON A TRIP!??
...NO... I KNOW THE ANSWER...
I...YES, EVEN I...

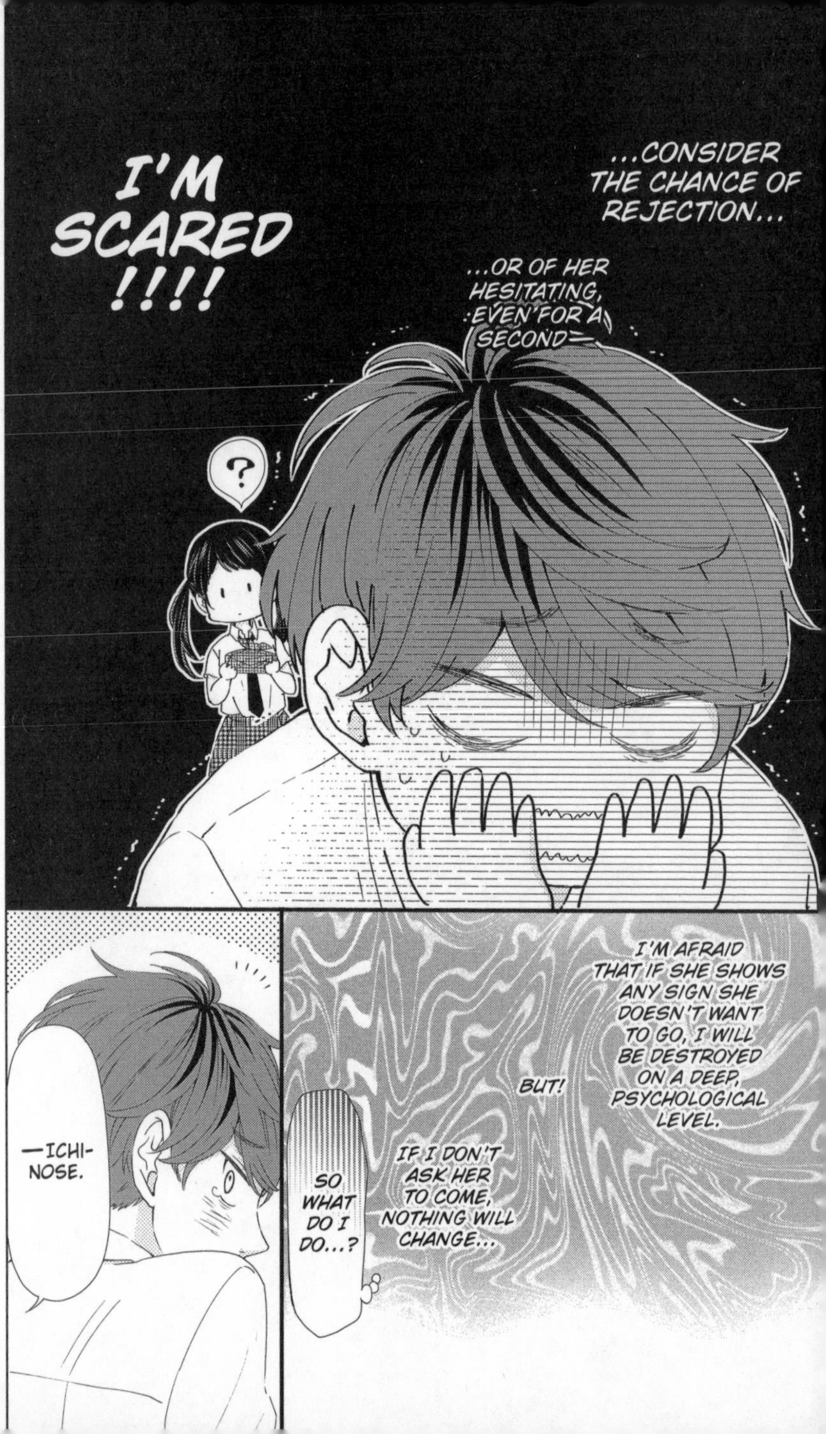
...CONSIDER THE CHANCE OF REJECTION...
...OR OF HER HESITATING, EVEN FOR A SECOND—
I'M SCARED!!!!
?
I'M AFRAID THAT IF SHE SHOWS ANY SIGN SHE DOESN'T WANT TO GO, I WILL BE DESTROYED ON A DEEP, PSYCHOLOGICAL LEVEL.
BUT!
IF I DON'T ASK HER TO COME, NOTHING WILL CHANGE...
SO WHAT DO I DO...?
—ICHI-NOSE.

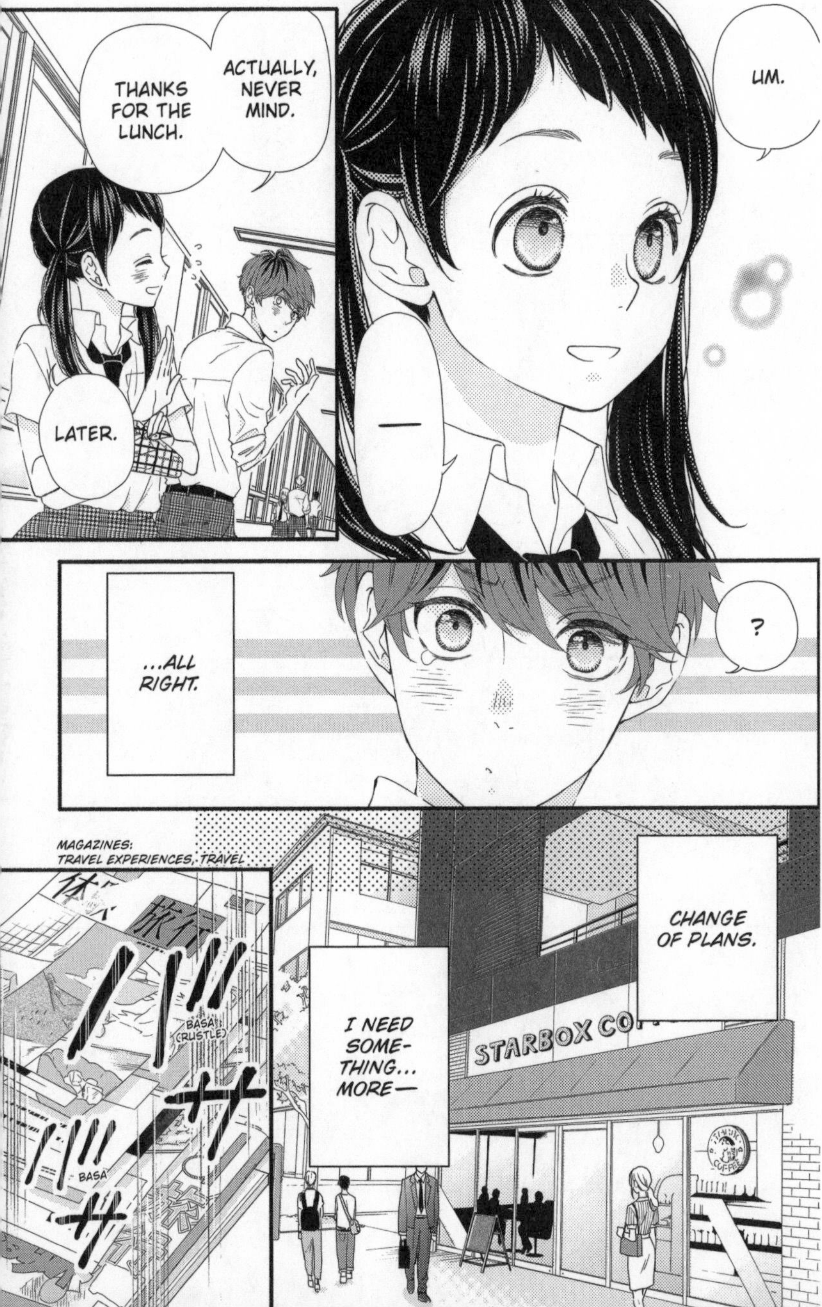
UM.
—
ACTUALLY, NEVER MIND.
THANKS FOR THE LUNCH.
LATER.
?
...ALL RIGHT.
CHANGE OF PLANS.
STARBOX CO
I NEED SOME-THING... MORE—
MAGAZINES: TRAVEL EXPERIENCES, TRAVEL
BASA (RUSTLE)
BASA

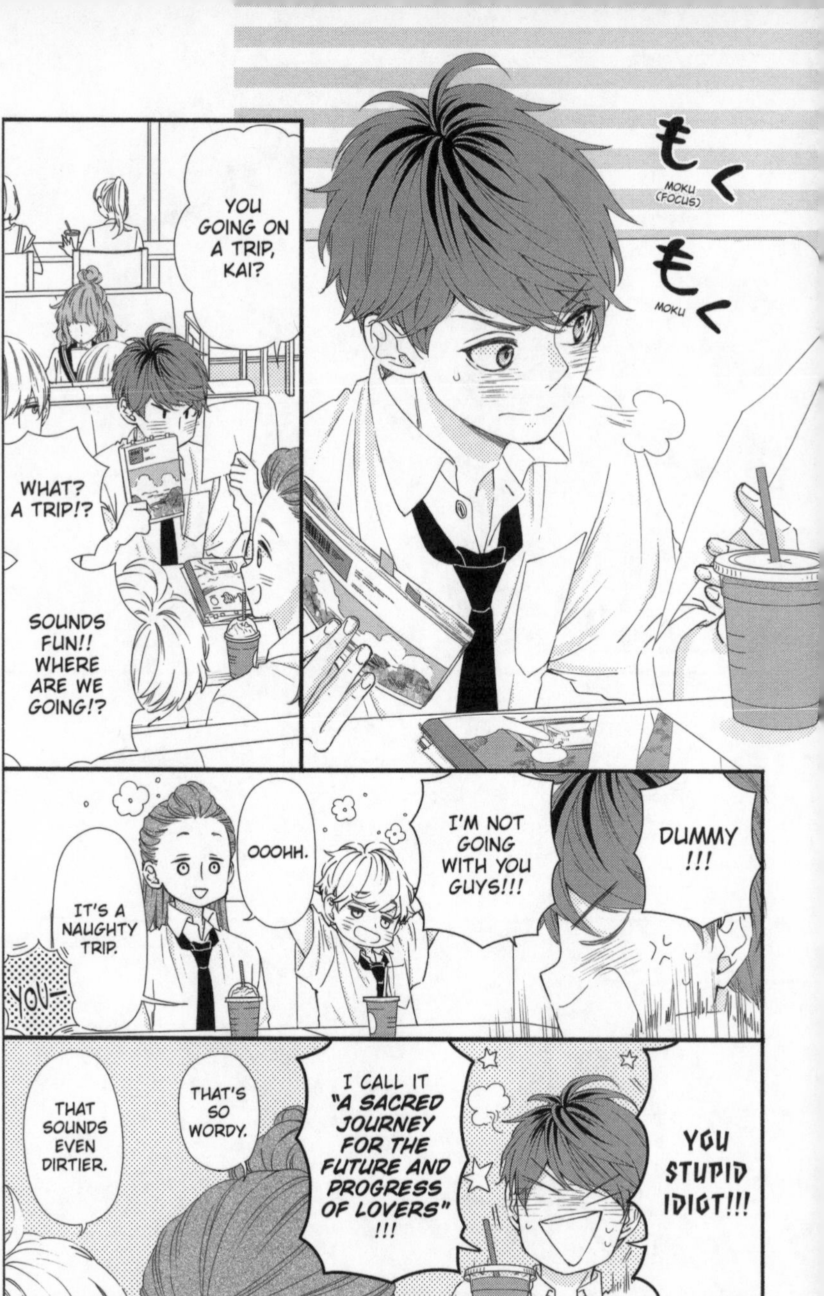
もく
MOKU (FOCUS)
もく
MOKU
YOU GOING ON A TRIP, KAI?
WHAT? A TRIP!?
SOUNDS FUN!! WHERE ARE WE GOING!?
DUMMY !!!
I'M NOT GOING WITH YOU GUYS!!!
OOOHH.
IT'S A NAUGHTY TRIP.
YOU—
YOU STUPID IDIOT!!!
I CALL IT *"A SACRED JOURNEY FOR THE FUTURE AND PROGRESS OF LOVERS"* !!!
THAT'S SO WORDY.
THAT SOUNDS EVEN DIRTIER.

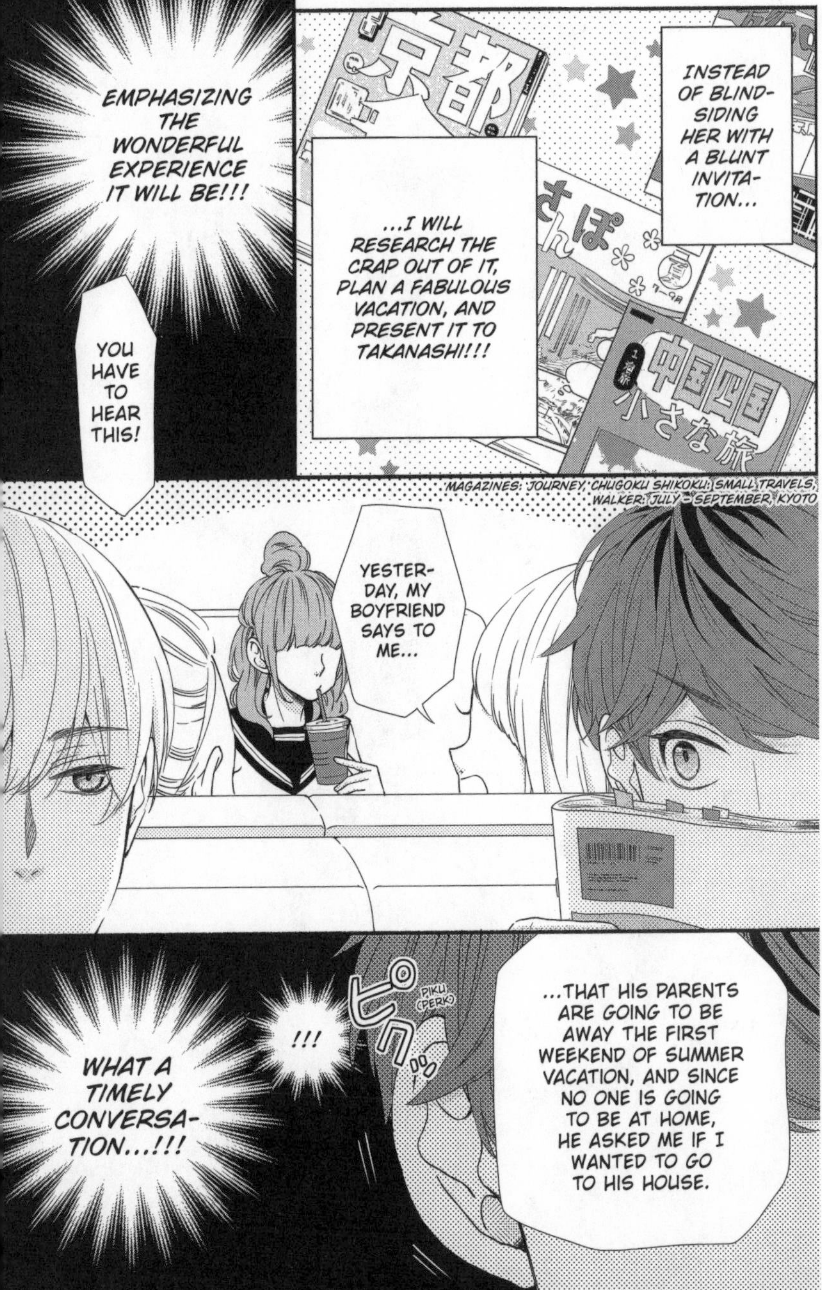
INSTEAD OF BLIND-SIDING HER WITH A BLUNT INVITA-TION...
...I WILL RESEARCH THE CRAP OUT OF IT, PLAN A FABULOUS VACATION, AND PRESENT IT TO TAKANASHI!!!
EMPHASIZING THE WONDERFUL EXPERIENCE IT WILL BE!!!
YOU HAVE TO HEAR THIS!
MAGAZINES: JOURNEY, CHUGOKU SHIKOKU: SMALL TRAVELS, WALKER: JULY - SEPTEMBER, KYOTO
YESTER-DAY, MY BOYFRIEND SAYS TO ME...
...THAT HIS PARENTS ARE GOING TO BE AWAY THE FIRST WEEKEND OF SUMMER VACATION, AND SINCE NO ONE IS GOING TO BE AT HOME, HE ASKED ME IF I WANTED TO GO TO HIS HOUSE.
PIKU (PERK)
!!!
WHAT A TIMELY CONVERSA-TION...!!!

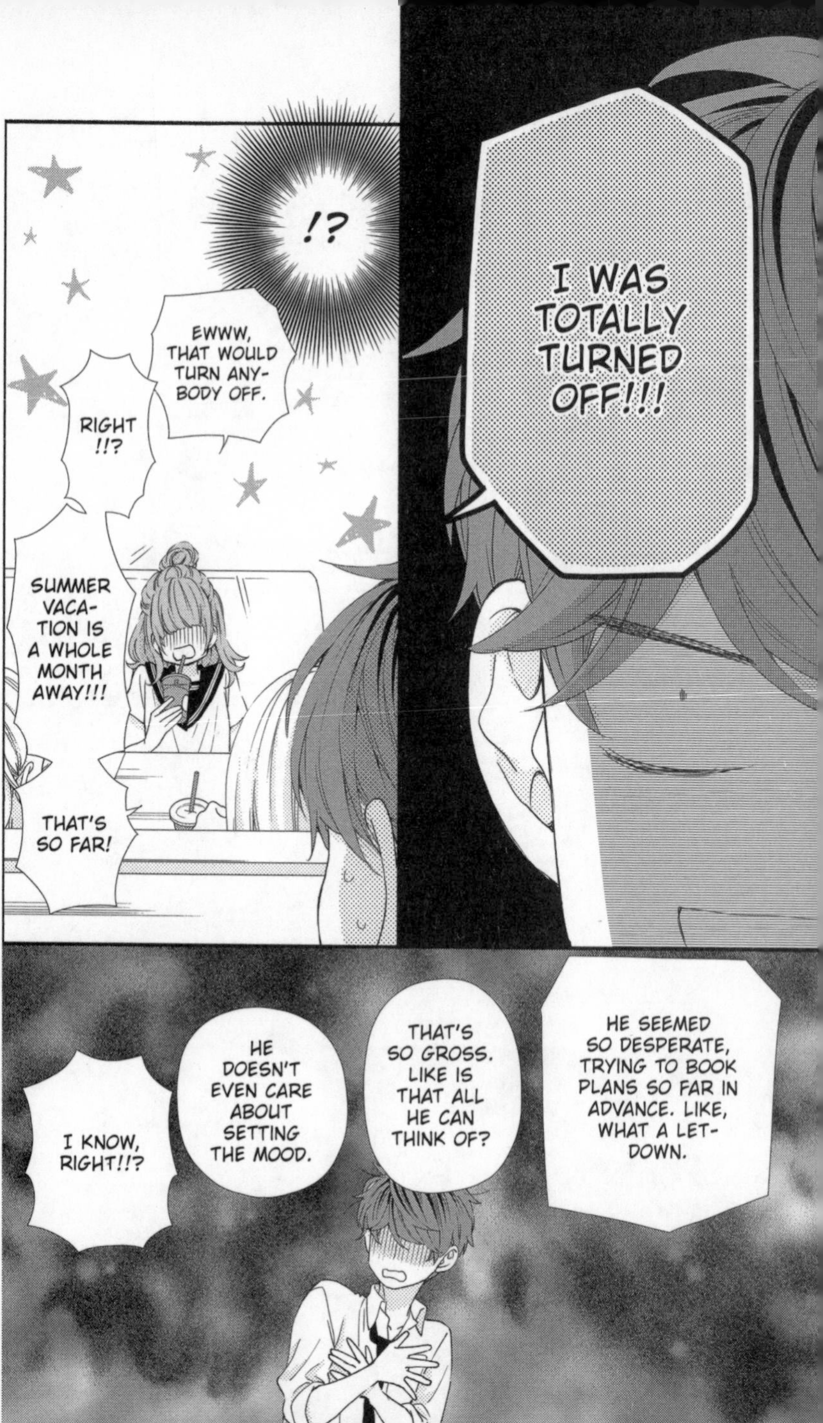
I WAS TOTALLY TURNED OFF!!!
!?
EWWW, THAT WOULD TURN ANY-BODY OFF.
RIGHT !!?
SUMMER VACA-TION IS A WHOLE MONTH AWAY!!!
THAT'S SO FAR!
HE SEEMED SO DESPERATE, TRYING TO BOOK PLANS SO FAR IN ADVANCE. LIKE, WHAT A LET-DOWN.
THAT'S SO GROSS. LIKE IS THAT ALL HE CAN THINK OF?
HE DOESN'T EVEN CARE ABOUT SETTING THE MOOD.
I KNOW, RIGHT!!?

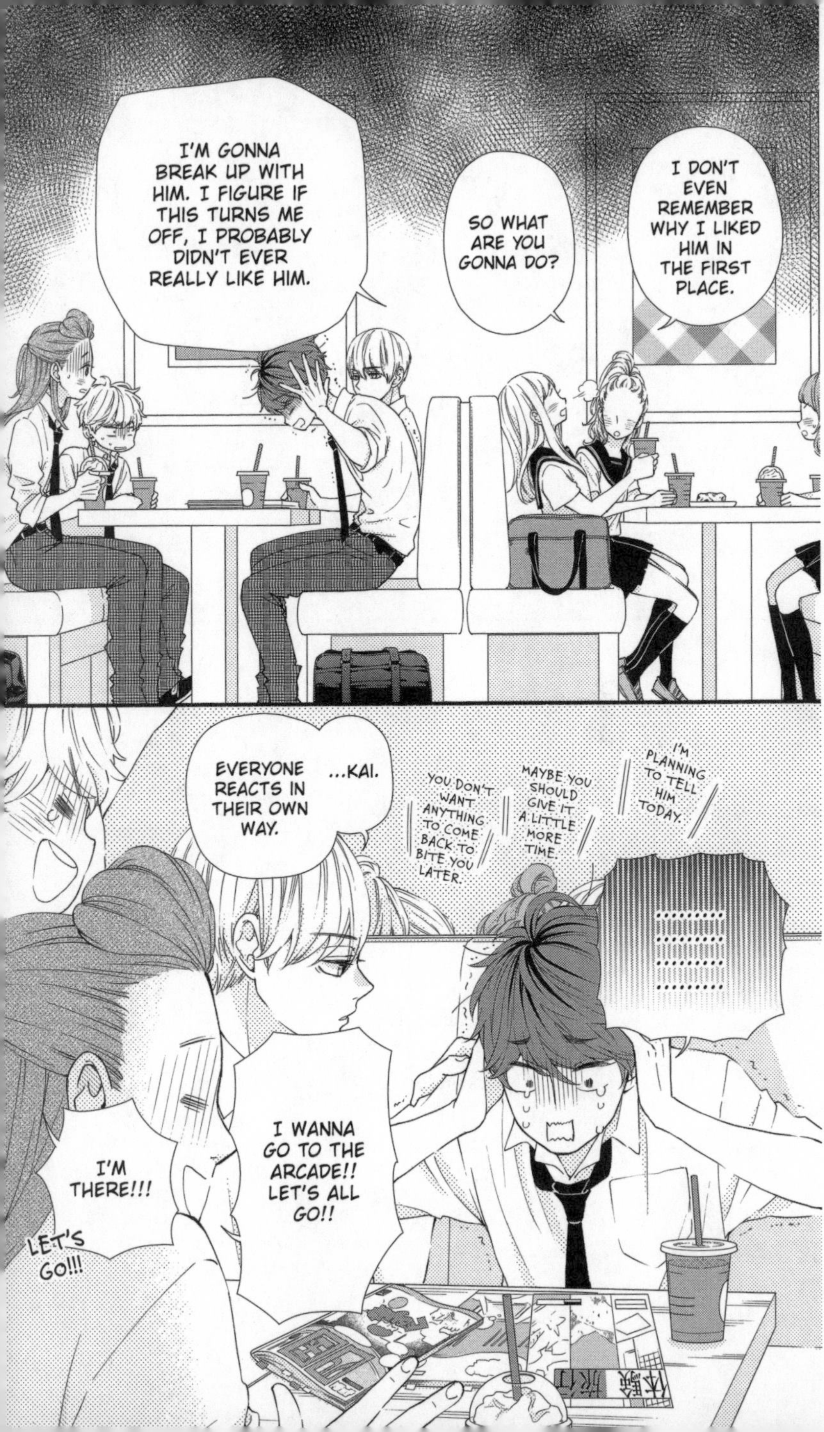
I DON'T EVEN REMEMBER WHY I LIKED HIM IN THE FIRST PLACE.
SO WHAT ARE YOU GONNA DO?
I'M GONNA BREAK UP WITH HIM. I FIGURE IF THIS TURNS ME OFF, I PROBABLY DIDN'T EVER REALLY LIKE HIM.
I'M PLANNING TO TELL HIM TODAY.
MAYBE YOU SHOULD GIVE IT A LITTLE MORE TIME.
YOU DON'T WANT ANYTHING TO COME BACK TO BITE YOU LATER.
...KAI.
EVERYONE REACTS IN THEIR OWN WAY.
I WANNA GO TO THE ARCADE!! LET'S ALL GO!!
I'M THERE!!!
LET'S GO!!!

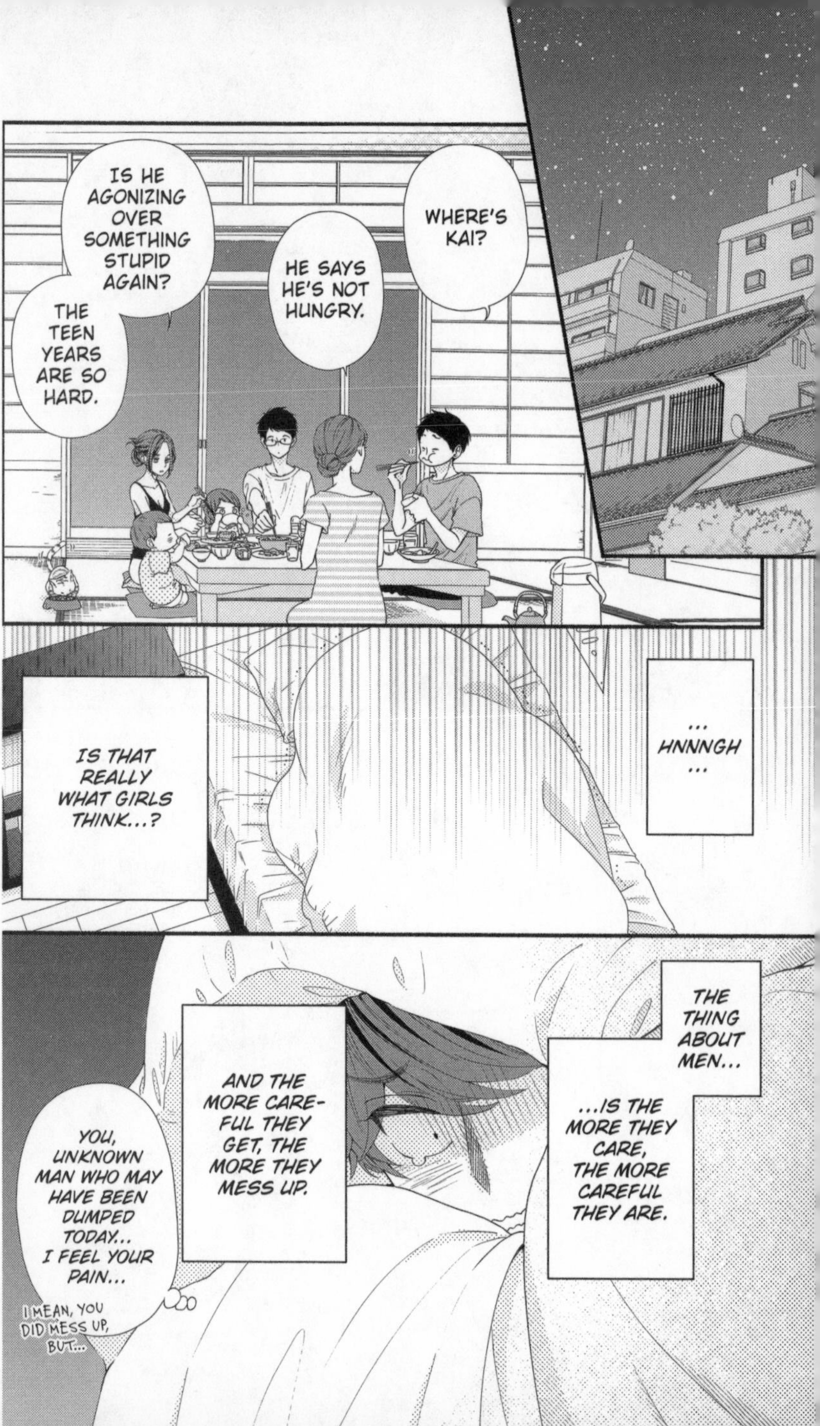
WHERE'S KAI?
HE SAYS HE'S NOT HUNGRY.
IS HE AGONIZING OVER SOMETHING STUPID AGAIN?
THE TEEN YEARS ARE SO HARD.
... HNNNGH ...
IS THAT REALLY WHAT GIRLS THINK...?
THE THING ABOUT MEN...
...IS THE MORE THEY CARE, THE MORE CAREFUL THEY ARE.
AND THE MORE CARE-FUL THEY GET, THE MORE THEY MESS UP.
YOU, UNKNOWN MAN WHO MAY HAVE BEEN DUMPED TODAY... I FEEL YOUR PAIN...
I MEAN, YOU DID MESS UP, BUT...

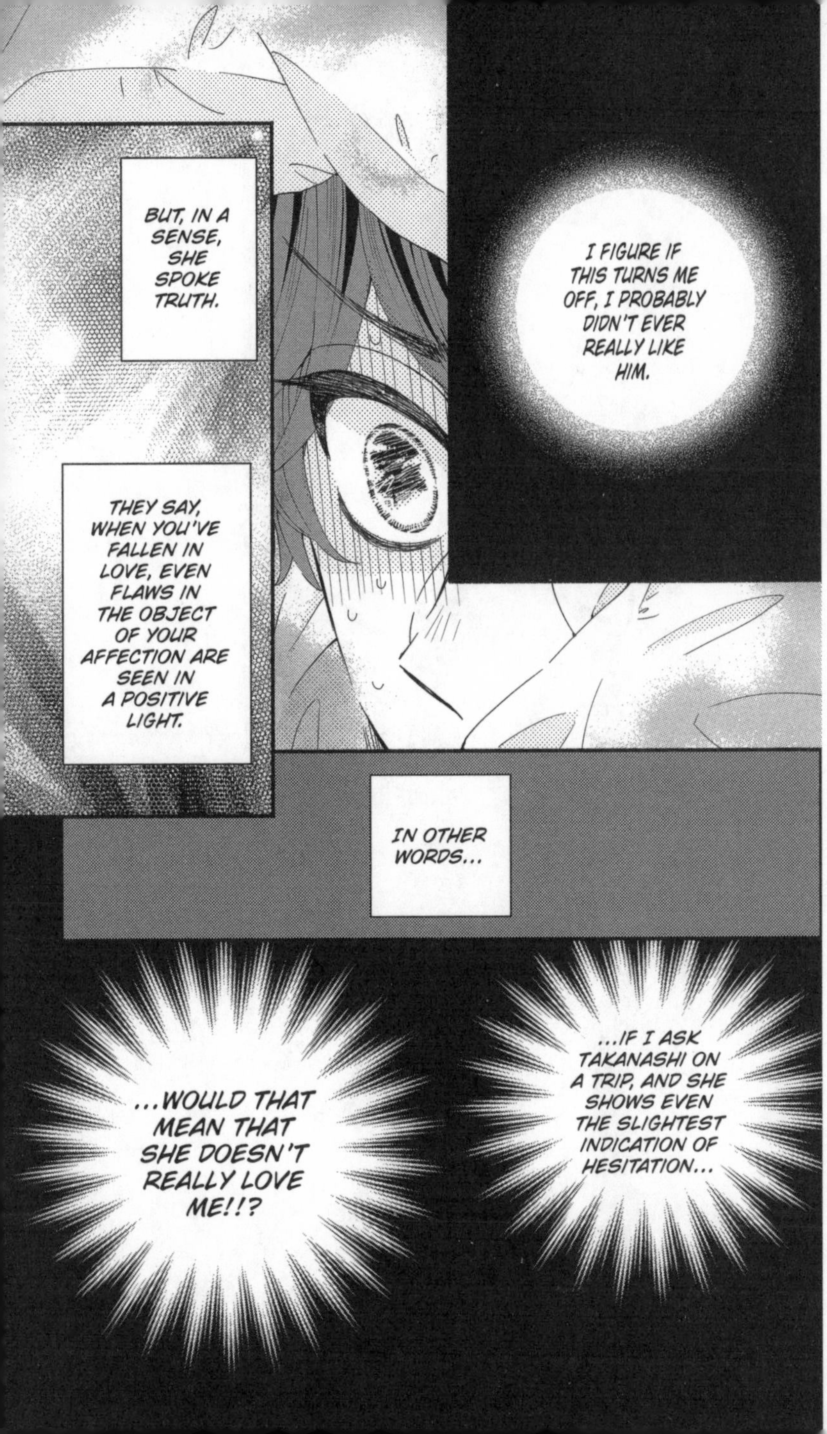
I FIGURE IF THIS TURNS ME OFF, I PROBABLY DIDN'T EVER REALLY LIKE HIM.
BUT, IN A SENSE, SHE SPOKE TRUTH.
THEY SAY, WHEN YOU'VE FALLEN IN LOVE, EVEN FLAWS IN THE OBJECT OF YOUR AFFECTION ARE SEEN IN A POSITIVE LIGHT.
IN OTHER WORDS...
...IF I ASK TAKANASHI ON A TRIP, AND SHE SHOWS EVEN THE SLIGHTEST INDICATION OF HESITATION...
...WOULD THAT MEAN THAT SHE DOESN'T REALLY LOVE ME!!?

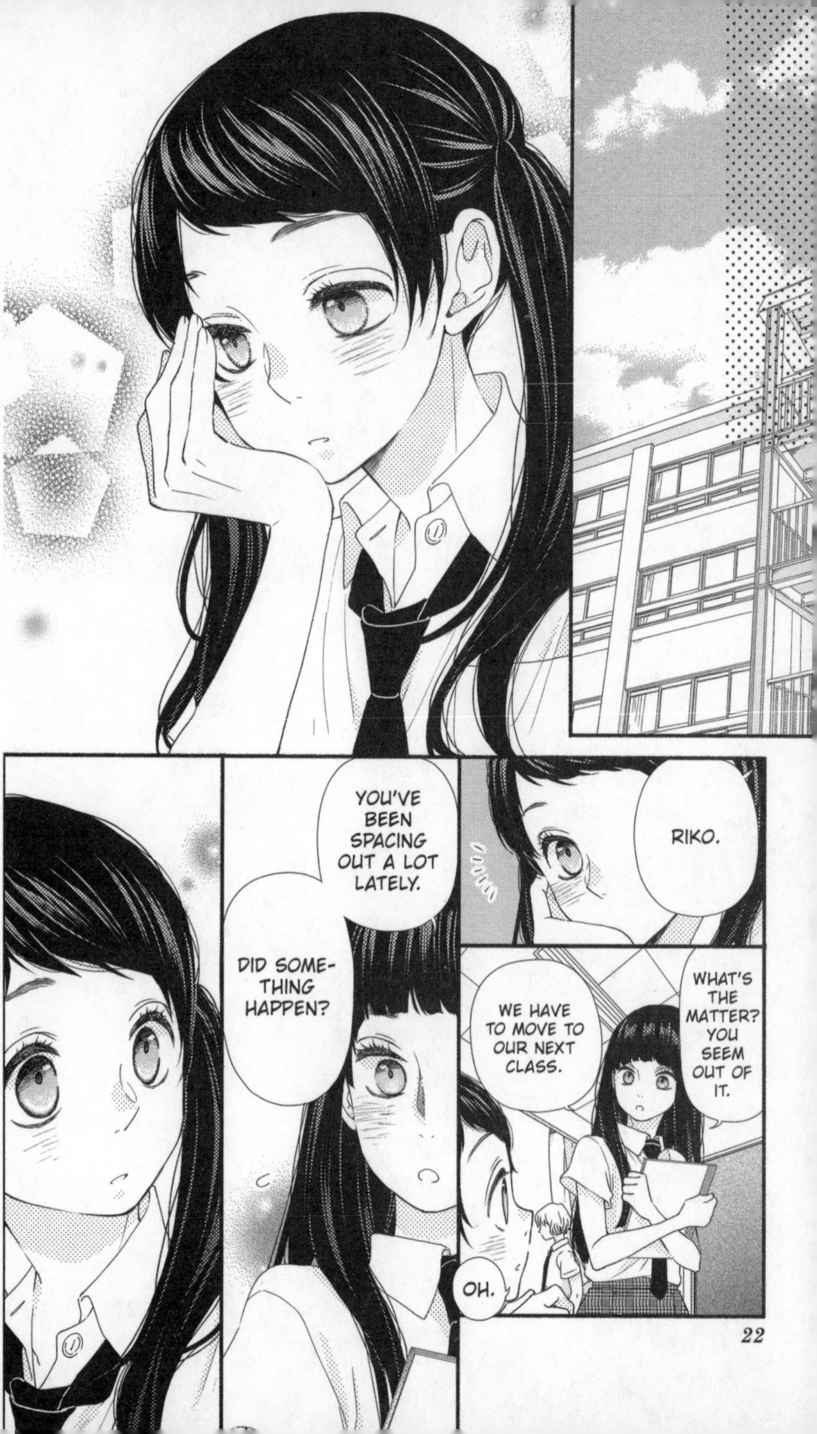
RIKO.
WHAT'S THE MATTER? YOU SEEM OUT OF IT.
WE HAVE TO MOVE TO OUR NEXT CLASS.
OH.
YOU'VE BEEN SPACING OUT A LOT LATELY.
DID SOME-THING HAPPEN?

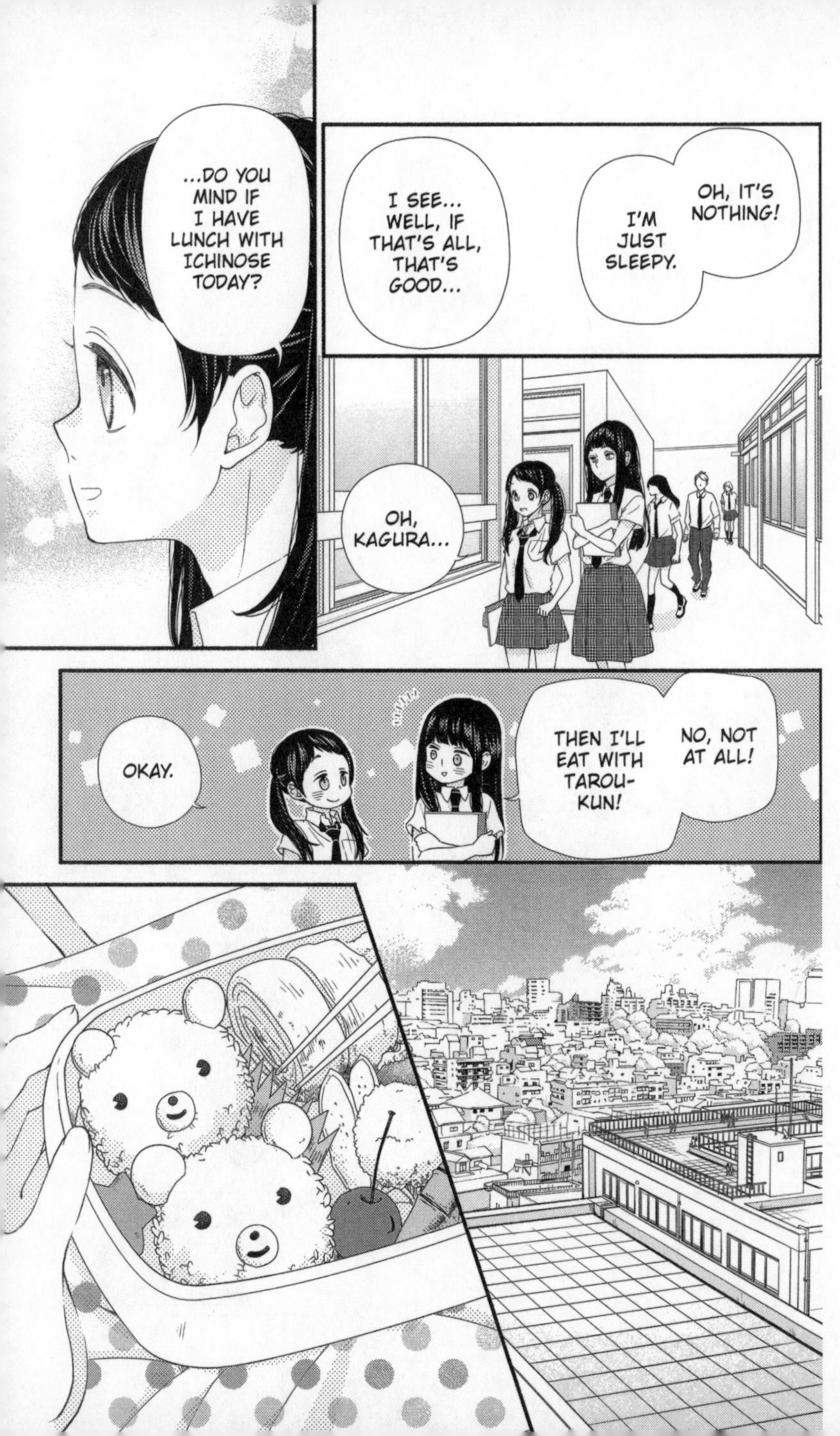
OH, IT'S NOTHING!
I'M JUST SLEEPY.
I SEE... WELL, IF THAT'S ALL, THAT'S GOOD...
OH, KAGURA...
...DO YOU MIND IF I HAVE LUNCH WITH ICHINOSE TODAY?
NO, NOT AT ALL!
THEN I'LL EAT WITH TAROU-KUN!
OKAY.

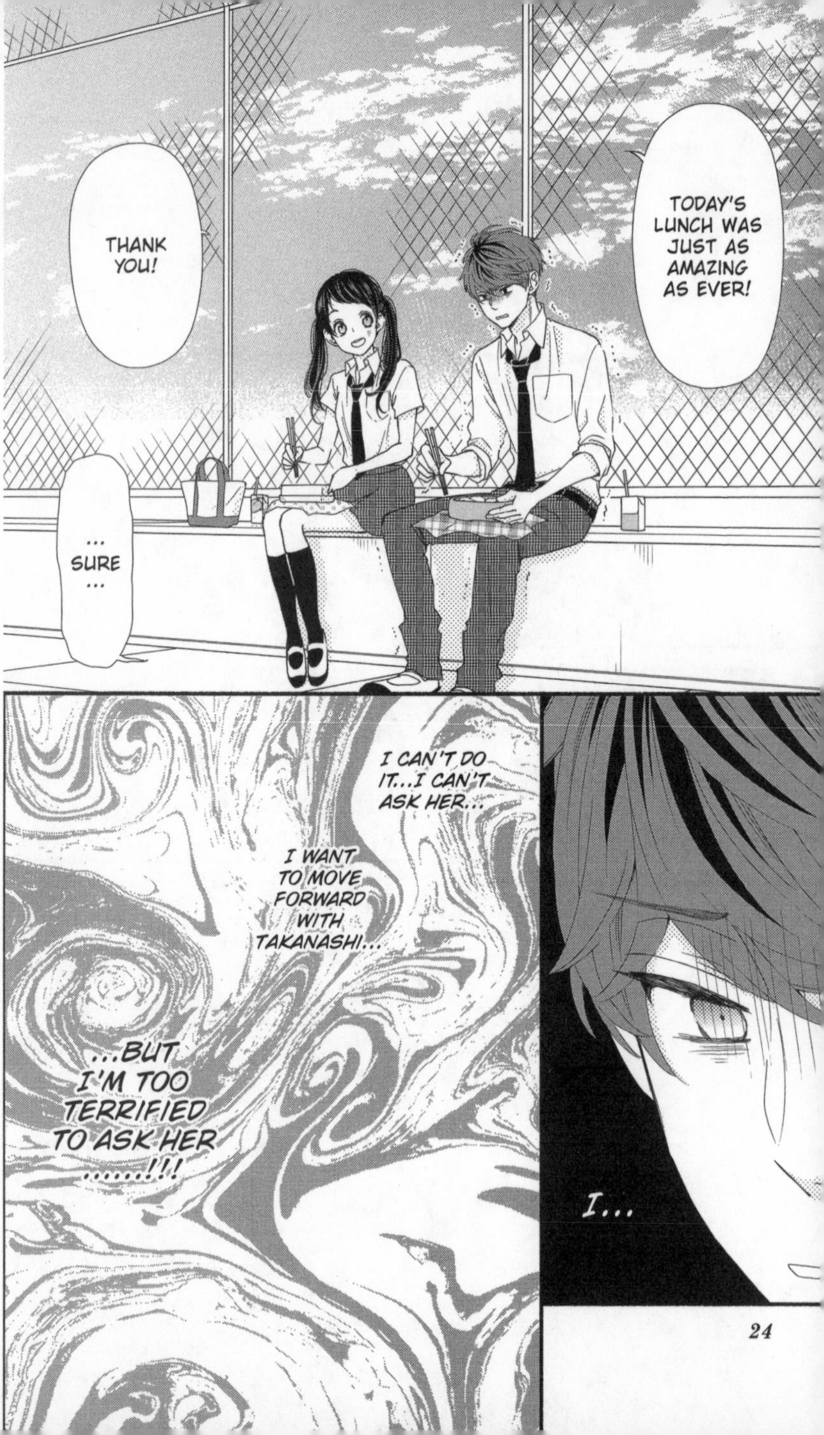
TODAY'S LUNCH WAS JUST AS AMAZING AS EVER!
THANK YOU!
... SURE ...
I...
I CAN'T DO IT...I CAN'T ASK HER...
I WANT TO MOVE FORWARD WITH TAKANASHI...
...BUT I'M TOO TERRIFIED TO ASK HER ....!!!

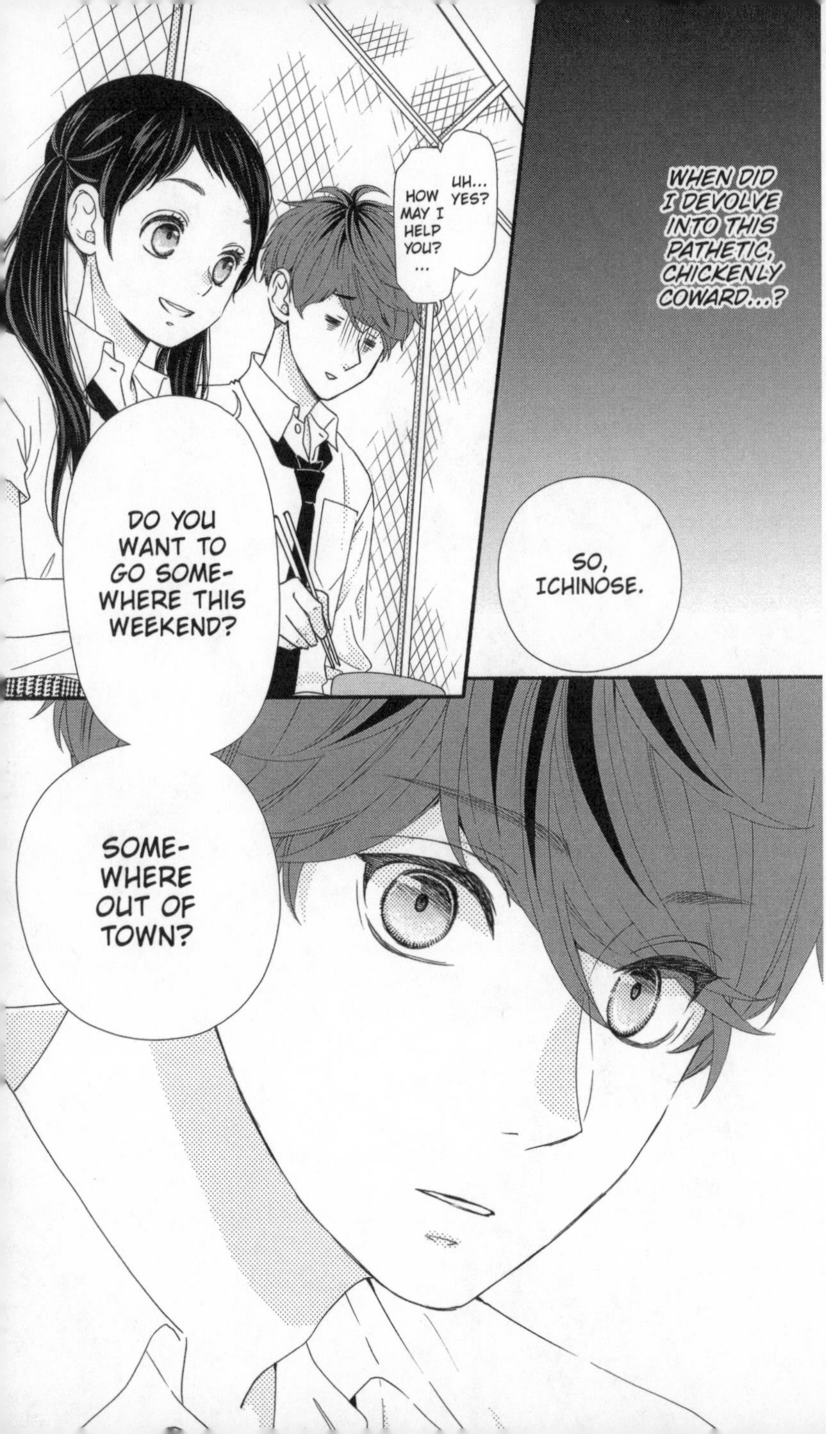
WHEN DID I DEVOLVE INTO THIS PATHETIC, CHICKENLY COWARD...?
SO, ICHINOSE.
UH... YES? HOW MAY I HELP YOU? ...
DO YOU WANT TO GO SOME-WHERE THIS WEEKEND?
SOME-WHERE OUT OF TOWN?

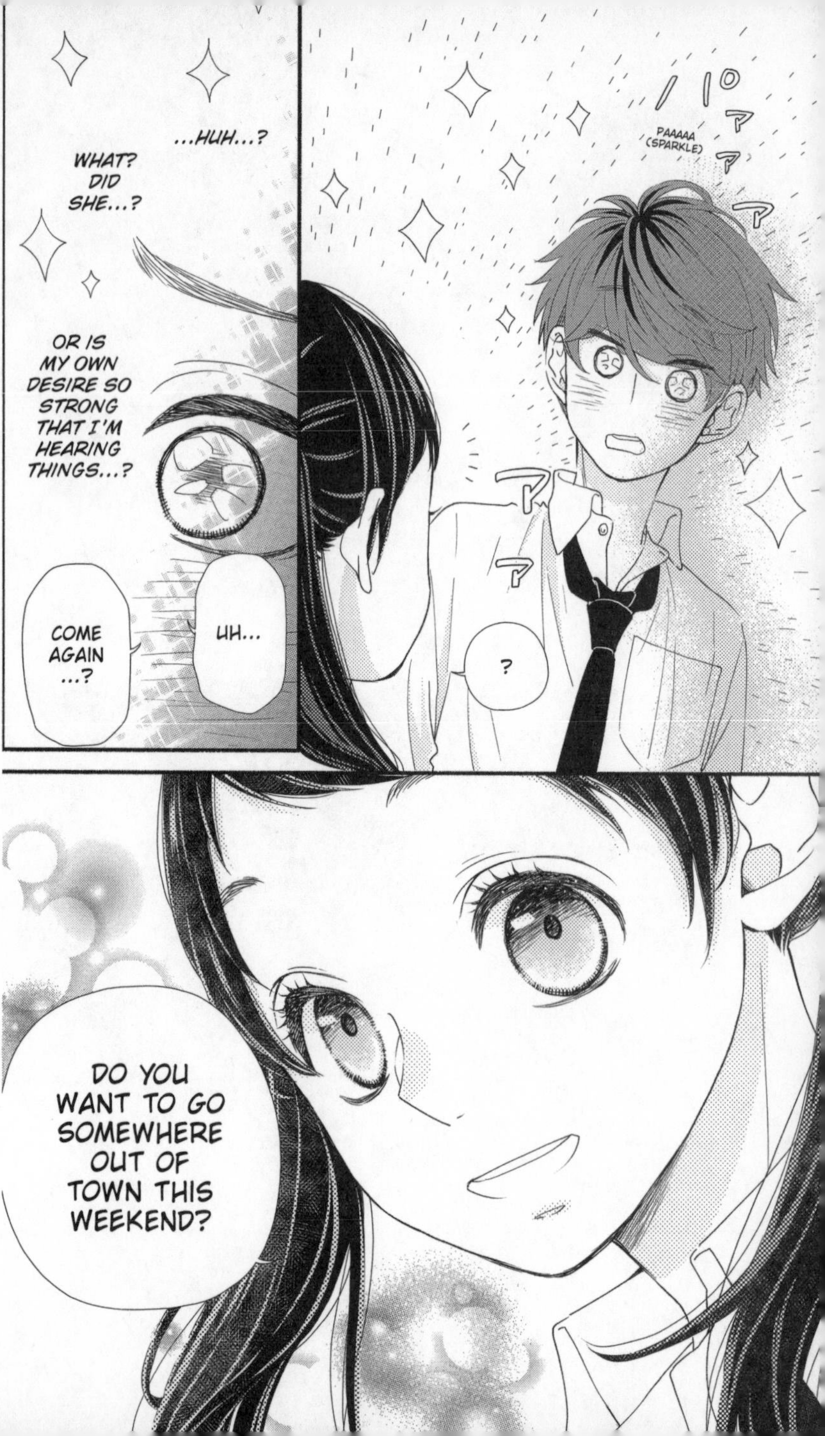
PAAAAA (SPARKLE)
?
...HUH...?
WHAT? DID SHE...?
OR IS MY OWN DESIRE SO STRONG THAT I'M HEARING THINGS...?
UH...
COME AGAIN ...?
DO YOU WANT TO GO SOMEWHERE OUT OF TOWN THIS WEEKEND?

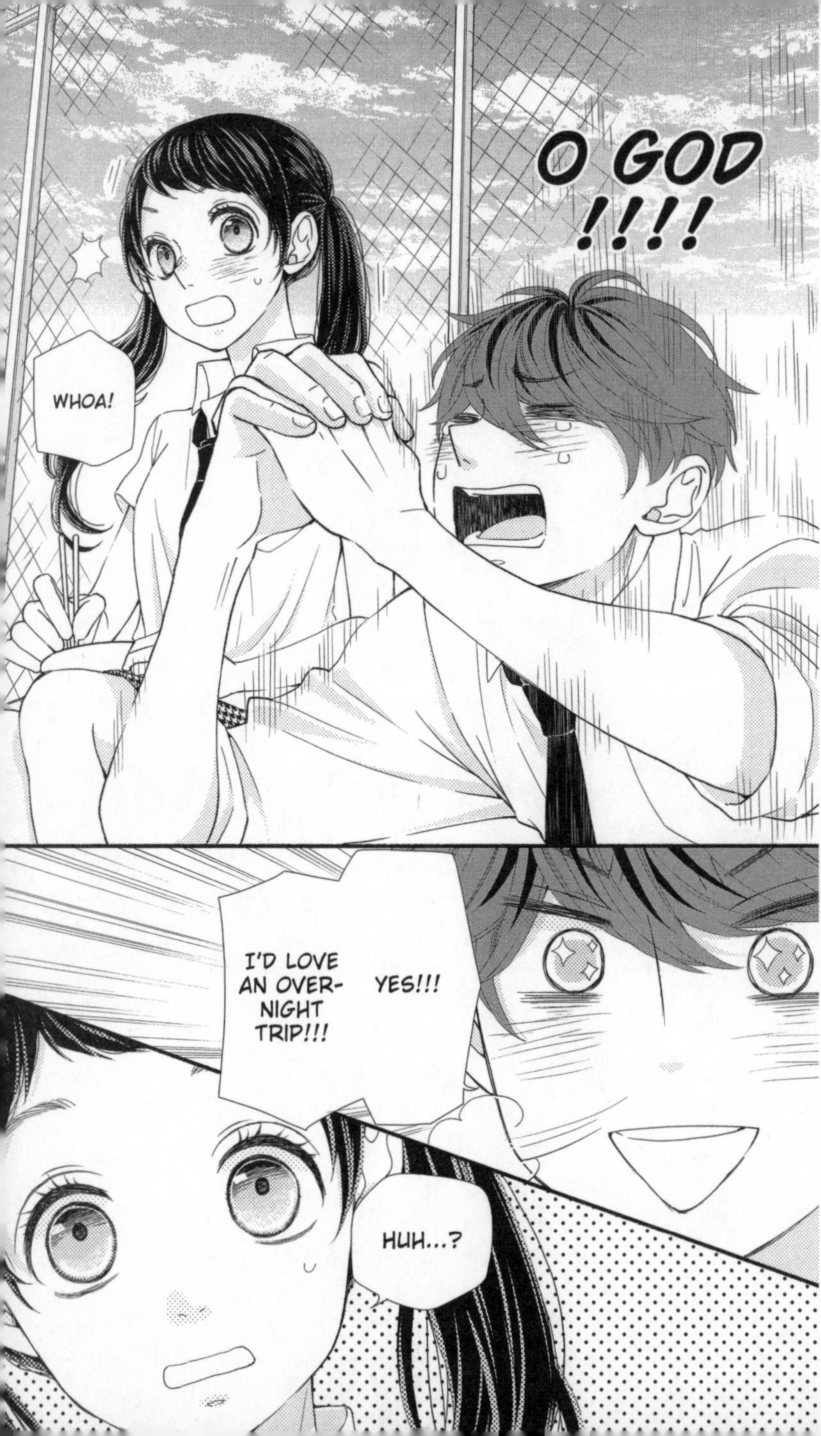
O GOD !!!!
WHOA!
YES!!!
I'D LOVE AN OVER-NIGHT TRIP!!!
HUH...?

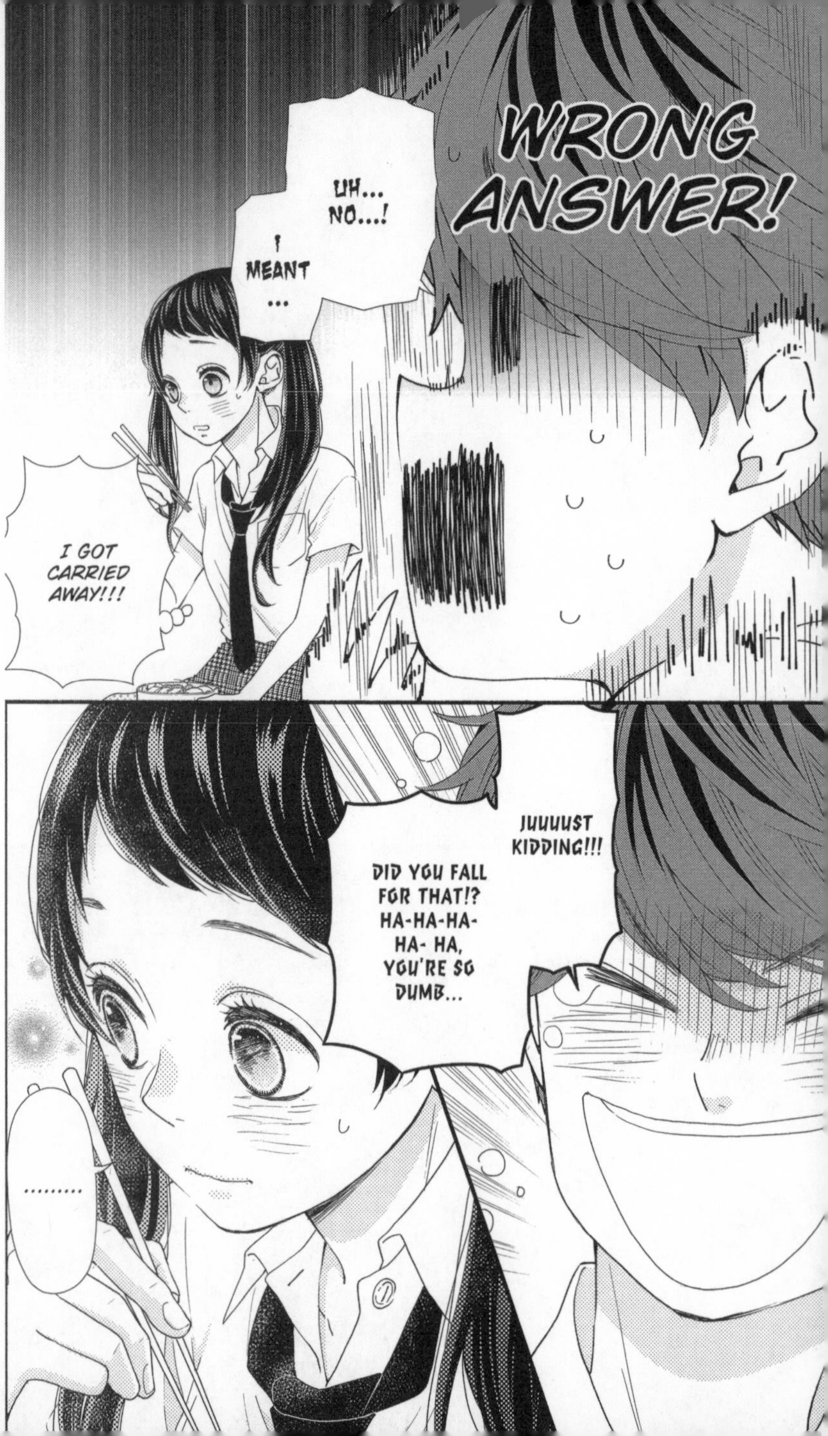
WRONG ANSWER!
UH... NO...!
I MEANT ...
I GOT CARRIED AWAY!!!
JUUUUST KIDDING!!!
DID YOU FALL FOR THAT!? HA-HA-HA-HA- HA, YOU'RE SO DUMB...
....

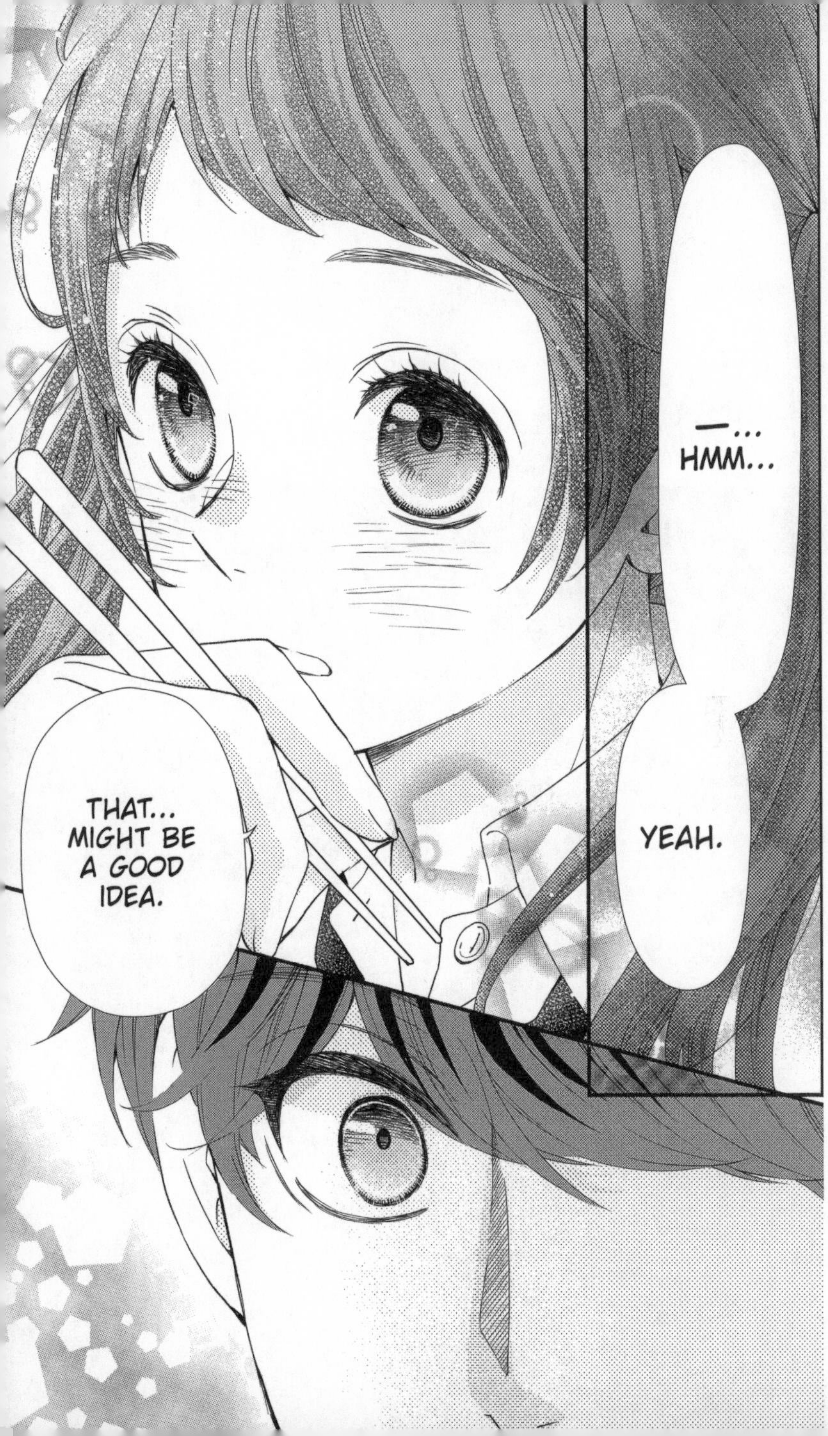
—...
HMM...
YEAH.
THAT... MIGHT BE A GOOD IDEA.

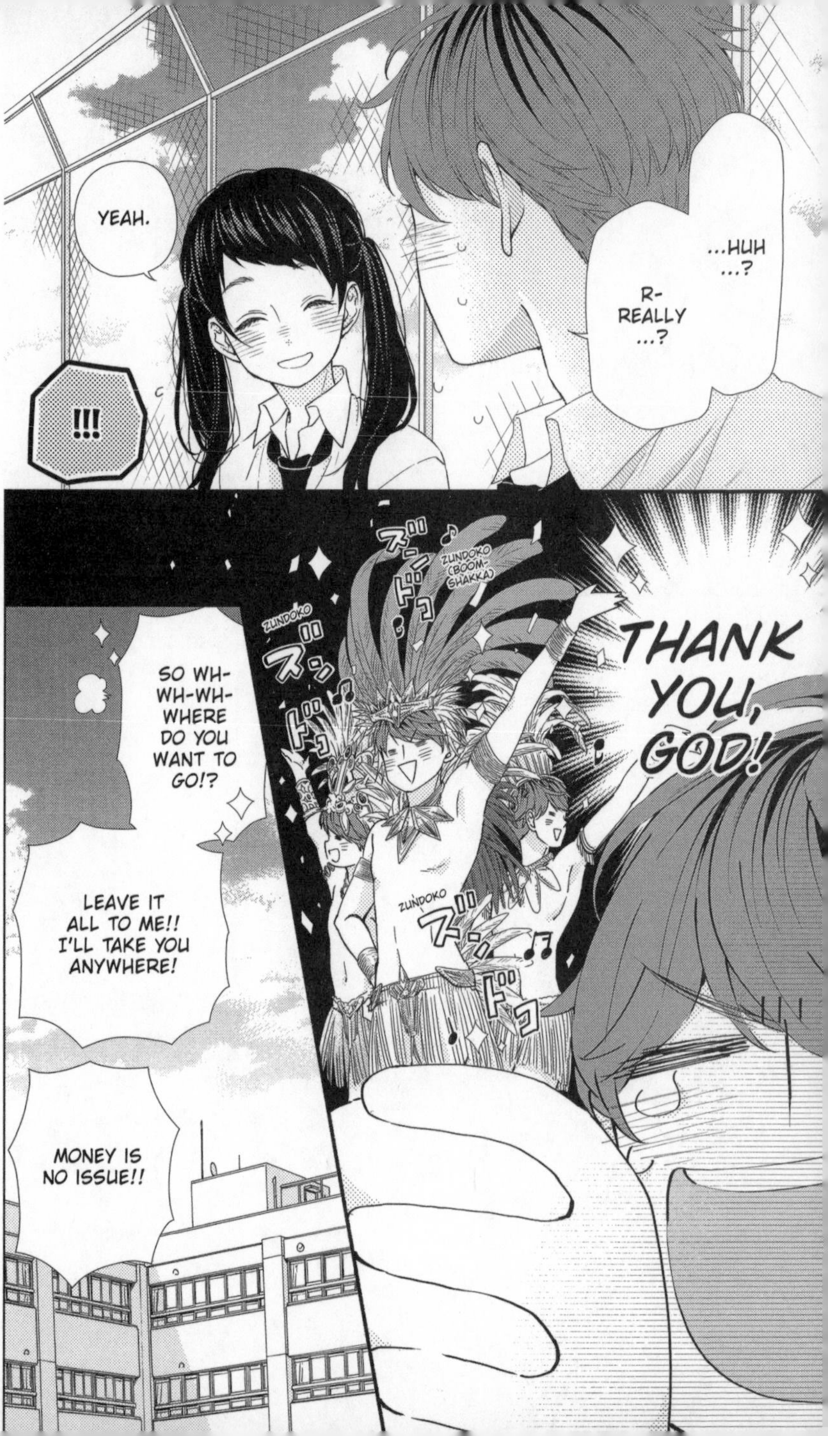
...HUH ...?
R-REALLY ...?
YEAH.
!!!
ZUNDOKO (BOOM-SHAKKA)
ZUNDOKO
THANK YOU, GOD!
ZUNDOKO
SO WH-WH-WH-WHERE DO YOU WANT TO GO!?
LEAVE IT ALL TO ME!! I'LL TAKE YOU ANYWHERE!
MONEY IS NO ISSUE!!

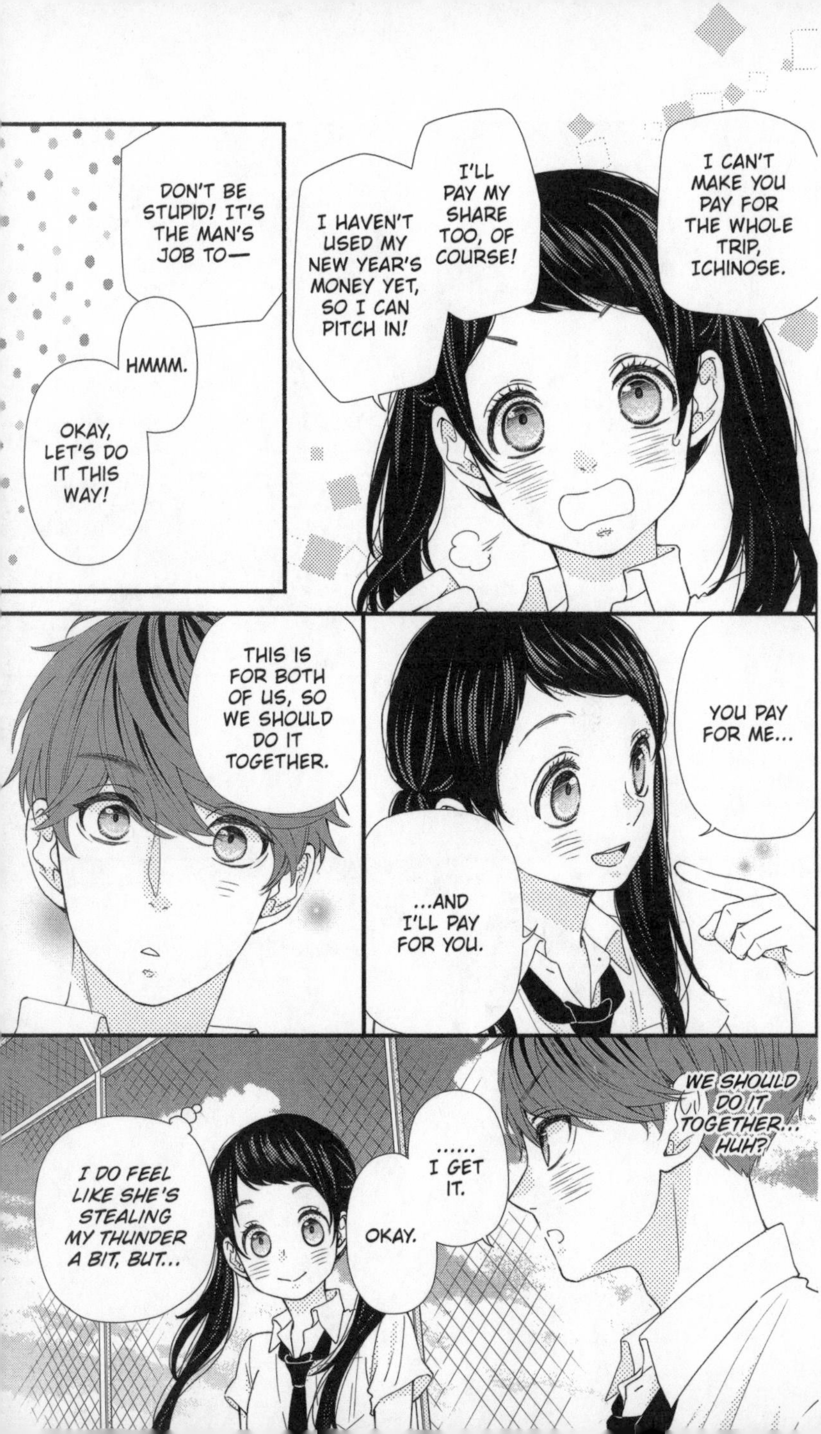
I CAN'T MAKE YOU PAY FOR THE WHOLE TRIP, ICHINOSE.
I'LL PAY MY SHARE TOO, OF COURSE!
I HAVEN'T USED MY NEW YEAR'S MONEY YET, SO I CAN PITCH IN!
DON'T BE STUPID! IT'S THE MAN'S JOB TO—
HMMM.
OKAY, LET'S DO IT THIS WAY!
YOU PAY FOR ME...
...AND I'LL PAY FOR YOU.
THIS IS FOR BOTH OF US, SO WE SHOULD DO IT TOGETHER.
WE SHOULD DO IT TOGETHER... HUH?
...... I GET IT.
OKAY.
I DO FEEL LIKE SHE'S STEALING MY THUNDER A BIT, BUT...

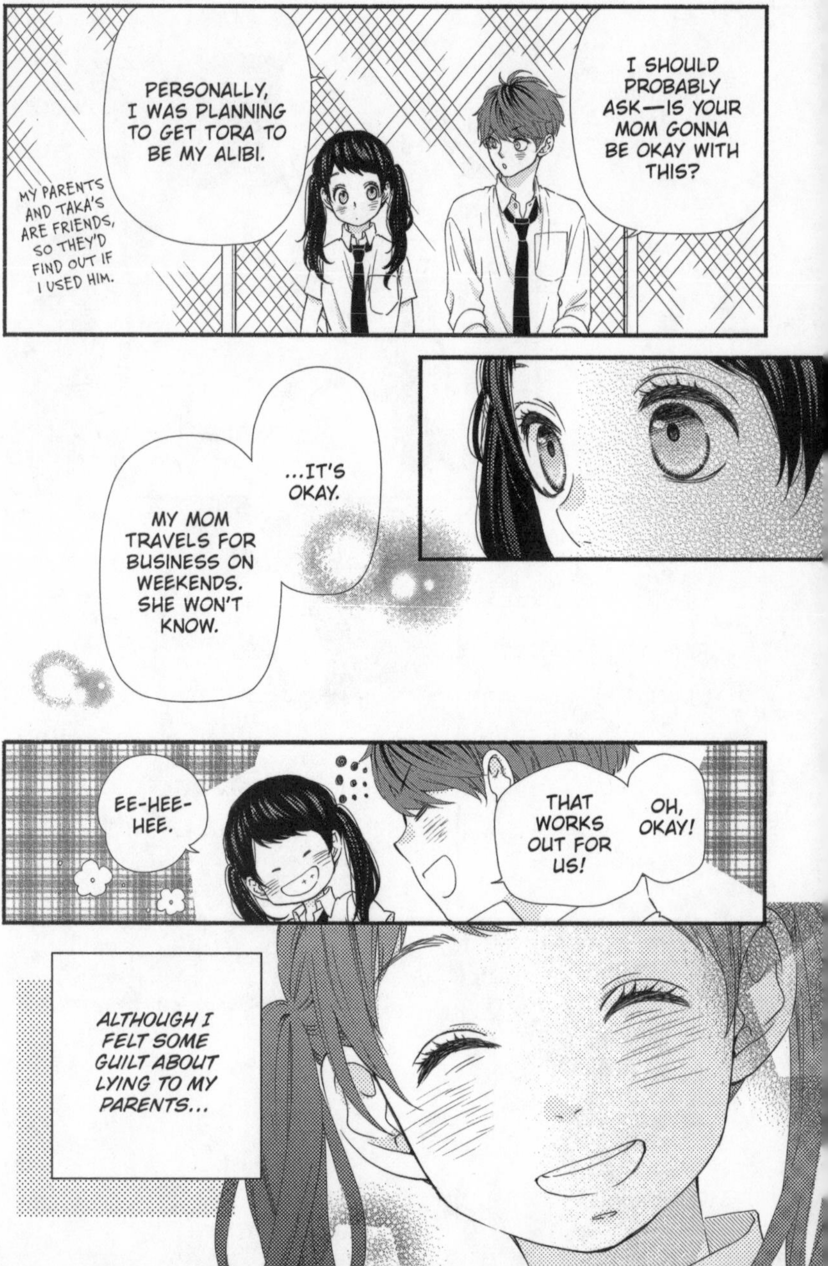
I SHOULD PROBABLY ASK—IS YOUR MOM GONNA BE OKAY WITH THIS?
PERSONALLY, I WAS PLANNING TO GET TORA TO BE MY ALIBI.
MY PARENTS AND TAKA'S ARE FRIENDS, SO THEY'D FIND OUT IF I USED HIM.
...IT'S OKAY.
MY MOM TRAVELS FOR BUSINESS ON WEEKENDS. SHE WON'T KNOW.
OH, OKAY!
THAT WORKS OUT FOR US!
EE-HEE-HEE.
ALTHOUGH I FELT SOME GUILT ABOUT LYING TO MY PARENTS...

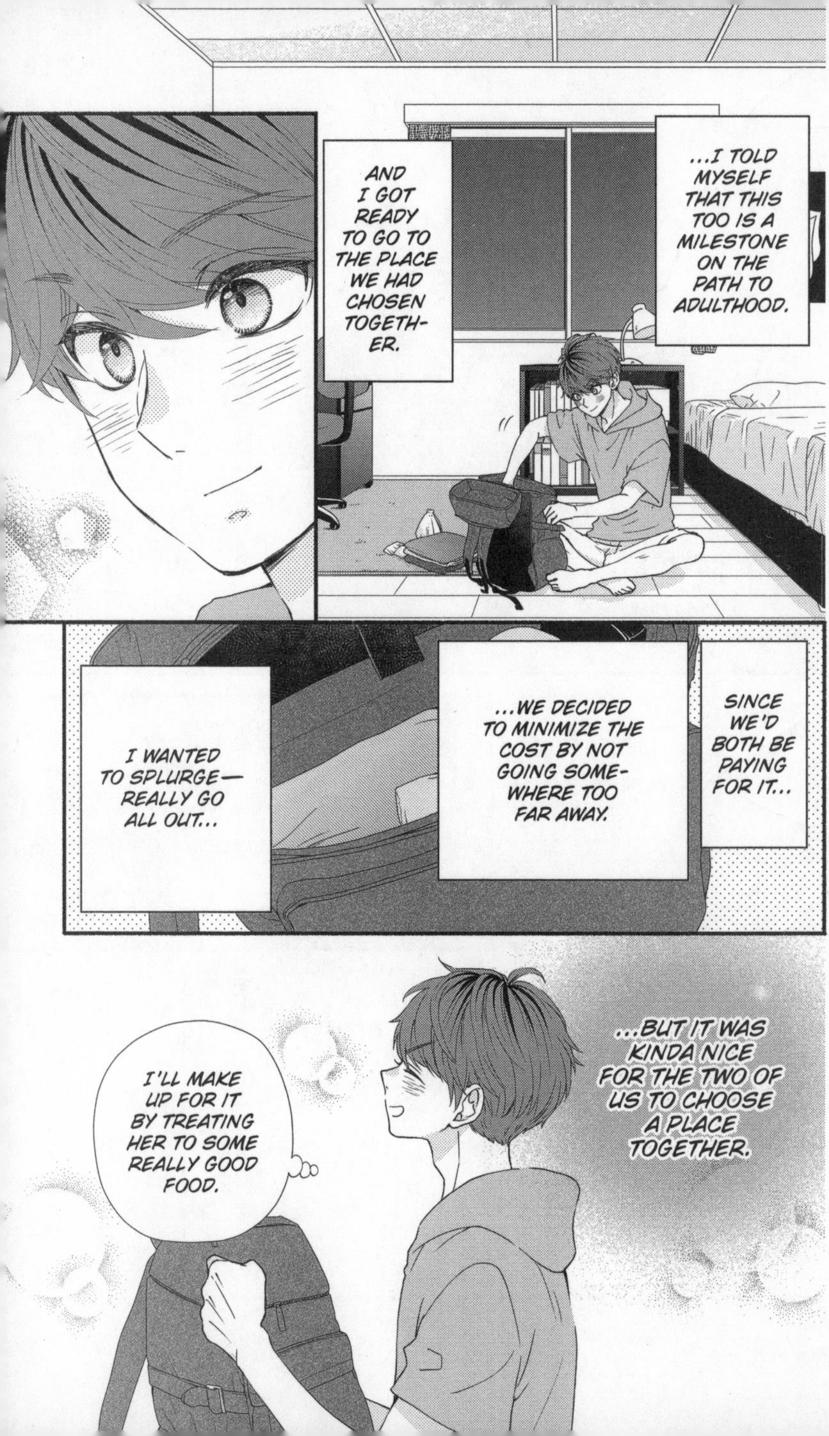
...I TOLD MYSELF THAT THIS TOO IS A MILESTONE ON THE PATH TO ADULTHOOD.
AND I GOT READY TO GO TO THE PLACE WE HAD CHOSEN TOGETH-ER.
SINCE WE'D BOTH BE PAYING FOR IT...
...WE DECIDED TO MINIMIZE THE COST BY NOT GOING SOME-WHERE TOO FAR AWAY.
I WANTED TO SPLURGE—REALLY GO ALL OUT...
...BUT IT WAS KINDA NICE FOR THE TWO OF US TO CHOOSE A PLACE TOGETHER.
I'LL MAKE UP FOR IT BY TREATING HER TO SOME REALLY GOOD FOOD.

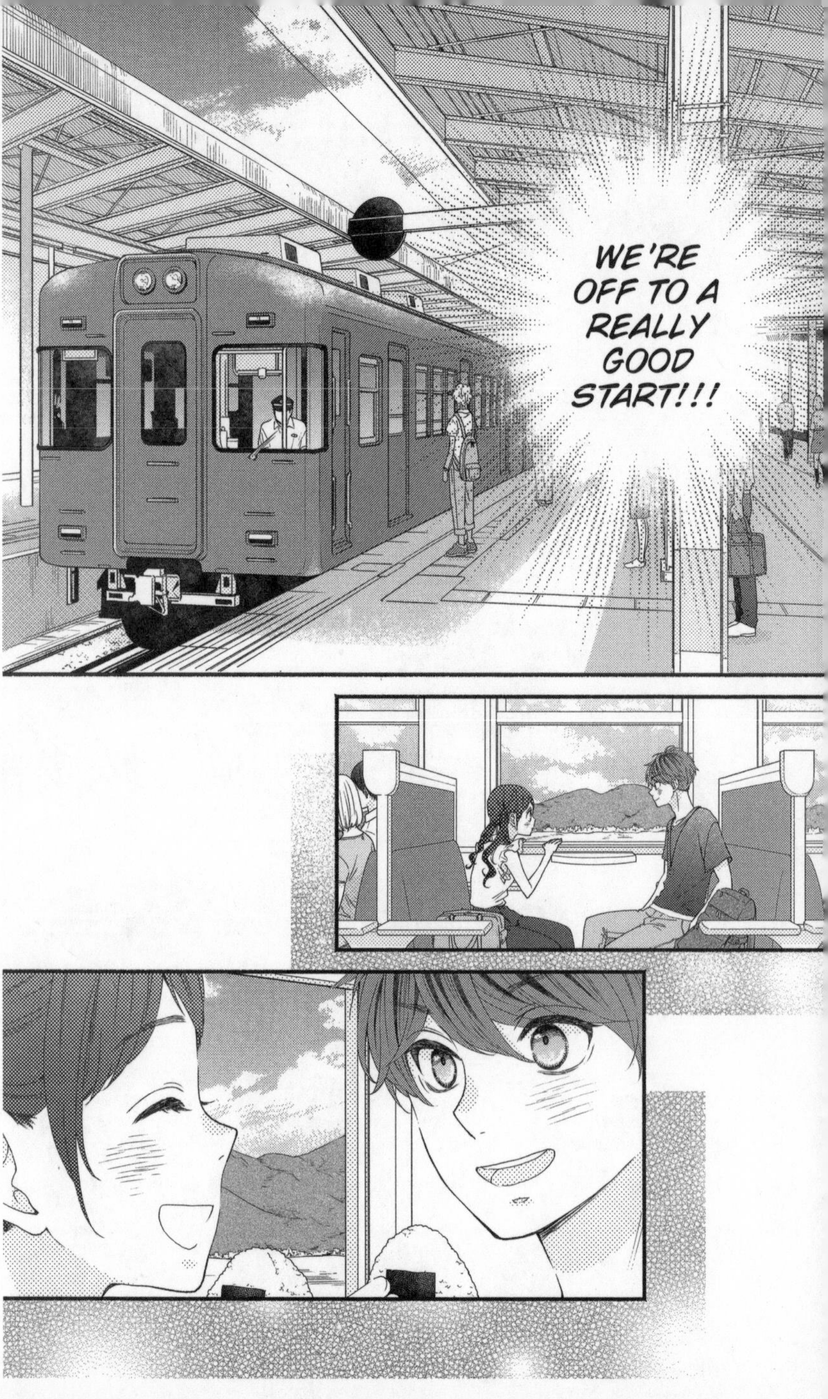
WE'RE OFF TO A REALLY GOOD START!!!

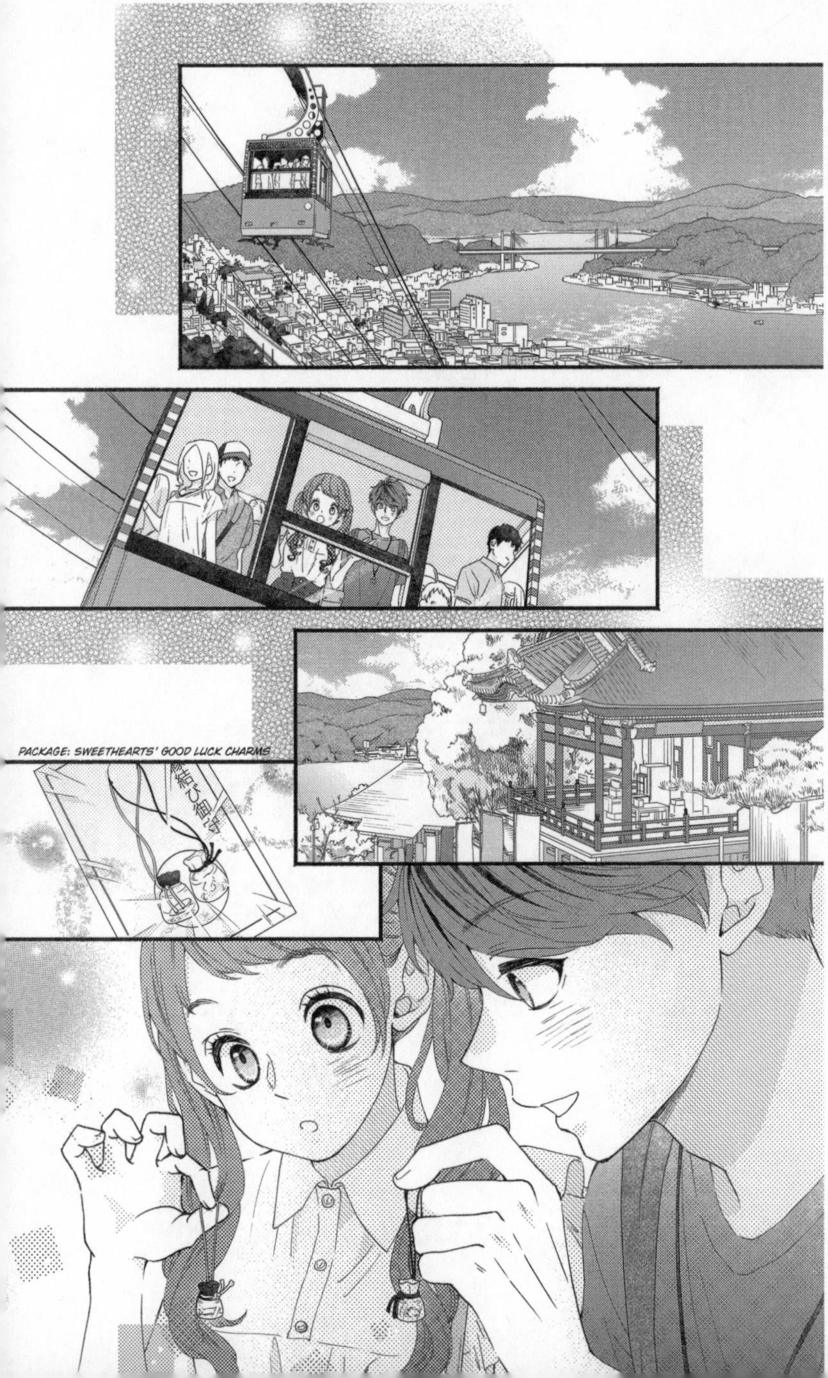
PACKAGE: SWEETHEARTS' GOOD LUCK CHARMS

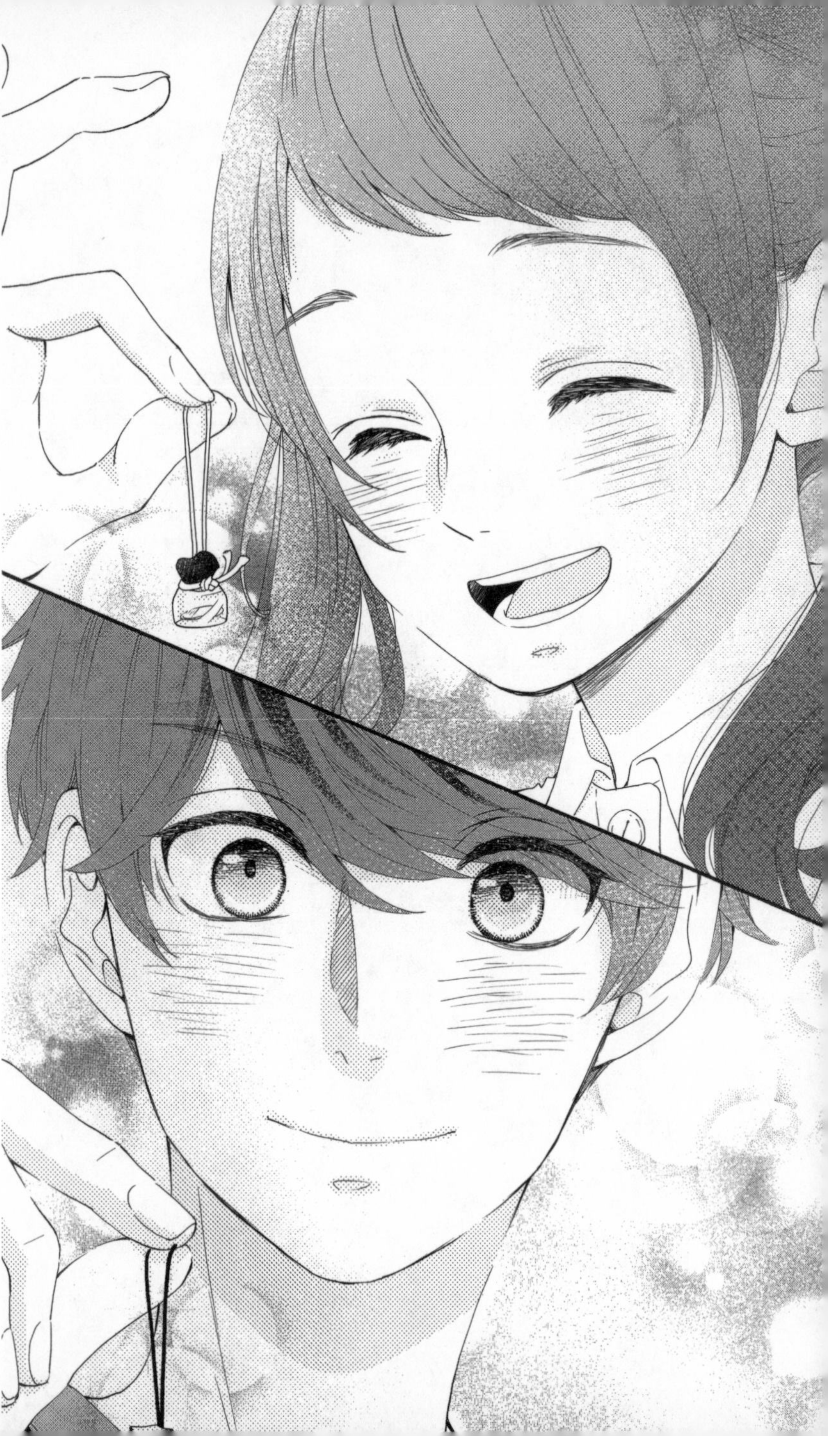

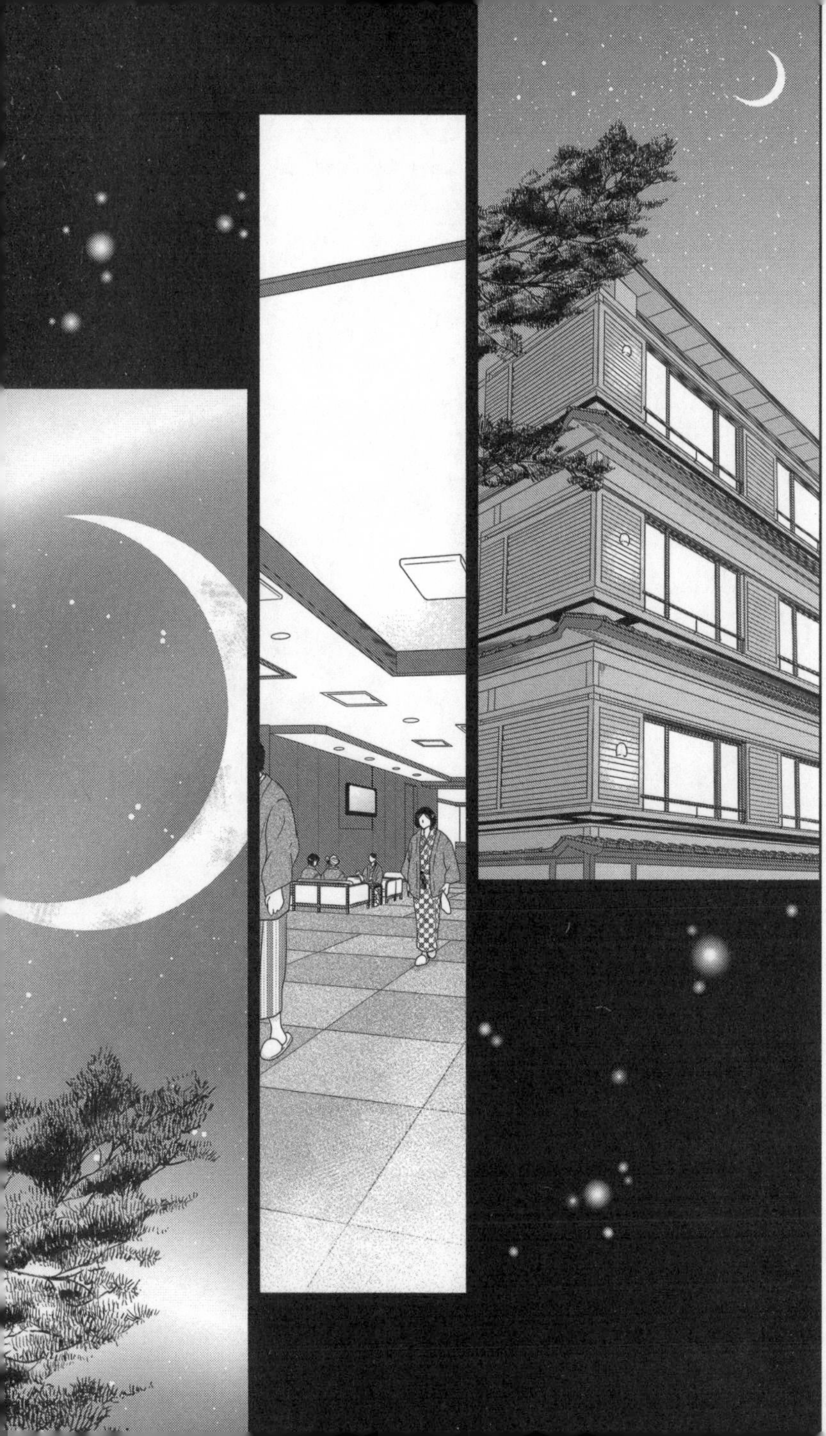

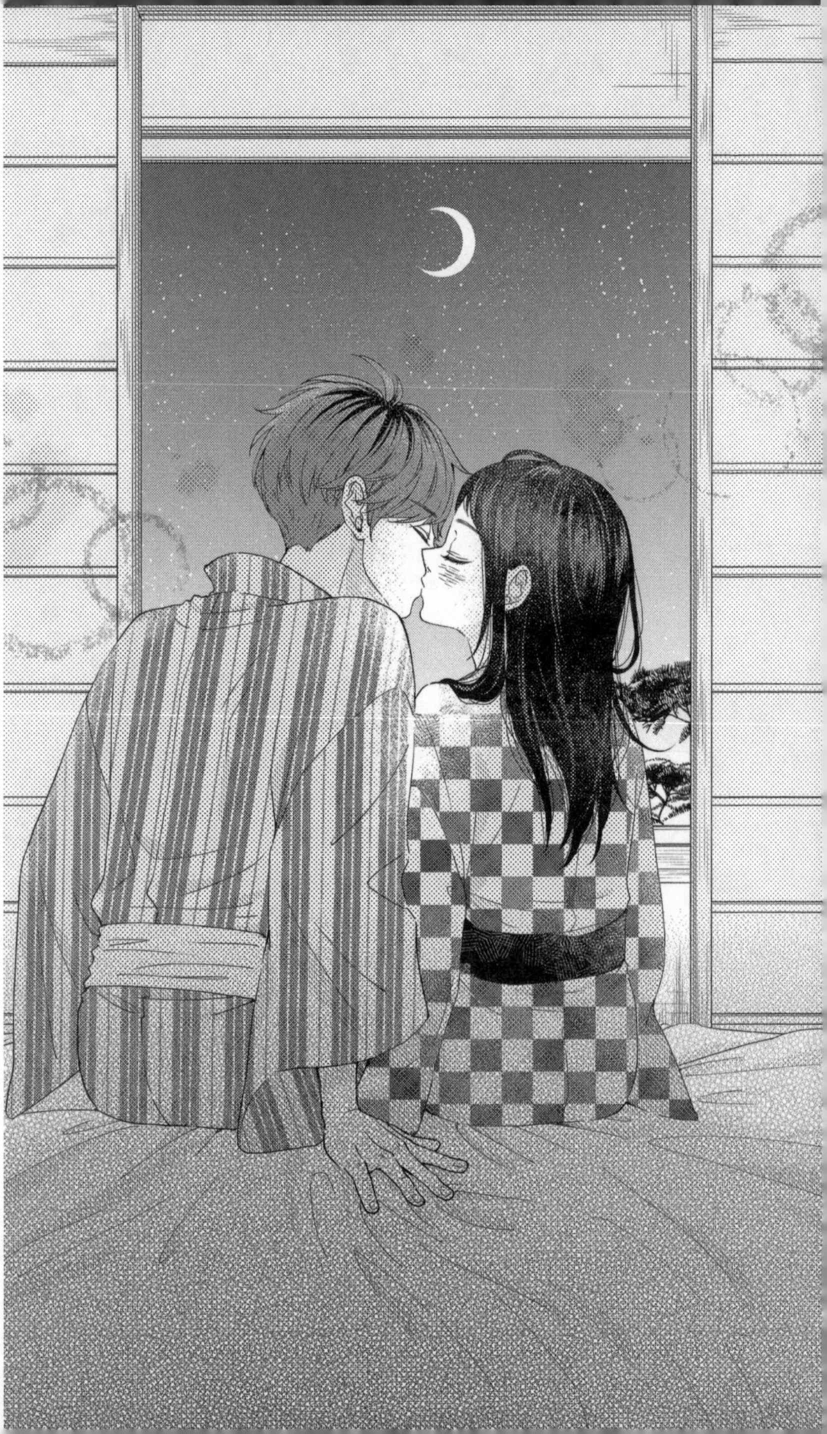

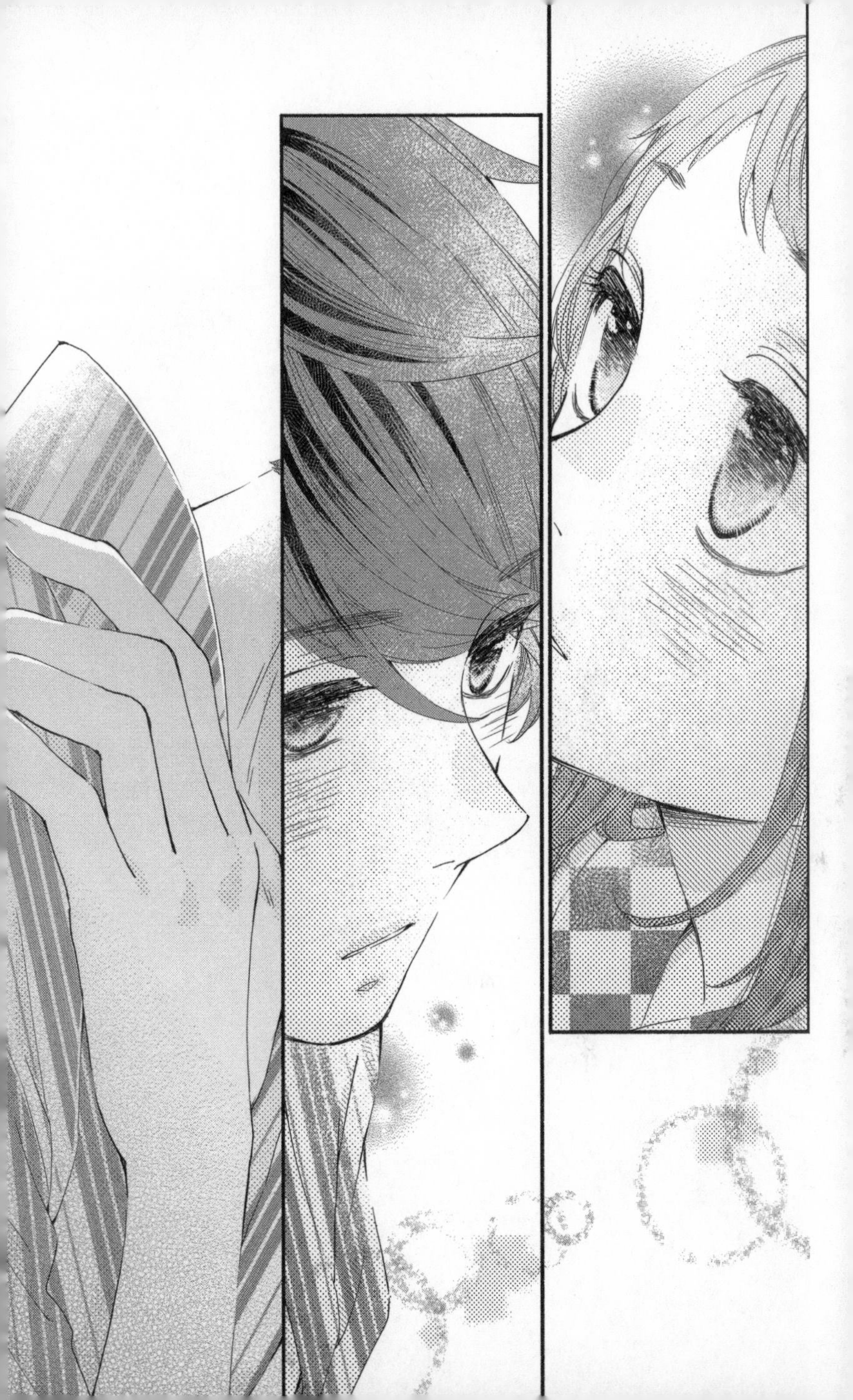

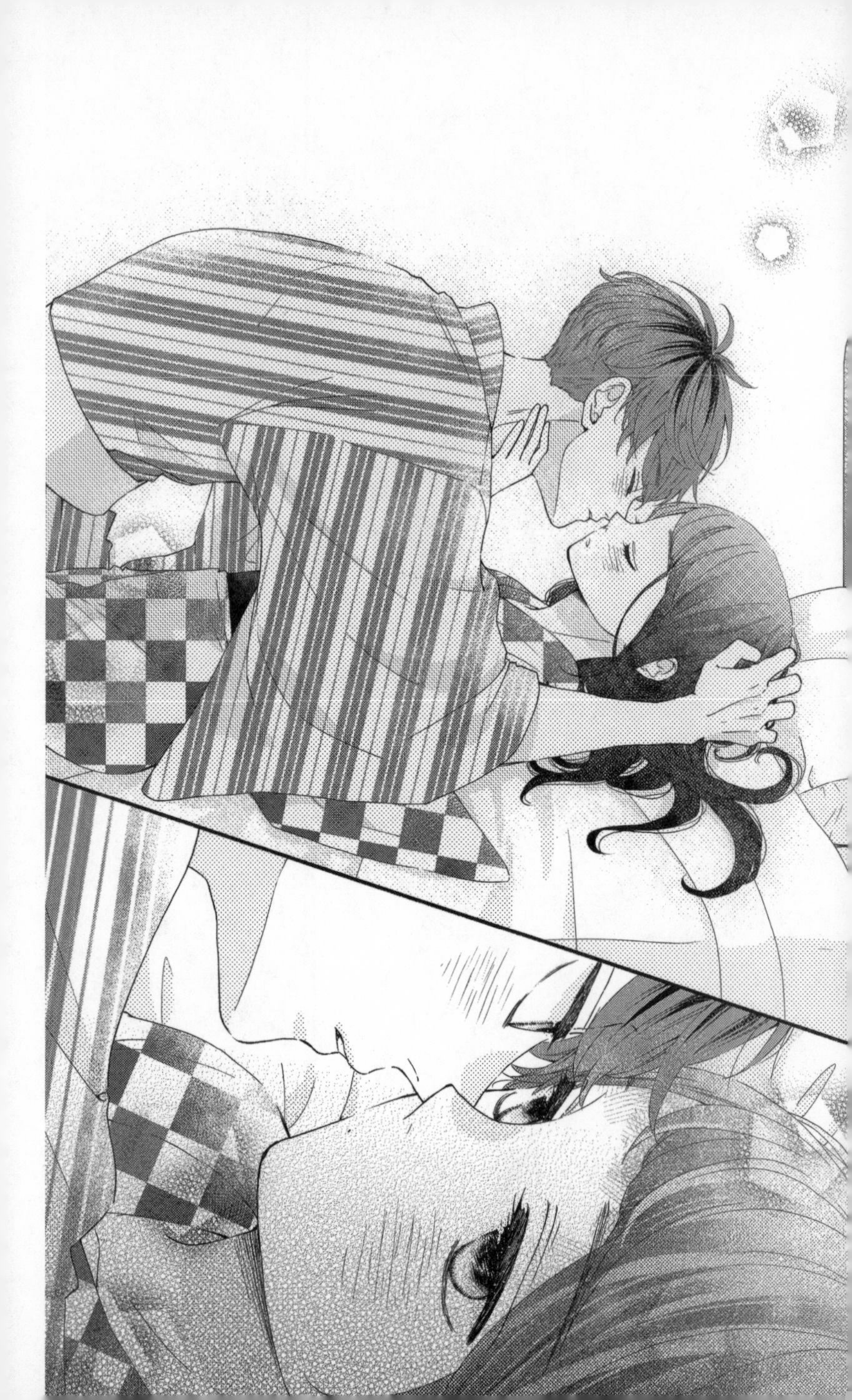

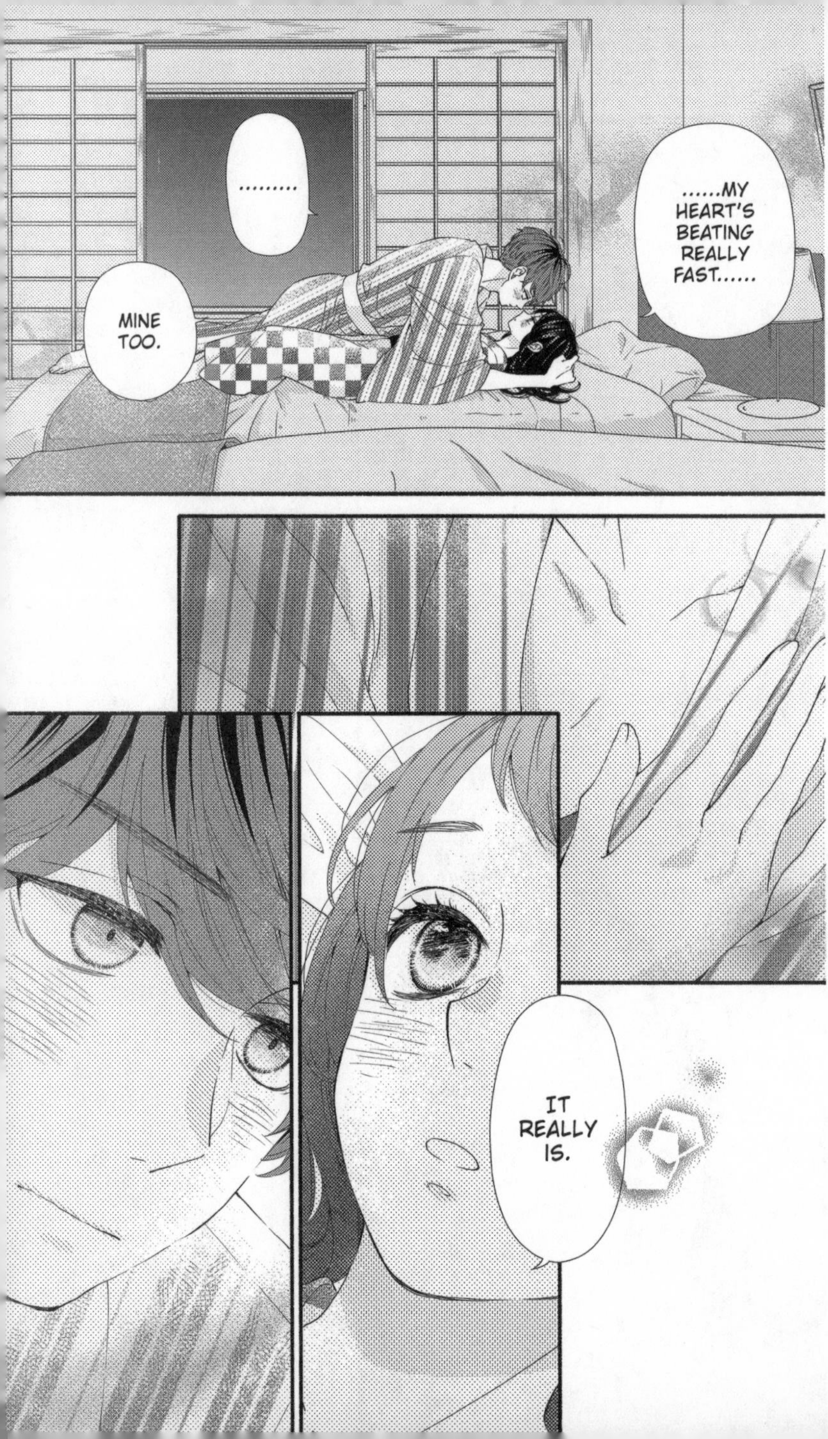
......MY HEART'S BEATING REALLY FAST......
....
MINE TOO.
IT REALLY IS.

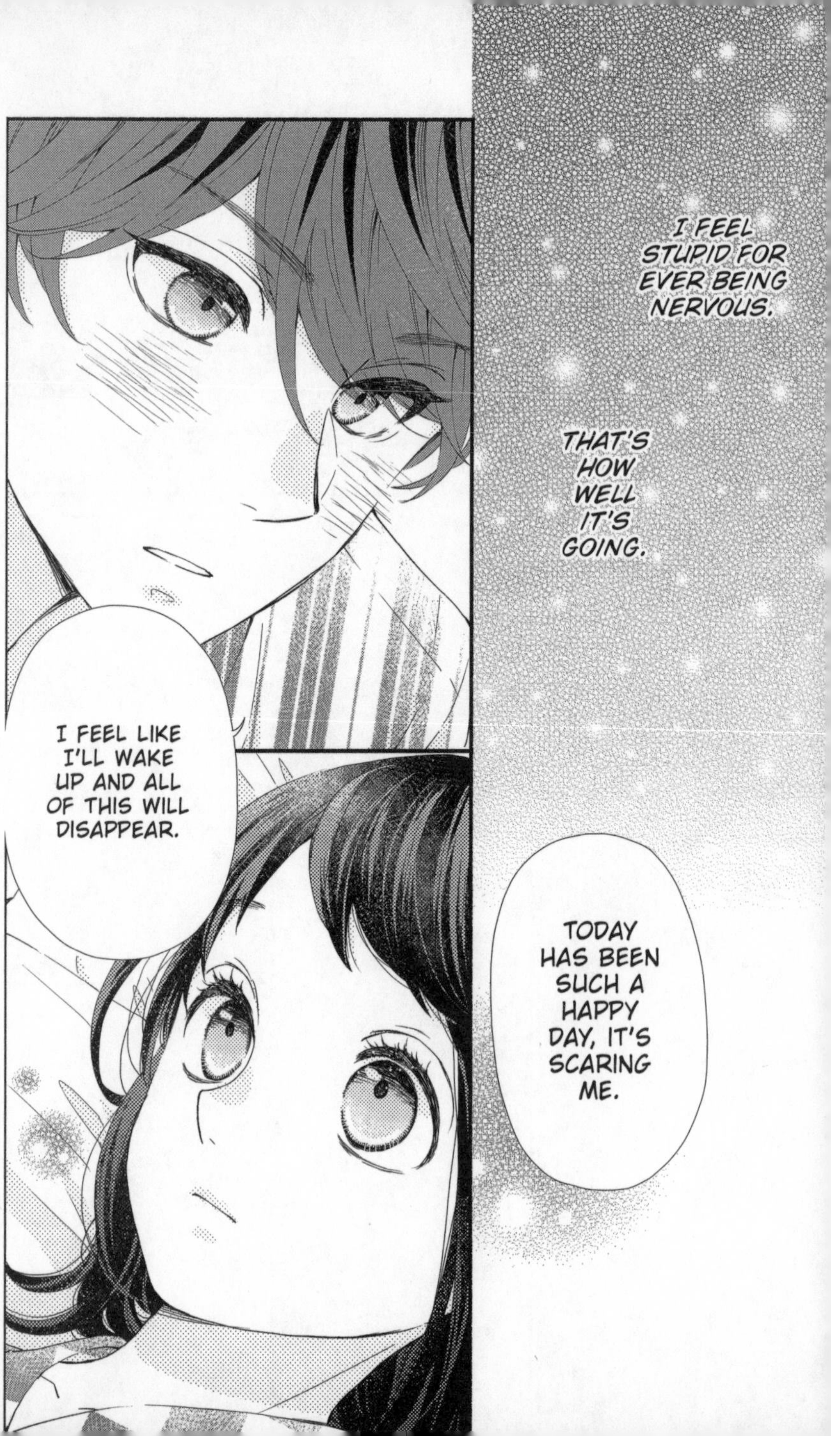
I FEEL STUPID FOR EVER BEING NERVOUS.
THAT'S HOW WELL IT'S GOING.
TODAY HAS BEEN SUCH A HAPPY DAY, IT'S SCARING ME.
I FEEL LIKE I'LL WAKE UP AND ALL OF THIS WILL DISAPPEAR.

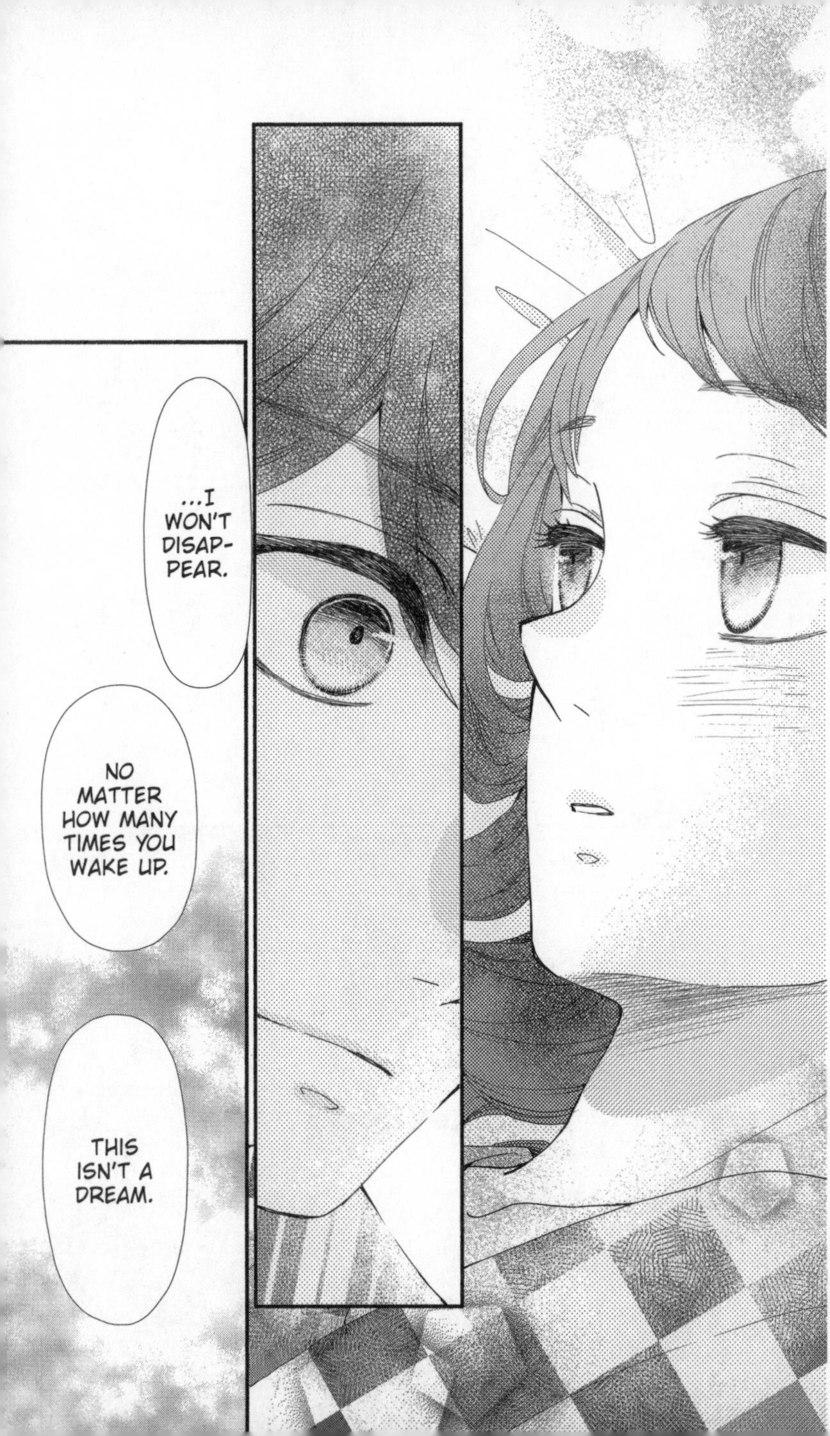
...I WON'T DISAP-PEAR.
NO MATTER HOW MANY TIMES YOU WAKE UP.
THIS ISN'T A DREAM.

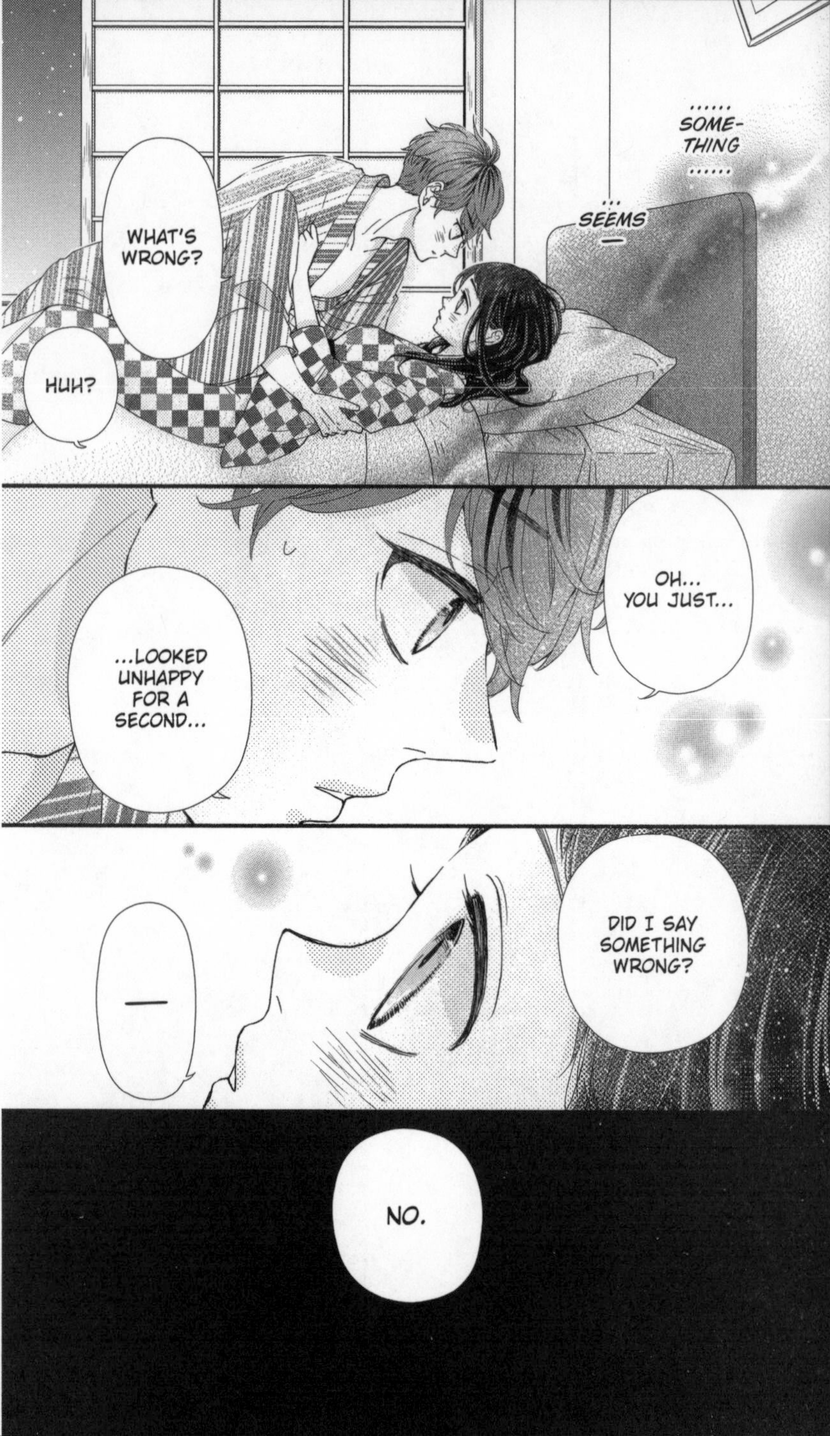

...... SOME-THING ......
... SEEMS —
WHAT'S WRONG?
HUH?
OH... YOU JUST...
...LOOKED UNHAPPY FOR A SECOND...
DID I SAY SOMETHING WRONG?
—
NO.

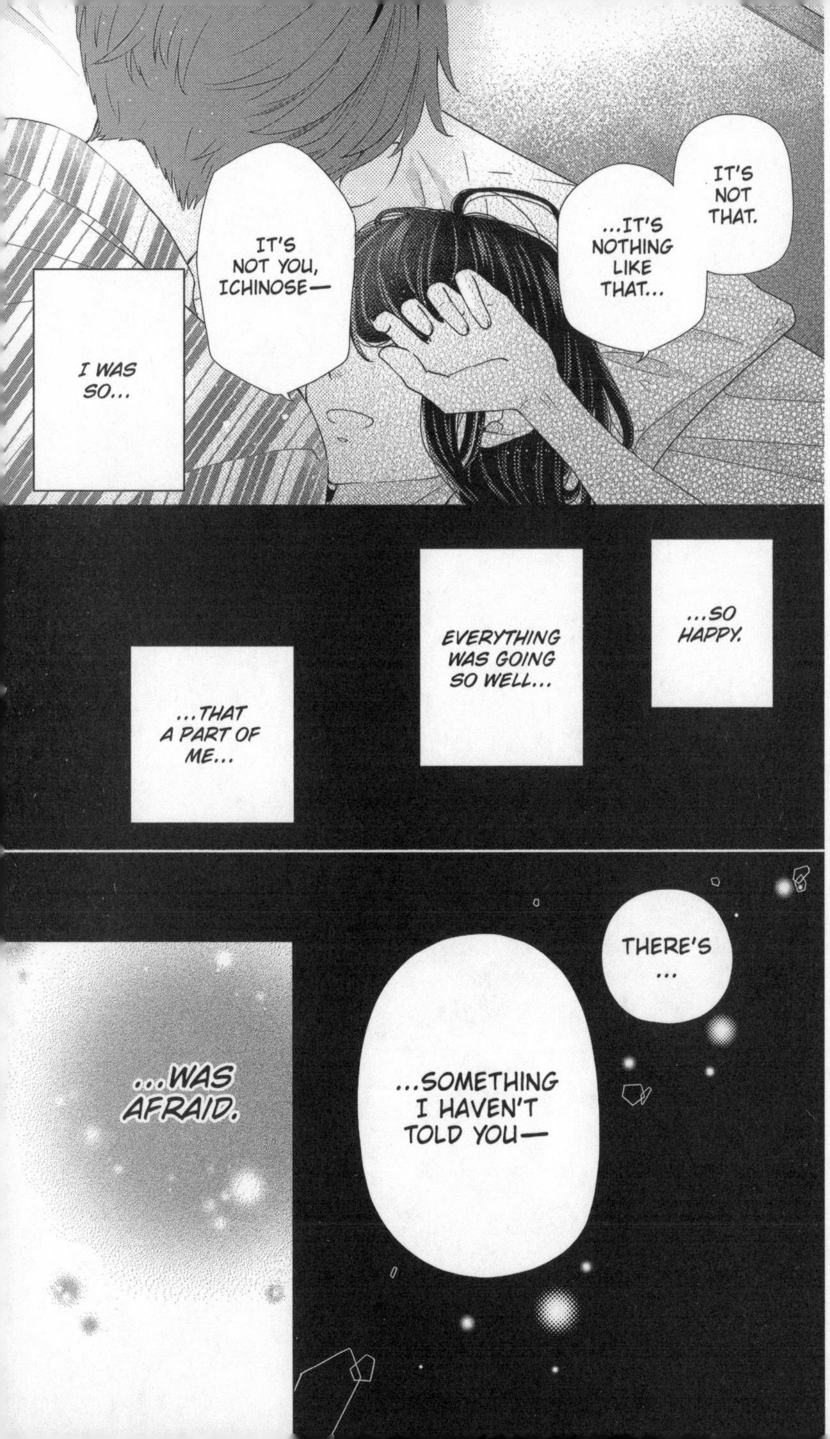
IT'S NOT THAT.
...IT'S NOTHING LIKE THAT...
IT'S NOT YOU, ICHINOSE—
I WAS SO...
...SO HAPPY.
EVERYTHING WAS GOING SO WELL...
...THAT A PART OF ME...
THERE'S...
...SOMETHING I HAVEN'T TOLD YOU—
...WAS AFRAID.

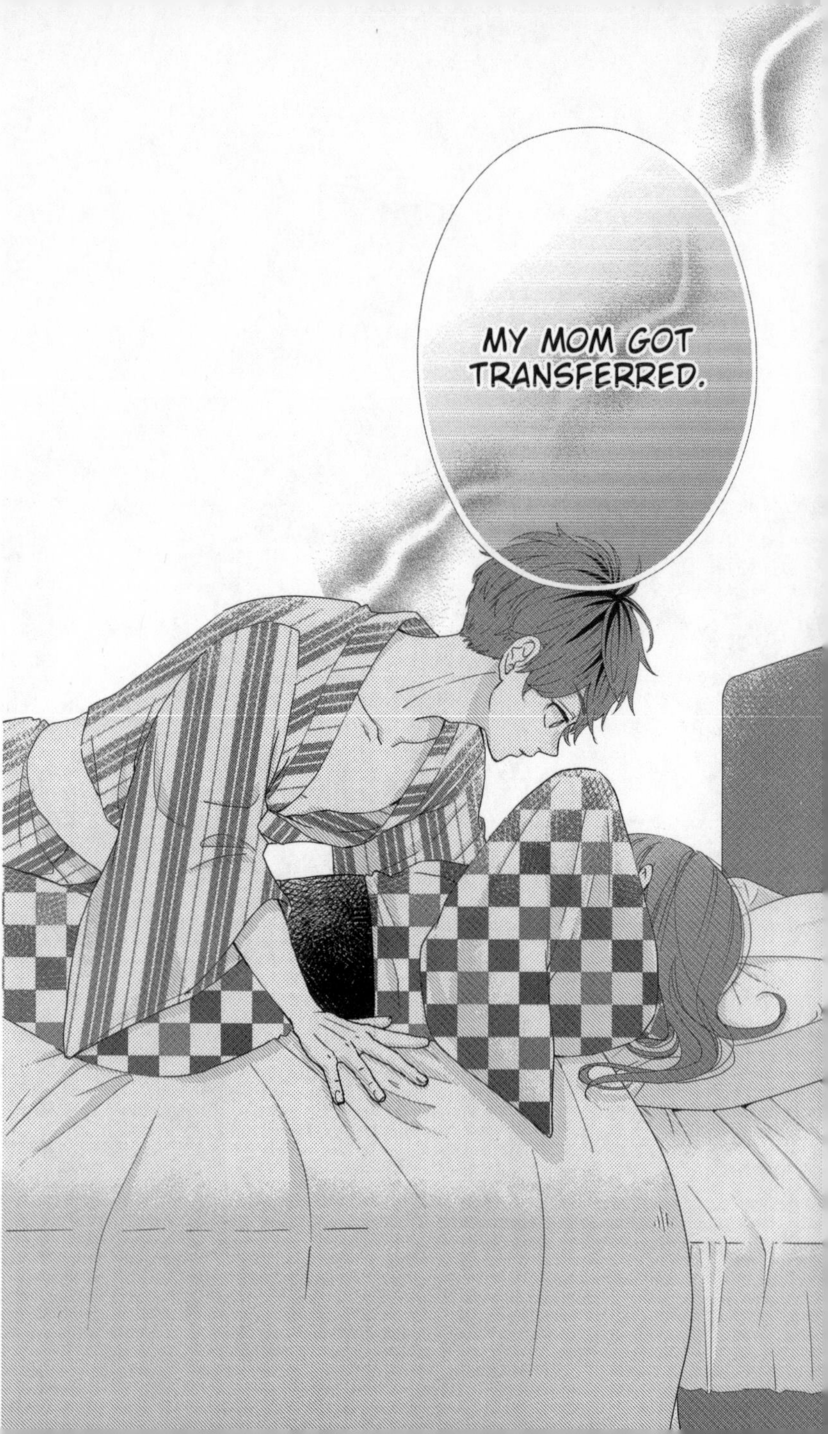
MY MOM GOT TRANSFERRED.

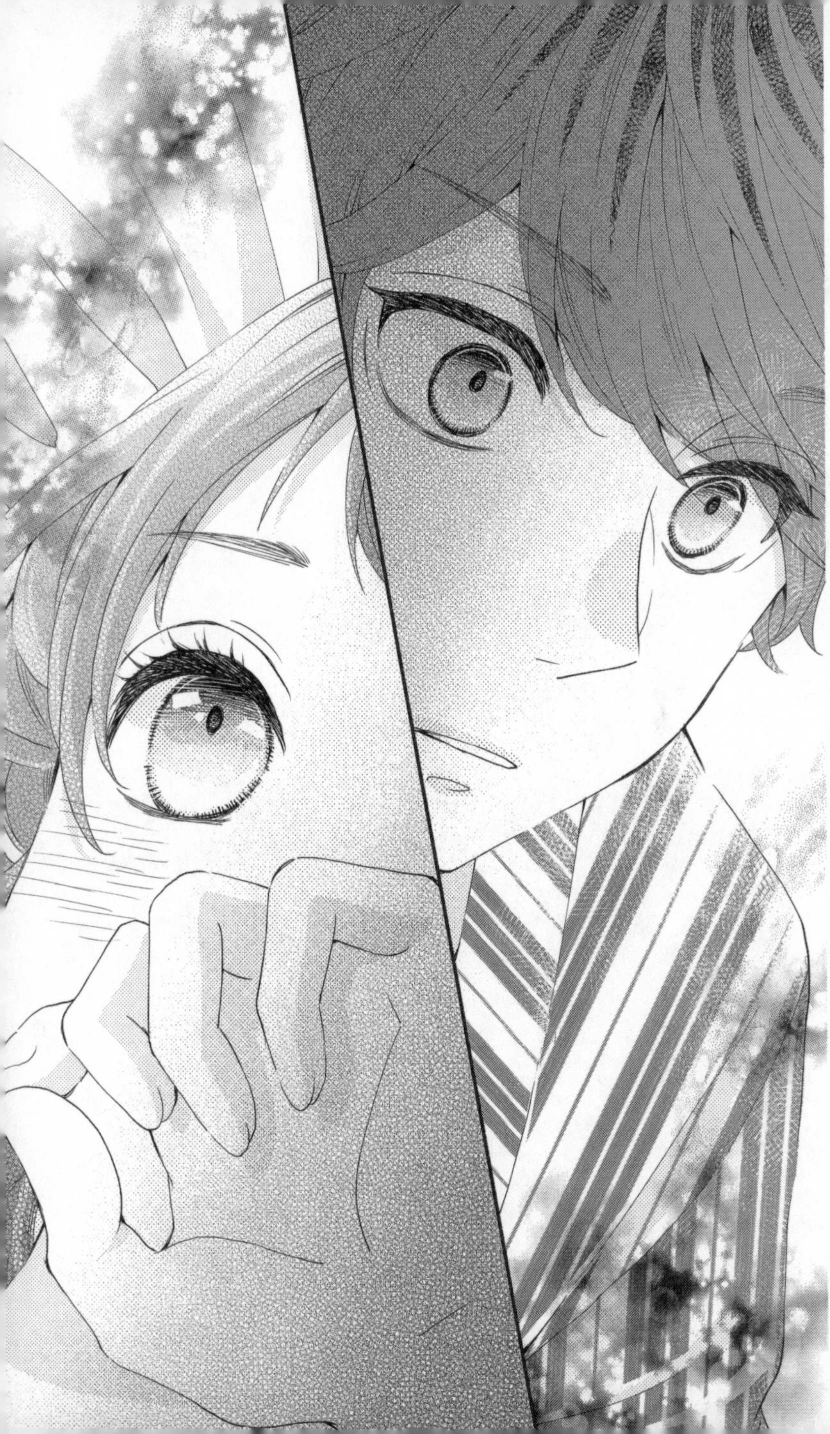

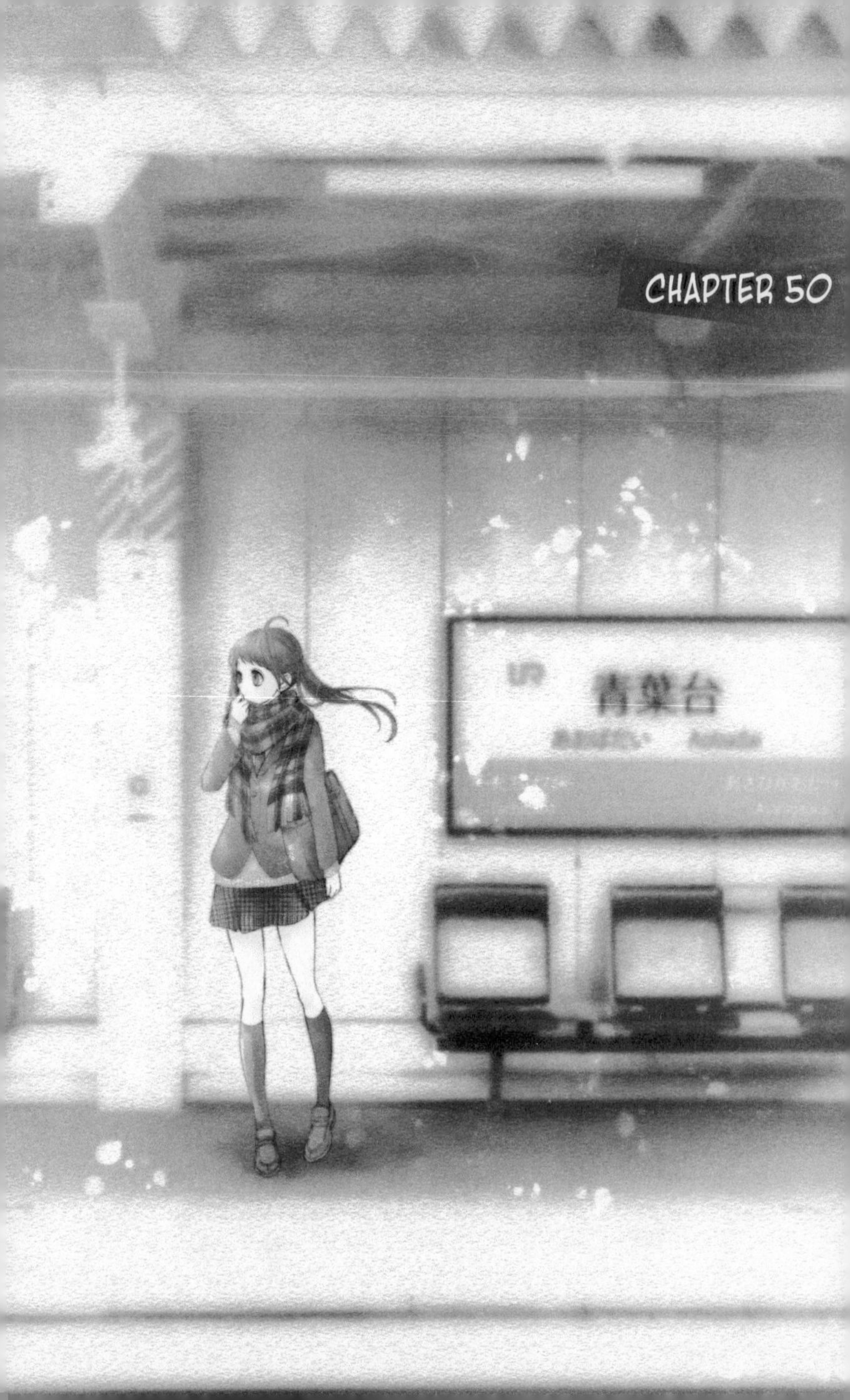
CHAPTER 50
青葉台

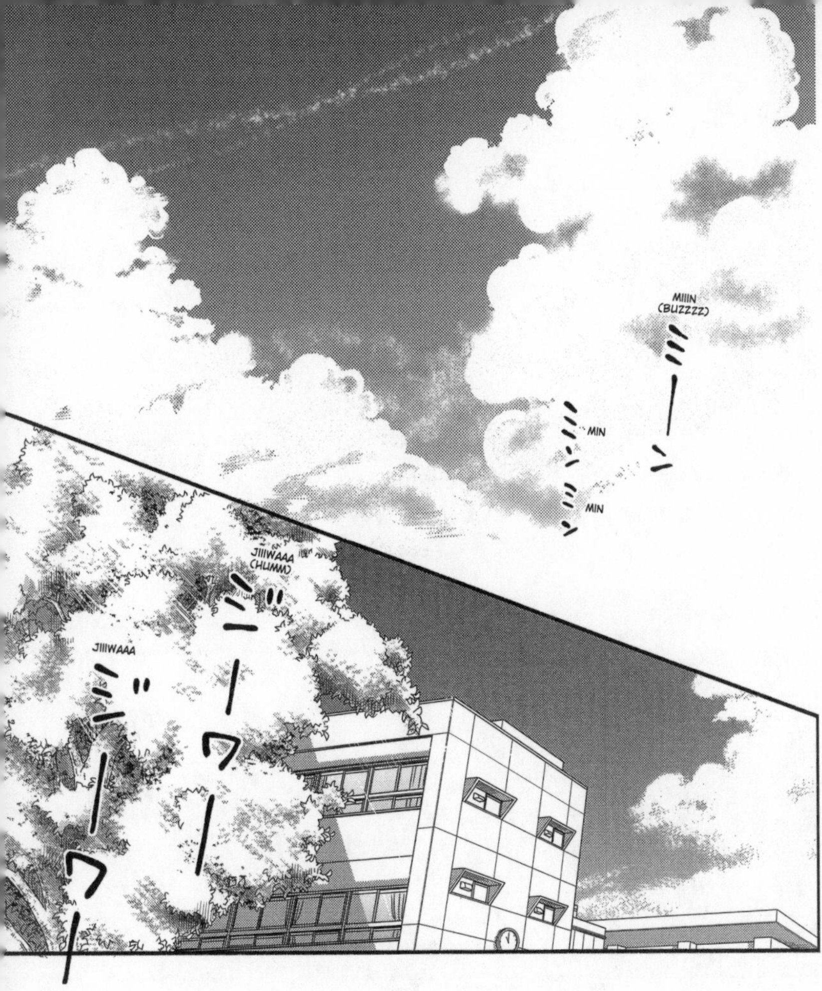
MIIIN (BUZZZZ)
MIN
MIN
JIIIWAAA (HUMM)
JIIIWAAA

hatsu haru

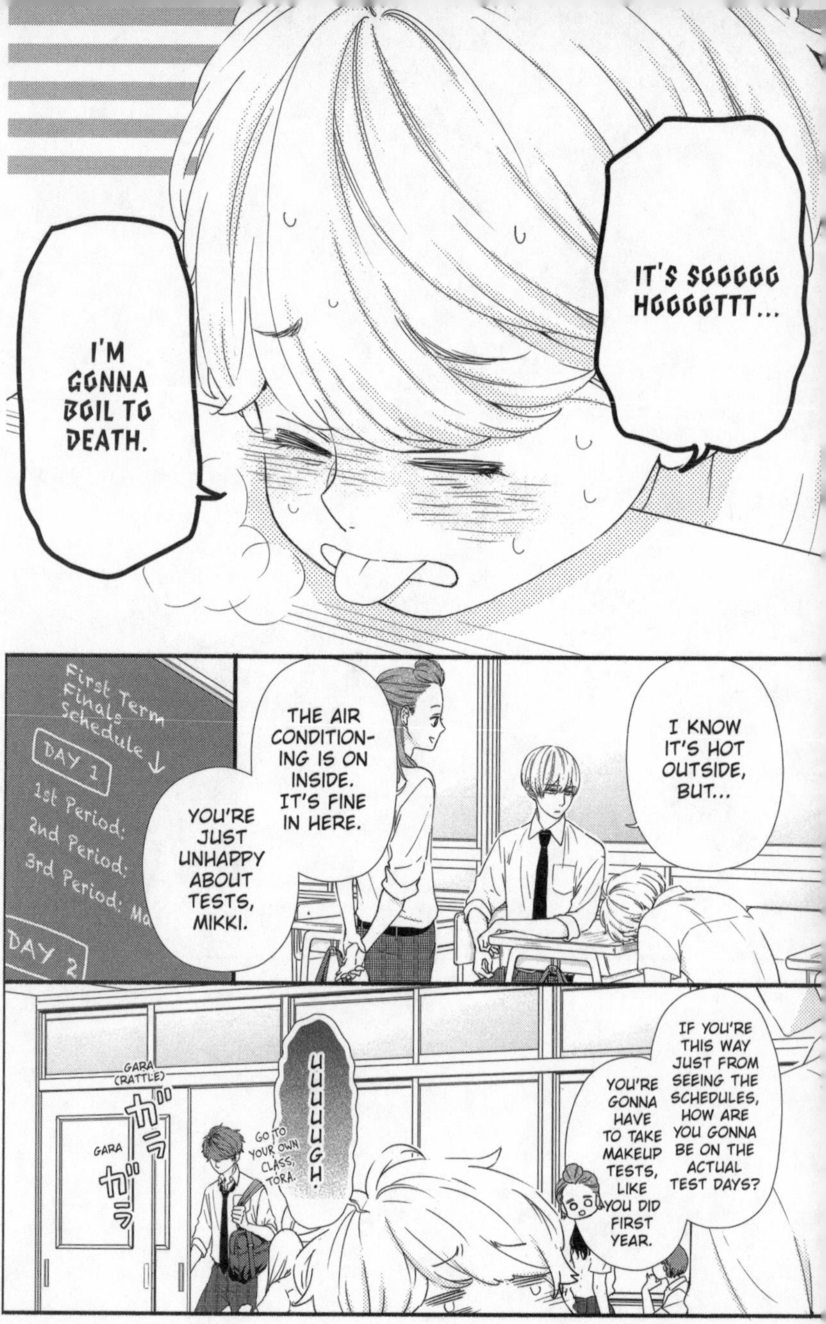
IT'S SOOOOO HOOOOTTT...
I'M GONNA BOIL TO DEATH.
I KNOW IT'S HOT OUTSIDE, BUT...
THE AIR CONDITIONING IS ON INSIDE. IT'S FINE IN HERE.
YOU'RE JUST UNHAPPY ABOUT TESTS, MIKKI.
First Term Finals Schedule ↓
DAY 1
1st Period:
2nd Period:
3rd Period: Ma
DAY 2
IF YOU'RE THIS WAY JUST FROM SEEING THE SCHEDULES, HOW ARE YOU GONNA BE ON THE ACTUAL TEST DAYS?
YOU'RE GONNA HAVE TO TAKE MAKEUP TESTS, LIKE YOU DID FIRST YEAR.
UUUUUGH!
GO TO YOUR OWN CLASS, TORA.
GARA (RATTLE)
GARA

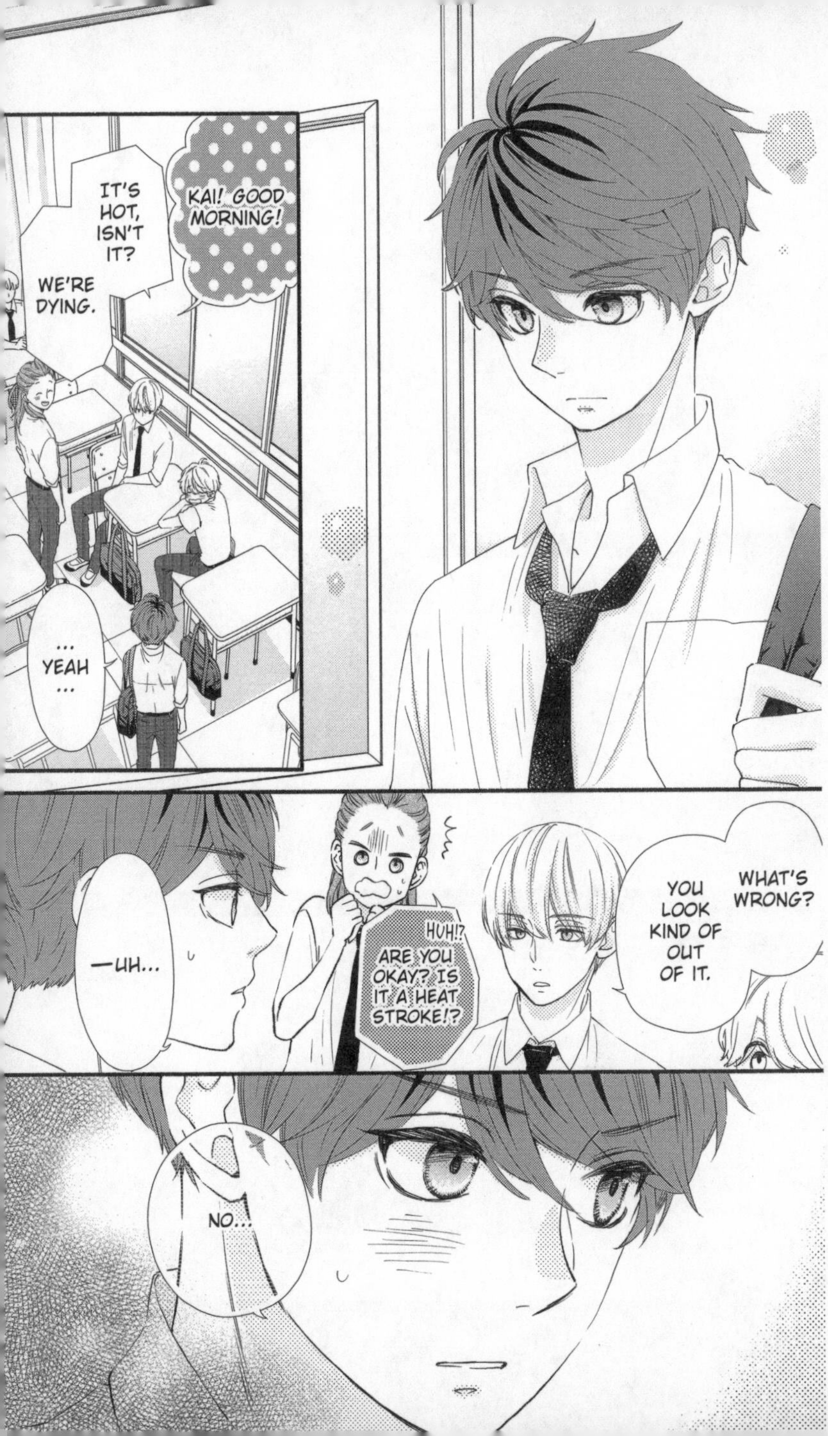
KAI! GOOD MORNING!
IT'S HOT, ISN'T IT?
WE'RE DYING.
... YEAH ...
WHAT'S WRONG? YOU LOOK KIND OF OUT OF IT.
HUH!?
ARE YOU OKAY? IS IT A HEAT STROKE!?
—UH...
NO...

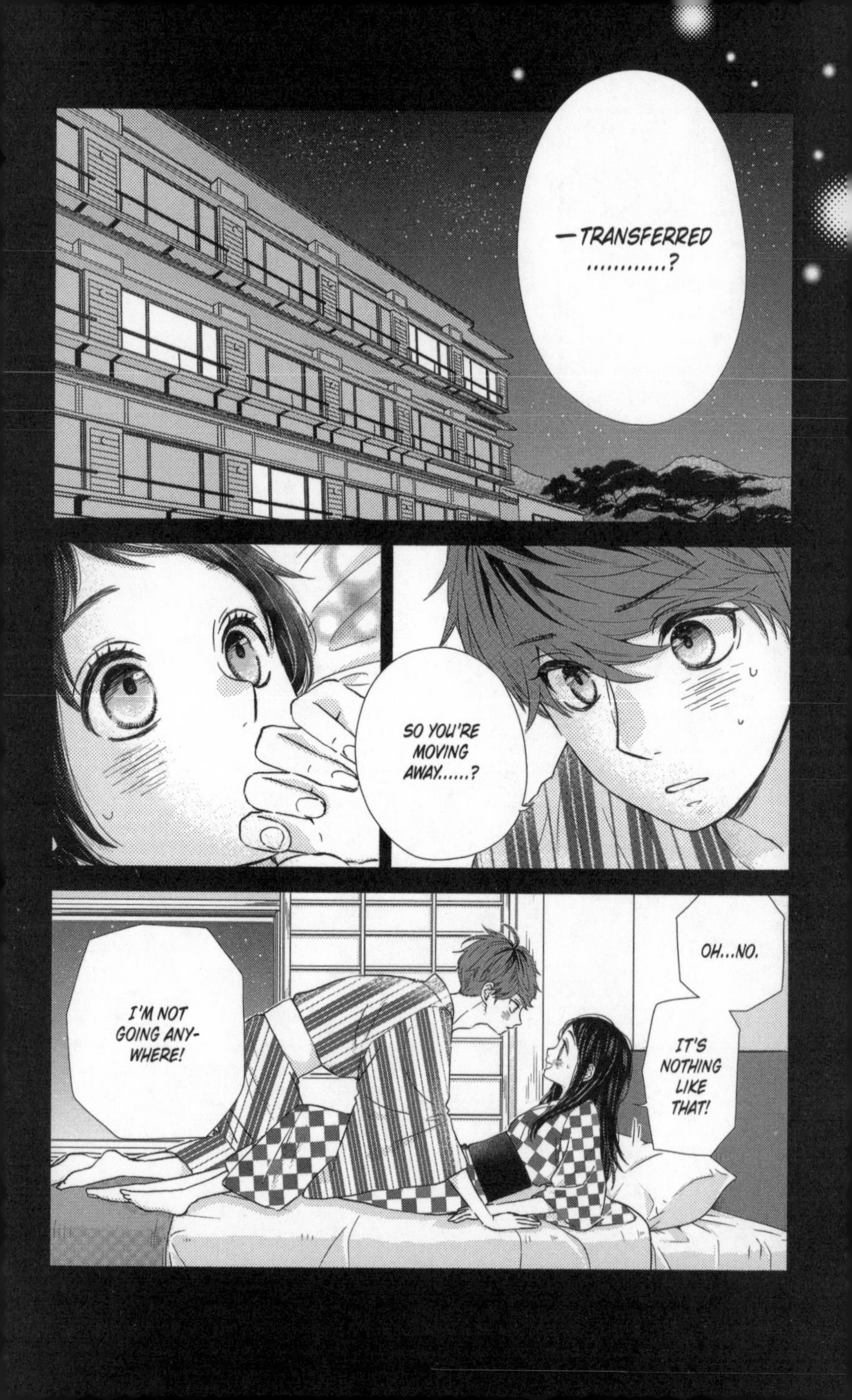
—TRANSFERRED ....?
SO YOU'RE MOVING AWAY......?
OH...NO.
IT'S NOTHING LIKE THAT!
I'M NOT GOING ANY-WHERE!

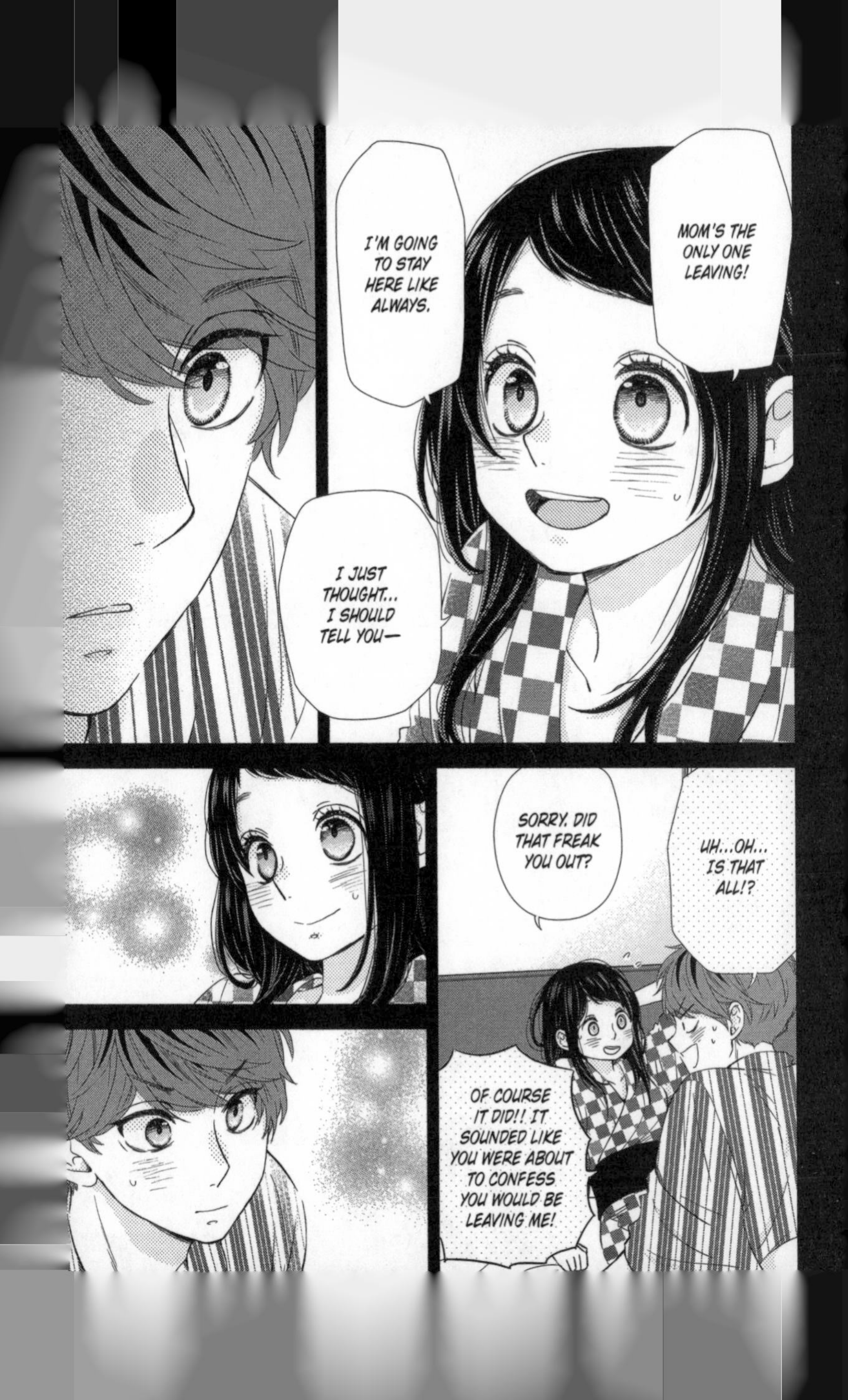
MOM'S THE ONLY ONE LEAVING!
I'M GOING TO STAY HERE LIKE ALWAYS.
I JUST THOUGHT... I SHOULD TELL YOU—
UH...OH... IS THAT ALL!?
SORRY. DID THAT FREAK YOU OUT?
OF COURSE IT DID!! IT SOUNDED LIKE YOU WERE ABOUT TO CONFESS YOU WOULD BE LEAVING ME!

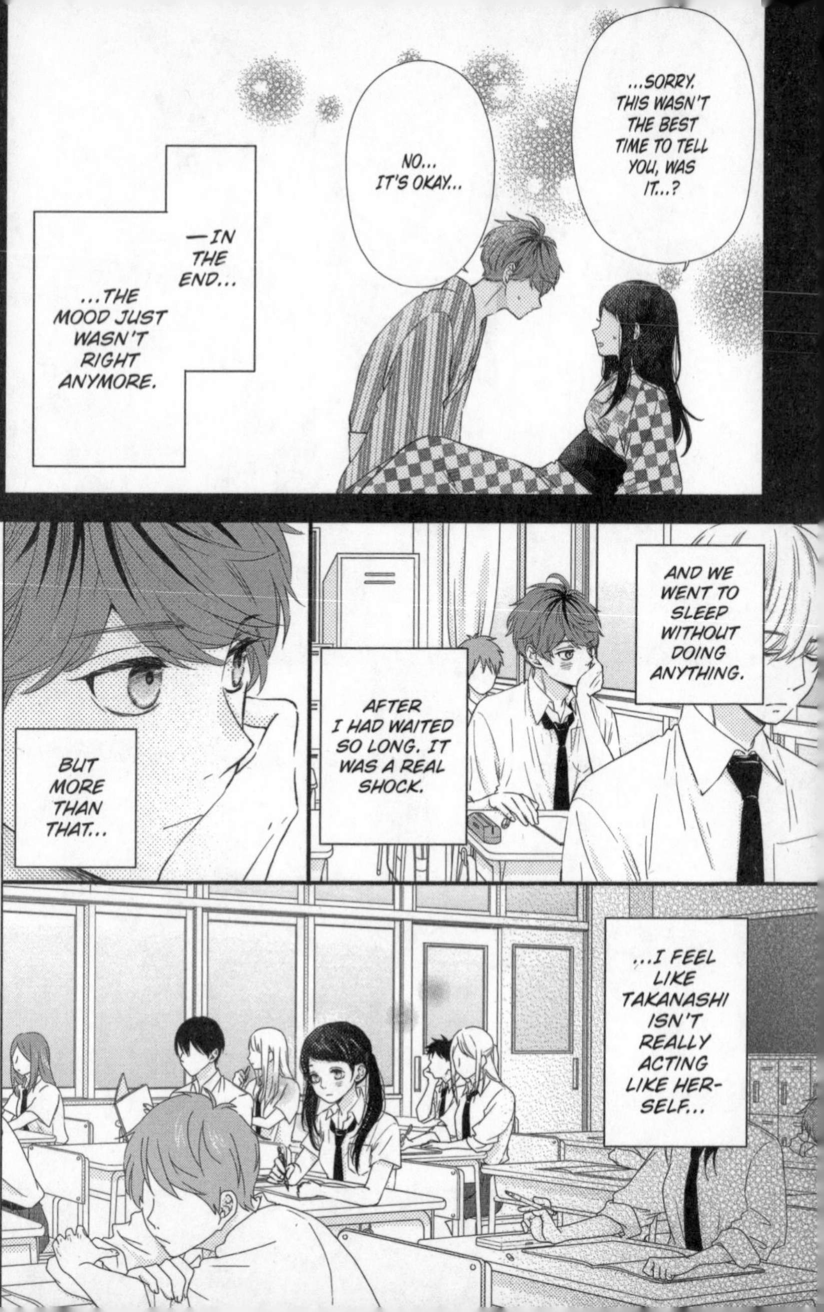
...SORRY. THIS WASN'T THE BEST TIME TO TELL YOU, WAS IT...?
NO... IT'S OKAY...
—IN THE END...
...THE MOOD JUST WASN'T RIGHT ANYMORE.
AND WE WENT TO SLEEP WITHOUT DOING ANYTHING.
AFTER I HAD WAITED SO LONG. IT WAS A REAL SHOCK.
BUT MORE THAN THAT...
...I FEEL LIKE TAKANASHI ISN'T REALLY ACTING LIKE HER-SELF...

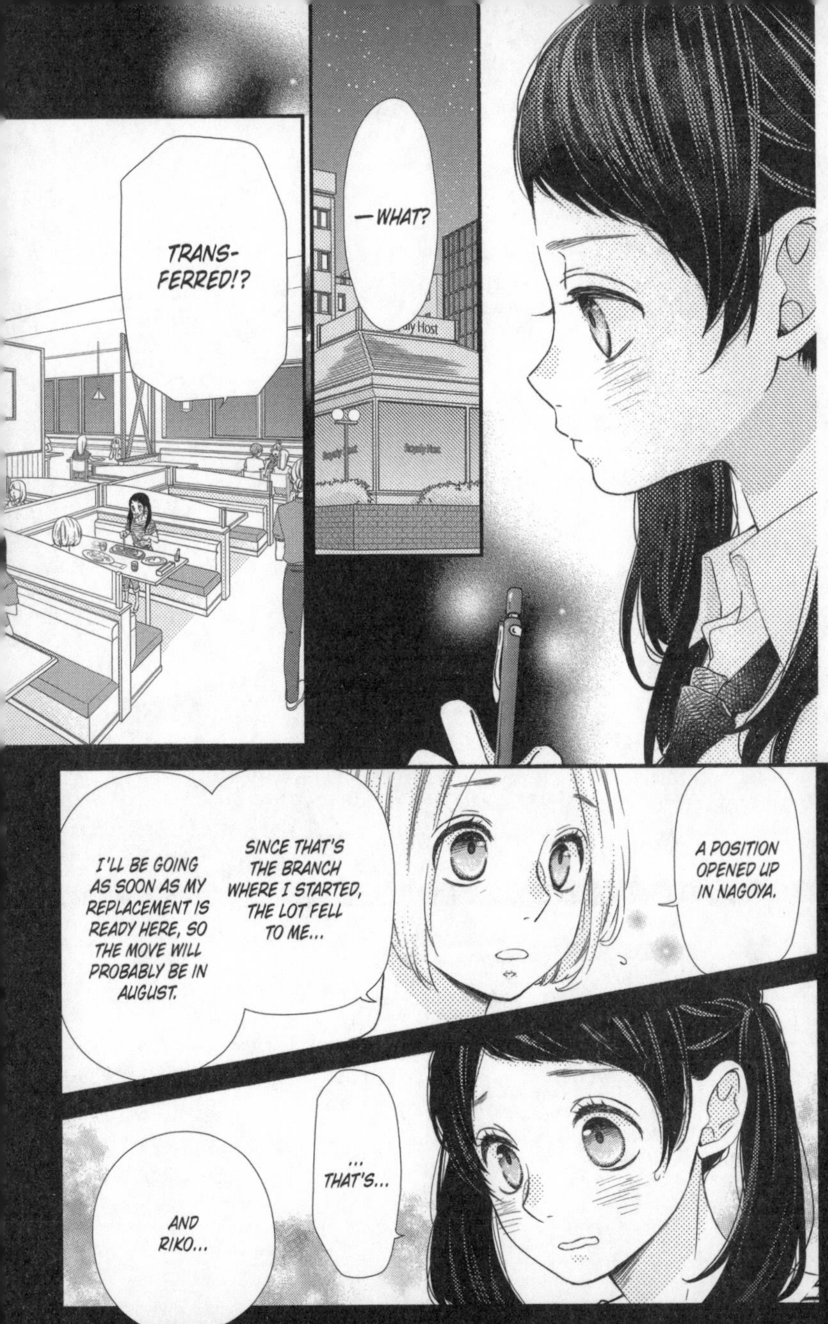
—WHAT?
TRANS-FERRED!?
A POSITION OPENED UP IN NAGOYA.
SINCE THAT'S THE BRANCH WHERE I STARTED, THE LOT FELL TO ME...
I'LL BE GOING AS SOON AS MY REPLACEMENT IS READY HERE, SO THE MOVE WILL PROBABLY BE IN AUGUST.
... THAT'S...
AND RIKO...

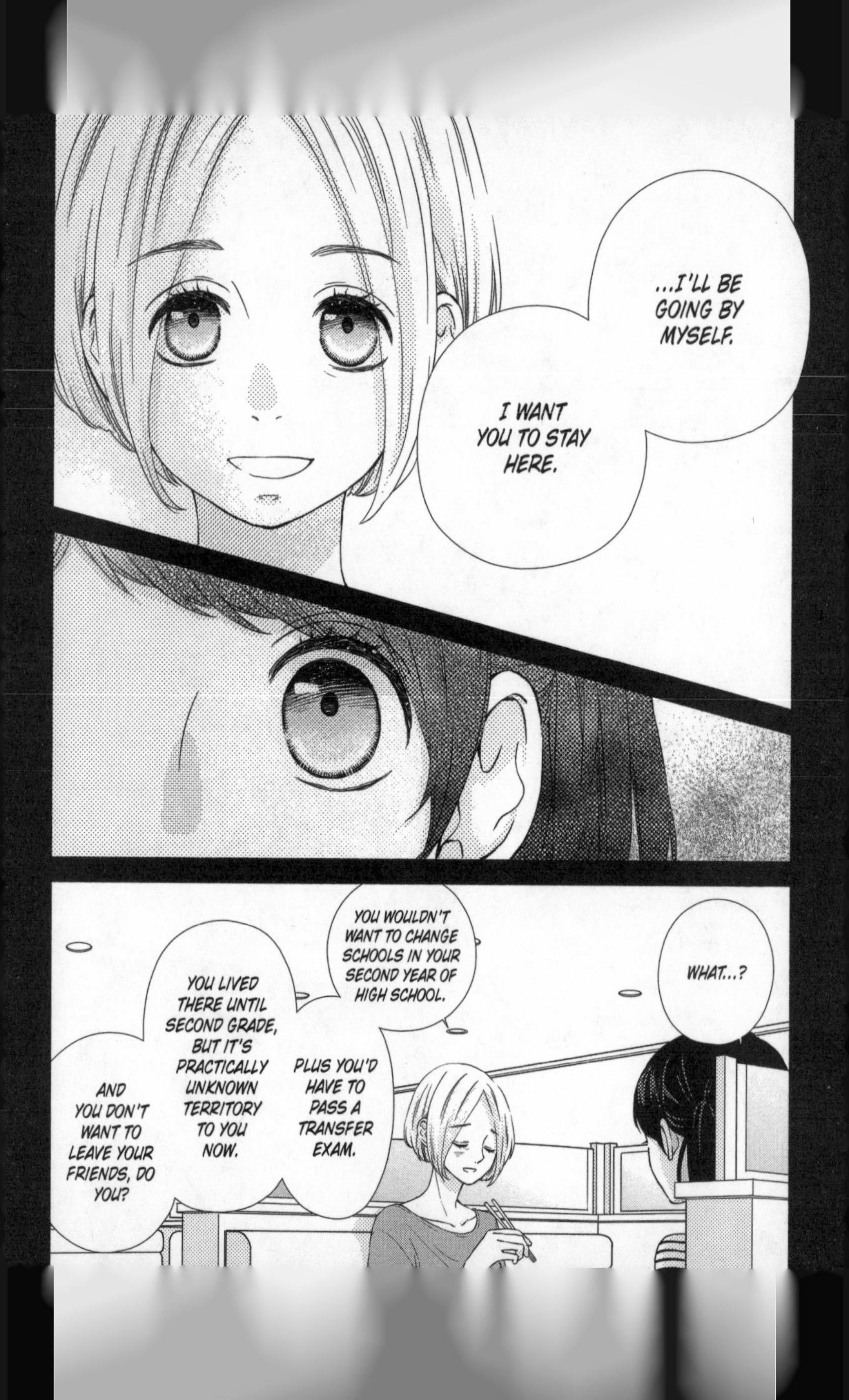
...I'LL BE GOING BY MYSELF.
I WANT YOU TO STAY HERE.
WHAT...?
YOU WOULDN'T WANT TO CHANGE SCHOOLS IN YOUR SECOND YEAR OF HIGH SCHOOL.
PLUS YOU'D HAVE TO PASS A TRANSFER EXAM.
YOU LIVED THERE UNTIL SECOND GRADE, BUT IT'S PRACTICALLY UNKNOWN TERRITORY TO YOU NOW.
AND YOU DON'T WANT TO LEAVE YOUR FRIENDS, DO YOU?

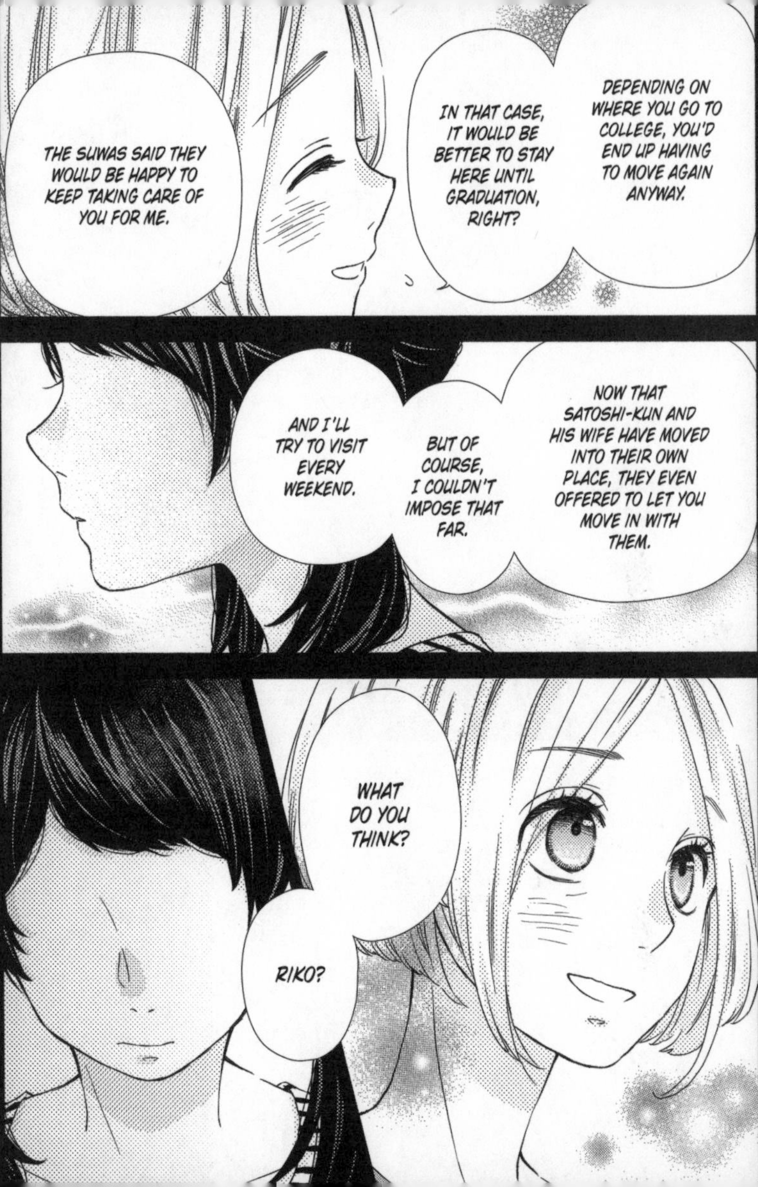
DEPENDING ON WHERE YOU GO TO COLLEGE, YOU'D END UP HAVING TO MOVE AGAIN ANYWAY.
IN THAT CASE, IT WOULD BE BETTER TO STAY HERE UNTIL GRADUATION, RIGHT?
THE SUWAS SAID THEY WOULD BE HAPPY TO KEEP TAKING CARE OF YOU FOR ME.
NOW THAT SATOSHI-KUN AND HIS WIFE HAVE MOVED INTO THEIR OWN PLACE, THEY EVEN OFFERED TO LET YOU MOVE IN WITH THEM.
BUT OF COURSE, I COULDN'T IMPOSE THAT FAR.
AND I'LL TRY TO VISIT EVERY WEEKEND.
WHAT DO YOU THINK?
RIKO?

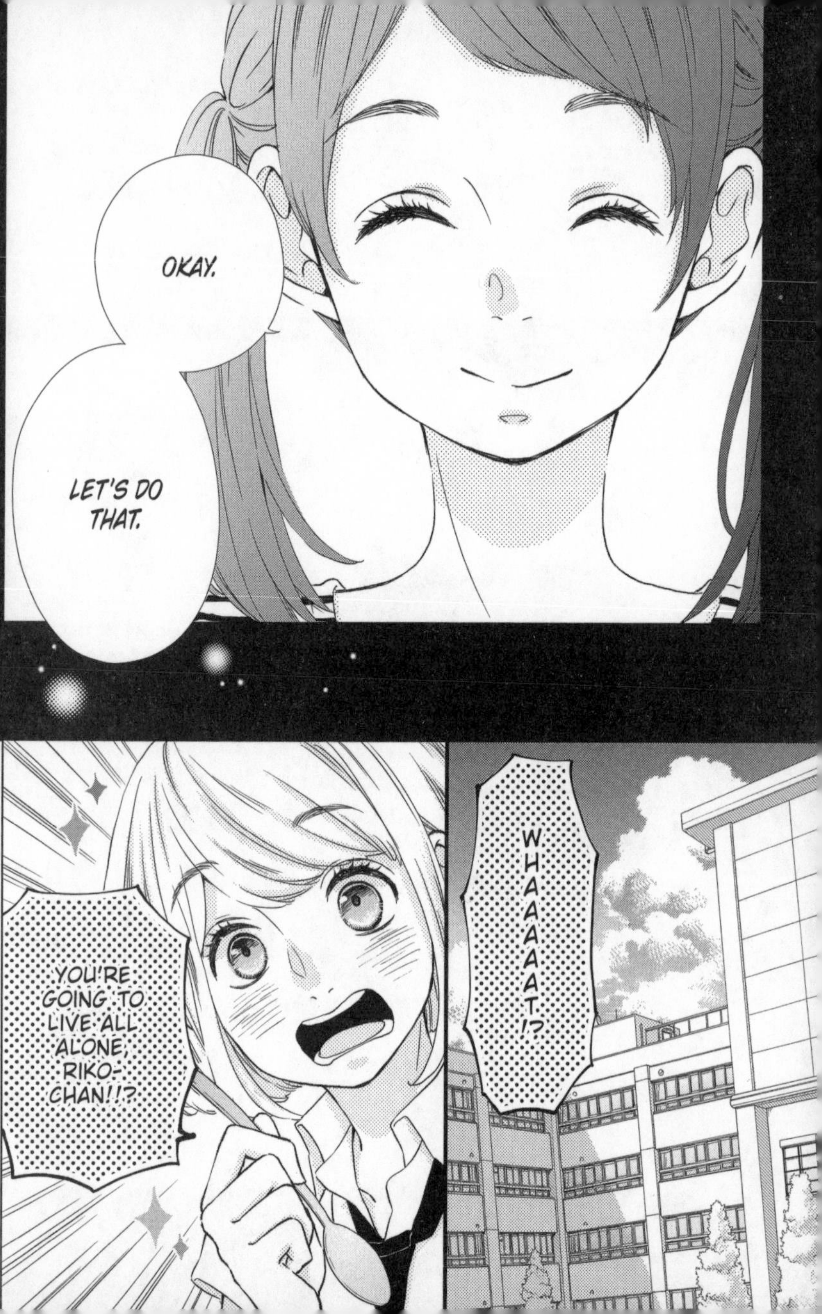
OKAY.
LET'S DO THAT.
WHAAAAAAT!?
YOU'RE GOING TO LIVE ALL ALONE, RIKO-CHAN!!?

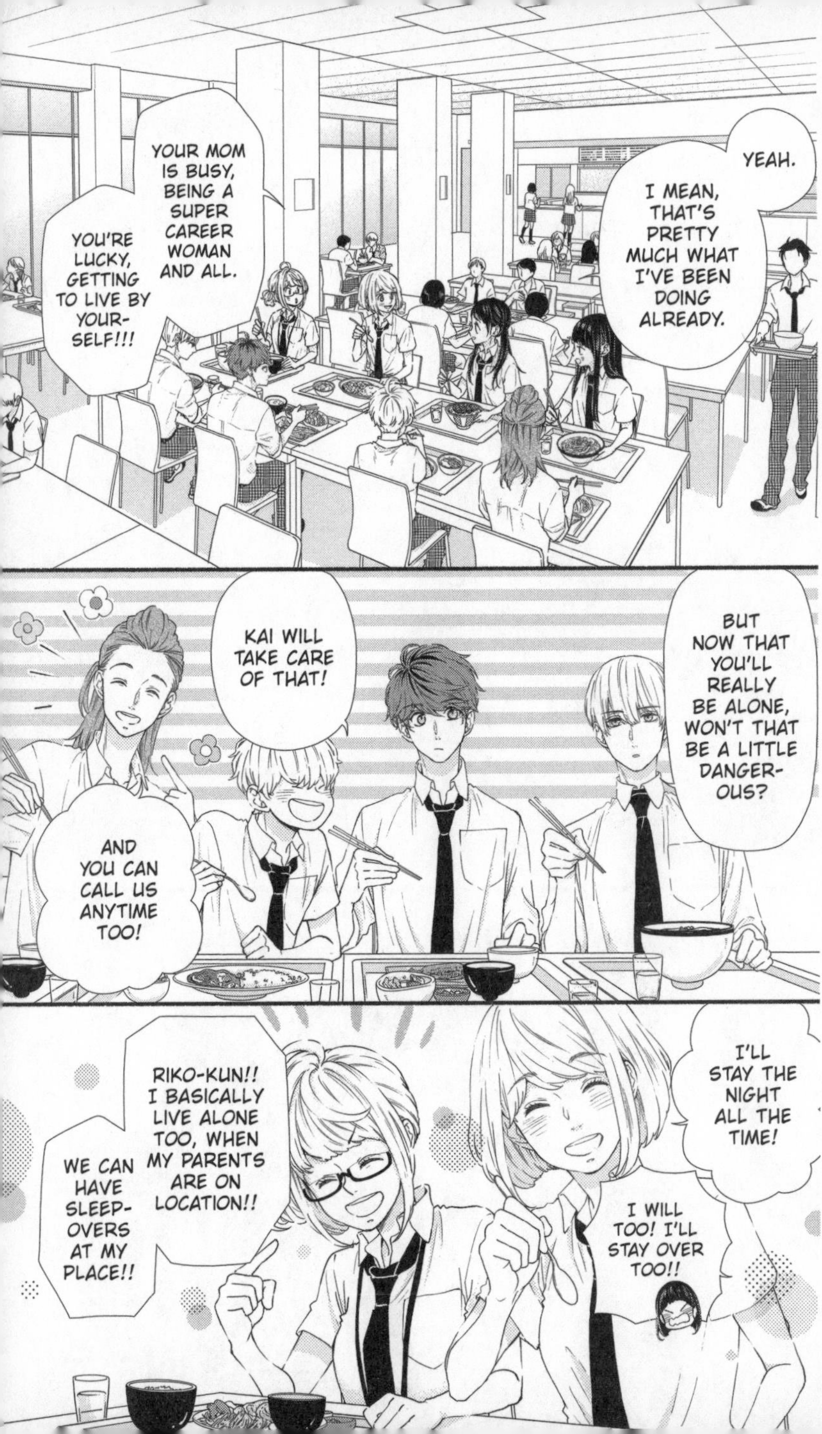
YEAH.
I MEAN, THAT'S PRETTY MUCH WHAT I'VE BEEN DOING ALREADY.
YOUR MOM IS BUSY, BEING A SUPER CAREER WOMAN AND ALL.
YOU'RE LUCKY, GETTING TO LIVE BY YOUR-SELF!!!
BUT NOW THAT YOU'LL REALLY BE ALONE, WON'T THAT BE A LITTLE DANGER-OUS?
KAI WILL TAKE CARE OF THAT!
AND YOU CAN CALL US ANYTIME TOO!
I'LL STAY THE NIGHT ALL THE TIME!
I WILL TOO! I'LL STAY OVER TOO!!
RIKO-KUN!! I BASICALLY LIVE ALONE TOO, WHEN MY PARENTS ARE ON LOCATION!!
WE CAN HAVE SLEEP-OVERS AT MY PLACE!!

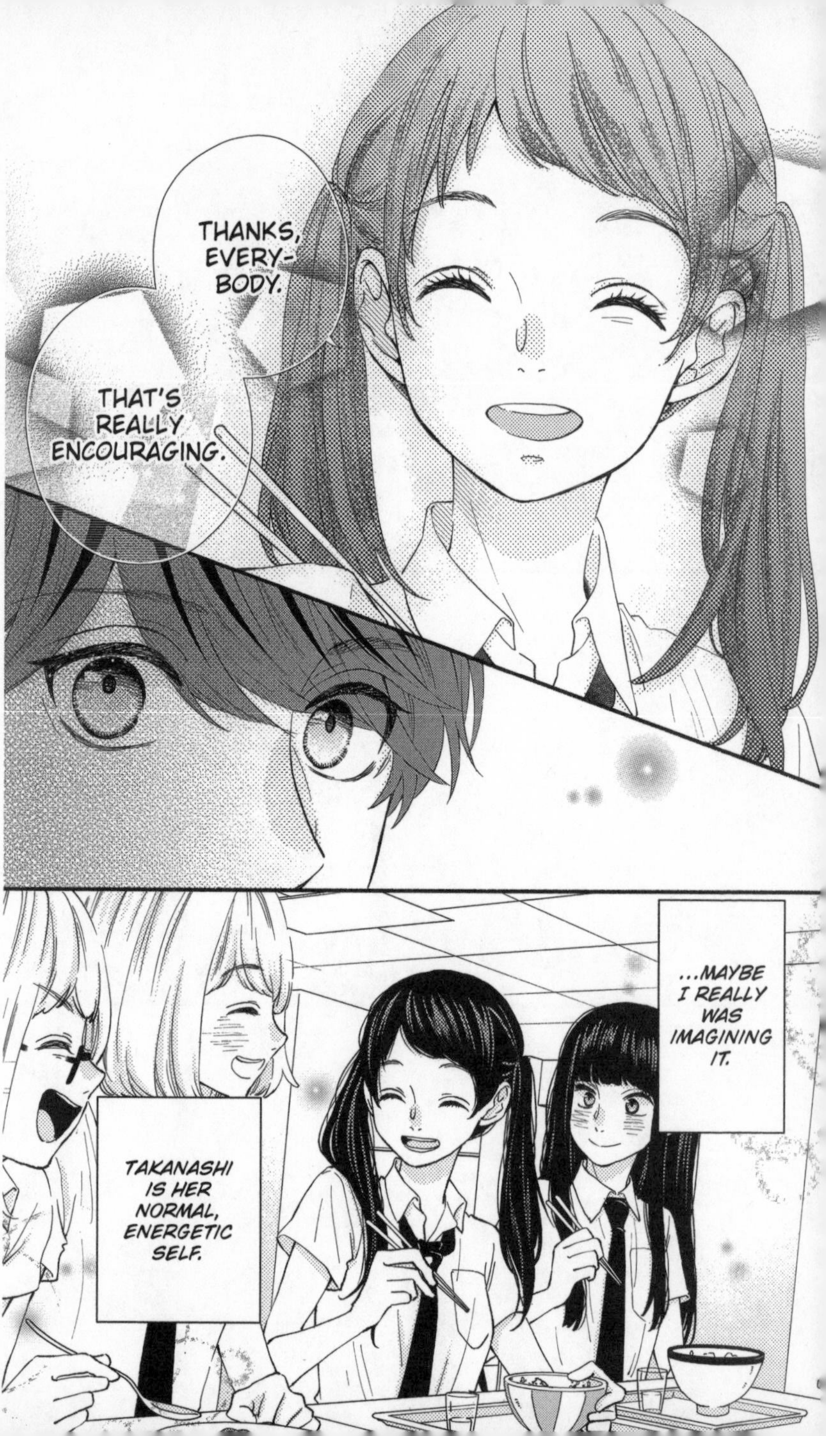
THANKS, EVERY-BODY.
THAT'S REALLY ENCOURAGING.
...MAYBE I REALLY WAS IMAGINING IT.
TAKANASHI IS HER NORMAL, ENERGETIC SELF.

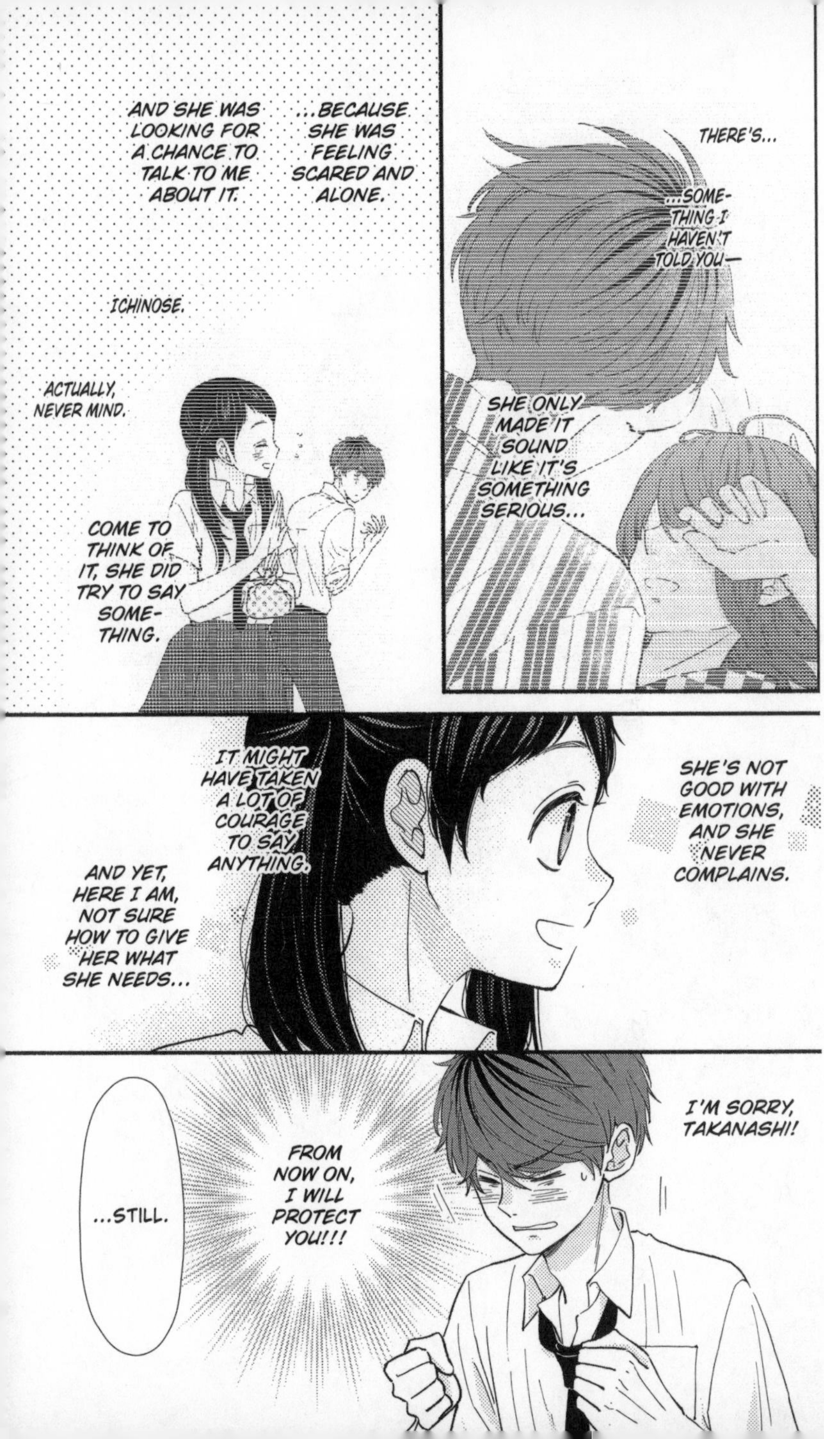
THERE'S...
...SOMETHING I HAVEN'T TOLD YOU—
SHE ONLY MADE IT SOUND LIKE IT'S SOMETHING SERIOUS...
...BECAUSE SHE WAS FEELING SCARED AND ALONE.
AND SHE WAS LOOKING FOR A CHANCE TO TALK TO ME ABOUT IT.
ICHINOSE.
ACTUALLY, NEVER MIND.
COME TO THINK OF IT, SHE DID TRY TO SAY SOMETHING.
SHE'S NOT GOOD WITH EMOTIONS, AND SHE NEVER COMPLAINS.
IT MIGHT HAVE TAKEN A LOT OF COURAGE TO SAY ANYTHING.
AND YET, HERE I AM, NOT SURE HOW TO GIVE HER WHAT SHE NEEDS...
I'M SORRY, TAKANASHI!
FROM NOW ON, I WILL PROTECT YOU!!!
...STILL.

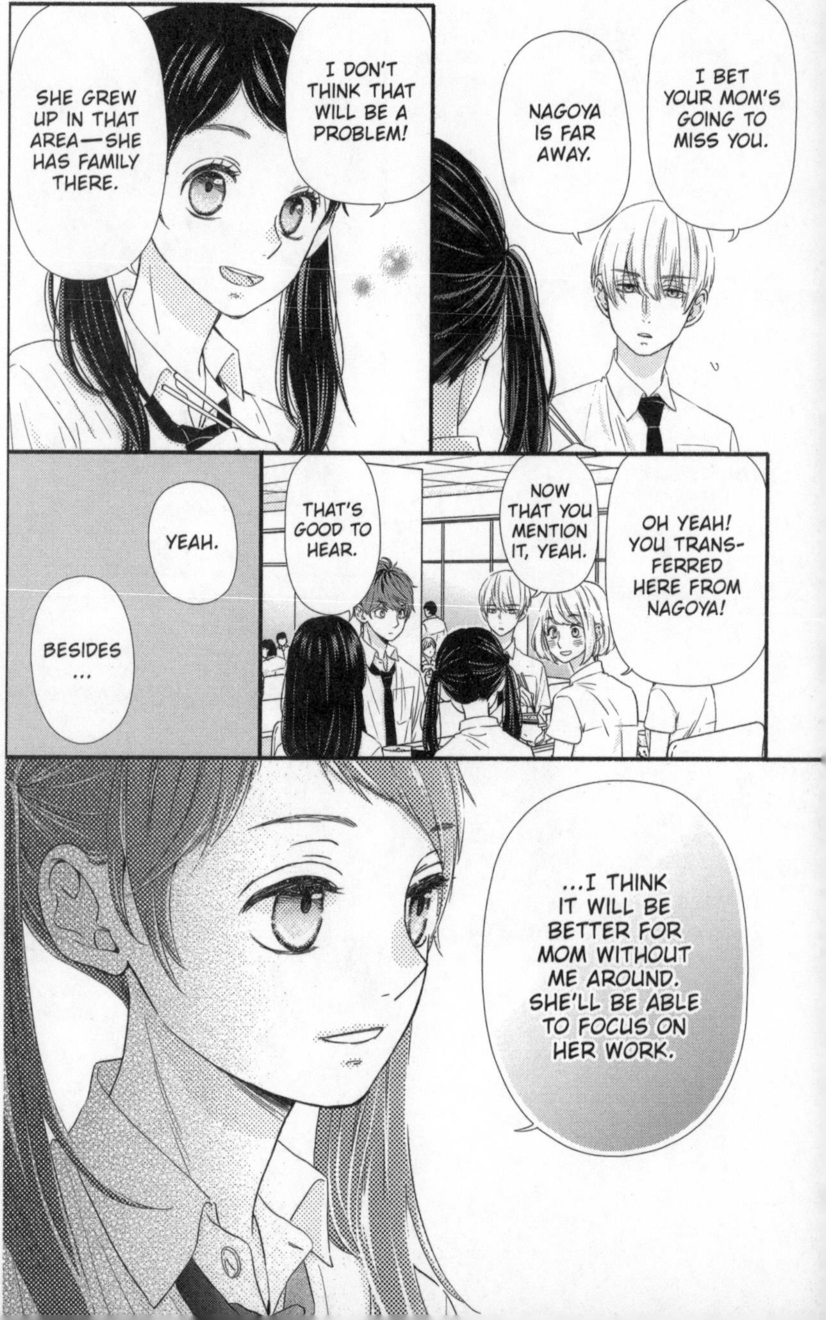
I BET YOUR MOM'S GOING TO MISS YOU.
NAGOYA IS FAR AWAY.
I DON'T THINK THAT WILL BE A PROBLEM!
SHE GREW UP IN THAT AREA—SHE HAS FAMILY THERE.
OH YEAH! YOU TRANS-FERRED HERE FROM NAGOYA!
NOW THAT YOU MENTION IT, YEAH.
THAT'S GOOD TO HEAR.
YEAH.
BESIDES...
...I THINK IT WILL BE BETTER FOR MOM WITHOUT ME AROUND. SHE'LL BE ABLE TO FOCUS ON HER WORK.

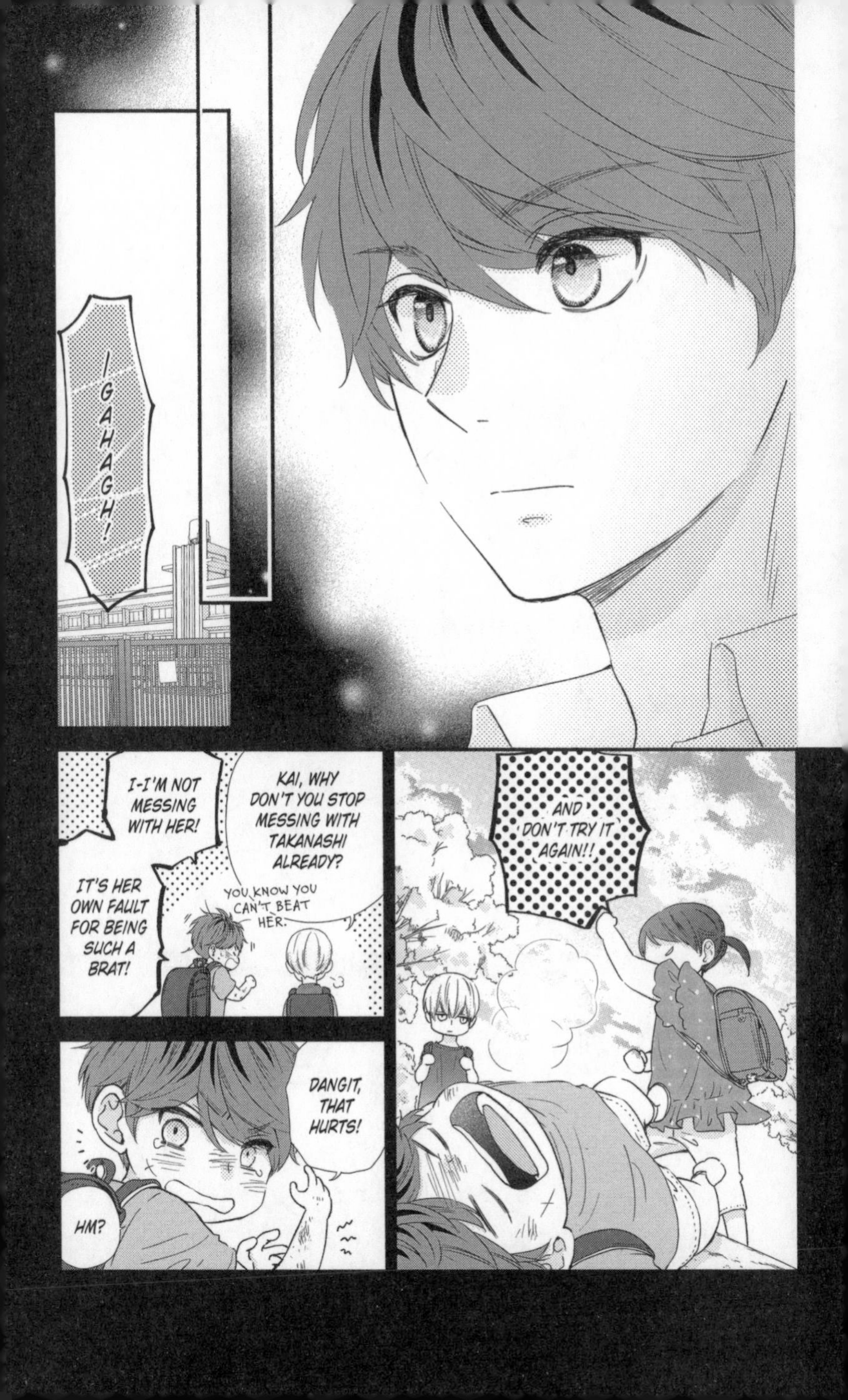
IGAHAGH!
AND DON'T TRY IT AGAIN!!
KAI, WHY DON'T YOU STOP MESSING WITH TAKANASHI ALREADY?
YOU KNOW YOU CAN'T BEAT HER.
I-I'M NOT MESSING WITH HER!
IT'S HER OWN FAULT FOR BEING SUCH A BRAT!
DANGIT, THAT HURTS!
HM?

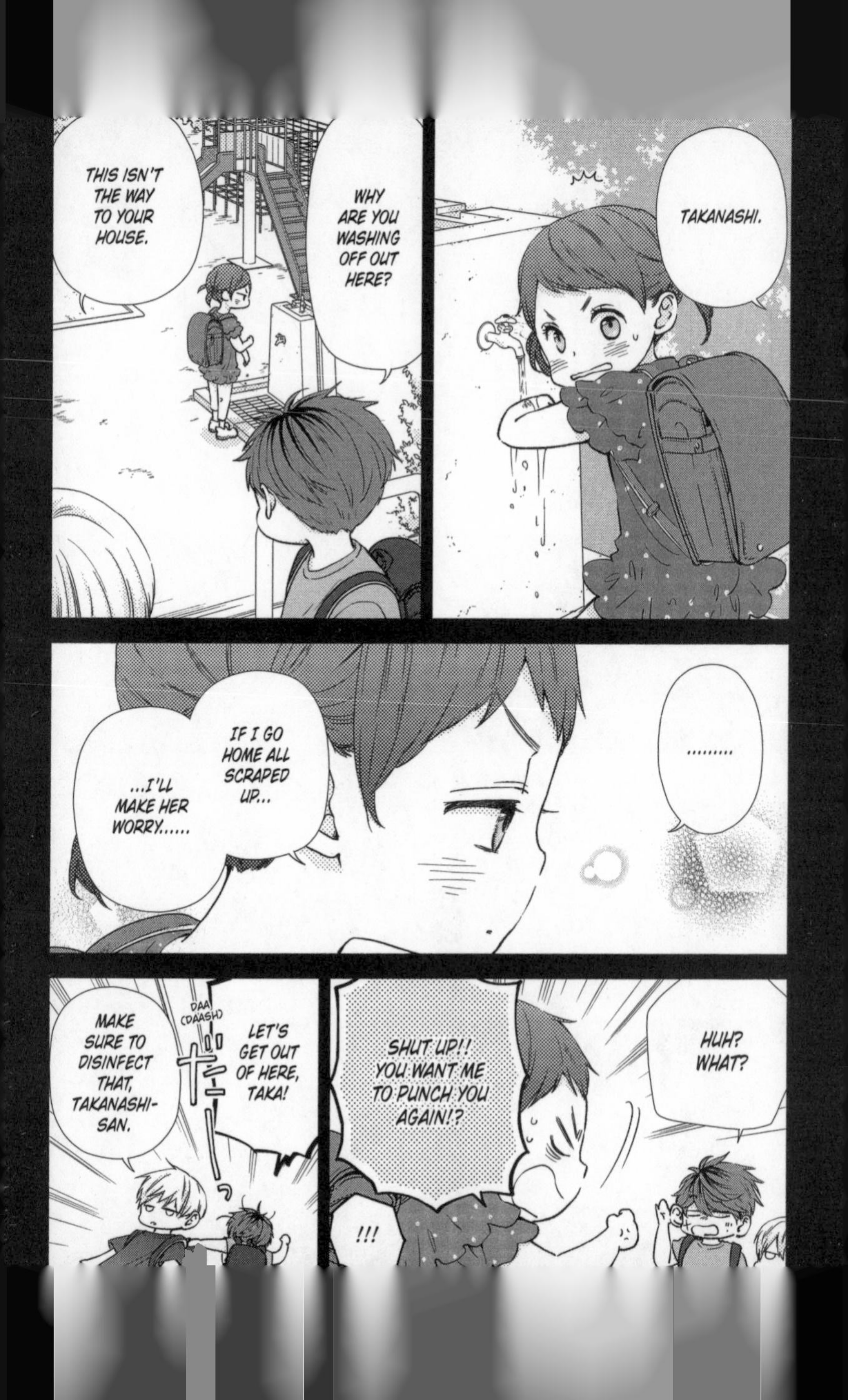
TAKANASHI.
WHY ARE YOU WASHING OFF OUT HERE?
THIS ISN'T THE WAY TO YOUR HOUSE.
....
IF I GO HOME ALL SCRAPED UP...
...I'LL MAKE HER WORRY......
HUH? WHAT?
SHUT UP!! YOU WANT ME TO PUNCH YOU AGAIN!?
!!!
LET'S GET OUT OF HERE, TAKA!
DAA (DAASH)
MAKE SURE TO DISINFECT THAT, TAKANASHI-SAN.

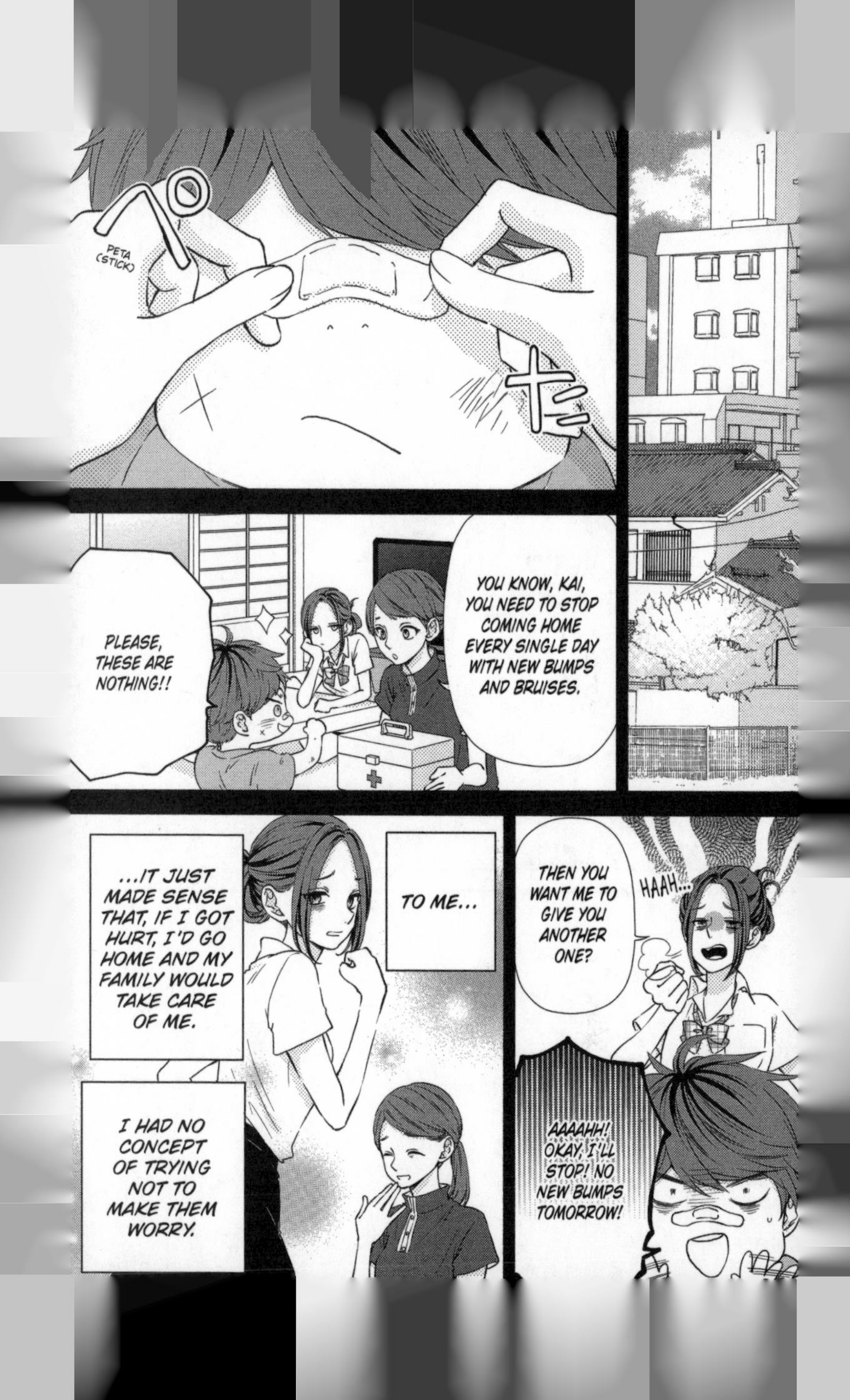
PETA (STICK)
YOU KNOW, KAI, YOU NEED TO STOP COMING HOME EVERY SINGLE DAY WITH NEW BUMPS AND BRUISES.
PLEASE, THESE ARE NOTHING!!
HAAH...
THEN YOU WANT ME TO GIVE YOU ANOTHER ONE?
AAAAHH! OKAY, I'LL STOP! NO NEW BUMPS TOMORROW!
TO ME...
...IT JUST MADE SENSE THAT, IF I GOT HURT, I'D GO HOME AND MY FAMILY WOULD TAKE CARE OF ME.
I HAD NO CONCEPT OF TRYING NOT TO MAKE THEM WORRY.

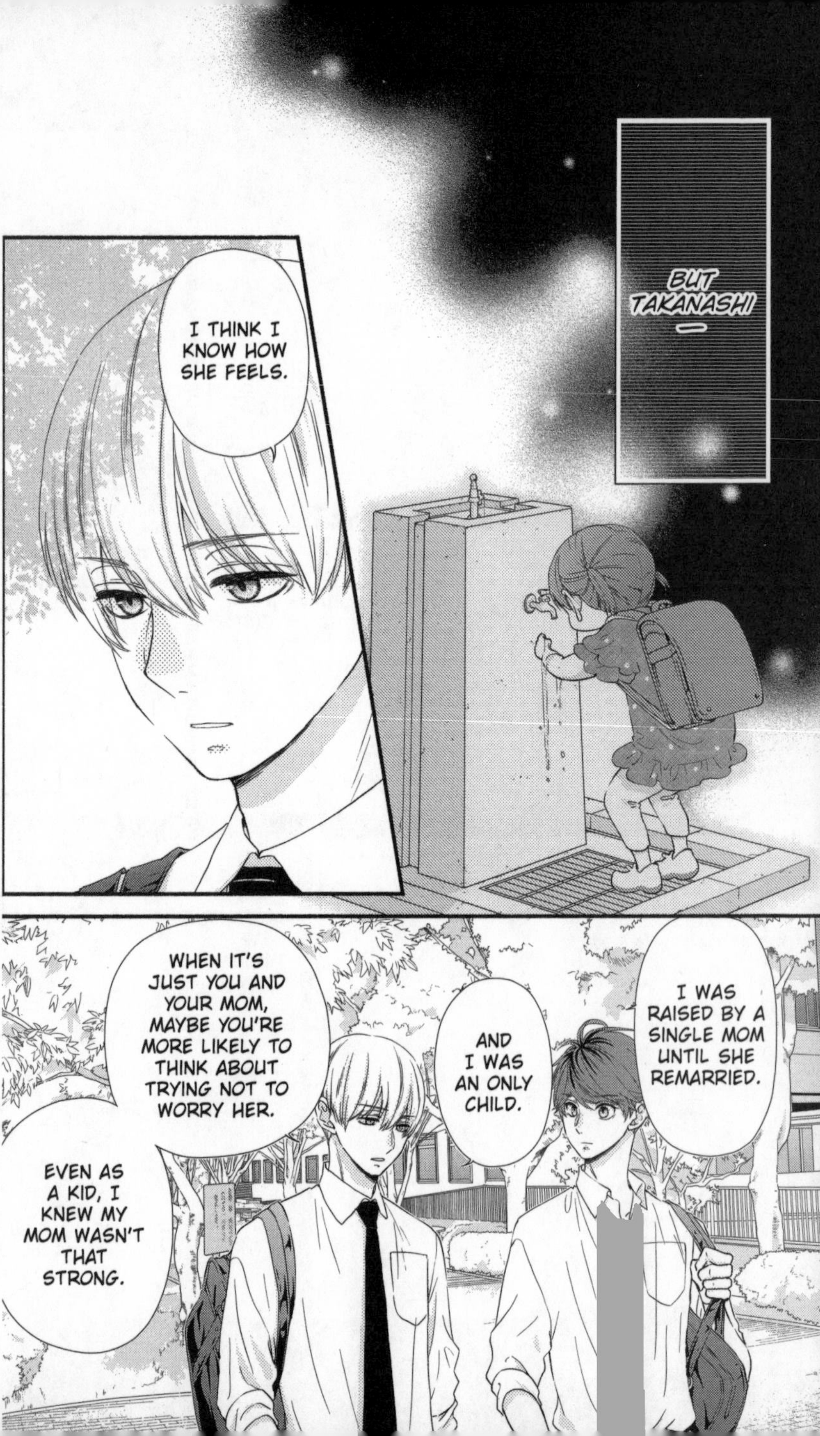
BUT TAKANASHI —
I THINK I KNOW HOW SHE FEELS.
I WAS RAISED BY A SINGLE MOM UNTIL SHE REMARRIED.
AND I WAS AN ONLY CHILD.
WHEN IT'S JUST YOU AND YOUR MOM, MAYBE YOU'RE MORE LIKELY TO THINK ABOUT TRYING NOT TO WORRY HER.
EVEN AS A KID, I KNEW MY MOM WASN'T THAT STRONG.

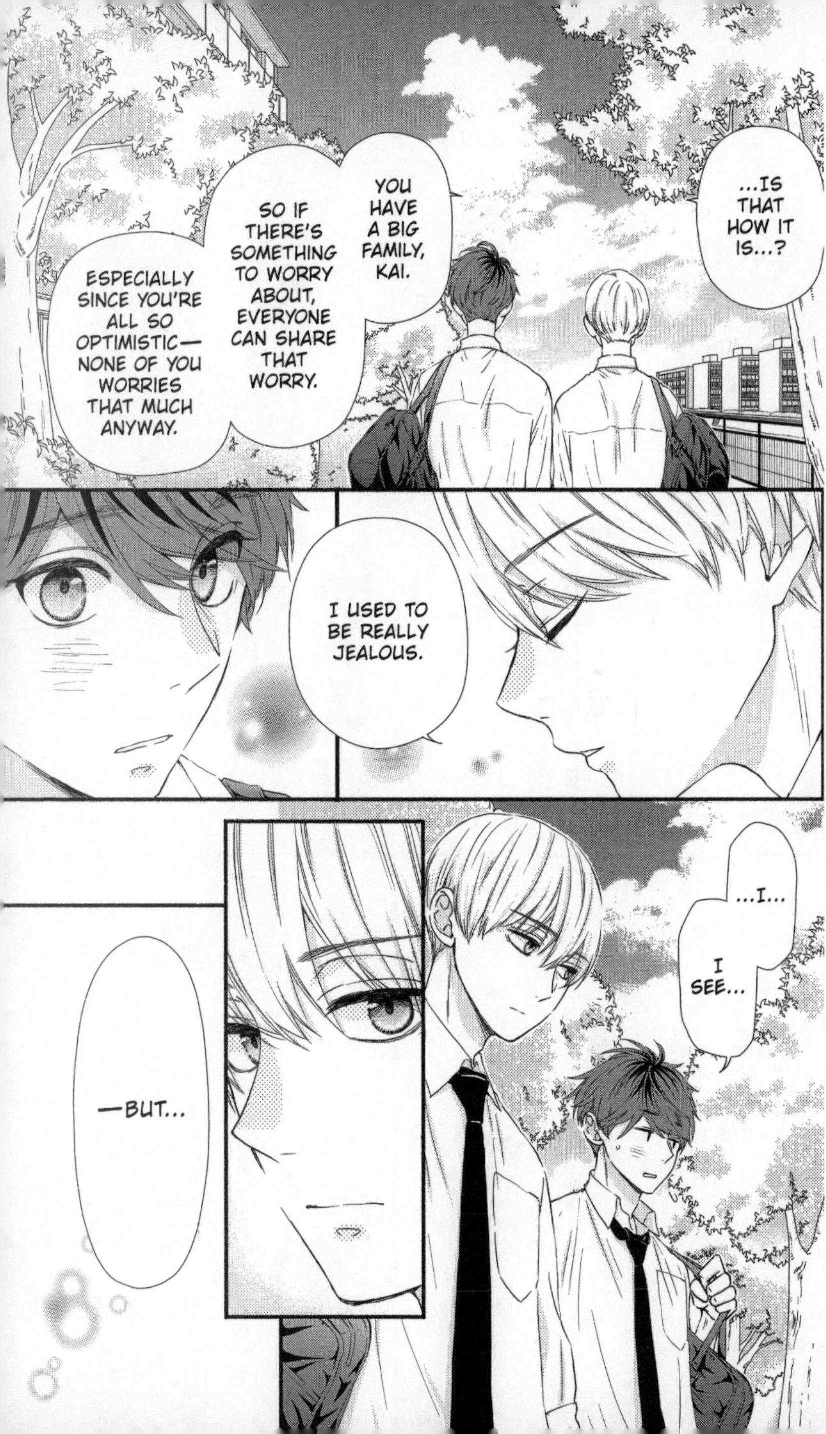
...IS THAT HOW IT IS...?
YOU HAVE A BIG FAMILY, KAI.
SO IF THERE'S SOMETHING TO WORRY ABOUT, EVERYONE CAN SHARE THAT WORRY.
ESPECIALLY SINCE YOU'RE ALL SO OPTIMISTIC—NONE OF YOU WORRIES THAT MUCH ANYWAY.
I USED TO BE REALLY JEALOUS.
...I... I SEE...
—BUT...

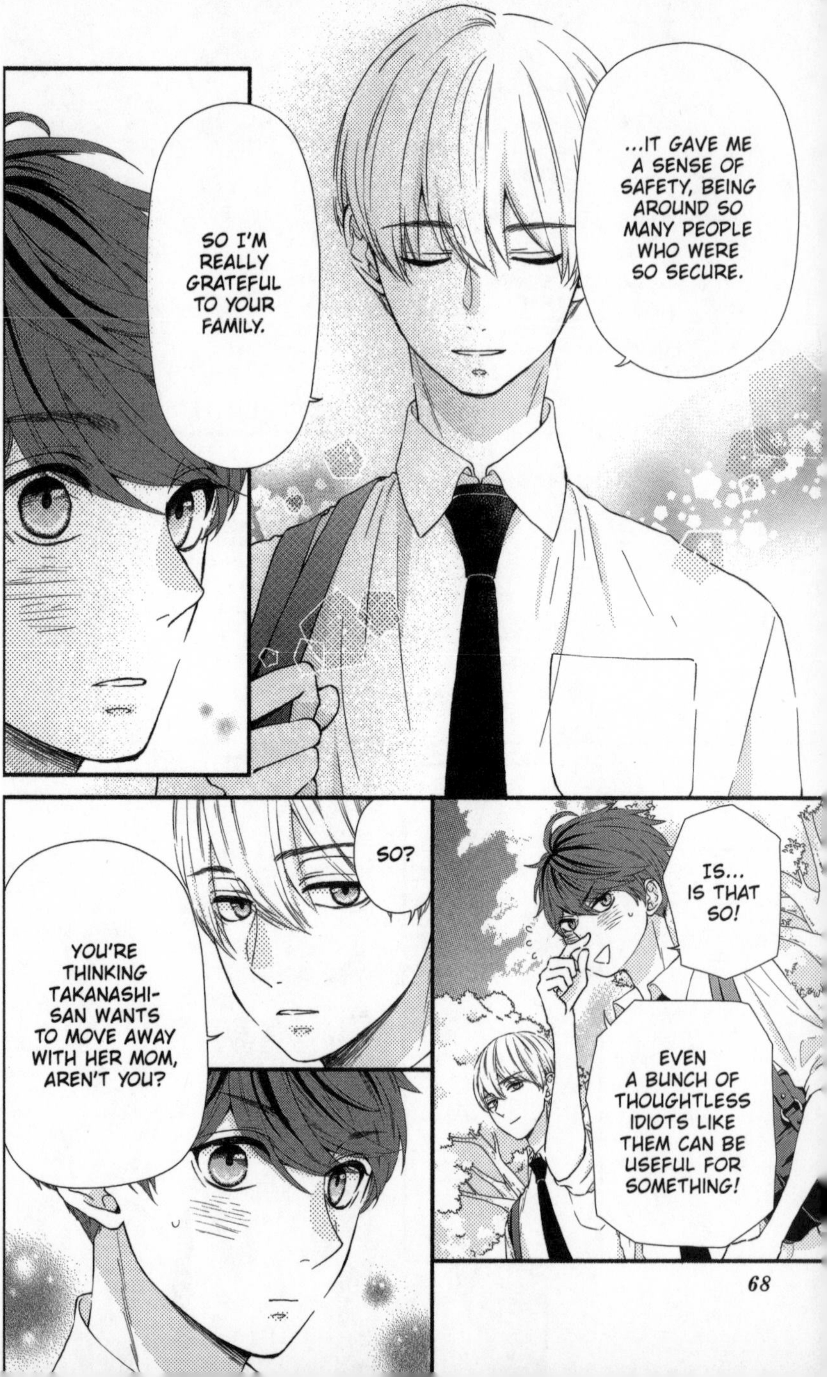
...IT GAVE ME A SENSE OF SAFETY, BEING AROUND SO MANY PEOPLE WHO WERE SO SECURE.
SO I'M REALLY GRATEFUL TO YOUR FAMILY.
IS... IS THAT SO!
EVEN A BUNCH OF THOUGHTLESS IDIOTS LIKE THEM CAN BE USEFUL FOR SOMETHING!
SO?
YOU'RE THINKING TAKANASHI-SAN WANTS TO MOVE AWAY WITH HER MOM, AREN'T YOU?

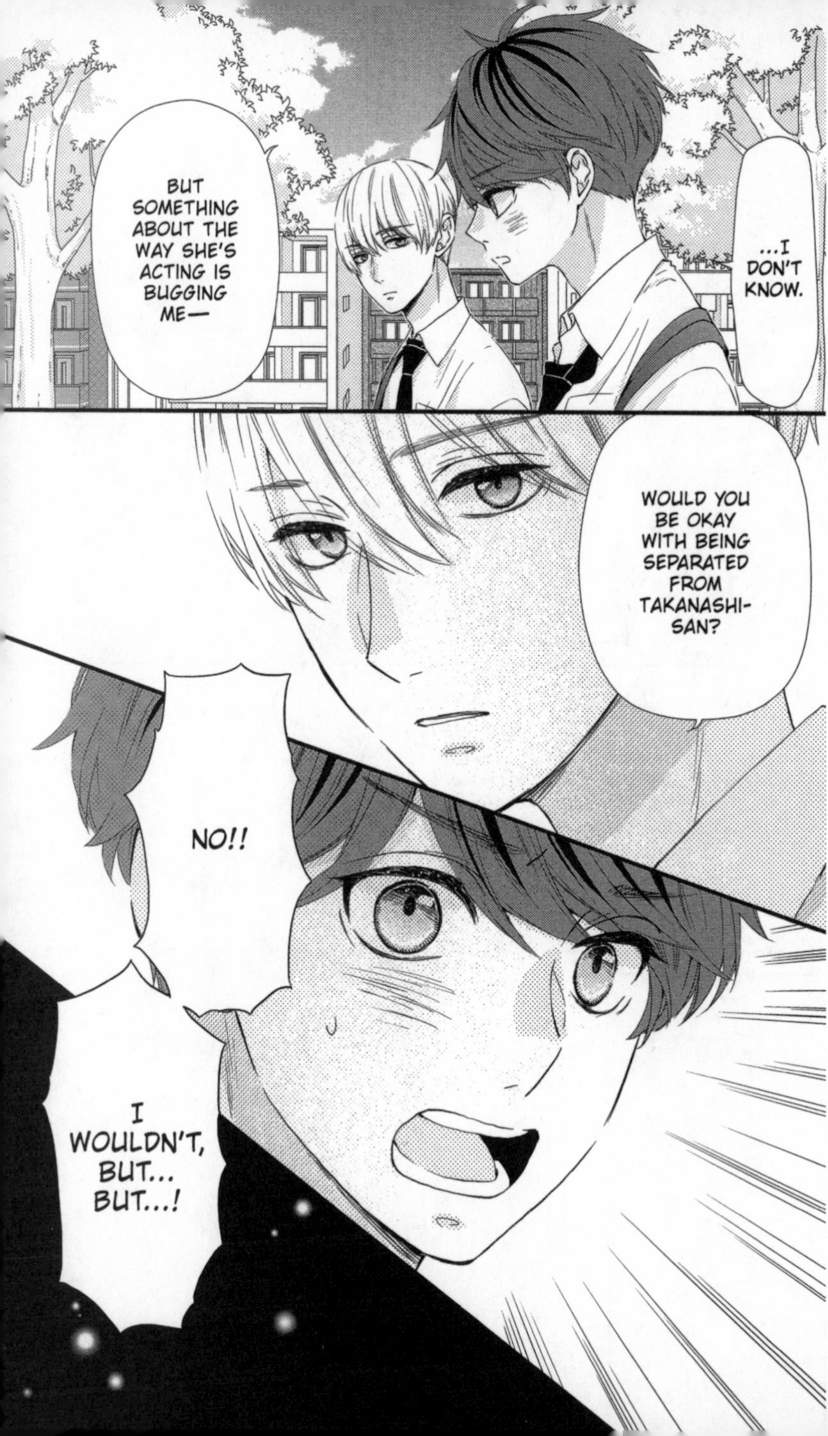
...I DON'T KNOW.
BUT SOMETHING ABOUT THE WAY SHE'S ACTING IS BUGGING ME—
WOULD YOU BE OKAY WITH BEING SEPARATED FROM TAKANASHI-SAN?
NO!!
I WOULDN'T, BUT... BUT...!

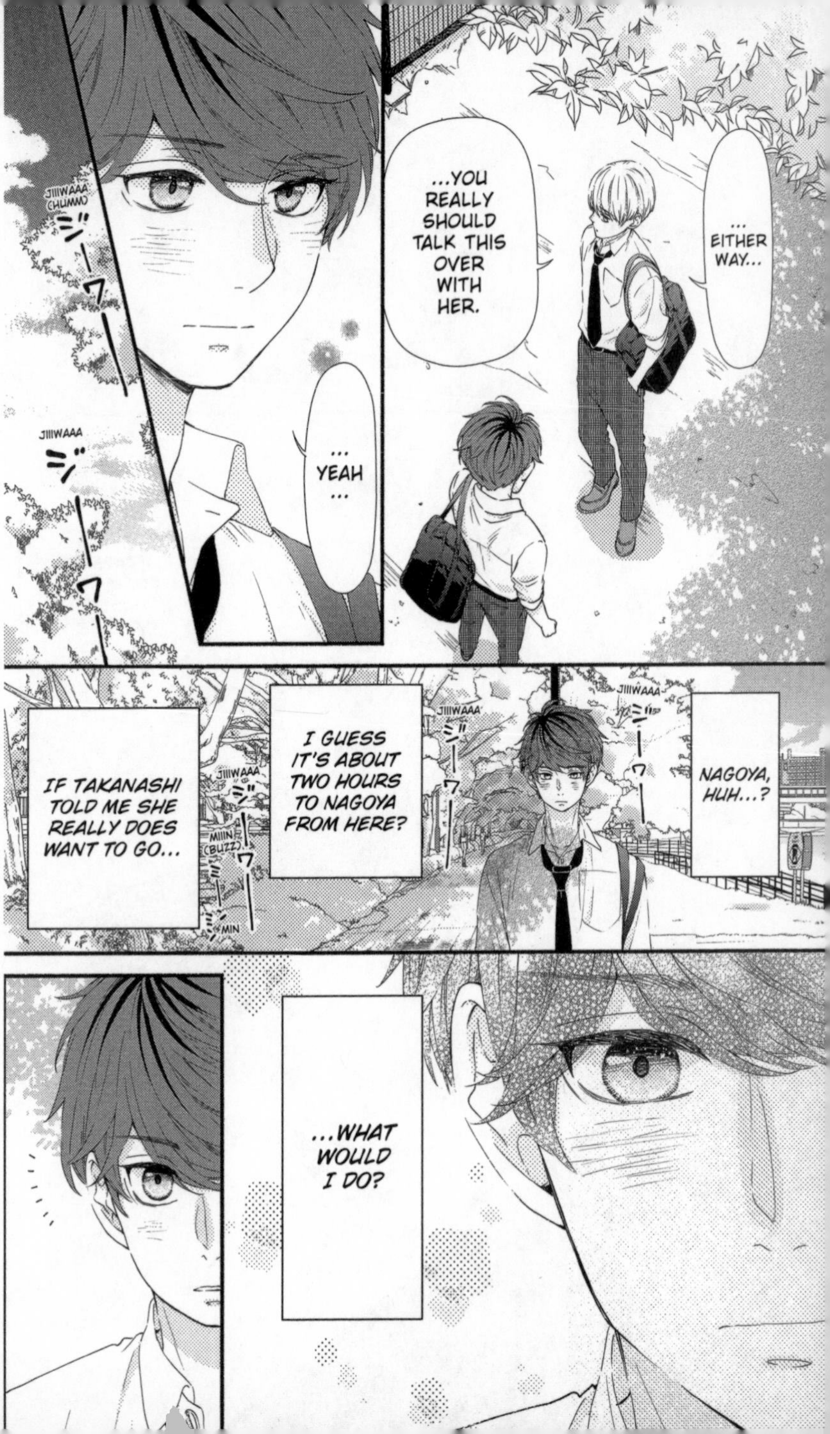

...EITHER WAY...
...YOU REALLY SHOULD TALK THIS OVER WITH HER.
JIIIWAAA (HUMM)
JIIIWAAA
...YEAH...
NAGOYA, HUH...?
JIIIWAAA
JIIIWAAA
I GUESS IT'S ABOUT TWO HOURS TO NAGOYA FROM HERE?
JIIIWAAA
MIIIN (BUZZ)
MIN
IF TAKANASHI TOLD ME SHE REALLY DOES WANT TO GO...
...WHAT WOULD I DO?

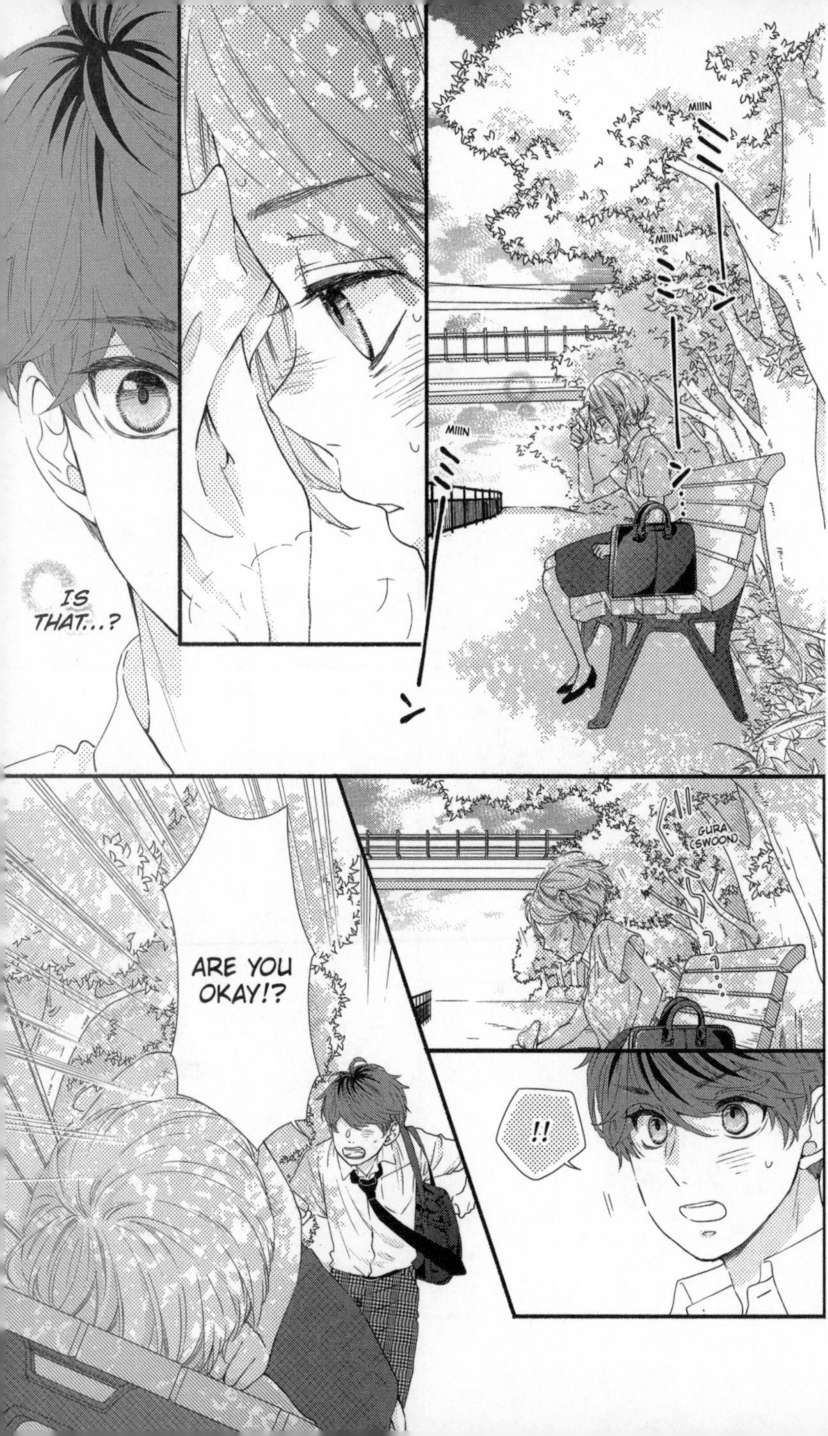
MIIIN
MIIIN
MIIIN
IS THAT...?
GURA (SWOON)
!!
ARE YOU OKAY!?

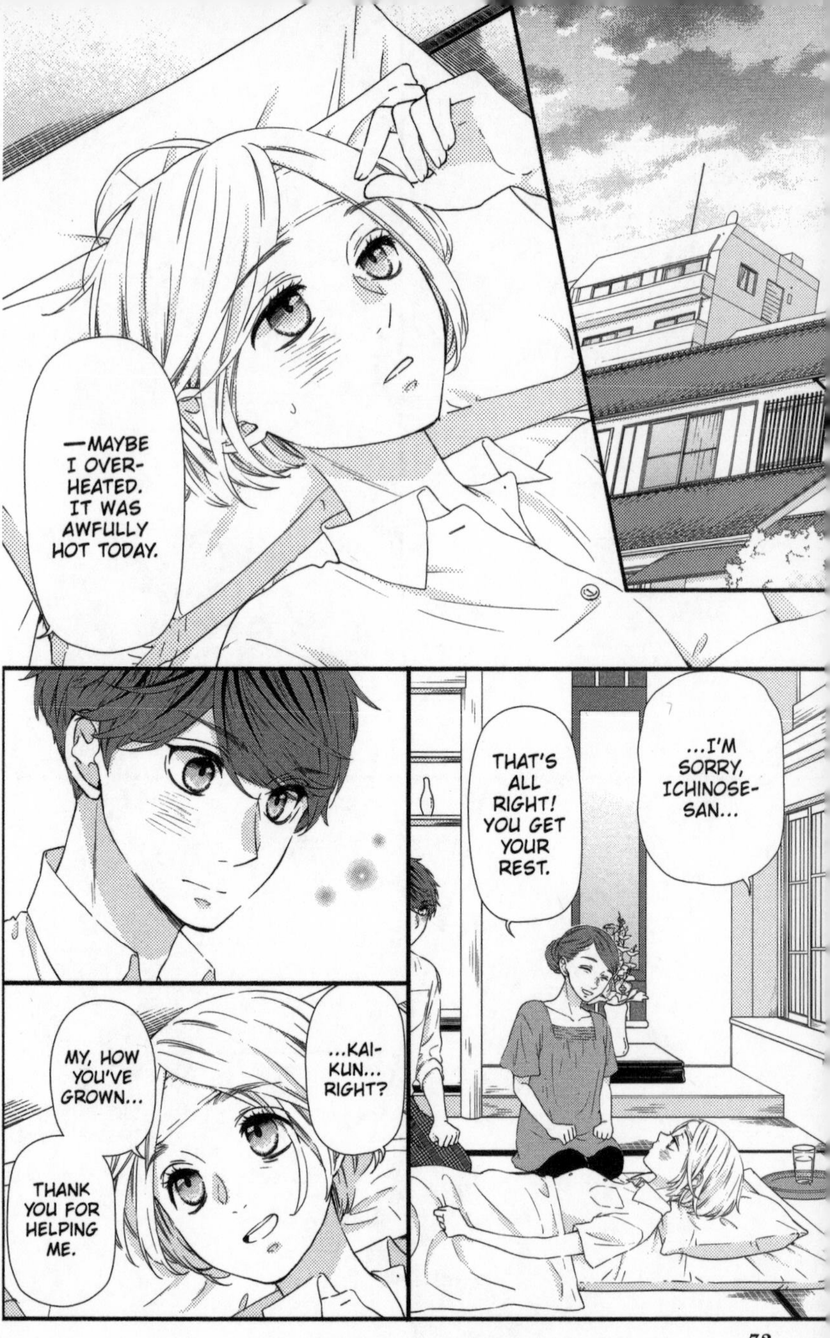
—MAYBE I OVER-HEATED. IT WAS AWFULLY HOT TODAY.
...I'M SORRY, ICHINOSE-SAN...
THAT'S ALL RIGHT! YOU GET YOUR REST.
...KAI-KUN... RIGHT?
MY, HOW YOU'VE GROWN...
THANK YOU FOR HELPING ME.

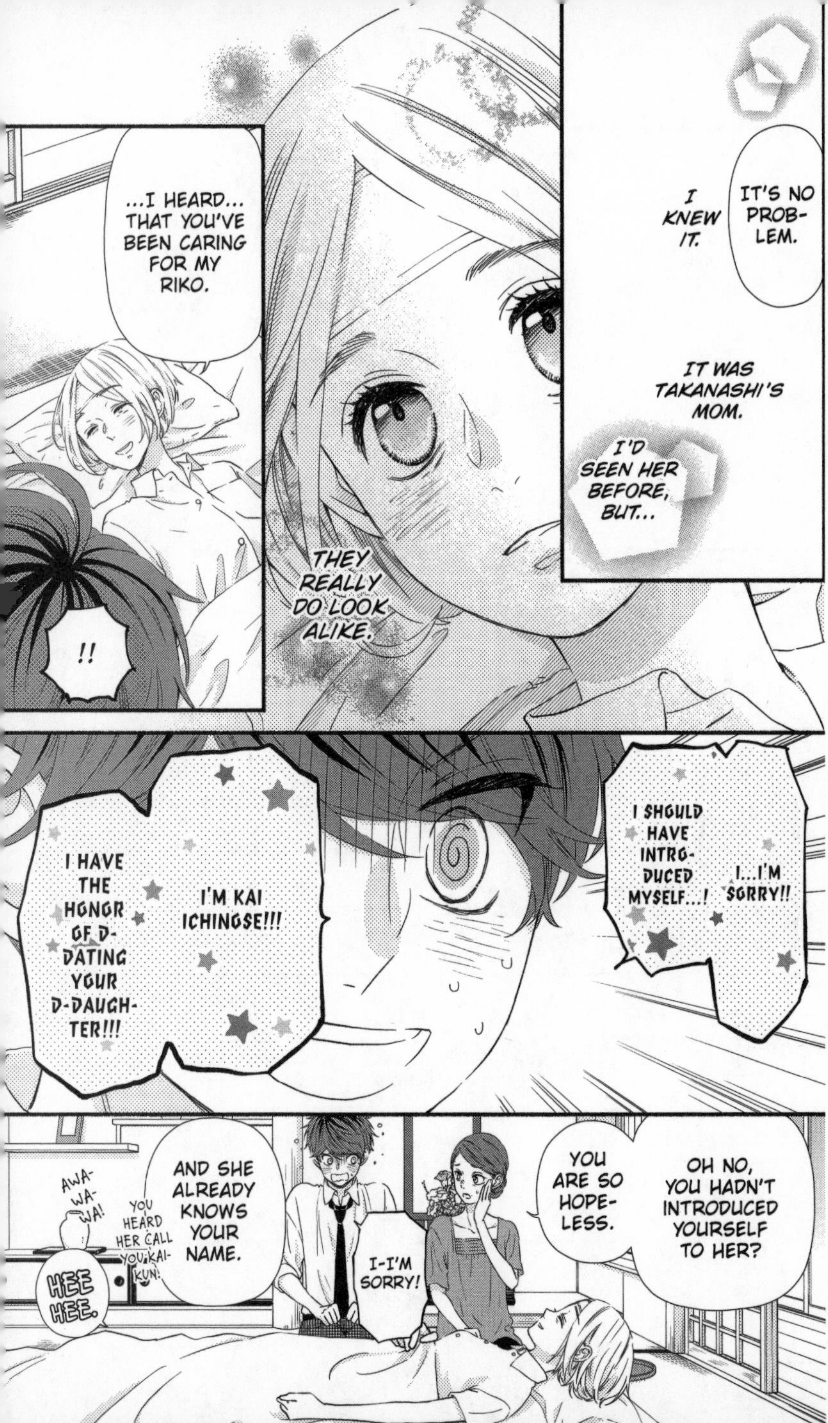
IT'S NO PROB-LEM.
I KNEW IT.
IT WAS TAKANASHI'S MOM.
I'D SEEN HER BEFORE, BUT...
THEY REALLY DO LOOK ALIKE.
...I HEARD... THAT YOU'VE BEEN CARING FOR MY RIKO.
!!
I...I'M SORRY!!
I SHOULD HAVE INTRO-DUCED MYSELF...!
I'M KAI ICHINOSE!!!
I HAVE THE HONOR OF D-DATING YOUR D-DAUGH-TER!!!
OH NO, YOU HADN'T INTRODUCED YOURSELF TO HER?
YOU ARE SO HOPE-LESS.
I-I'M SORRY!
AND SHE ALREADY KNOWS YOUR NAME.
YOU HEARD HER CALL YOU KAI-KUN!
AWA-WA-WA!
HEE HEE.

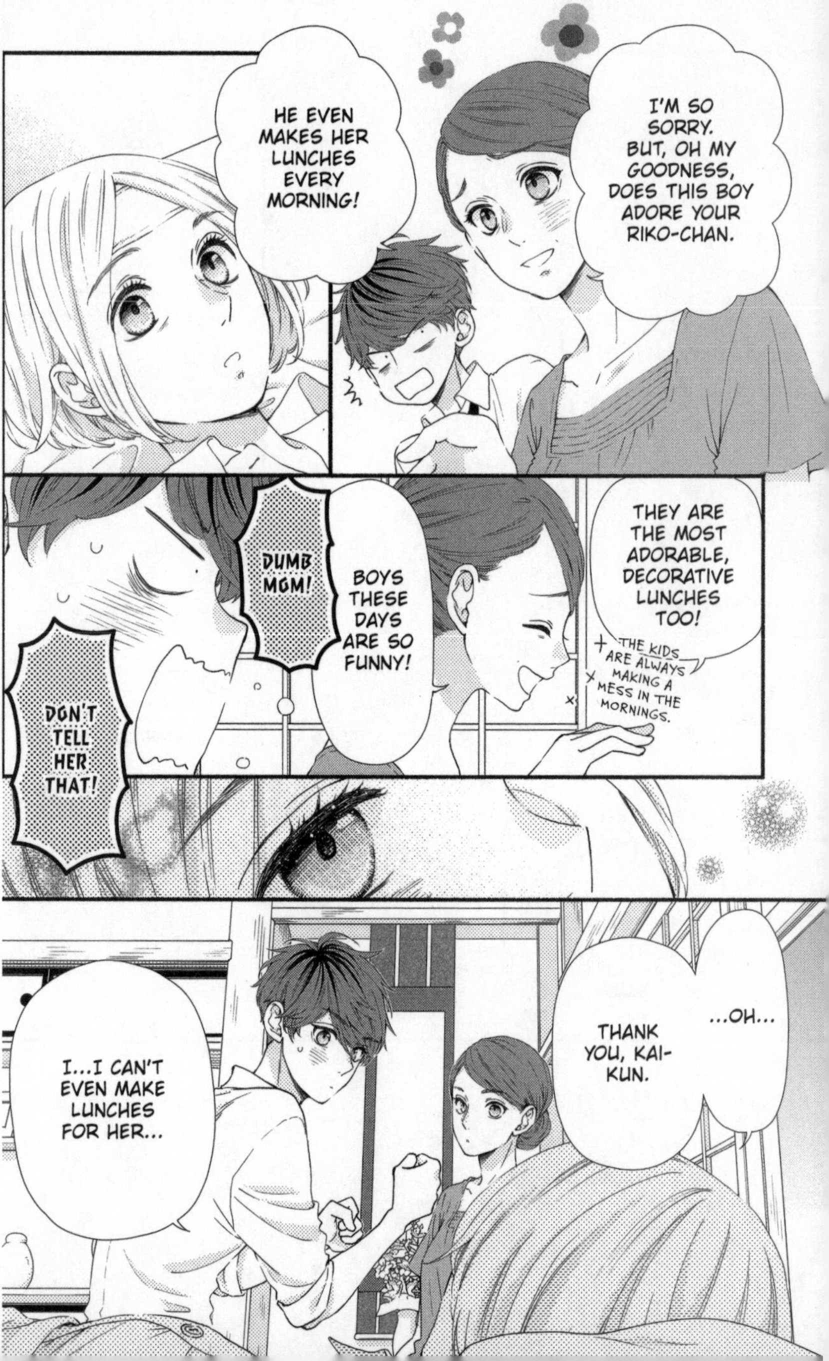
I'M SO SORRY.
BUT, OH MY GOODNESS, DOES THIS BOY ADORE YOUR RIKO-CHAN.
HE EVEN MAKES HER LUNCHES EVERY MORNING!
THEY ARE THE MOST ADORABLE, DECORATIVE LUNCHES TOO!
THE KIDS ARE ALWAYS MAKING A MESS IN THE MORNINGS.
BOYS THESE DAYS ARE SO FUNNY!
DUMB MOM!
DON'T TELL HER THAT!
...OH...
THANK YOU, KAI-KUN.
I...I CAN'T EVEN MAKE LUNCHES FOR HER...

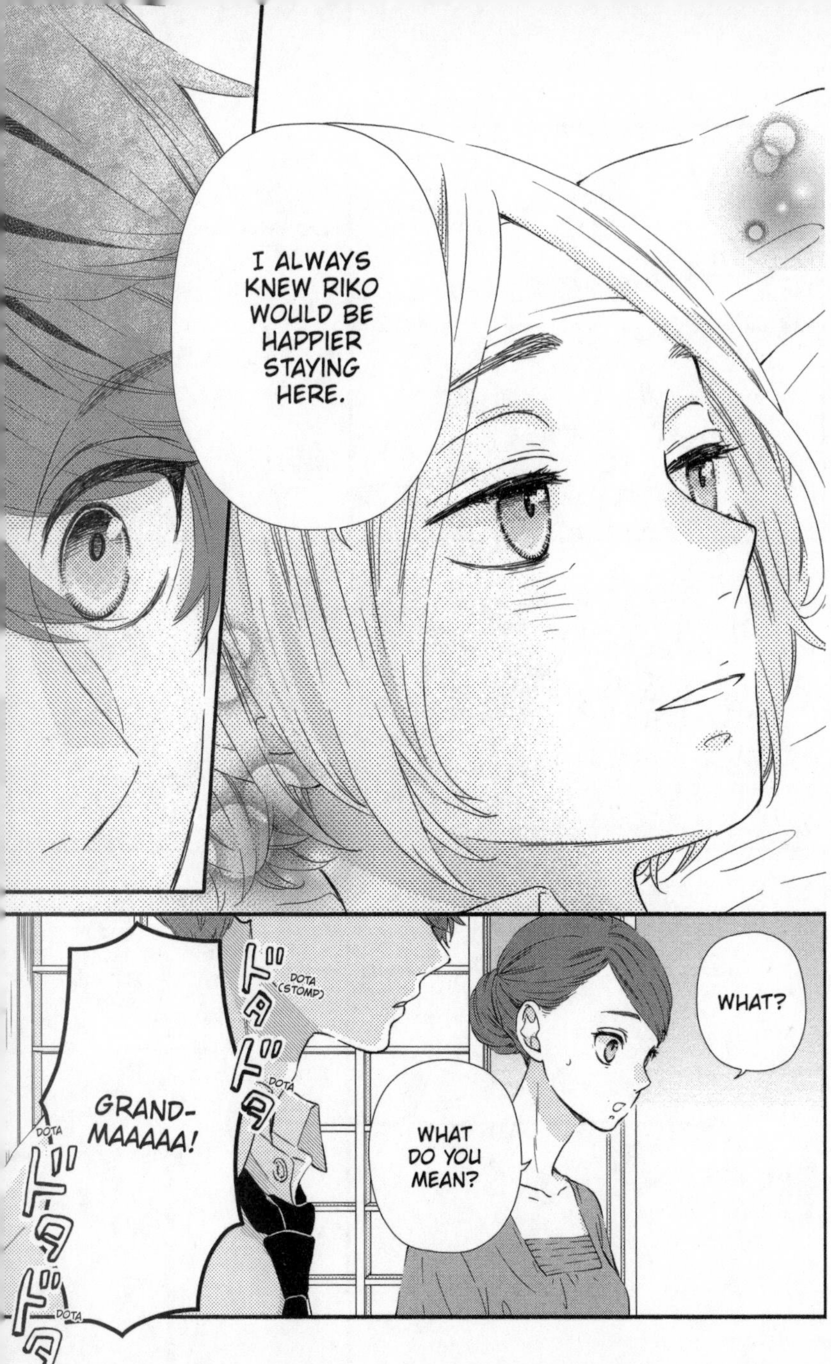
I ALWAYS KNEW RIKO WOULD BE HAPPIER STAYING HERE.
WHAT?
WHAT DO YOU MEAN?
DOTA (STOMP)
DOTA
GRAND-MAAAAAA!
DOTA
DOTA

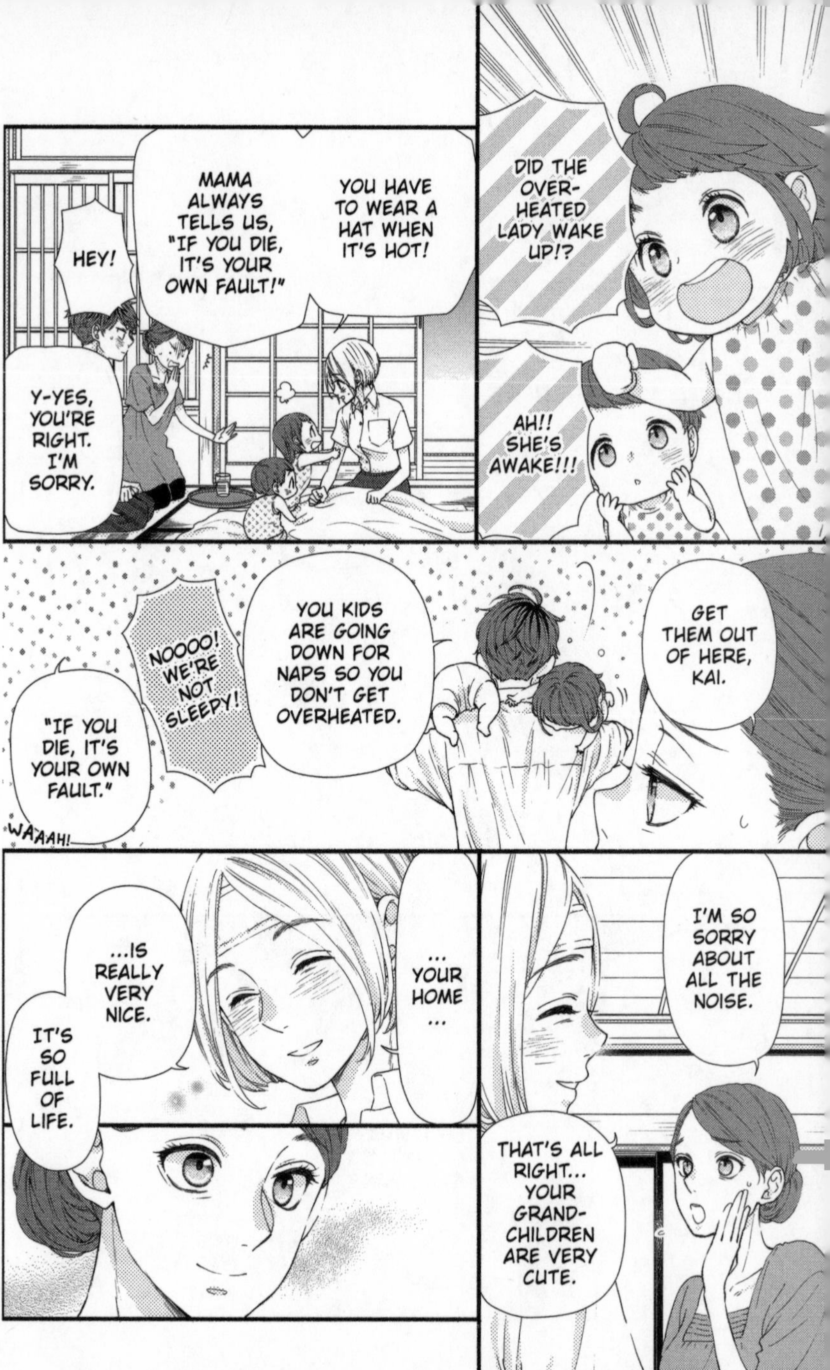
DID THE OVER-HEATED LADY WAKE UP!?
AH!! SHE'S AWAKE!!!
YOU HAVE TO WEAR A HAT WHEN IT'S HOT!
MAMA ALWAYS TELLS US, "IF YOU DIE, IT'S YOUR OWN FAULT!"
HEY!
Y-YES, YOU'RE RIGHT. I'M SORRY.
GET THEM OUT OF HERE, KAI.
YOU KIDS ARE GOING DOWN FOR NAPS SO YOU DON'T GET OVERHEATED.
NOOOO! WE'RE NOT SLEEPY!
"IF YOU DIE, IT'S YOUR OWN FAULT."
WAAAH!
I'M SO SORRY ABOUT ALL THE NOISE.
THAT'S ALL RIGHT... YOUR GRANDCHILDREN ARE VERY CUTE.
...YOUR HOME...
...IS REALLY VERY NICE.
IT'S SO FULL OF LIFE.

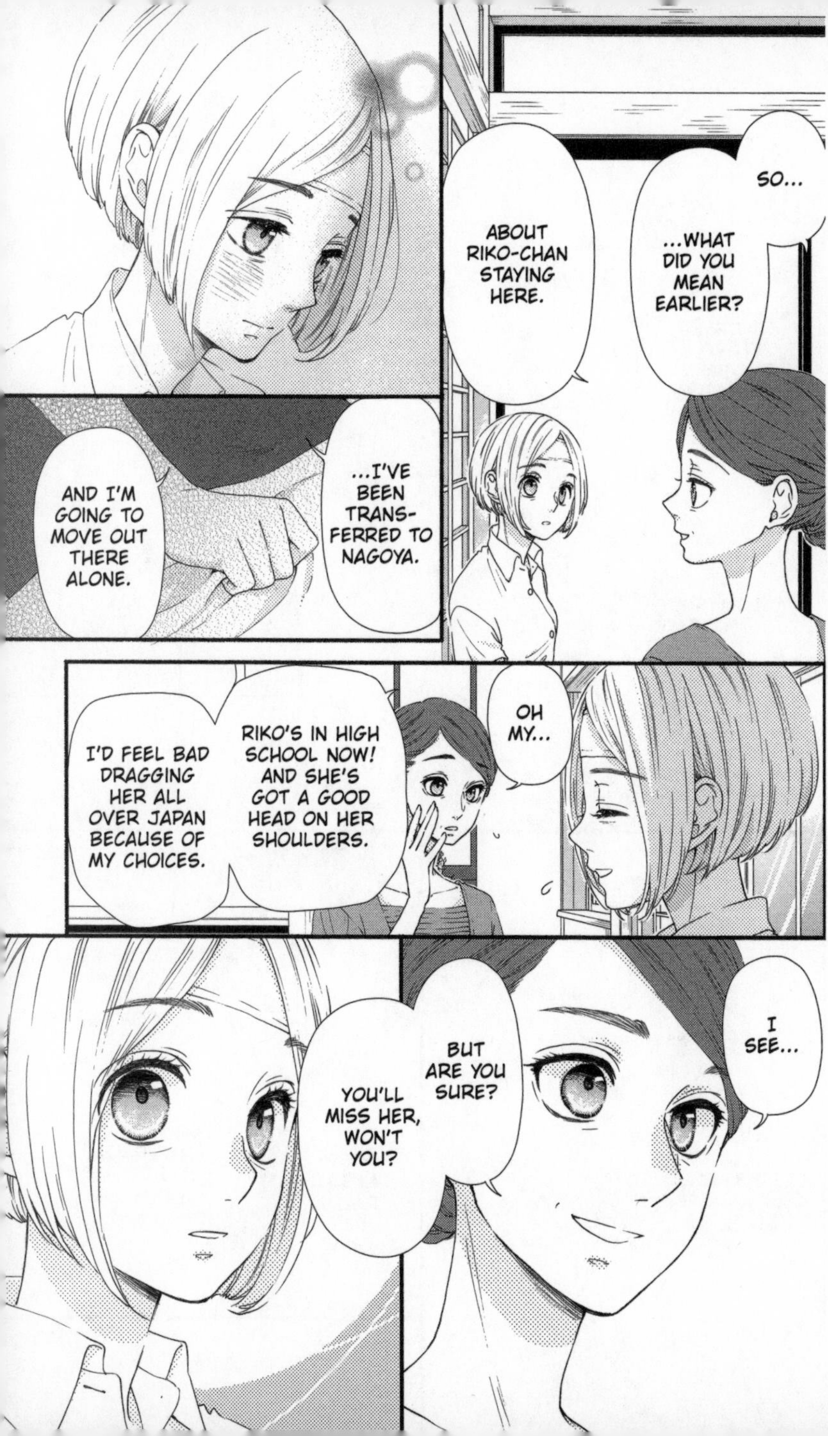
SO...
...WHAT DID YOU MEAN EARLIER?
ABOUT RIKO-CHAN STAYING HERE.
...I'VE BEEN TRANS-FERRED TO NAGOYA.
AND I'M GOING TO MOVE OUT THERE ALONE.
OH MY...
RIKO'S IN HIGH SCHOOL NOW! AND SHE'S GOT A GOOD HEAD ON HER SHOULDERS.
I'D FEEL BAD DRAGGING HER ALL OVER JAPAN BECAUSE OF MY CHOICES.
I SEE...
BUT ARE YOU SURE?
YOU'LL MISS HER, WON'T YOU?

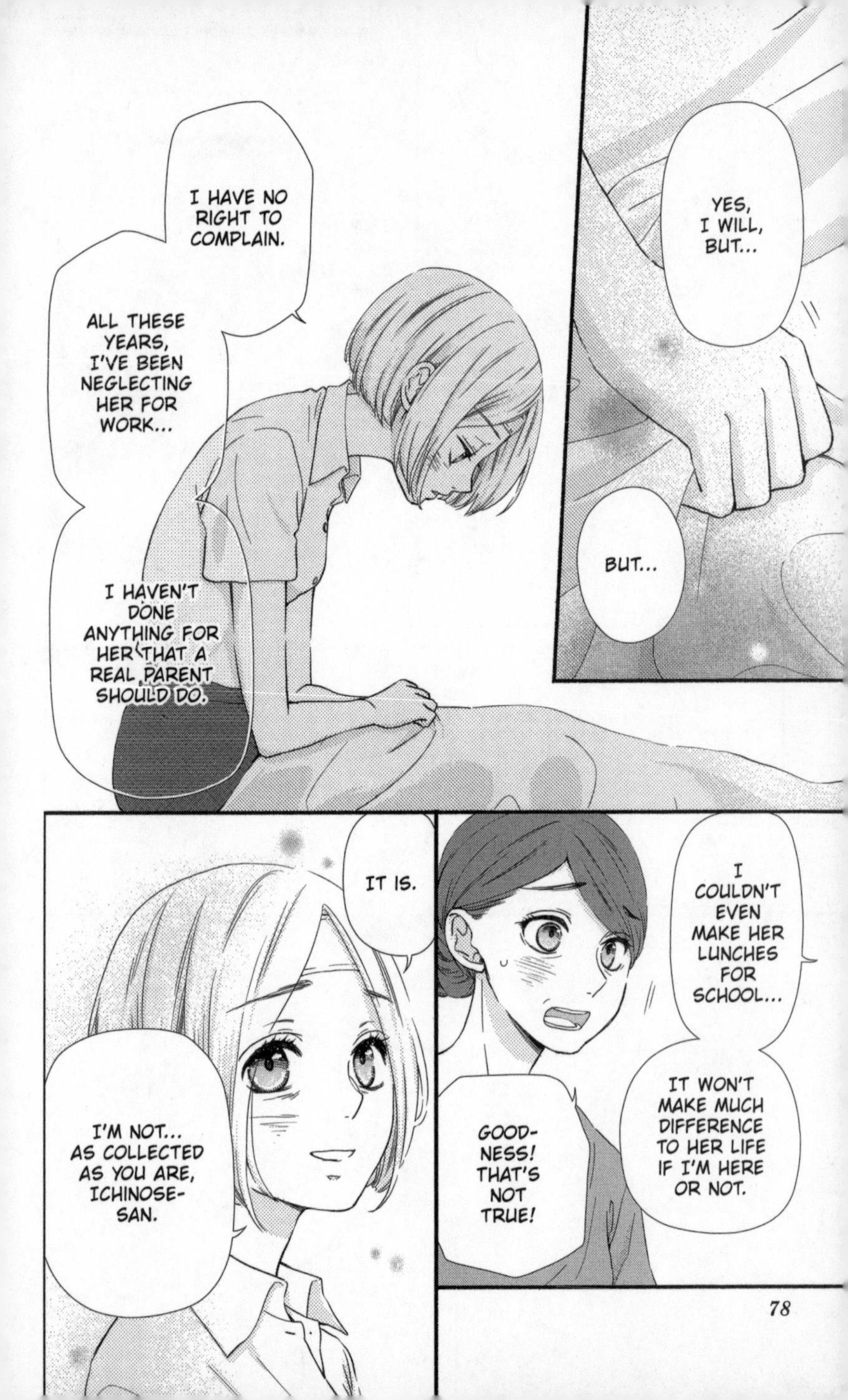
YES, I WILL, BUT...
BUT...
I HAVE NO RIGHT TO COMPLAIN.
ALL THESE YEARS, I'VE BEEN NEGLECTING HER FOR WORK...
I HAVEN'T DONE ANYTHING FOR HER THAT A REAL PARENT SHOULD DO.
I COULDN'T EVEN MAKE HER LUNCHES FOR SCHOOL...
IT WON'T MAKE MUCH DIFFERENCE TO HER LIFE IF I'M HERE OR NOT.
GOOD-NESS! THAT'S NOT TRUE!
IT IS.
I'M NOT... AS COLLECTED AS YOU ARE, ICHINOSE-SAN.

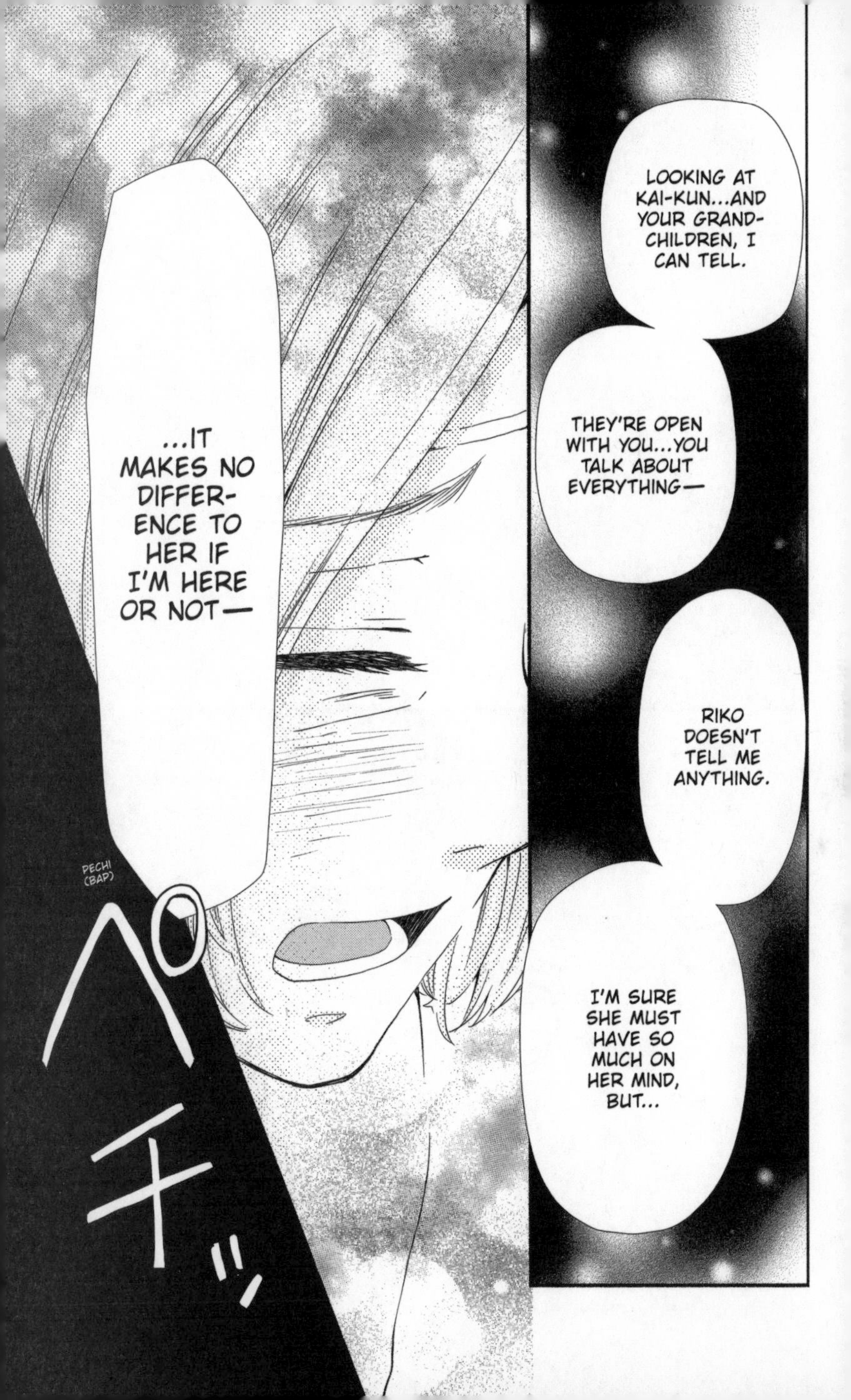
LOOKING AT KAI-KUN...AND YOUR GRAND-CHILDREN, I CAN TELL.
THEY'RE OPEN WITH YOU...YOU TALK ABOUT EVERYTHING—
RIKO DOESN'T TELL ME ANYTHING.
I'M SURE SHE MUST HAVE SO MUCH ON HER MIND, BUT...
...IT MAKES NO DIFFER-ENCE TO HER IF I'M HERE OR NOT—
PECHI (BAP)

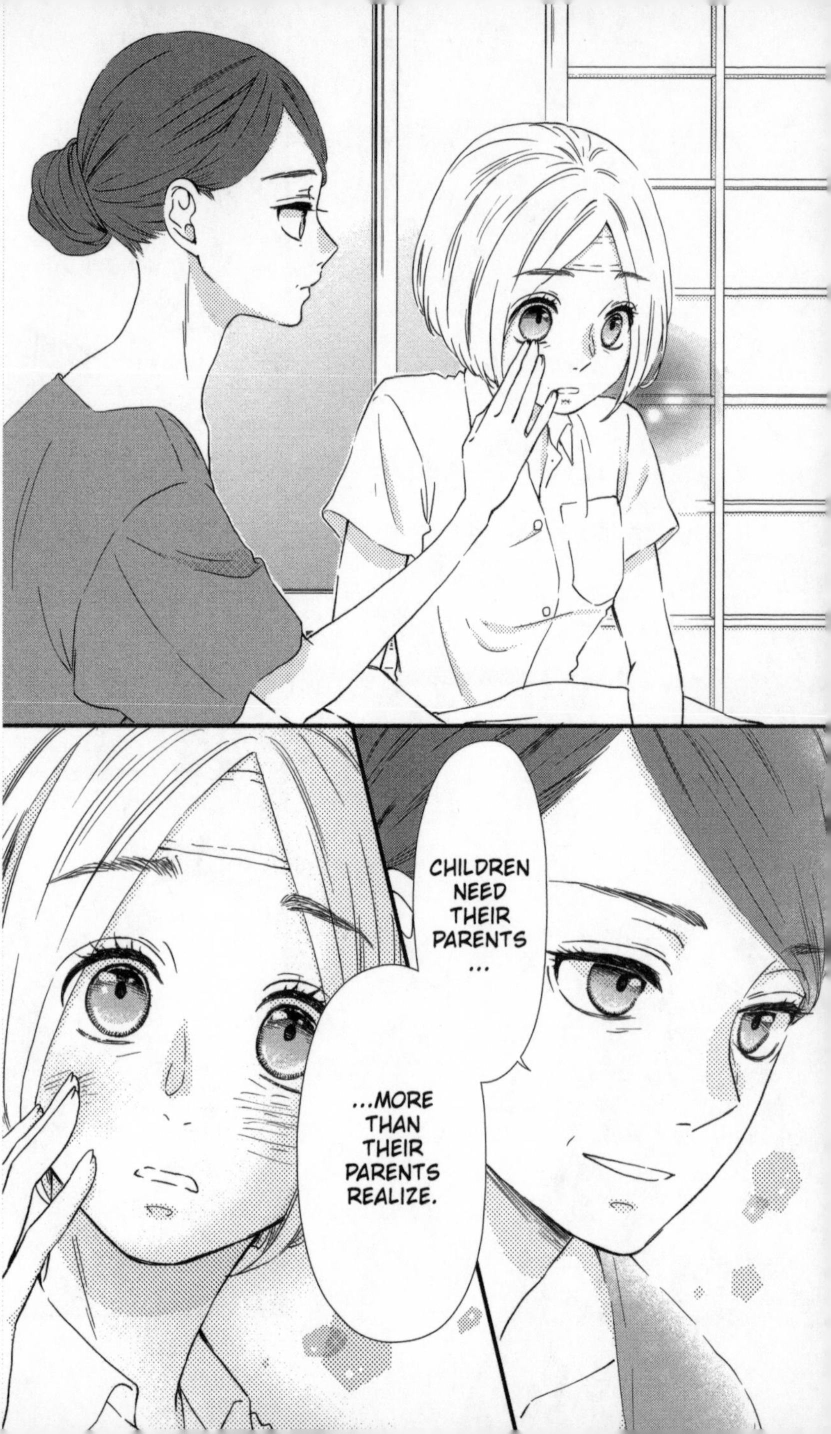
CHILDREN NEED THEIR PARENTS ...
...MORE THAN THEIR PARENTS REALIZE.

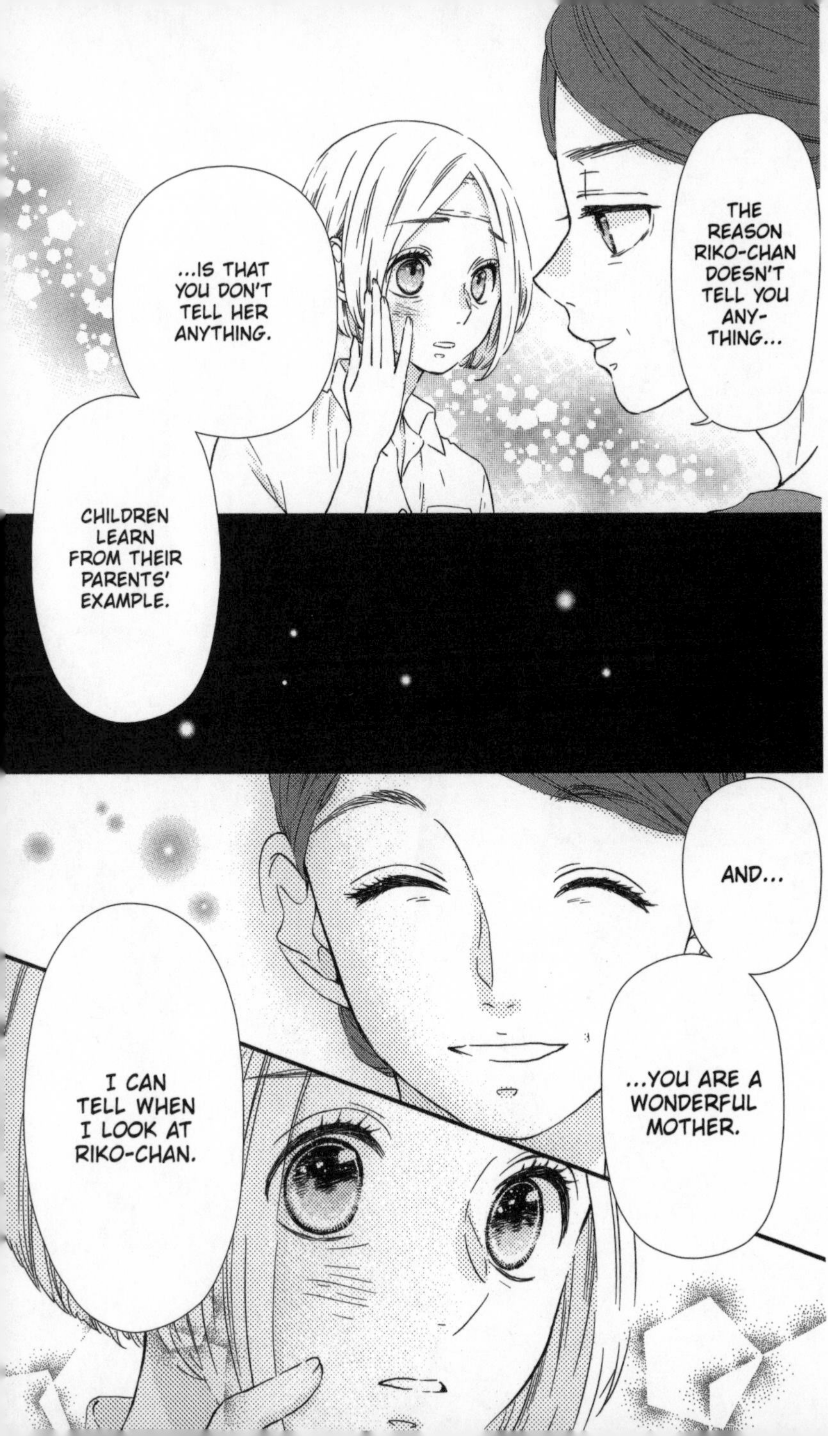
THE REASON RIKO-CHAN DOESN'T TELL YOU ANYTHING...
...IS THAT YOU DON'T TELL HER ANYTHING.
CHILDREN LEARN FROM THEIR PARENTS' EXAMPLE.
AND...
...YOU ARE A WONDERFUL MOTHER.
I CAN TELL WHEN I LOOK AT RIKO-CHAN.

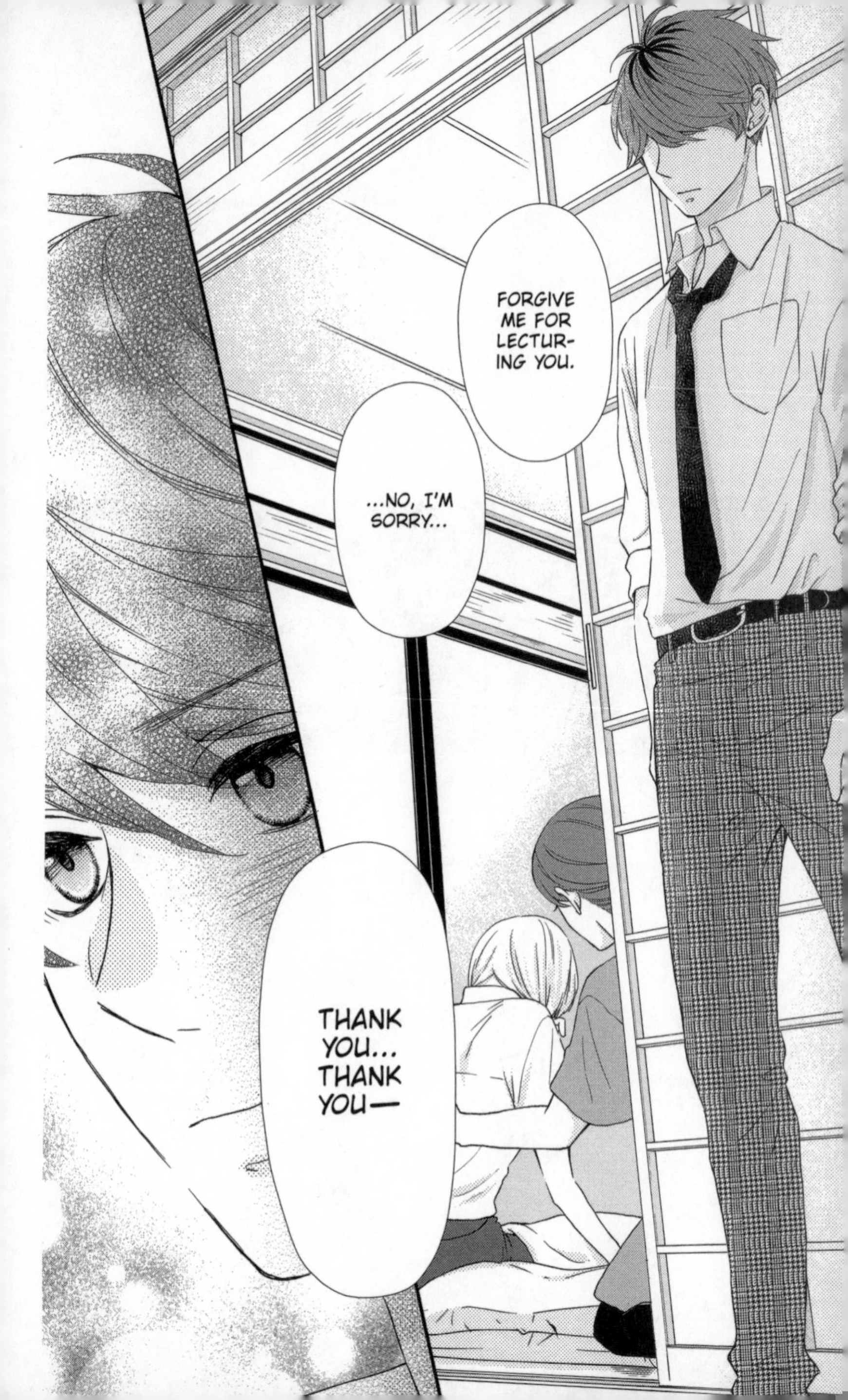
FORGIVE ME FOR LECTURING YOU.
...NO, I'M SORRY...
THANK YOU... THANK YOU—

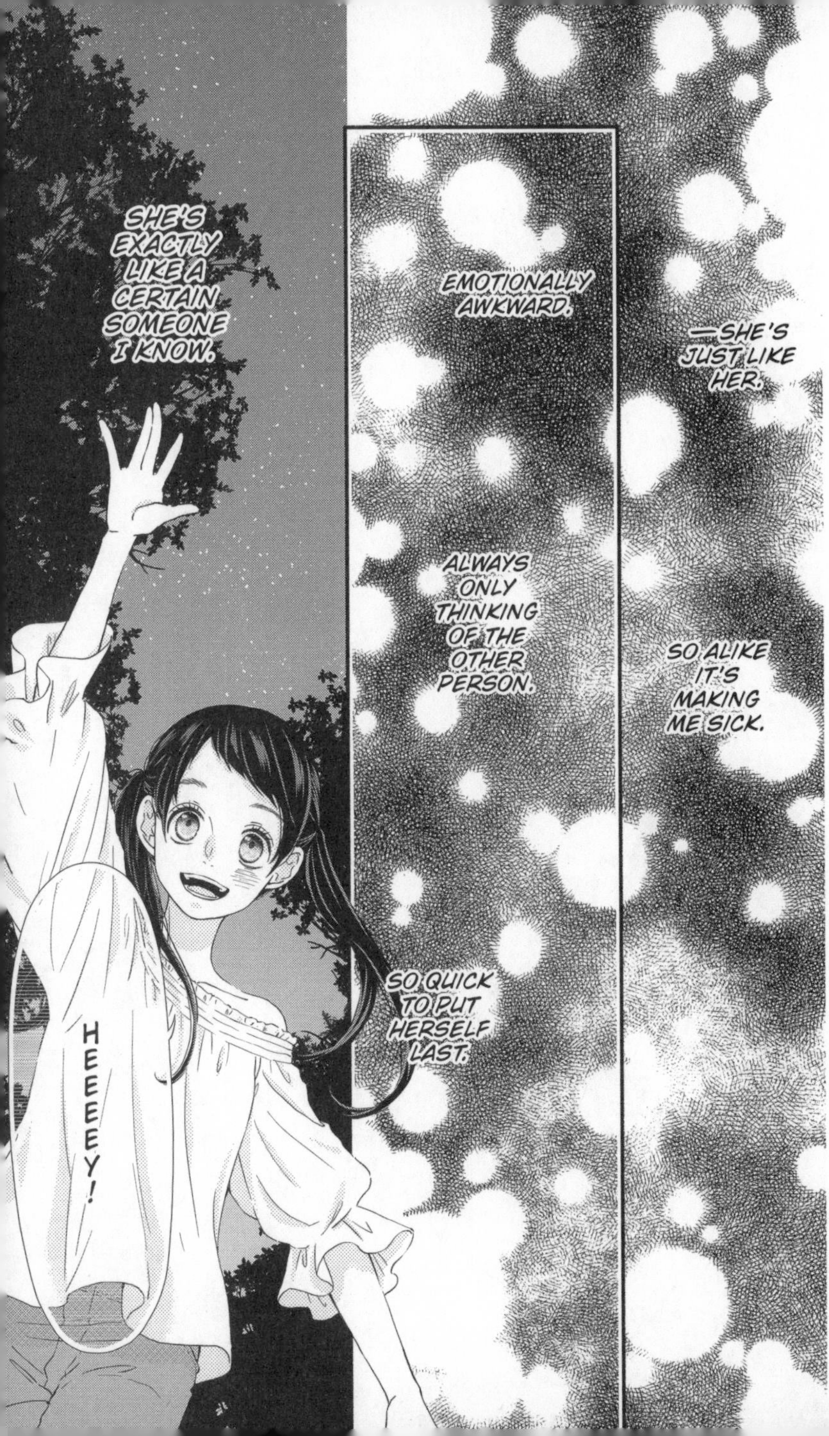
—SHE'S JUST LIKE HER.
SO ALIKE IT'S MAKING ME SICK.
EMOTIONALLY AWKWARD.
ALWAYS ONLY THINKING OF THE OTHER PERSON.
SO QUICK TO PUT HERSELF LAST.
SHE'S EXACTLY LIKE A CERTAIN SOMEONE I KNOW.
HEEEEEY!

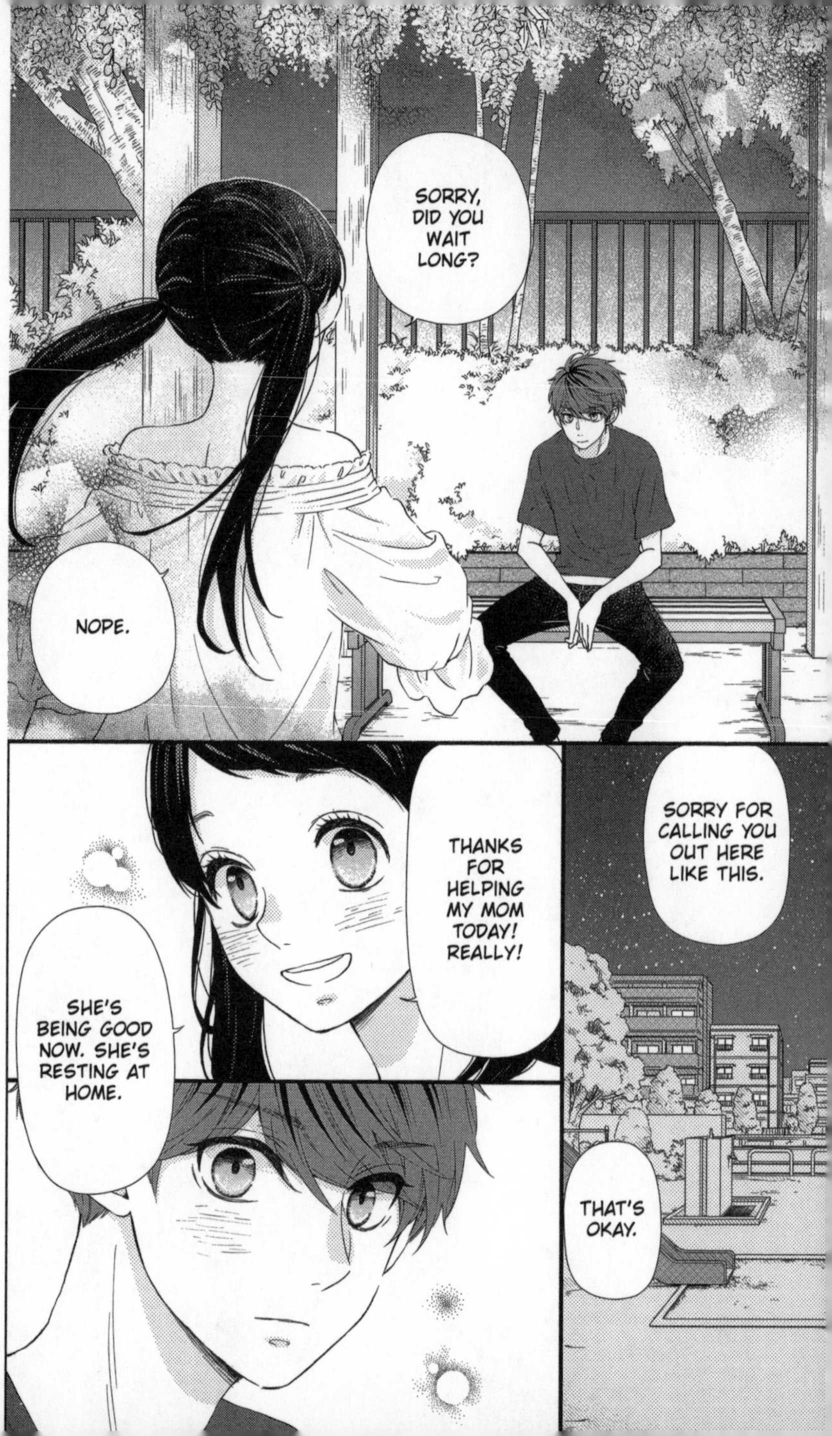
SORRY, DID YOU WAIT LONG?
NOPE.
SORRY FOR CALLING YOU OUT HERE LIKE THIS.
THAT'S OKAY.
THANKS FOR HELPING MY MOM TODAY! REALLY!
SHE'S BEING GOOD NOW. SHE'S RESTING AT HOME.

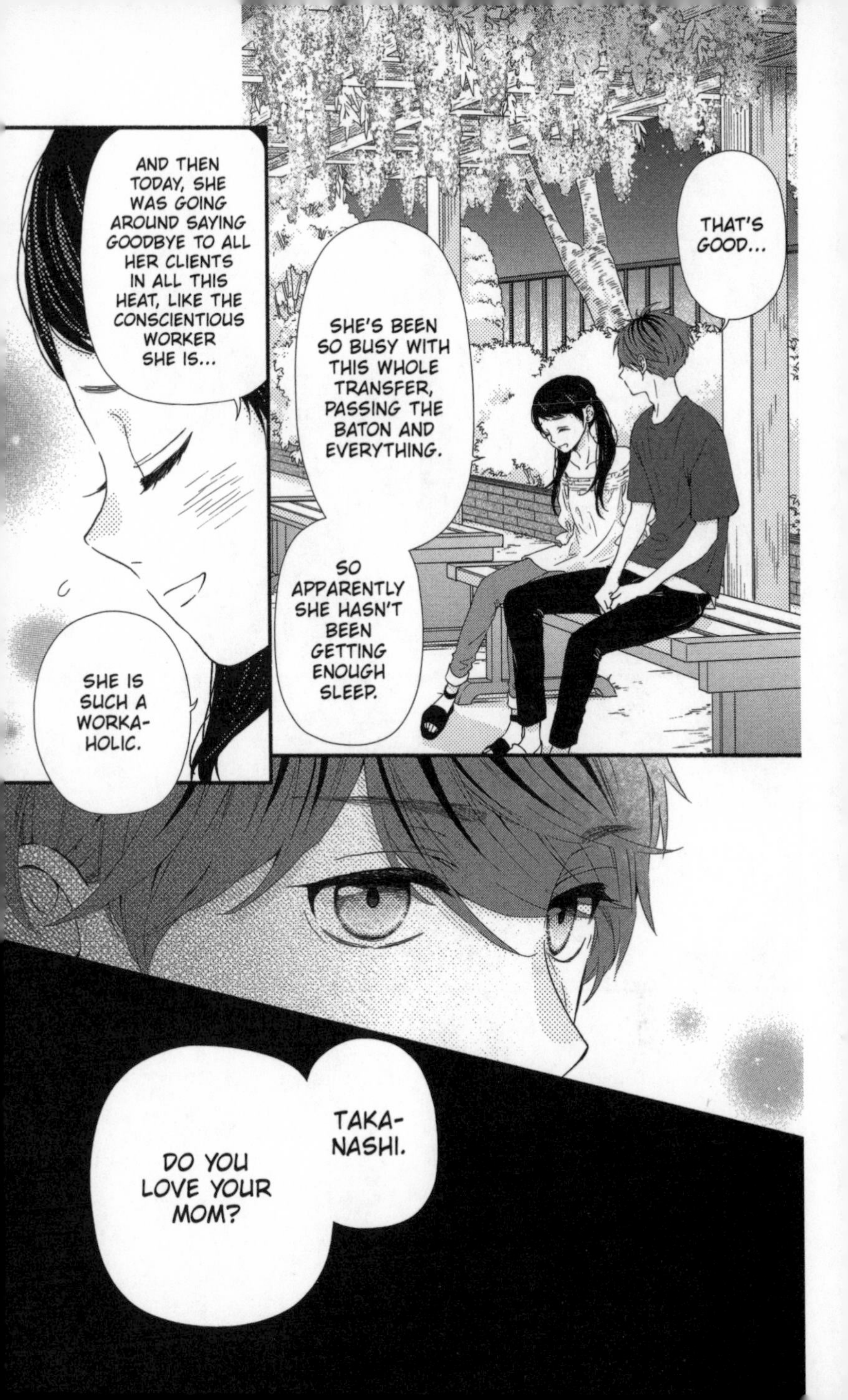
THAT'S GOOD...
SHE'S BEEN SO BUSY WITH THIS WHOLE TRANSFER, PASSING THE BATON AND EVERYTHING.
SO APPARENTLY SHE HASN'T BEEN GETTING ENOUGH SLEEP.
AND THEN TODAY, SHE WAS GOING AROUND SAYING GOODBYE TO ALL HER CLIENTS IN ALL THIS HEAT, LIKE THE CONSCIENTIOUS WORKER SHE IS...
SHE IS SUCH A WORKA-HOLIC.
TAKA-NASHI.
DO YOU LOVE YOUR MOM?

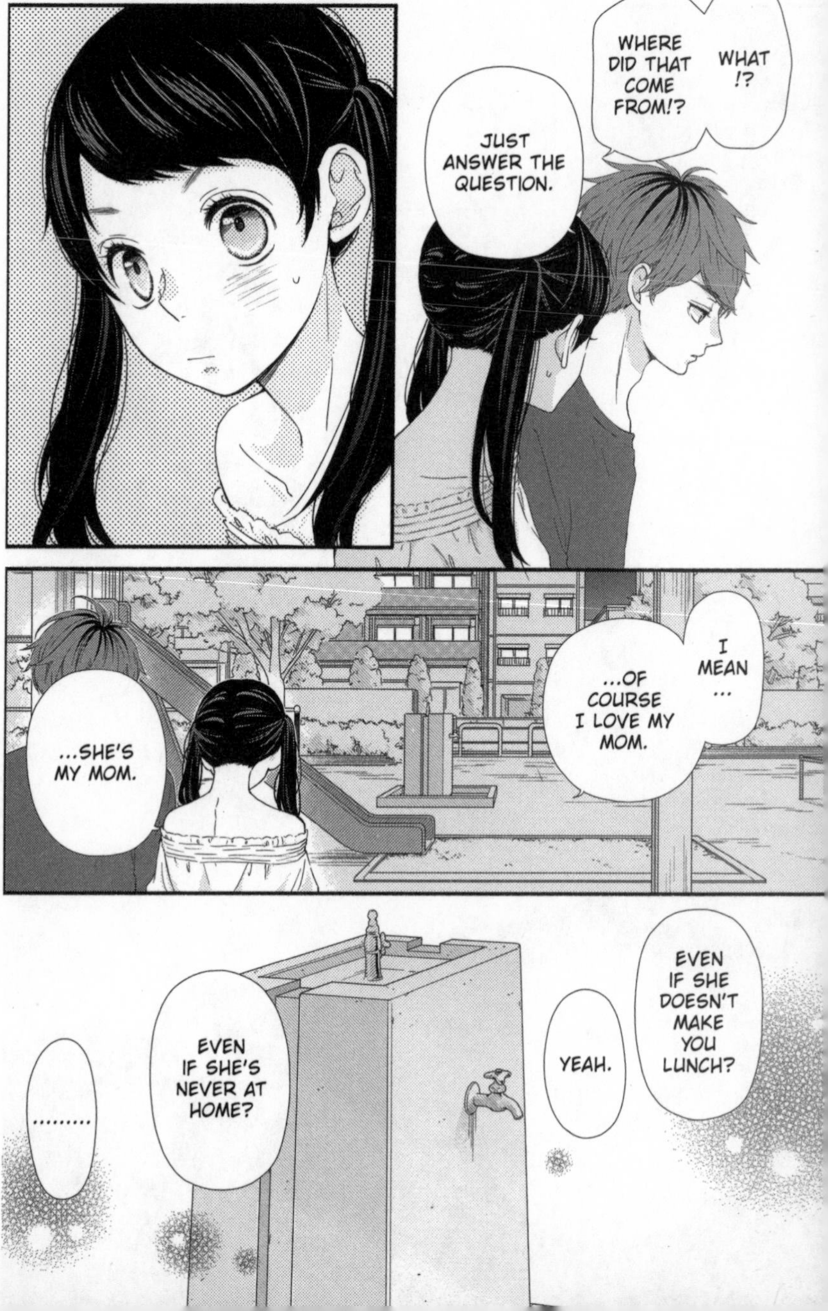
WHAT!?
WHERE DID THAT COME FROM!?
JUST ANSWER THE QUESTION.
I MEAN...
...OF COURSE I LOVE MY MOM.
...SHE'S MY MOM.
EVEN IF SHE DOESN'T MAKE YOU LUNCH?
YEAH.
EVEN IF SHE'S NEVER AT HOME?
....

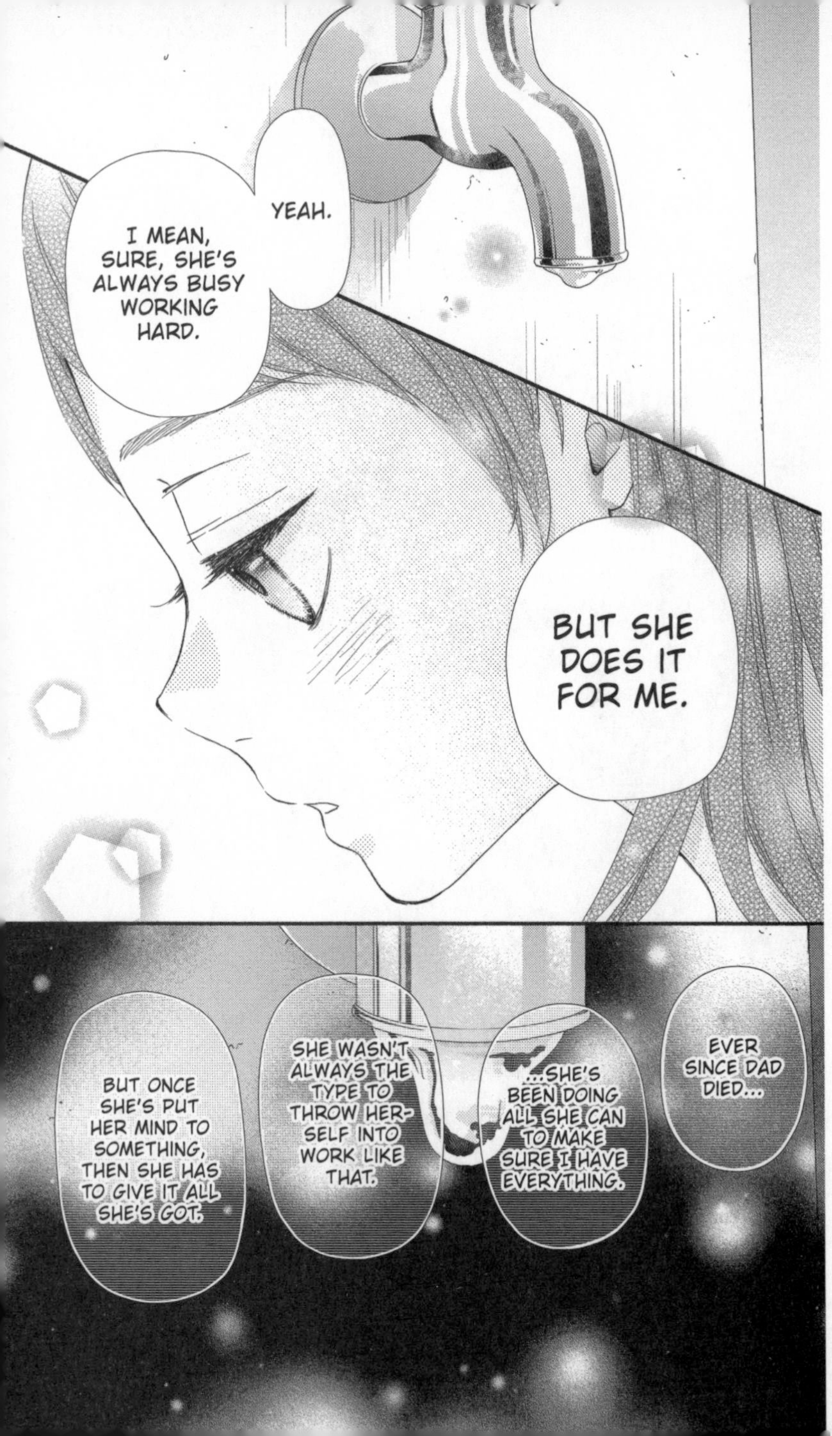
YEAH.
I MEAN, SURE, SHE'S ALWAYS BUSY WORKING HARD.
BUT SHE DOES IT FOR ME.
EVER SINCE DAD DIED...
...SHE'S BEEN DOING ALL SHE CAN TO MAKE SURE I HAVE EVERYTHING.
SHE WASN'T ALWAYS THE TYPE TO THROW HER-SELF INTO WORK LIKE THAT.
BUT ONCE SHE'S PUT HER MIND TO SOMETHING, THEN SHE HAS TO GIVE IT ALL SHE'S GOT.

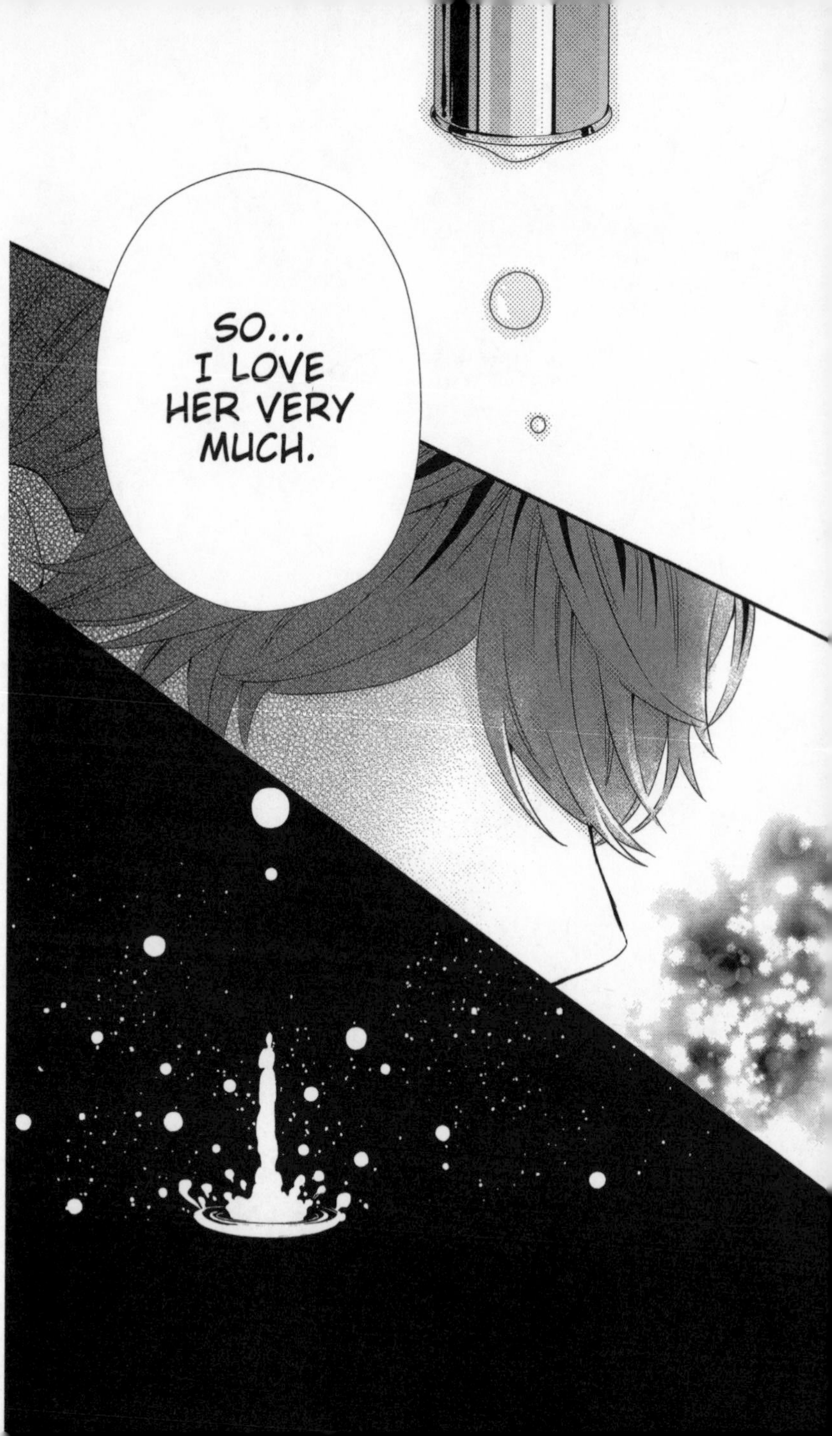
SO... I LOVE HER VERY MUCH.

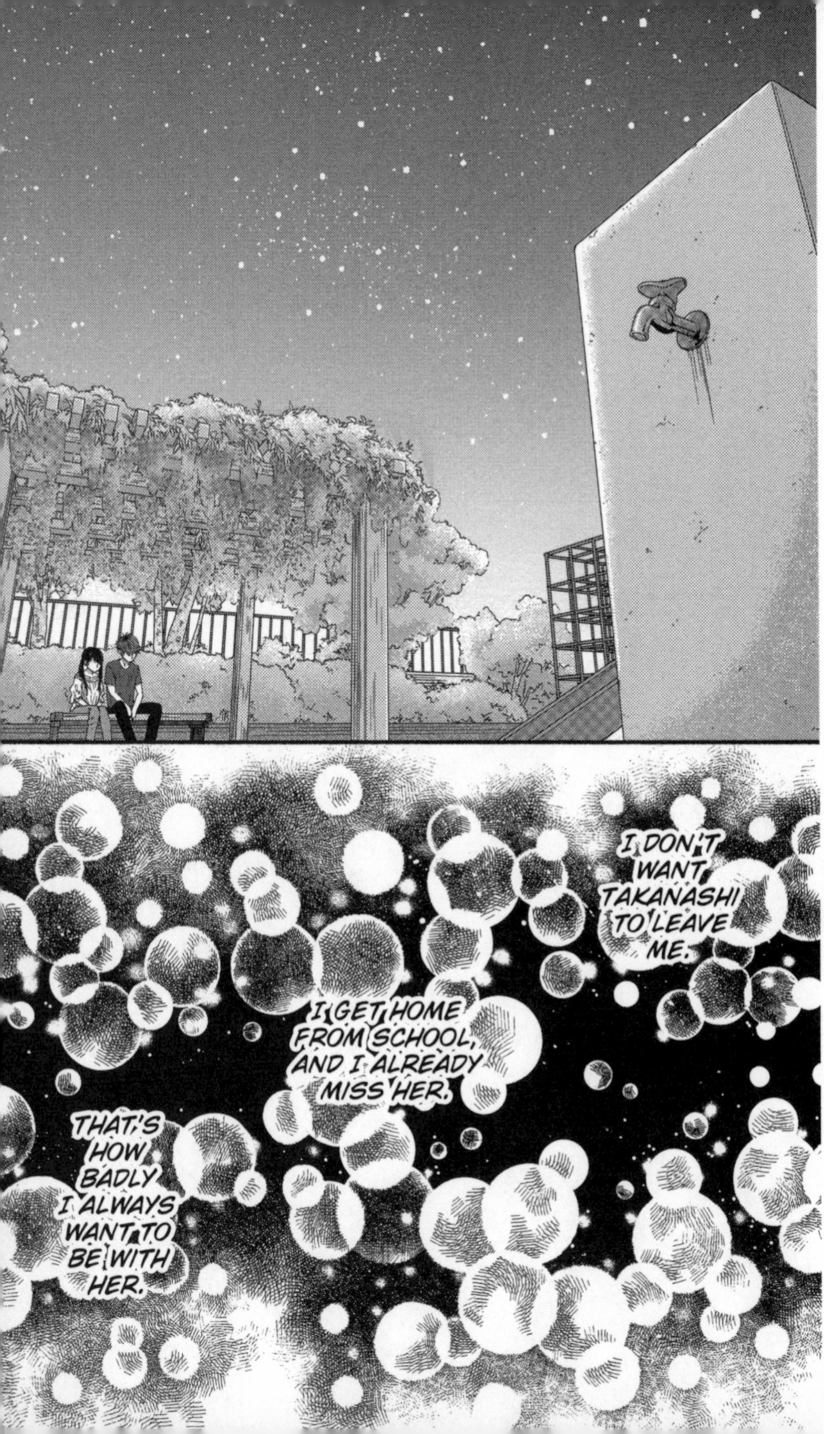
I DON'T WANT TAKANASHI TO LEAVE ME.
I GET HOME FROM SCHOOL, AND I ALREADY MISS HER.
THAT'S HOW BADLY I ALWAYS WANT TO BE WITH HER.

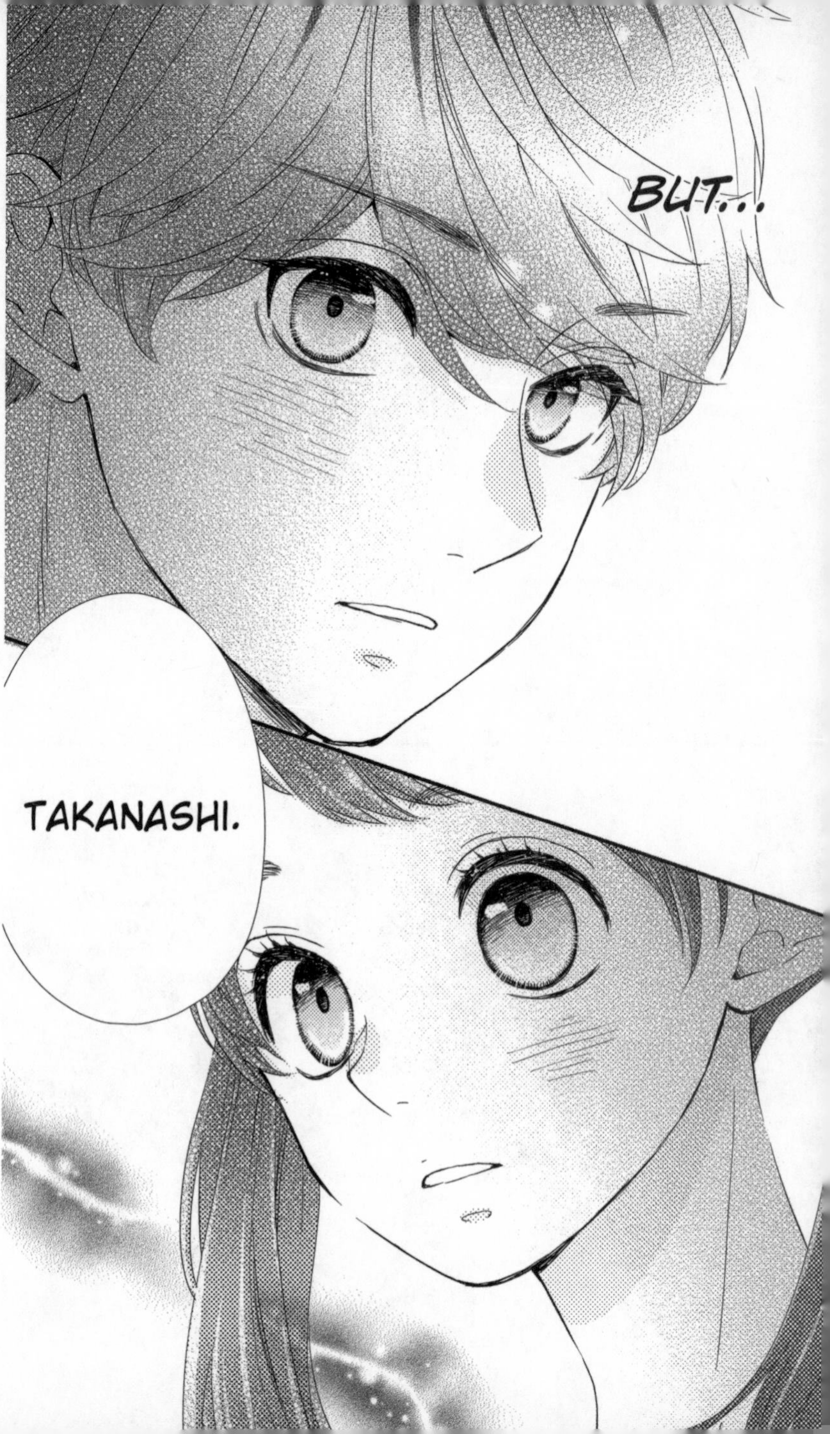
BUT...
TAKANASHI.

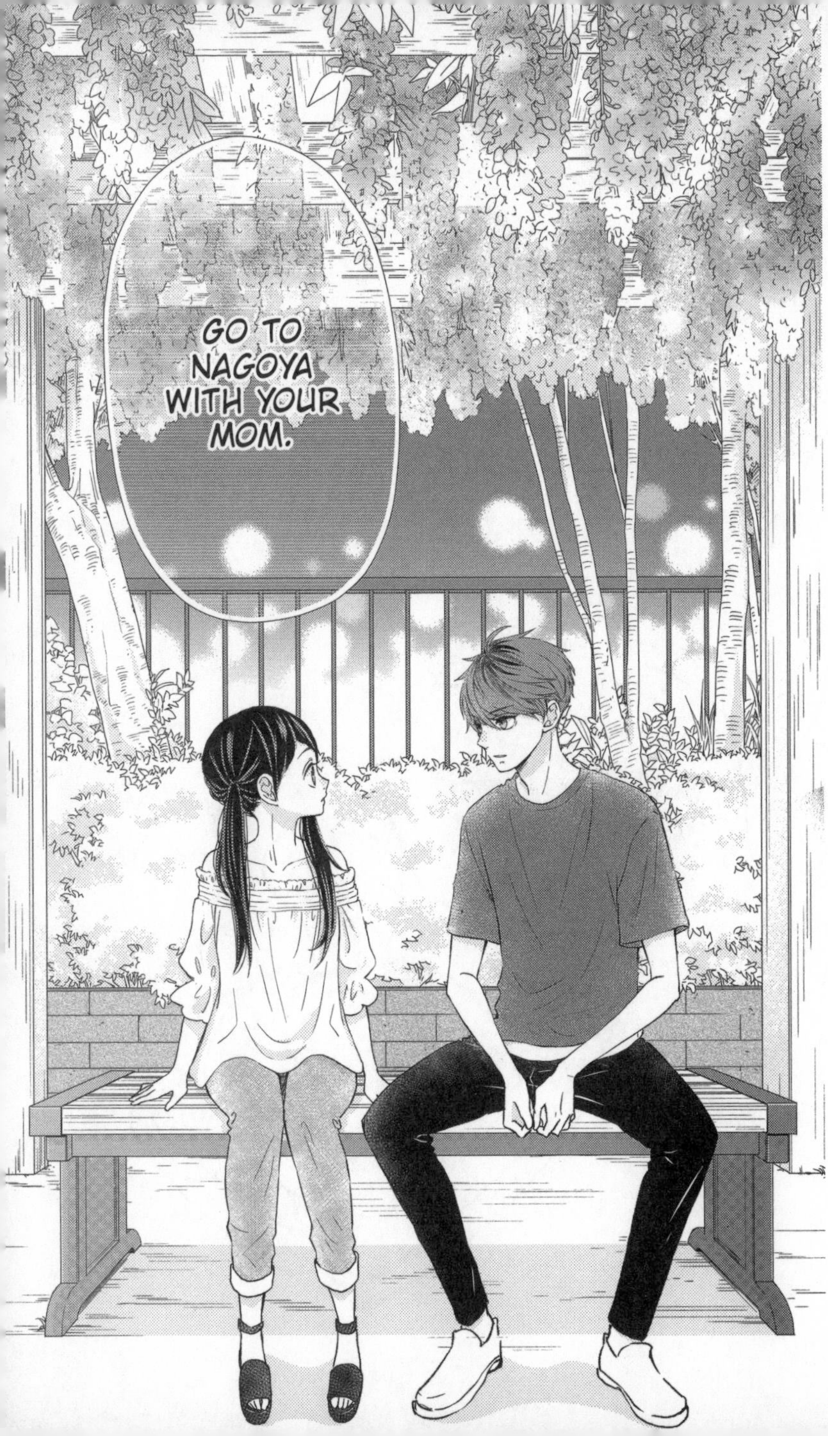
GO TO NAGOYA WITH YOUR MOM.

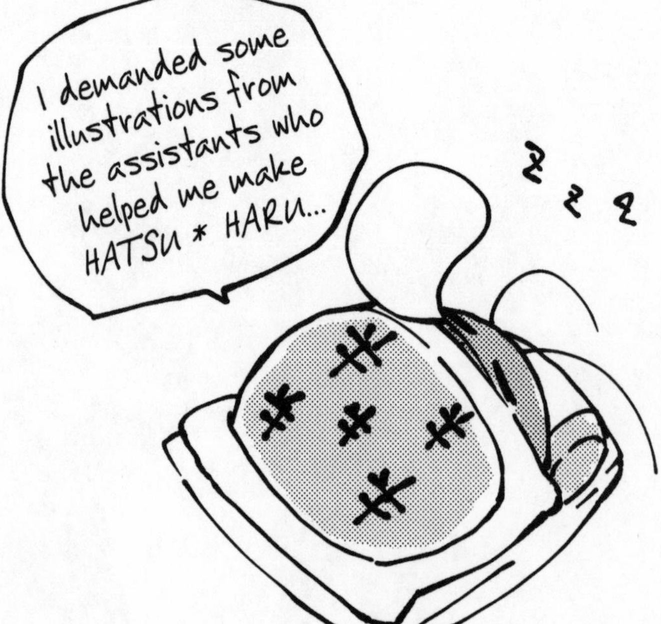
I demanded some illustrations from the assistants who helped me make HATSU * HARU...
Z Z Z

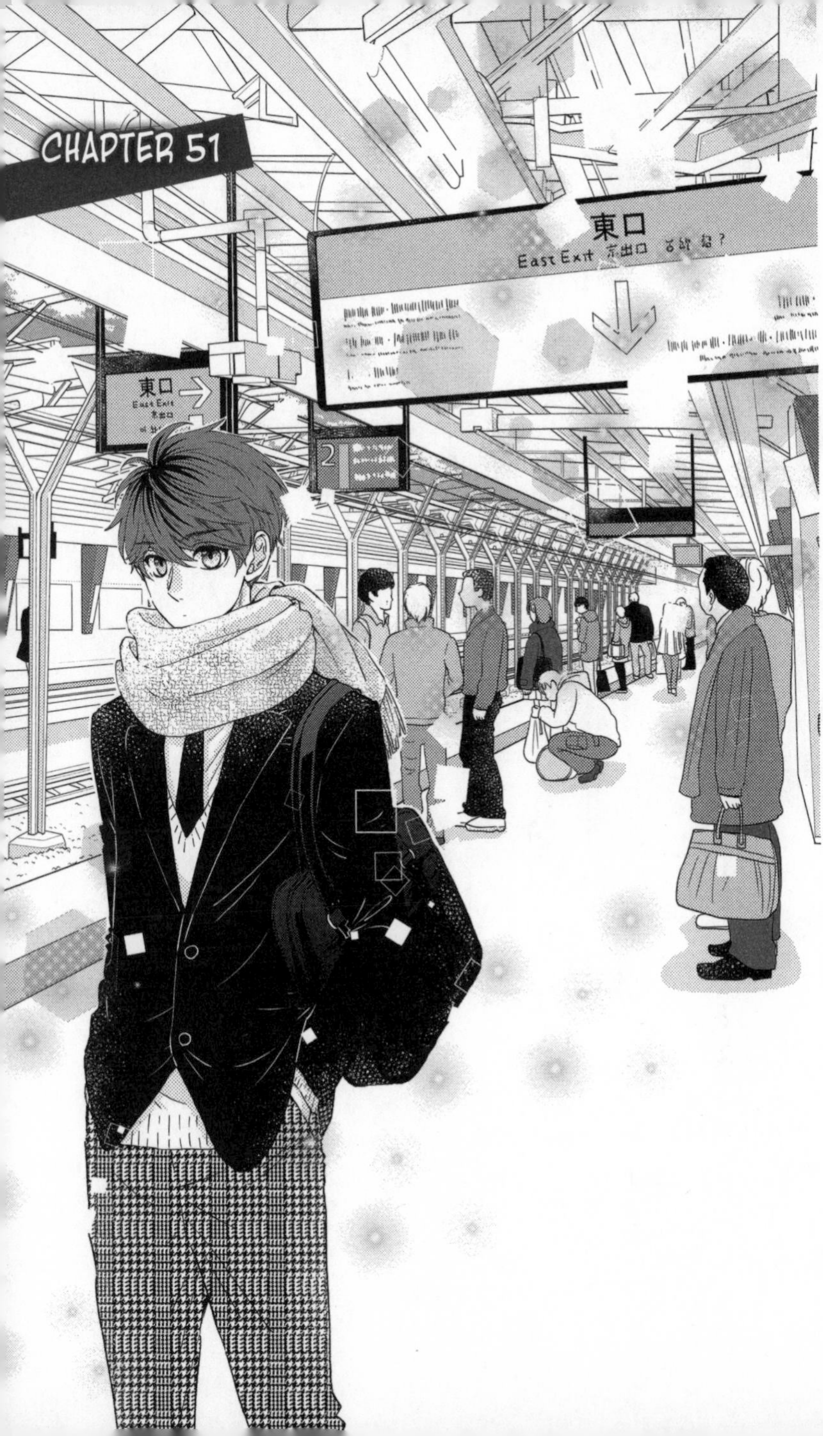
CHAPTER 51
東口
East Exit
東口
East Exit

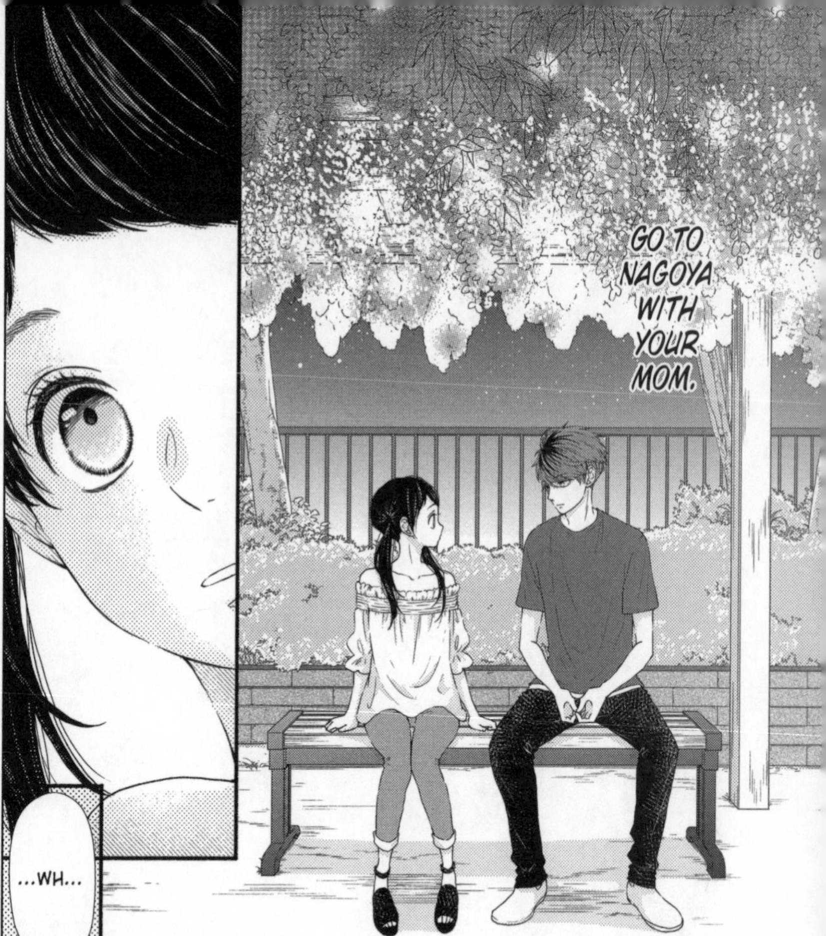
GO TO NAGOYA WITH YOUR MOM.
...WH...

hatsu haru

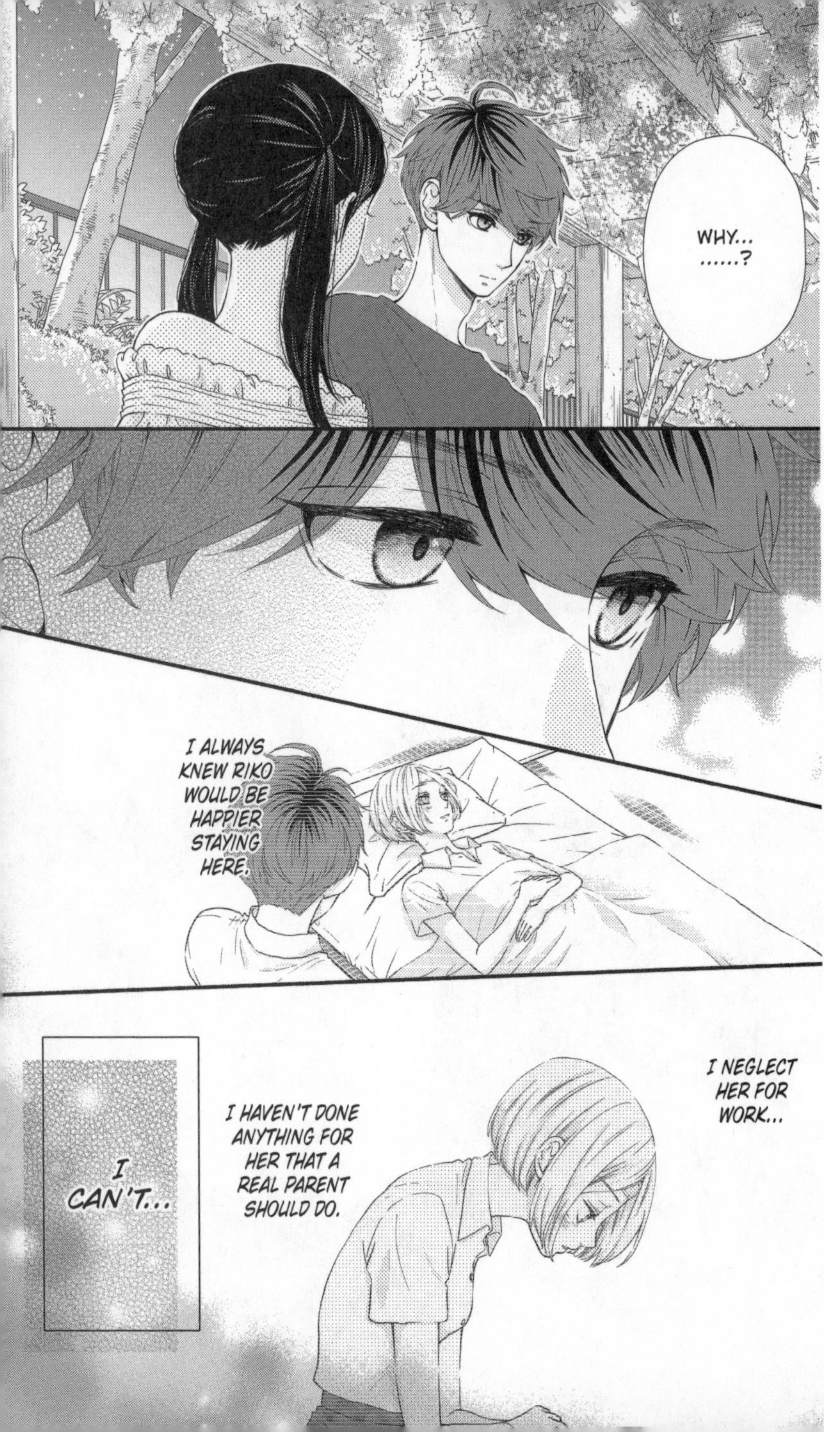
WHY... ......?
I ALWAYS KNEW RIKO WOULD BE HAPPIER STAYING HERE.
I NEGLECT HER FOR WORK...
I HAVEN'T DONE ANYTHING FOR HER THAT A REAL PARENT SHOULD DO.
I CAN'T...

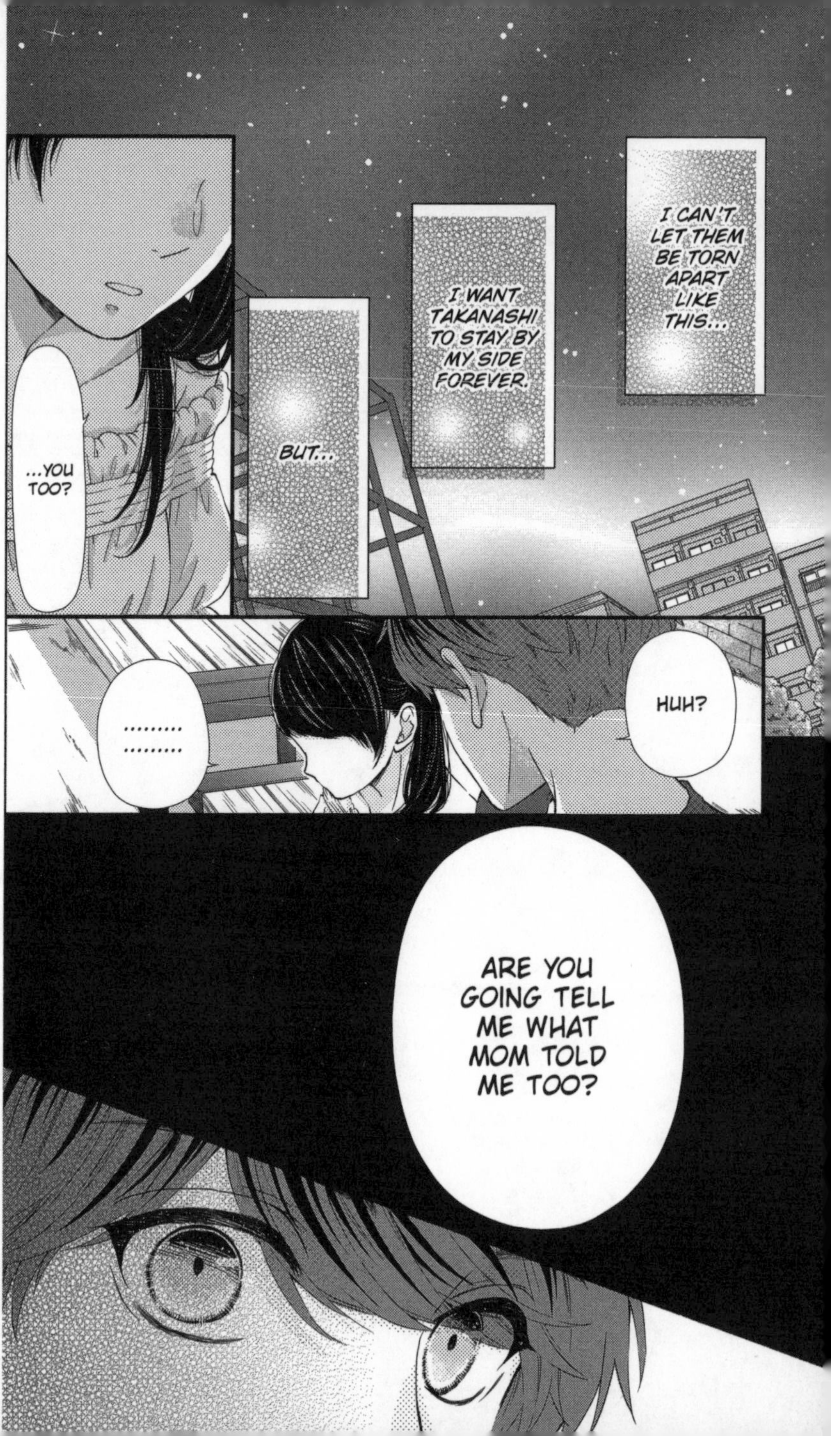
I CAN'T LET THEM BE TORN APART LIKE THIS...
I WANT TAKANASHI TO STAY BY MY SIDE FOREVER.
BUT...
...YOU TOO?
HUH?
....
....
ARE YOU GOING TELL ME WHAT MOM TOLD ME TOO?

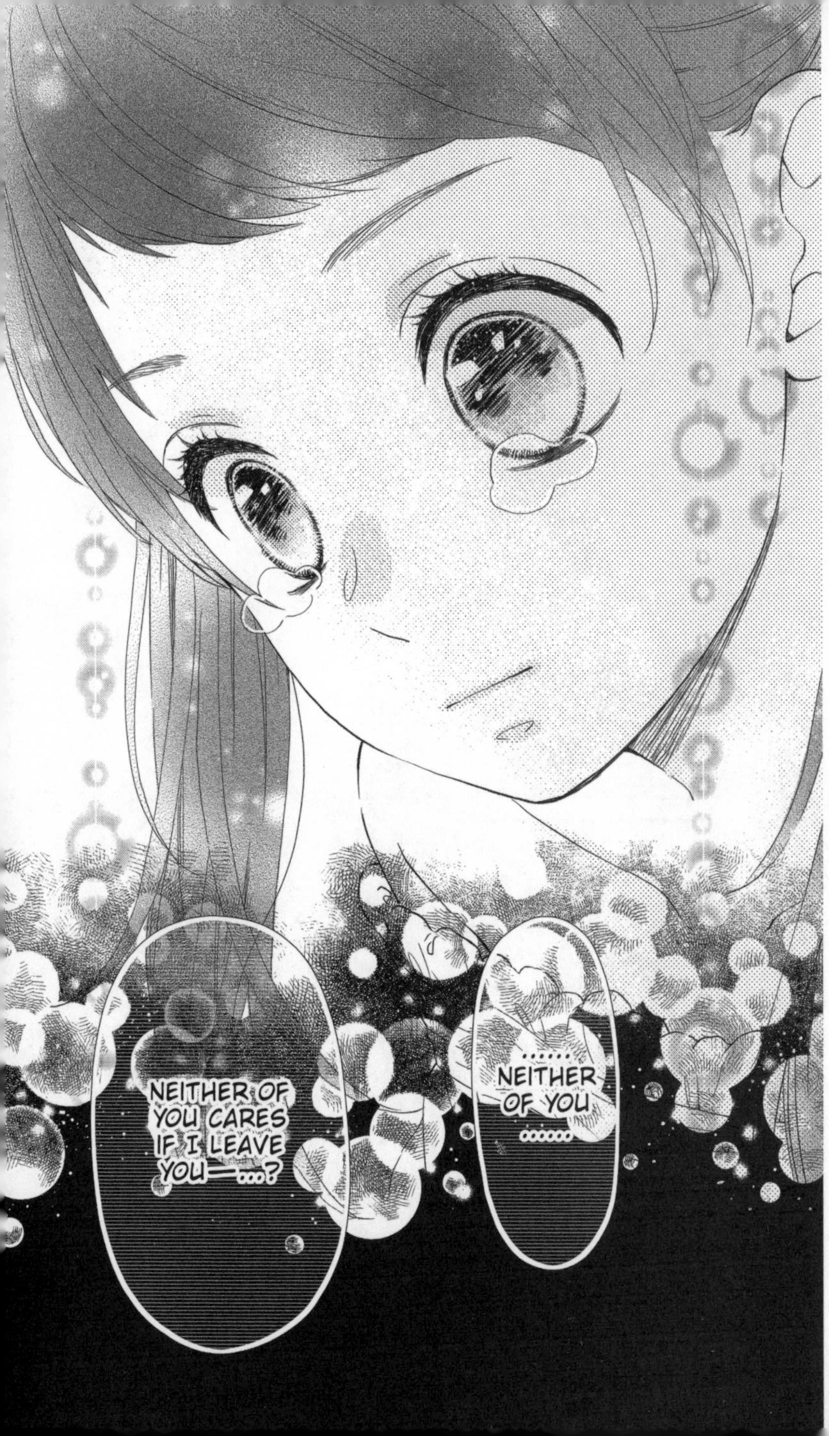
......NEITHER OF YOU ......
NEITHER OF YOU CARES IF I LEAVE YOU—...?

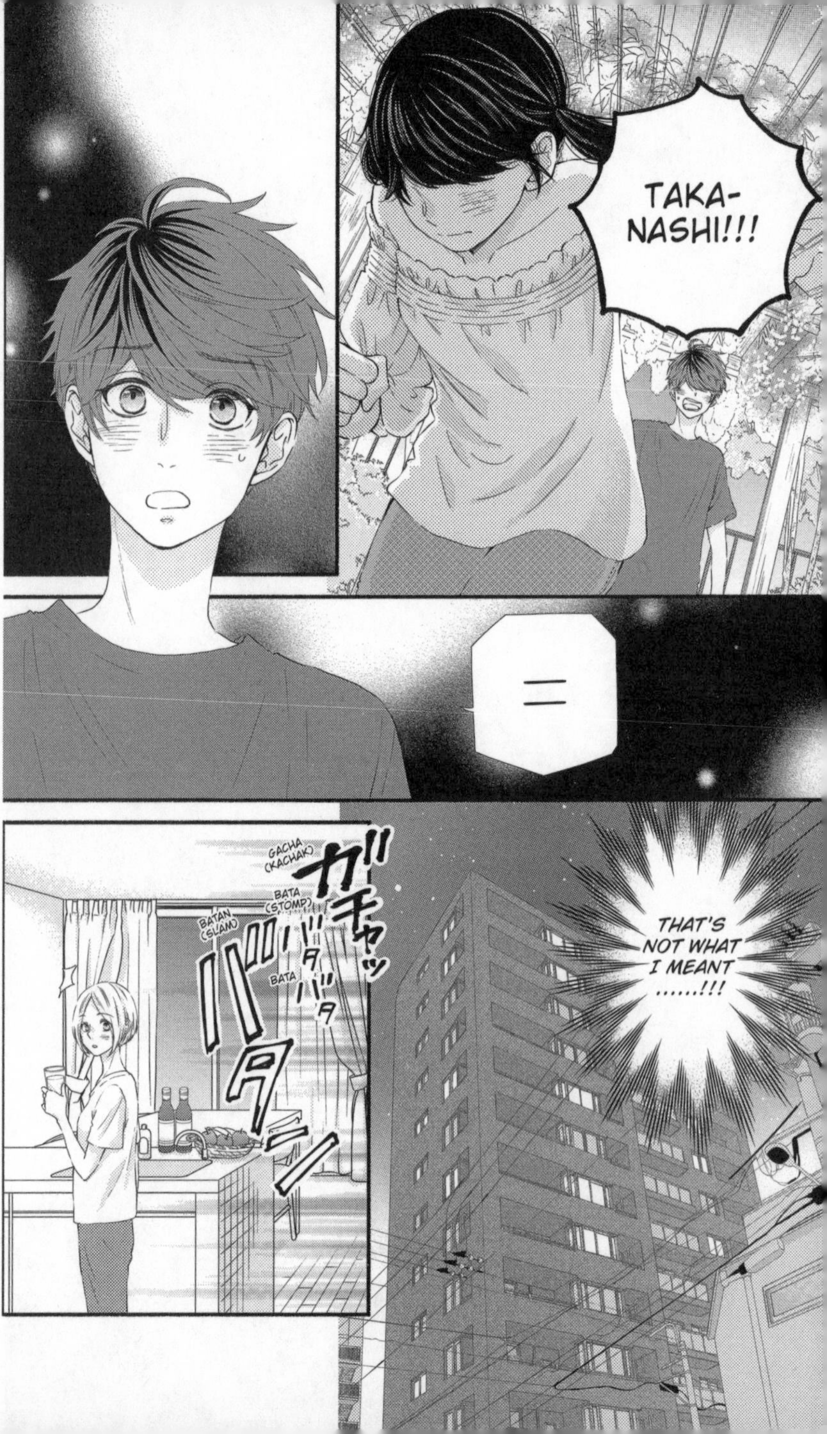
TAKA-
NASHI!!!
—
THAT'S NOT WHAT I MEANT ......!!!
GACHA (KACHAK)
BATA (STOMP)
BATA
BATAN (SLAM)

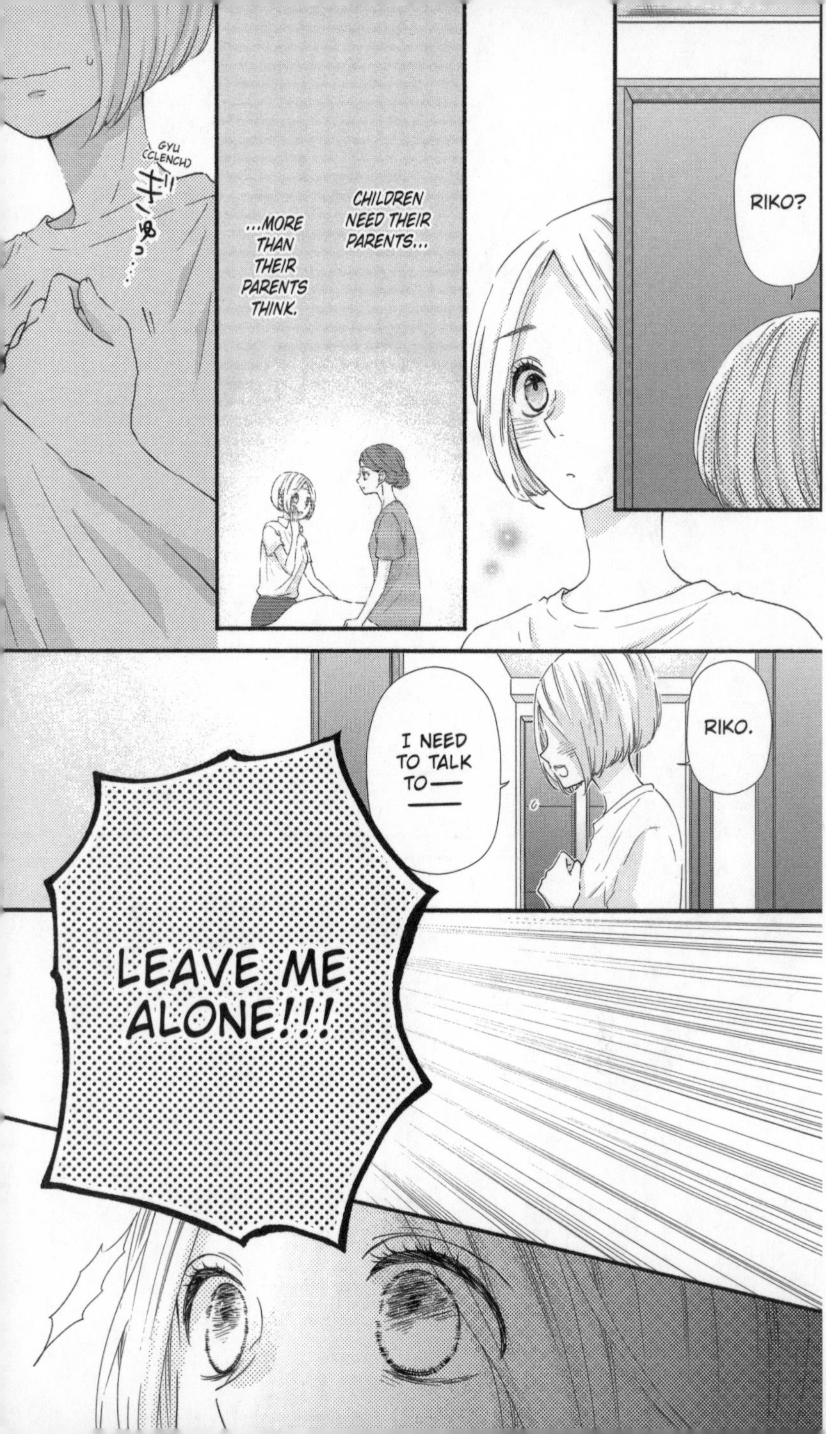
RIKO?
CHILDREN NEED THEIR PARENTS...
...MORE THAN THEIR PARENTS THINK.
GYU (CLENCH)
RIKO.
I NEED TO TALK TO— —
LEAVE ME ALONE!!!

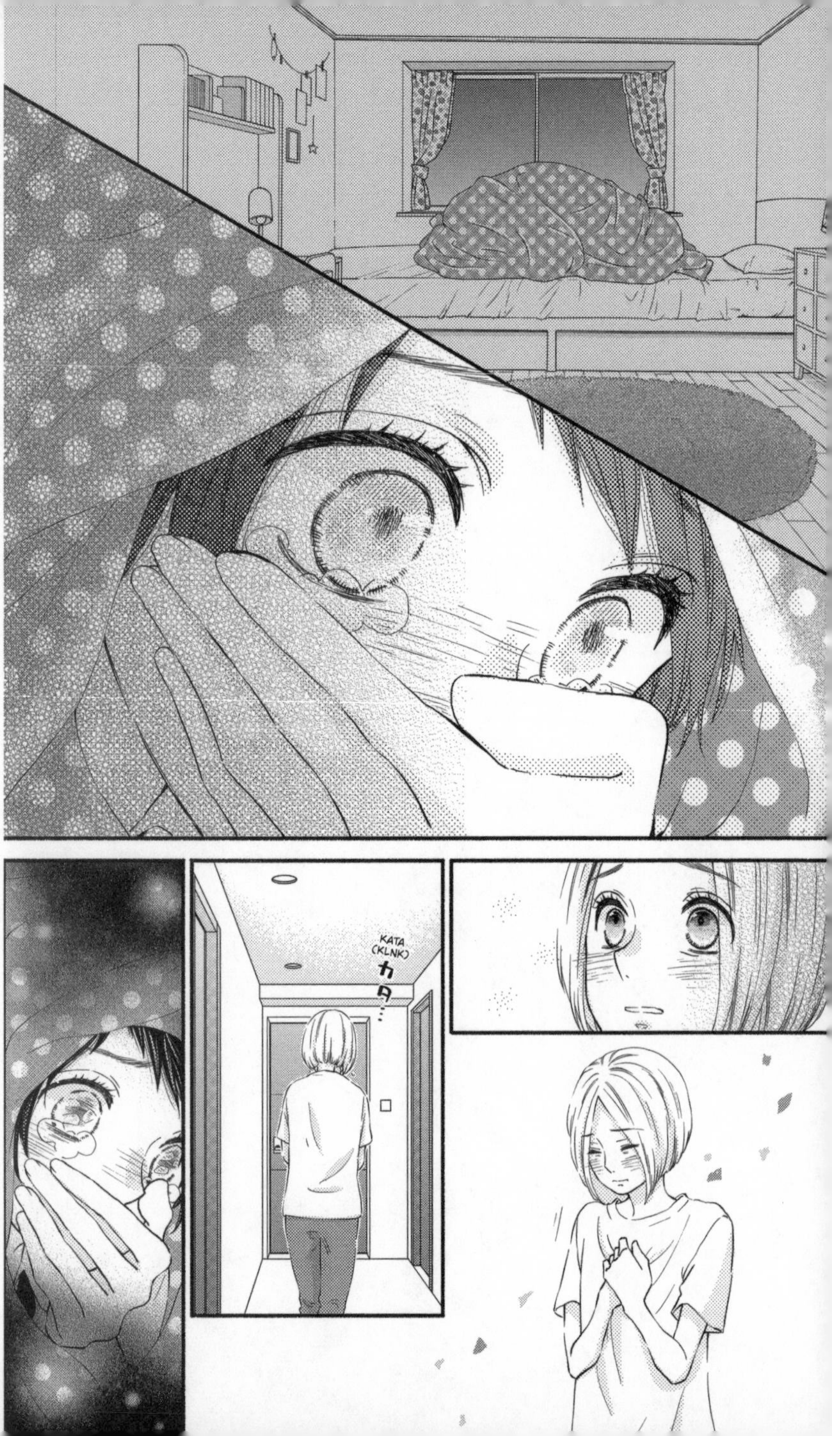
KATA
(KLNK)
カタ…

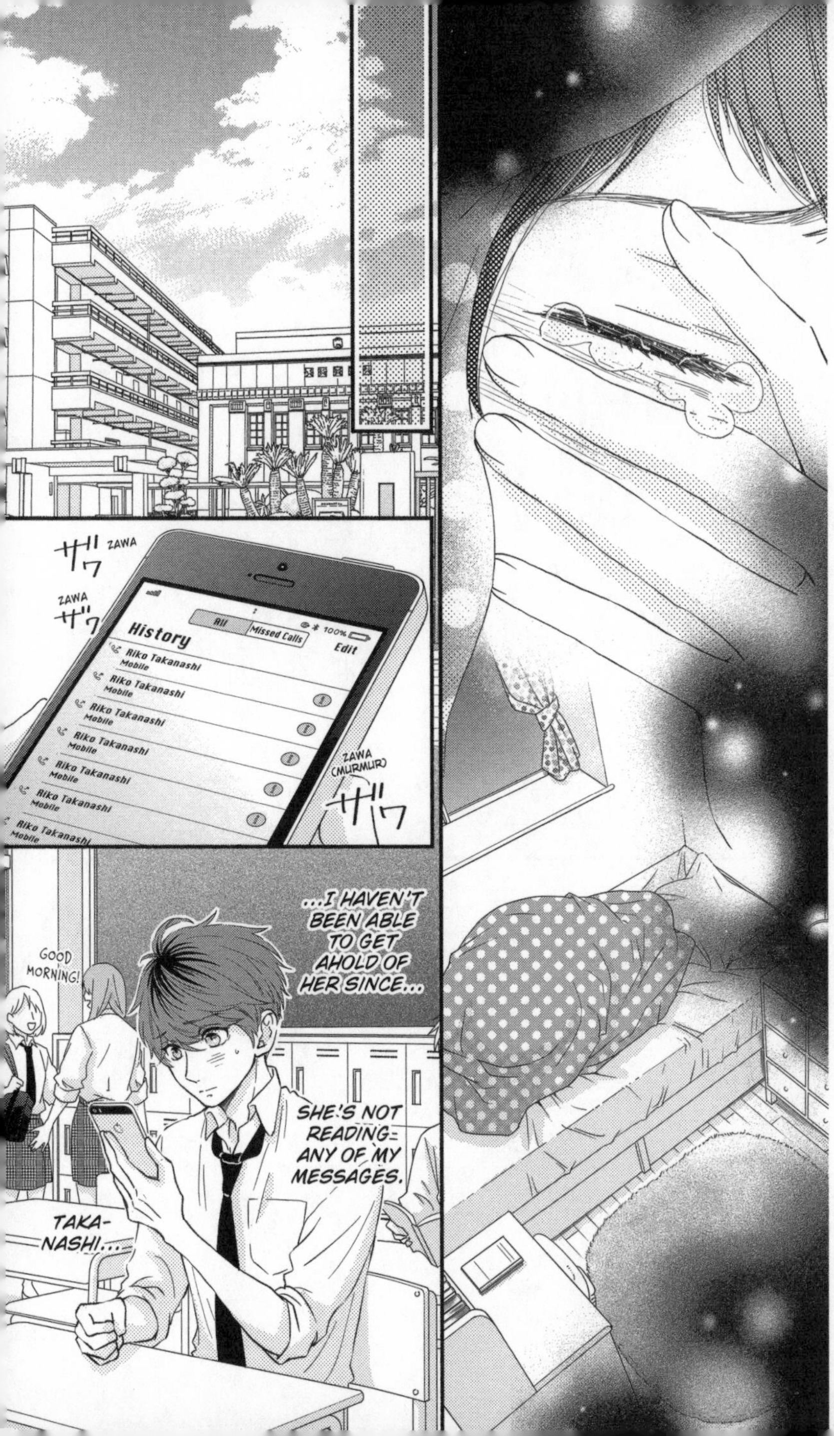
ザワ ZAWA
ZAWA ザワ
History
All
Missed Calls
100%
Edit
Riko Takanashi Mobile
Riko Takanashi Mobile
Riko Takanashi Mobile
Riko Takanashi Mobile
Riko Takanashi Mobile
Riko Takanashi Mobile
Riko Takanashi Mobile
ZAWA (MURMUR) ザワ
...I HAVEN'T BEEN ABLE TO GET AHOLD OF HER SINCE...
GOOD MORNING!
SHE'S NOT READING ANY OF MY MESSAGES.
TAKA-NASHI...

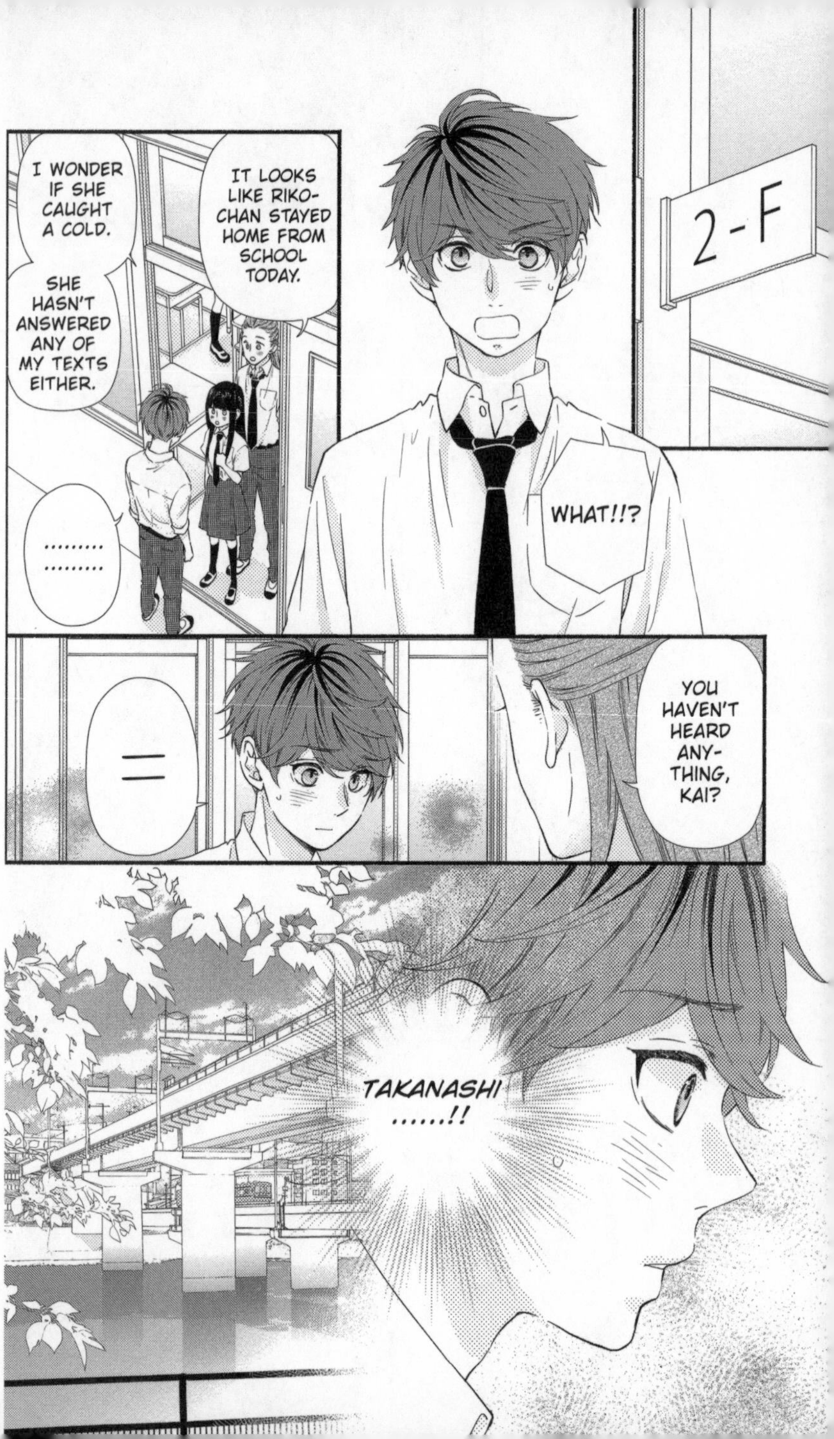
2-F
WHAT!!?
IT LOOKS LIKE RIKO-CHAN STAYED HOME FROM SCHOOL TODAY.
I WONDER IF SHE CAUGHT A COLD.
SHE HASN'T ANSWERED ANY OF MY TEXTS EITHER.
....
YOU HAVEN'T HEARD ANY-THING, KAI?
—
TAKANASHI ......!!

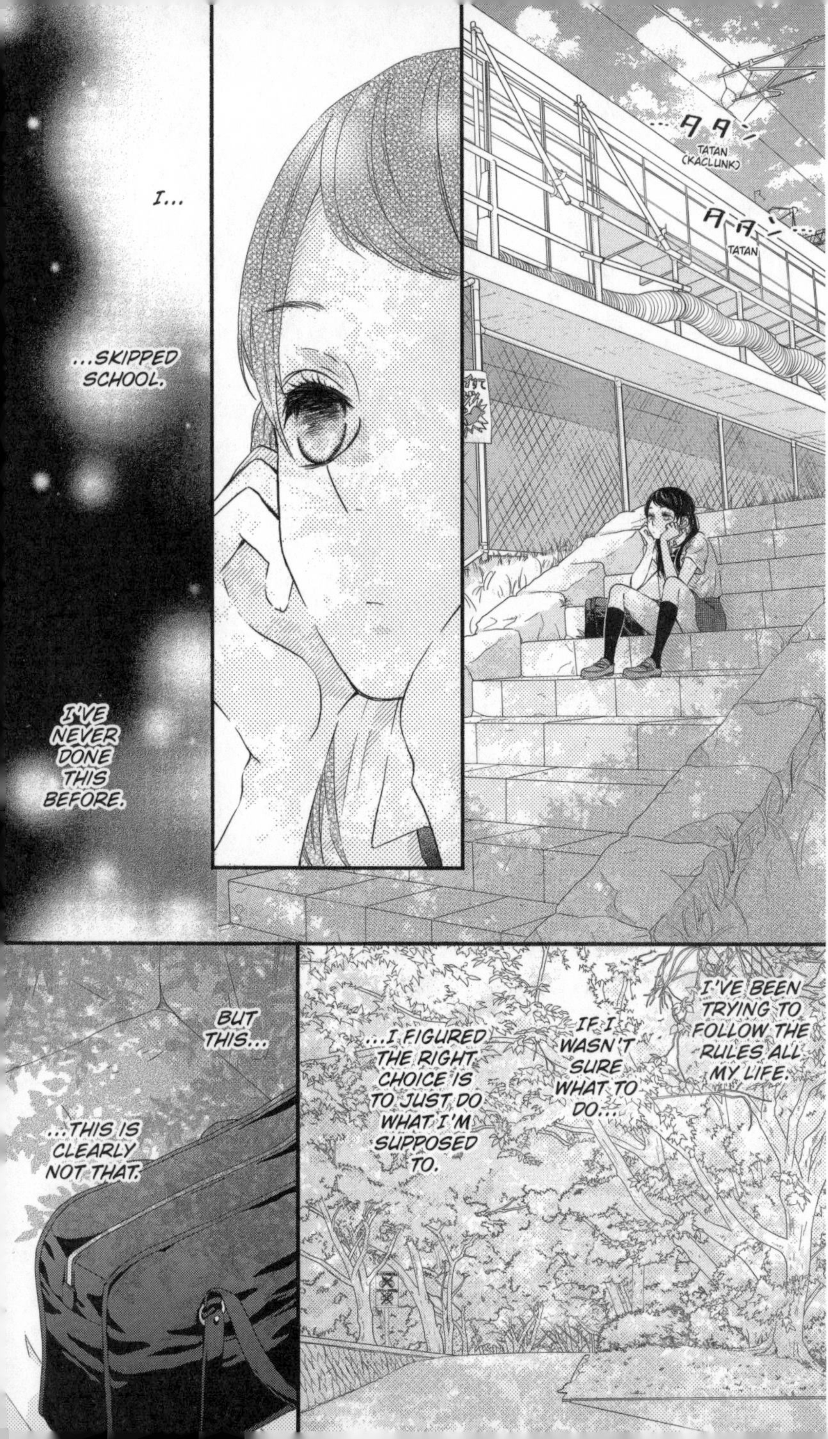

TATAN (KACLUNK)
TATAN
I...
...SKIPPED SCHOOL.
I'VE NEVER DONE THIS BEFORE.
I'VE BEEN TRYING TO FOLLOW THE RULES ALL MY LIFE.
IF I WASN'T SURE WHAT TO DO...
...I FIGURED THE RIGHT CHOICE IS TO JUST DO WHAT I'M SUPPOSED TO.
BUT THIS...
...THIS IS CLEARLY NOT THAT.

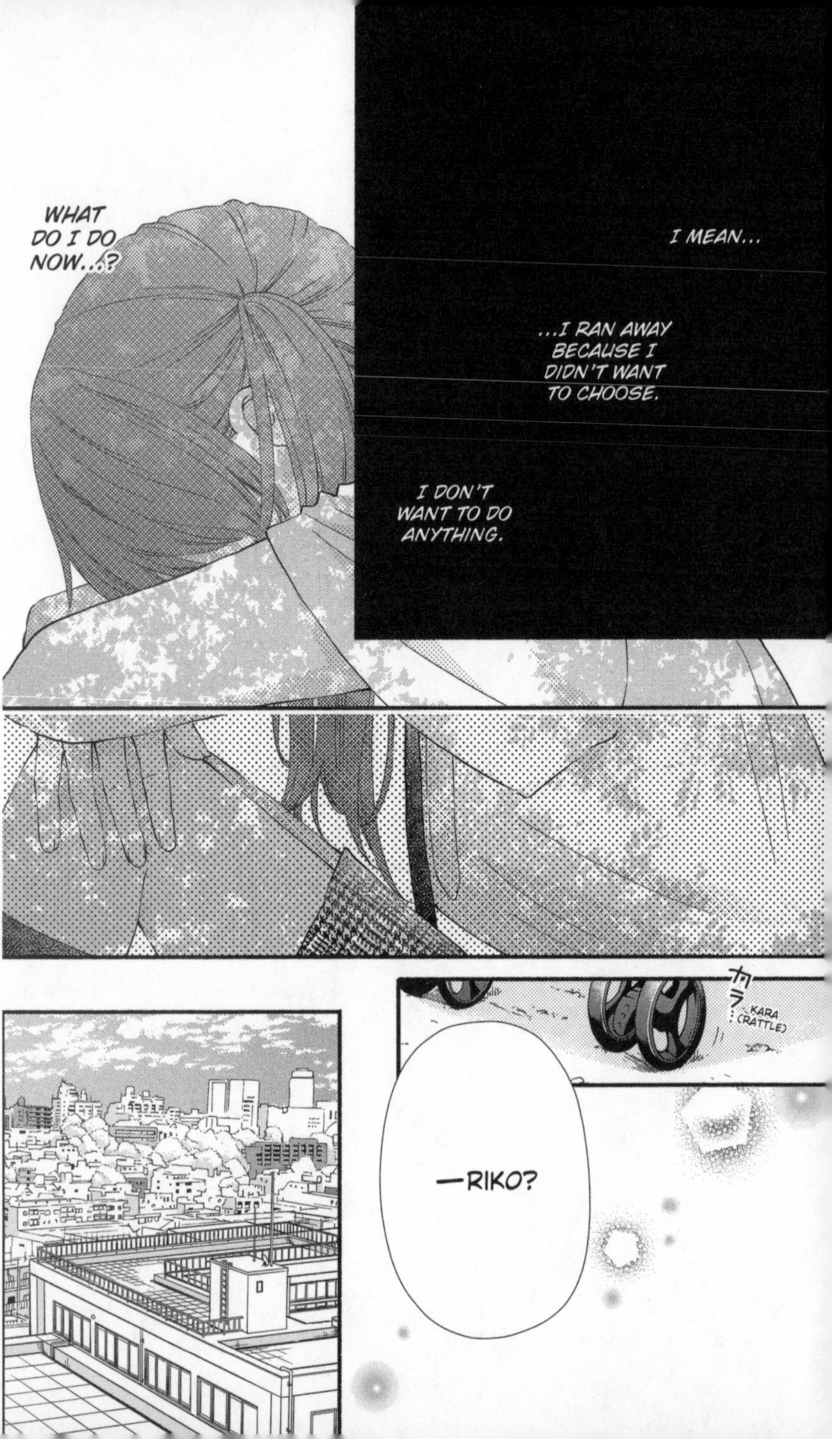
I MEAN...
...I RAN AWAY BECAUSE I DIDN'T WANT TO CHOOSE.
I DON'T WANT TO DO ANYTHING.
WHAT DO I DO NOW...?
カラ
KARA (RATTLE)
—RIKO?

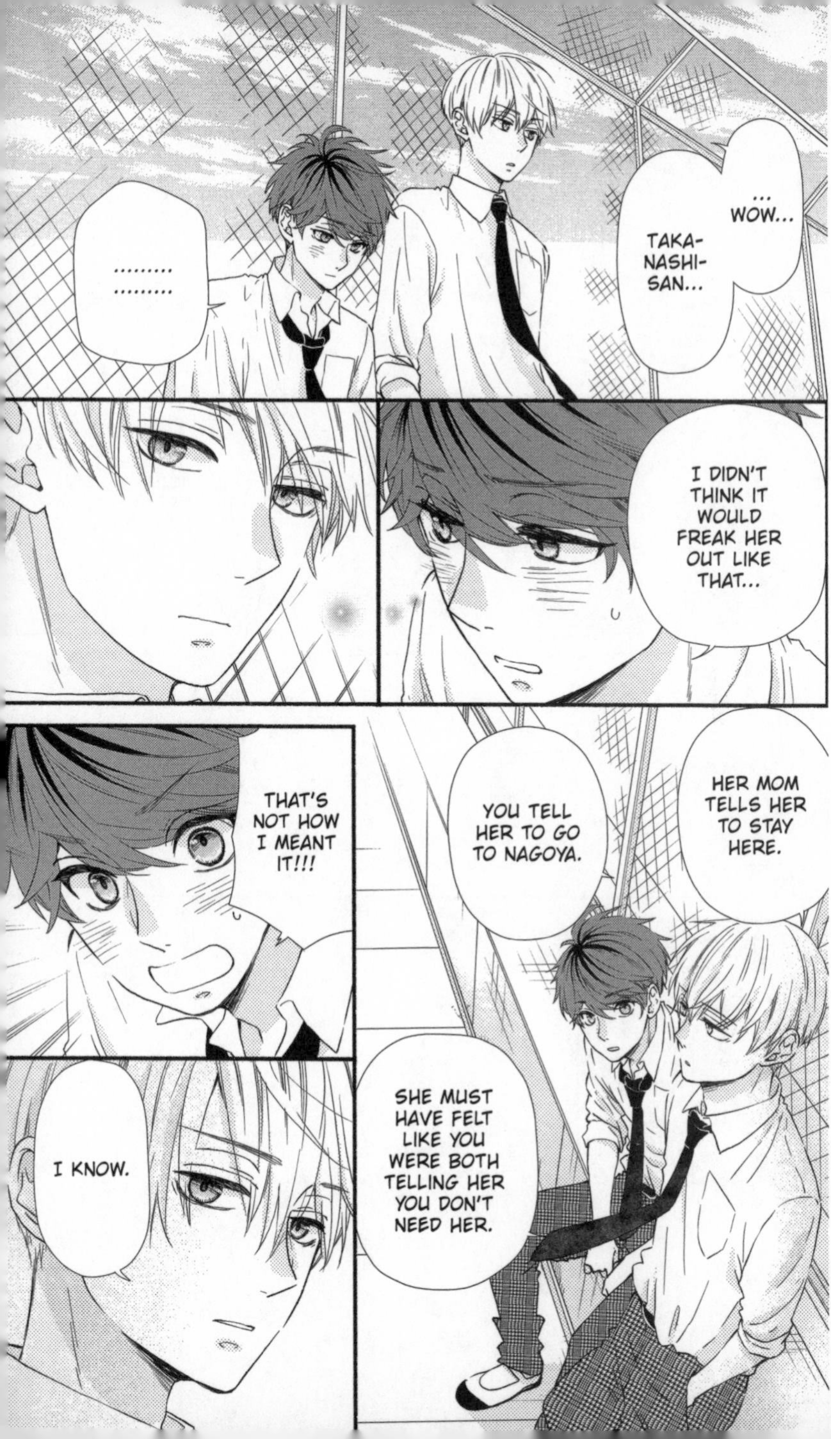

... WOW... TAKA-NASHI-SAN...
....
....
I DIDN'T THINK IT WOULD FREAK HER OUT LIKE THAT...
HER MOM TELLS HER TO STAY HERE.
YOU TELL HER TO GO TO NAGOYA.
SHE MUST HAVE FELT LIKE YOU WERE BOTH TELLING HER YOU DON'T NEED HER.
THAT'S NOT HOW I MEANT IT!!!
I KNOW.

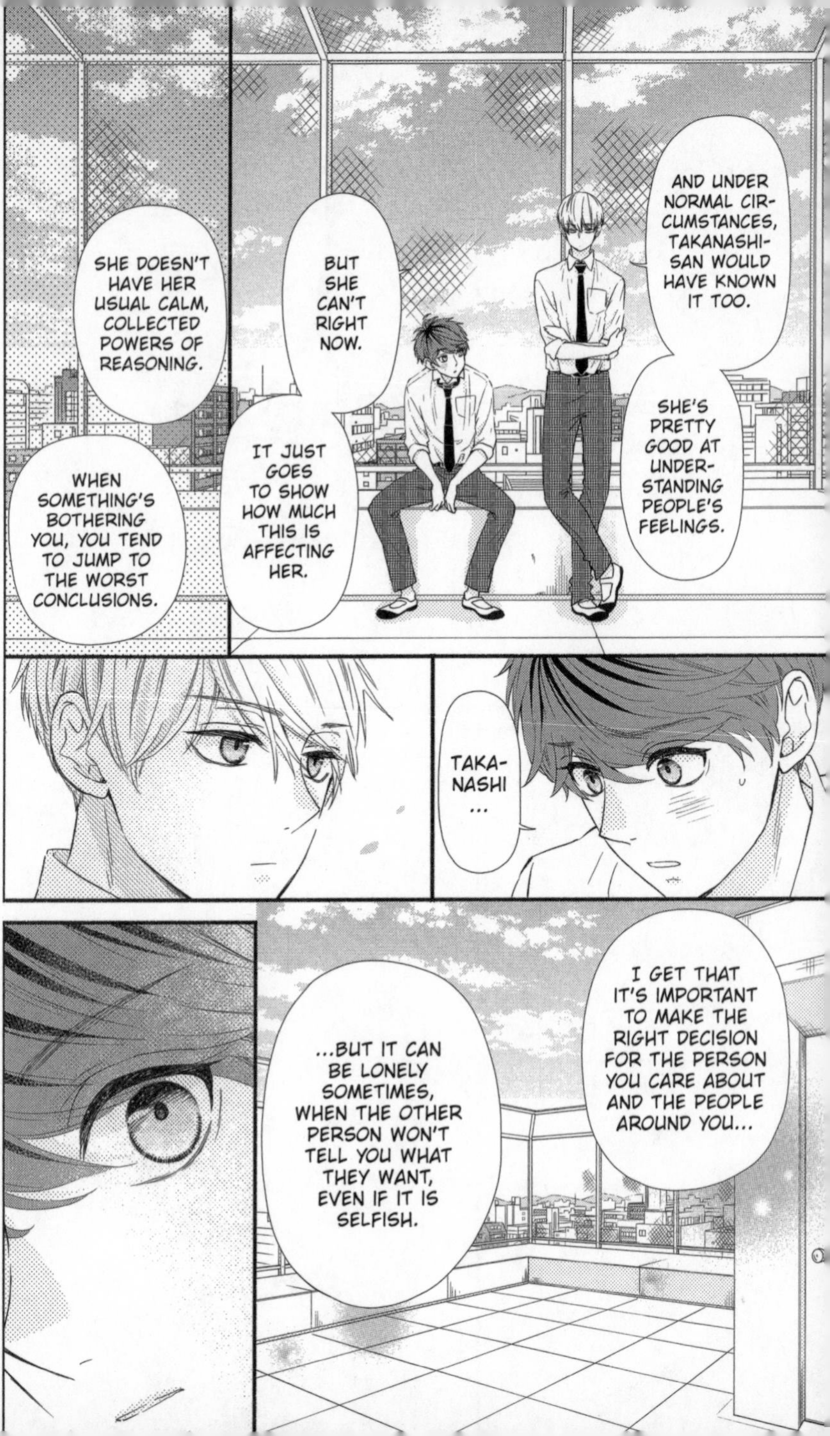
AND UNDER NORMAL CIR-CUMSTANCES, TAKANASHI-SAN WOULD HAVE KNOWN IT TOO.
SHE'S PRETTY GOOD AT UNDER-STANDING PEOPLE'S FEELINGS.
BUT SHE CAN'T RIGHT NOW.
IT JUST GOES TO SHOW HOW MUCH THIS IS AFFECTING HER.
SHE DOESN'T HAVE HER USUAL CALM, COLLECTED POWERS OF REASONING.
WHEN SOMETHING'S BOTHERING YOU, YOU TEND TO JUMP TO THE WORST CONCLUSIONS.
TAKA-NASHI...
I GET THAT IT'S IMPORTANT TO MAKE THE RIGHT DECISION FOR THE PERSON YOU CARE ABOUT AND THE PEOPLE AROUND YOU...
...BUT IT CAN BE LONELY SOMETIMES, WHEN THE OTHER PERSON WON'T TELL YOU WHAT THEY WANT, EVEN IF IT IS SELFISH.

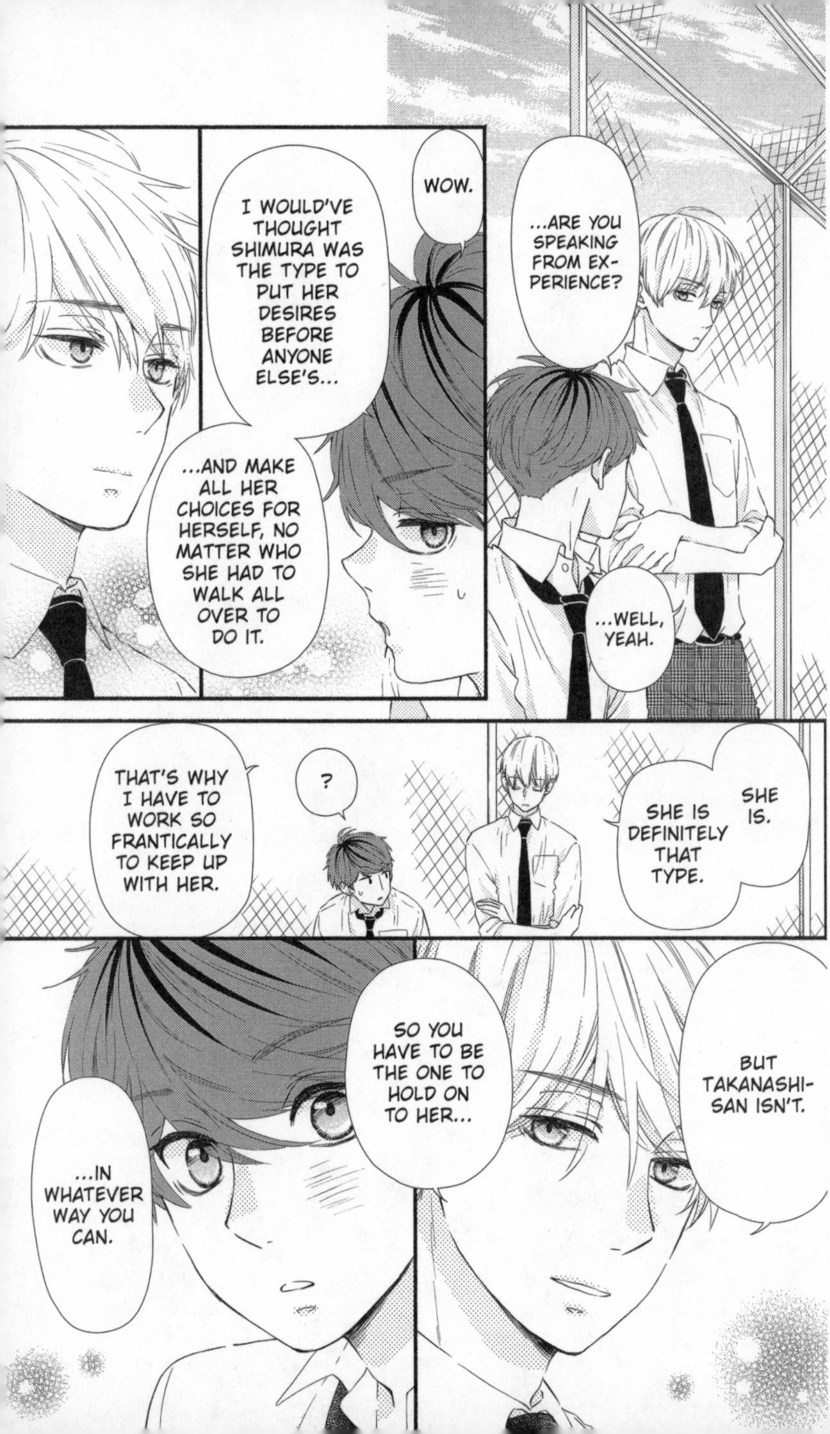
...ARE YOU SPEAKING FROM EX-PERIENCE?
...WELL, YEAH.
WOW.
I WOULD'VE THOUGHT SHIMURA WAS THE TYPE TO PUT HER DESIRES BEFORE ANYONE ELSE'S...
...AND MAKE ALL HER CHOICES FOR HERSELF, NO MATTER WHO SHE HAD TO WALK ALL OVER TO DO IT.
SHE IS.
SHE IS DEFINITELY THAT TYPE.
?
THAT'S WHY I HAVE TO WORK SO FRANTICALLY TO KEEP UP WITH HER.
BUT TAKANASHI-SAN ISN'T.
SO YOU HAVE TO BE THE ONE TO HOLD ON TO HER...
...IN WHATEVER WAY YOU CAN.

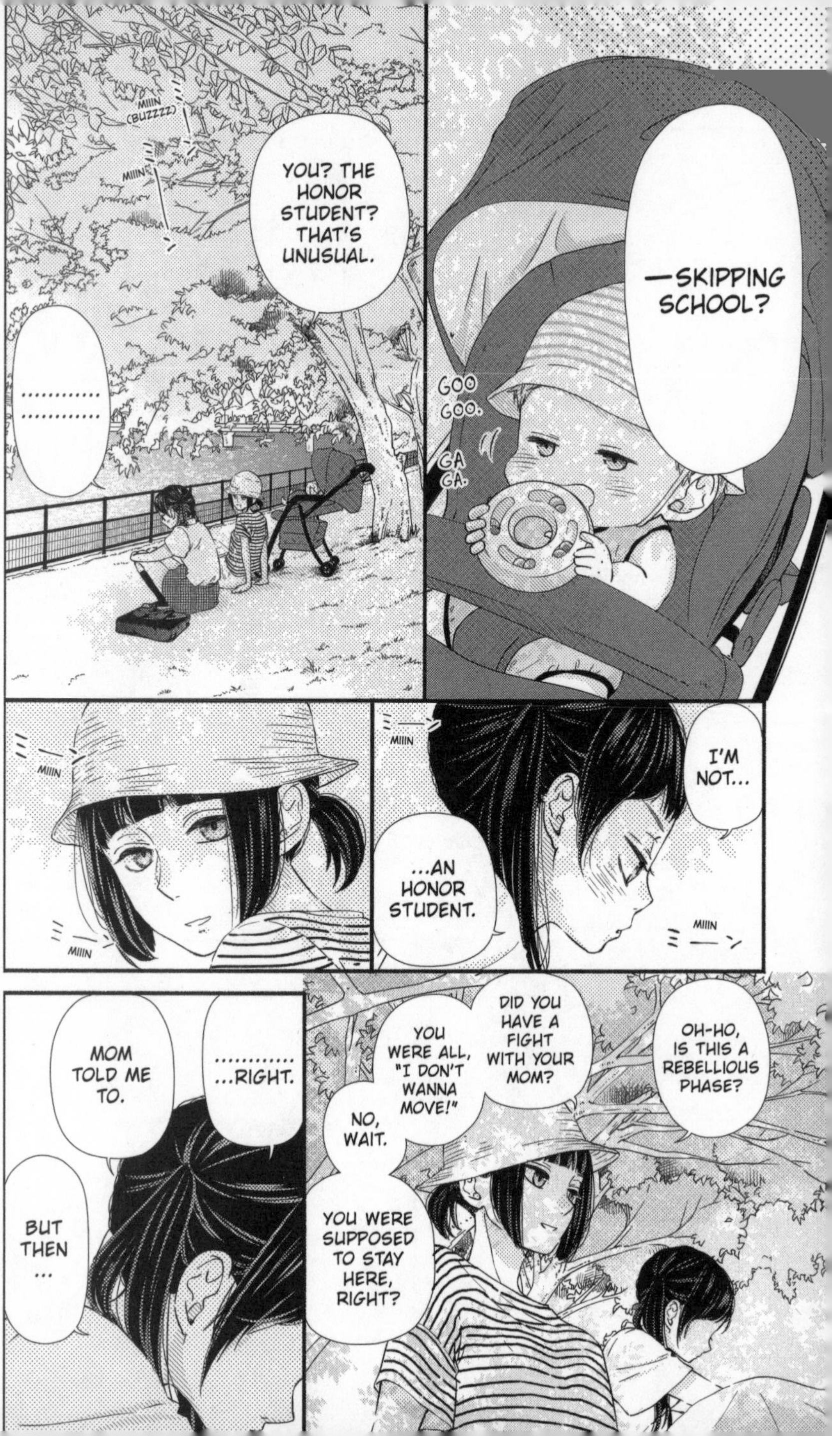
—SKIPPING SCHOOL?
GOO GOO.
GA GA.
MIIIN (BUZZZZ)
MIIIN
YOU? THE HONOR STUDENT? THAT'S UNUSUAL.
....
MIIIN
I'M NOT...
...AN HONOR STUDENT.
MIIIN
MIIIN
MIIIN
OH-HO, IS THIS A REBELLIOUS PHASE?
DID YOU HAVE A FIGHT WITH YOUR MOM?
YOU WERE ALL, "I DON'T WANNA MOVE!"
NO, WAIT.
YOU WERE SUPPOSED TO STAY HERE, RIGHT?
....RIGHT.
MOM TOLD ME TO.
BUT THEN ...

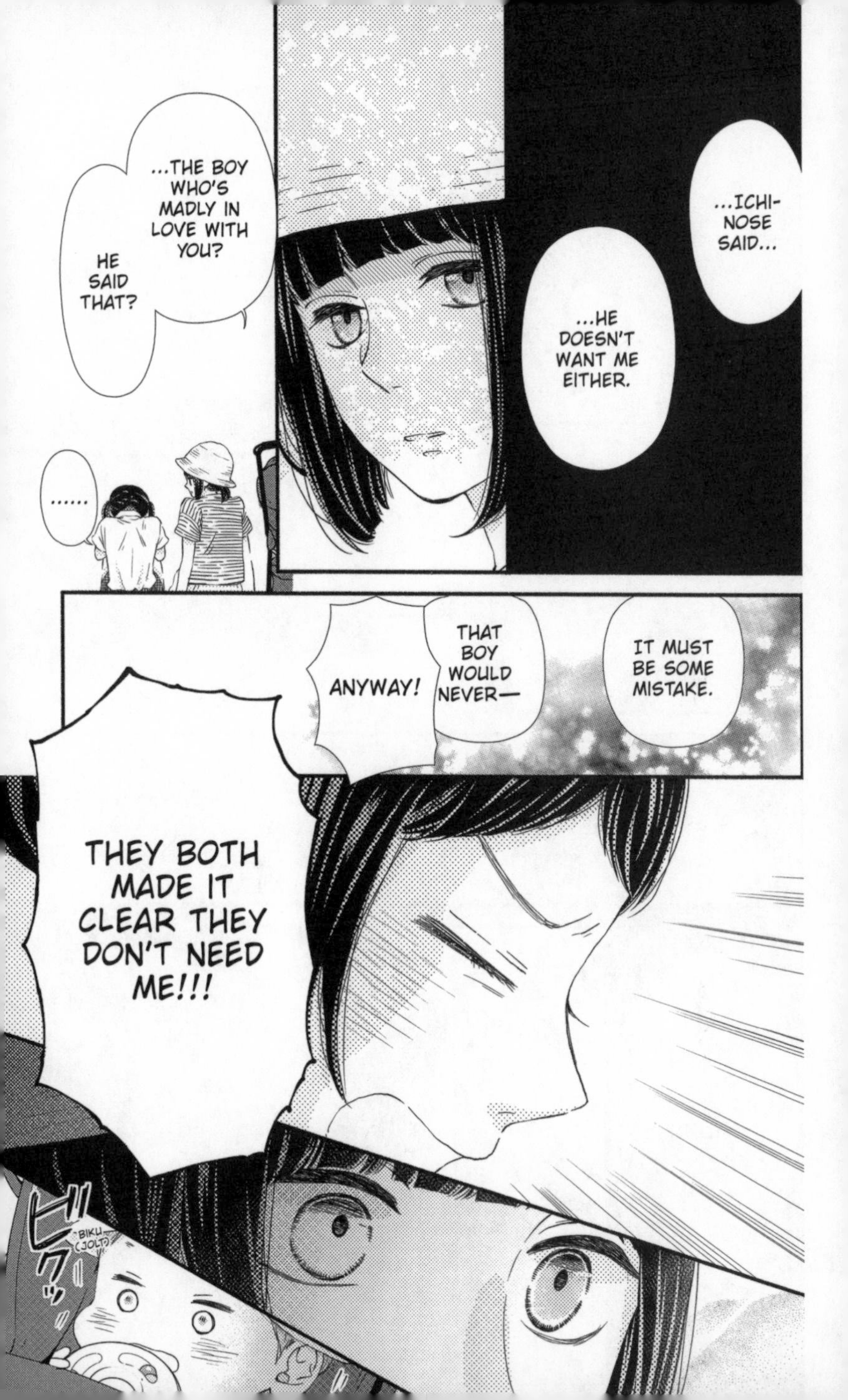
...ICHI-NOSE SAID...
...HE DOESN'T WANT ME EITHER.
...THE BOY WHO'S MADLY IN LOVE WITH YOU?
HE SAID THAT?
......
IT MUST BE SOME MISTAKE.
THAT BOY WOULD NEVER—
ANYWAY!
THEY BOTH MADE IT CLEAR THEY DON'T NEED ME!!!
ビクッ
BIKU (JOLT)

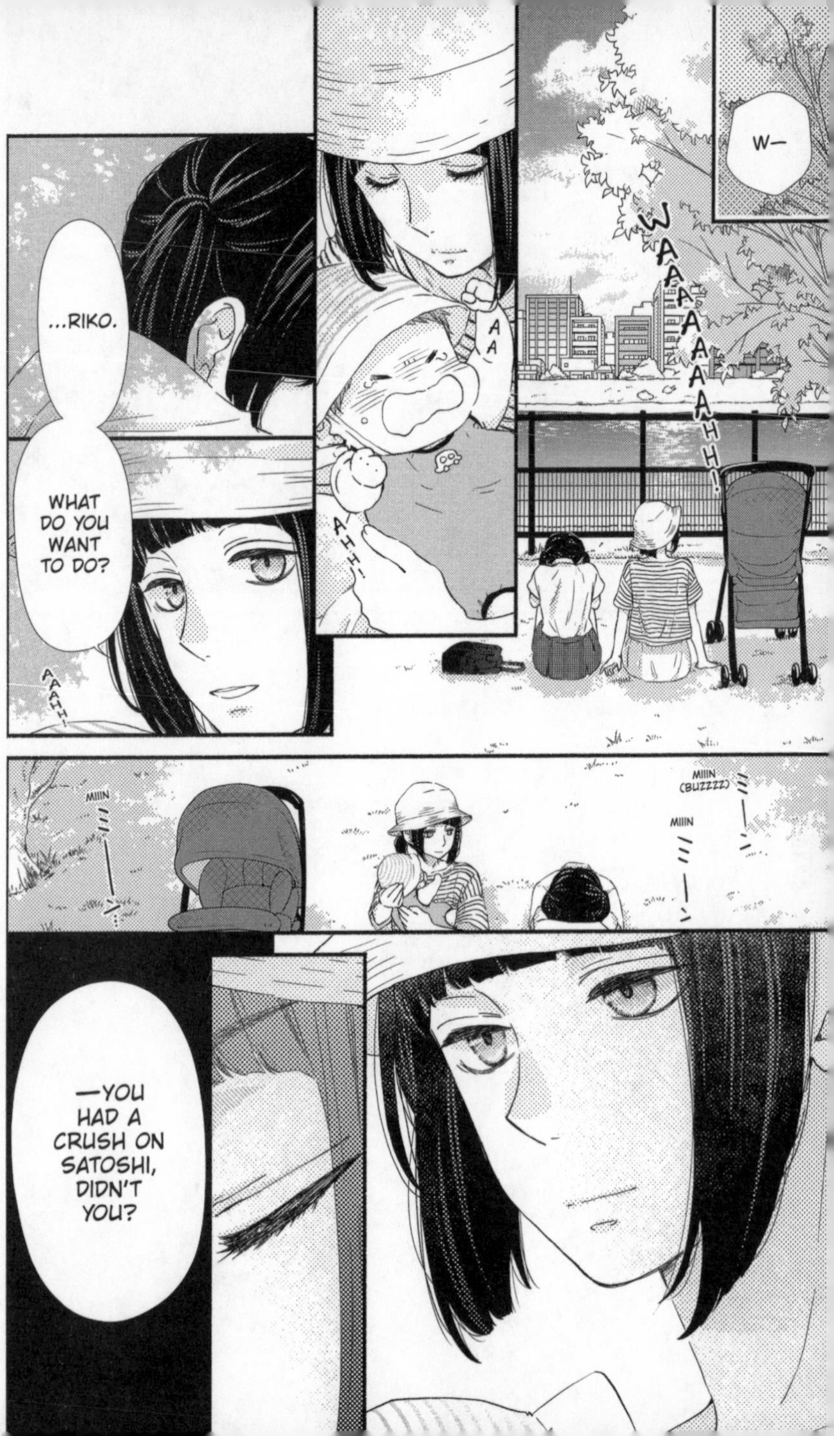
W—
WAAAAAAAHH!
AA
AHH!
...RIKO.
WHAT DO YOU WANT TO DO?
AAAHH!
MIIIN (BUZZZZ)
MIIIN
MIIIN
—YOU HAD A CRUSH ON SATOSHI, DIDN'T YOU?

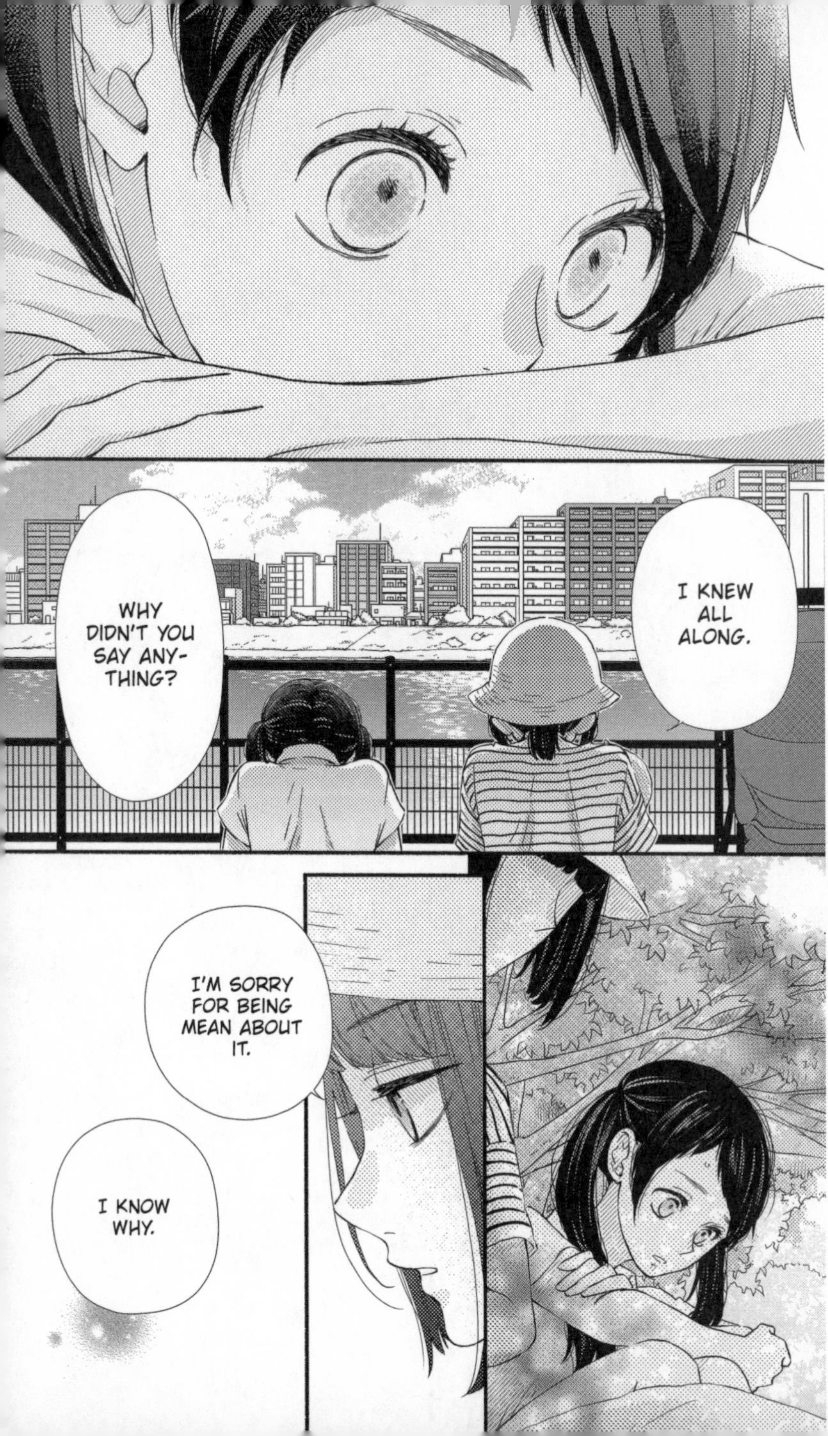
I KNEW ALL ALONG.
WHY DIDN'T YOU SAY ANY-THING?
I'M SORRY FOR BEING MEAN ABOUT IT.
I KNOW WHY.

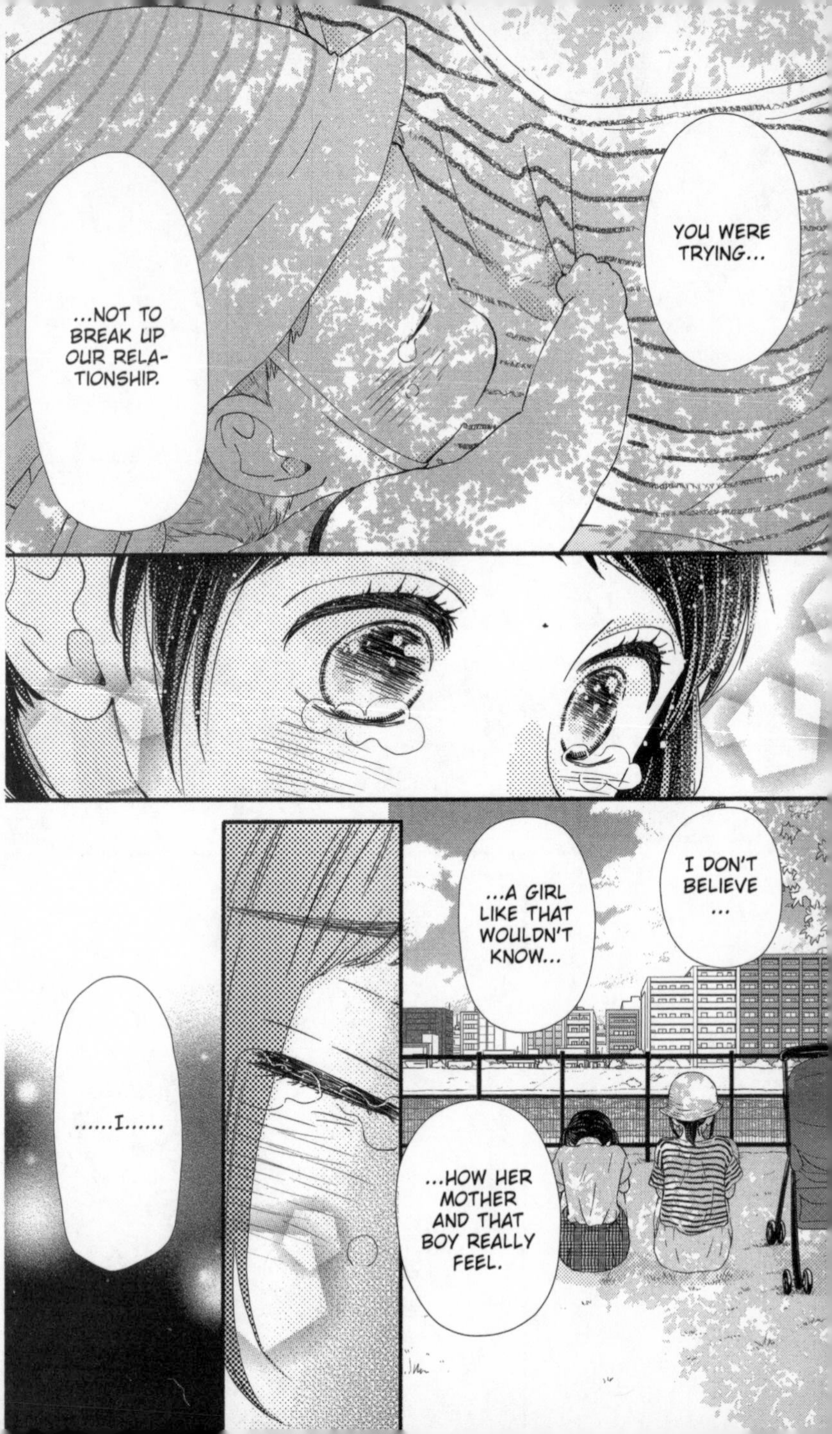
YOU WERE TRYING...
...NOT TO BREAK UP OUR RELA-TIONSHIP.
I DON'T BELIEVE ...
...A GIRL LIKE THAT WOULDN'T KNOW...
...HOW HER MOTHER AND THAT BOY REALLY FEEL.
......I......

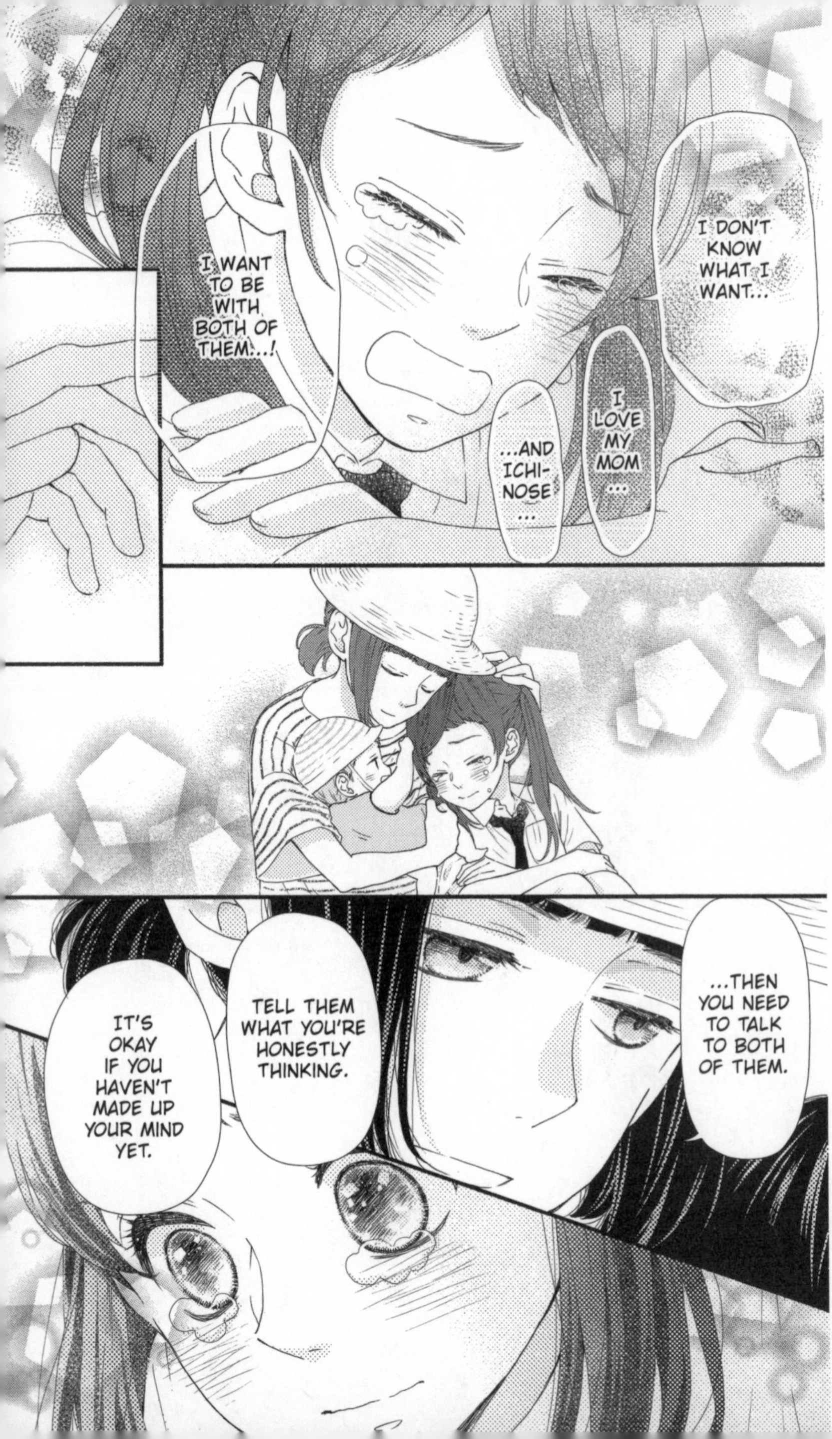
I DON'T KNOW WHAT I WANT...
I LOVE MY MOM ...
...AND ICHINOSE ...
I WANT TO BE WITH BOTH OF THEM...!
...THEN YOU NEED TO TALK TO BOTH OF THEM.
TELL THEM WHAT YOU'RE HONESTLY THINKING.
IT'S OKAY IF YOU HAVEN'T MADE UP YOUR MIND YET.

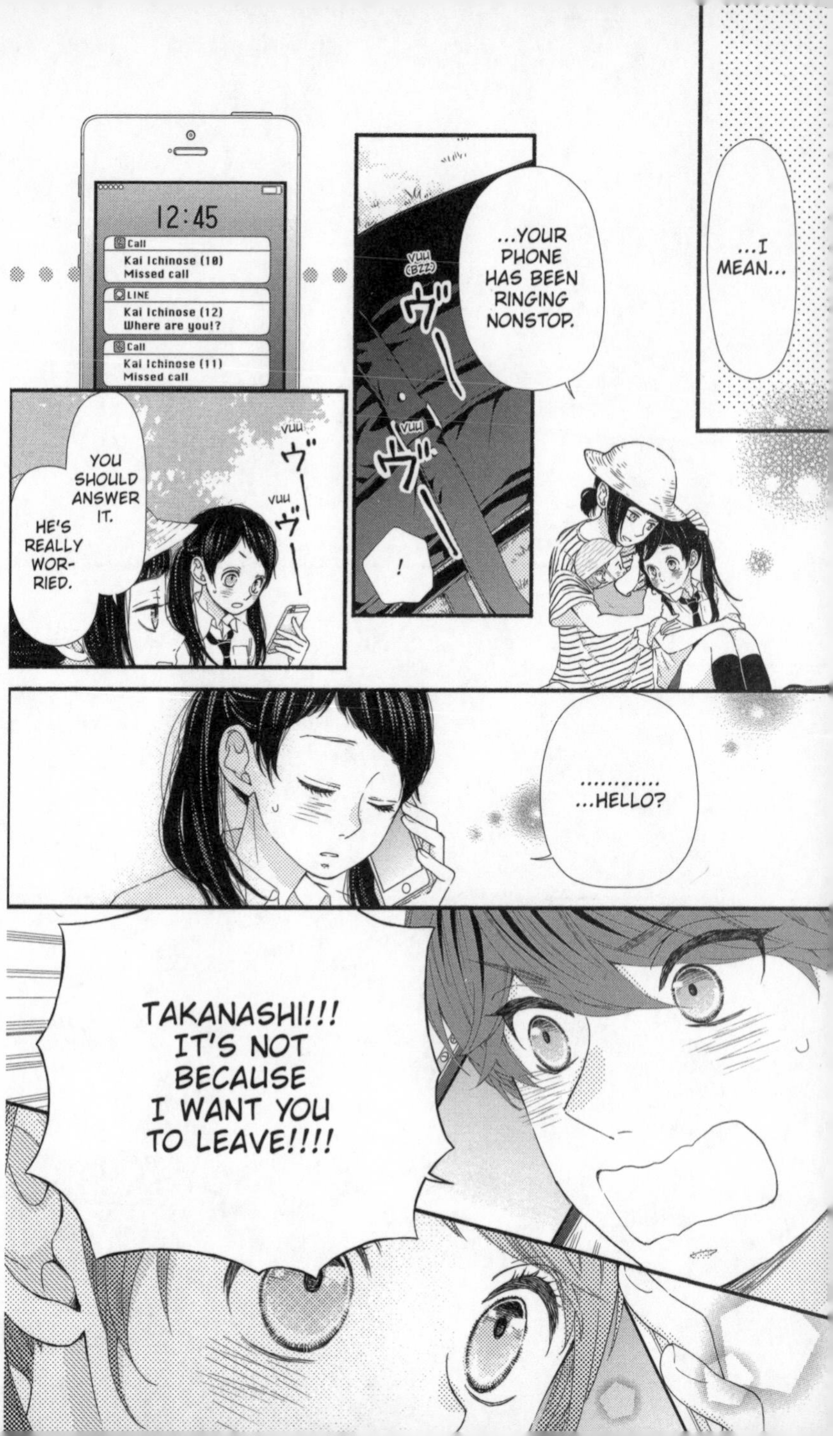
...I MEAN...
...YOUR PHONE HAS BEEN RINGING NONSTOP.
VUU (BZZ)
VUU
!
12:45
Call
Kai Ichinose (10)
Missed call
LINE
Kai Ichinose (12)
Where are you!?
Call
Kai Ichinose (11)
Missed call
VUU
VUU
YOU SHOULD ANSWER IT.
HE'S REALLY WOR-RIED.
....HELLO?
TAKANASHI!!!! IT'S NOT BECAUSE I WANT YOU TO LEAVE!!!!

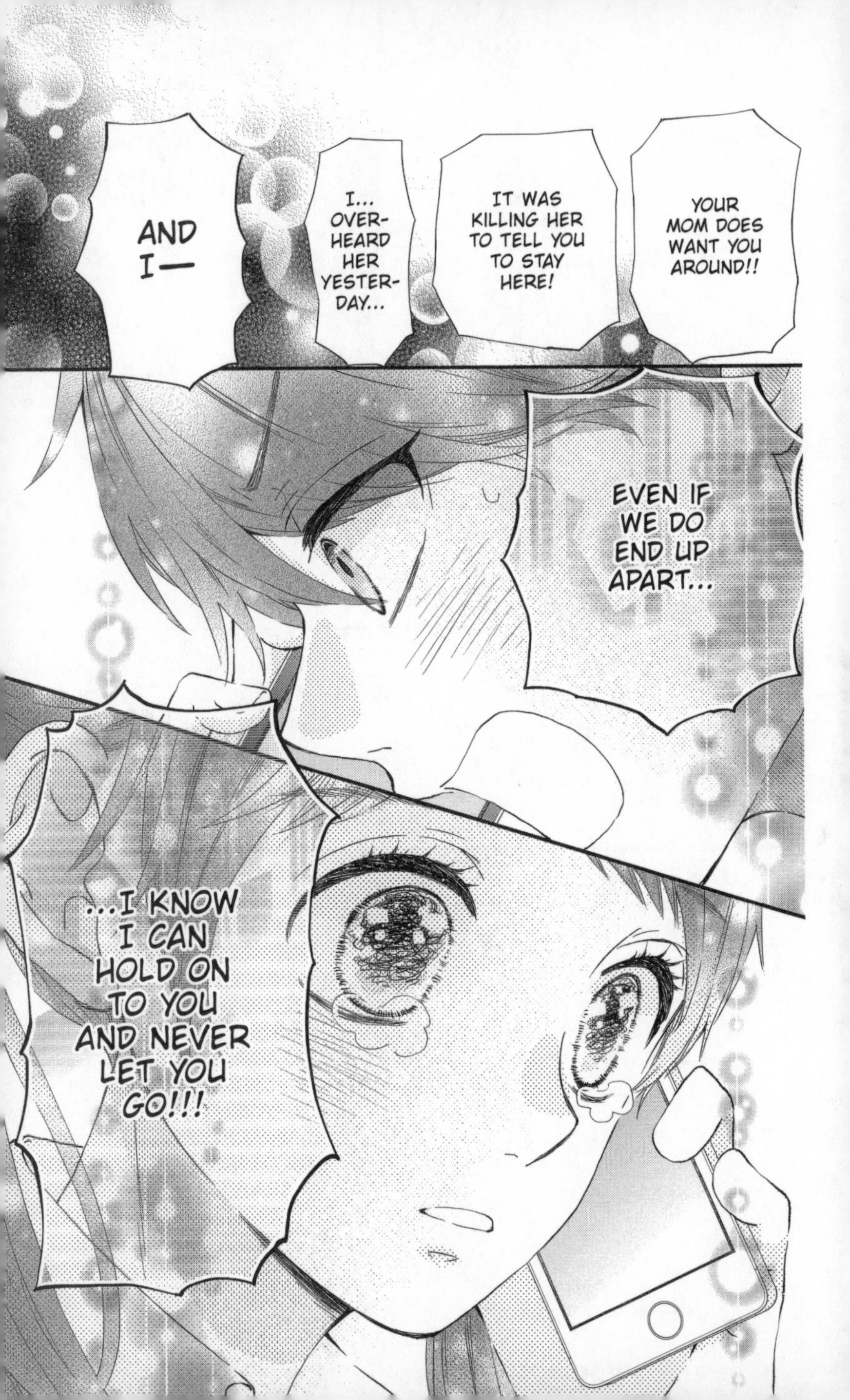
YOUR MOM DOES WANT YOU AROUND!!
IT WAS KILLING HER TO TELL YOU TO STAY HERE!
I... OVER-HEARD HER YESTER-DAY...
AND I—
EVEN IF WE DO END UP APART...
...I KNOW I CAN HOLD ON TO YOU AND NEVER LET YOU GO!!!

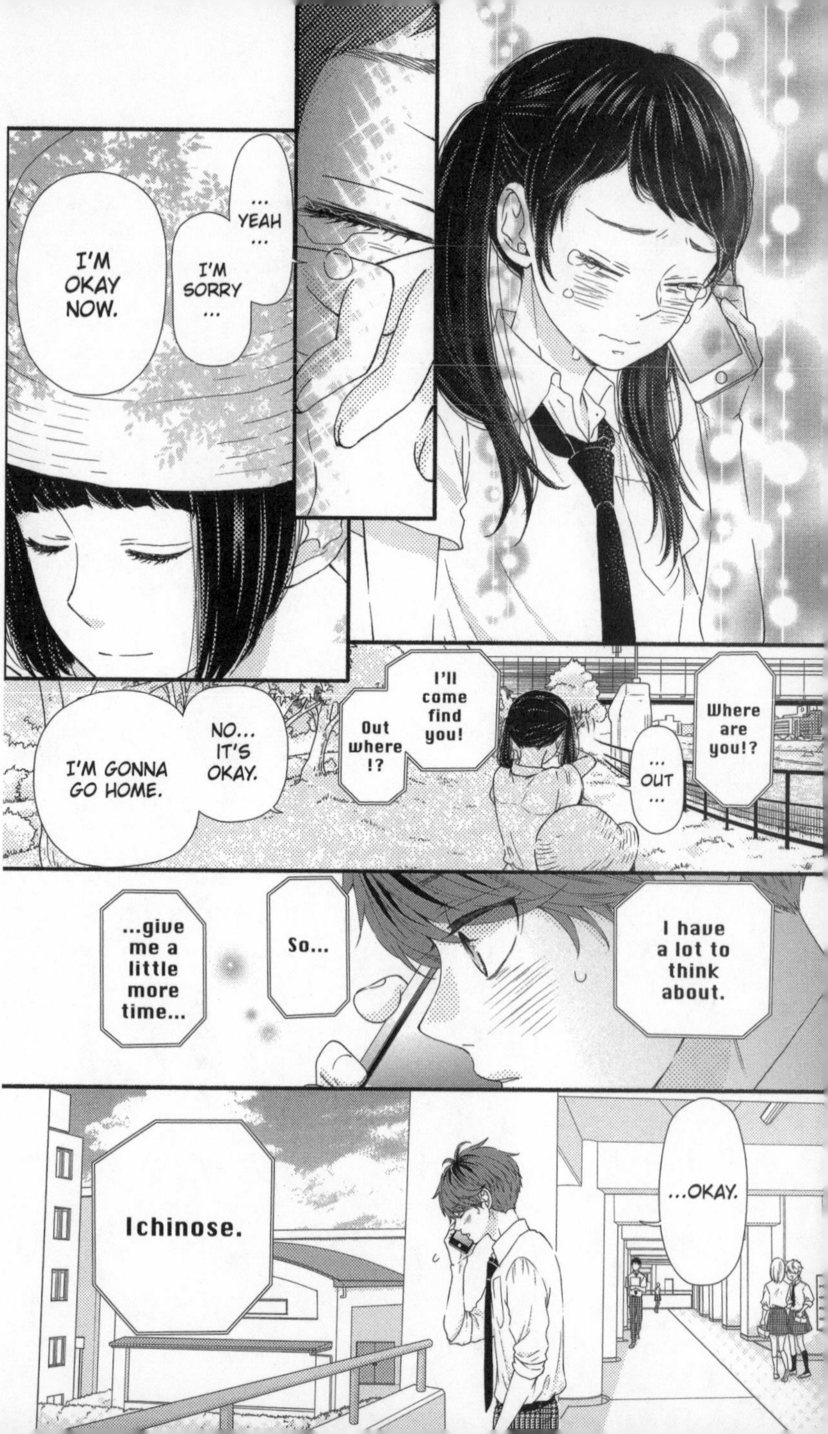
... YEAH ...
I'M SORRY ...
I'M OKAY NOW.
Where are you!?
... OUT ...
I'll come find you!
Out where !?
NO... IT'S OKAY.
I'M GONNA GO HOME.
I have a lot to think about.
So...
...give me a little more time...
...OKAY.
Ichinose.

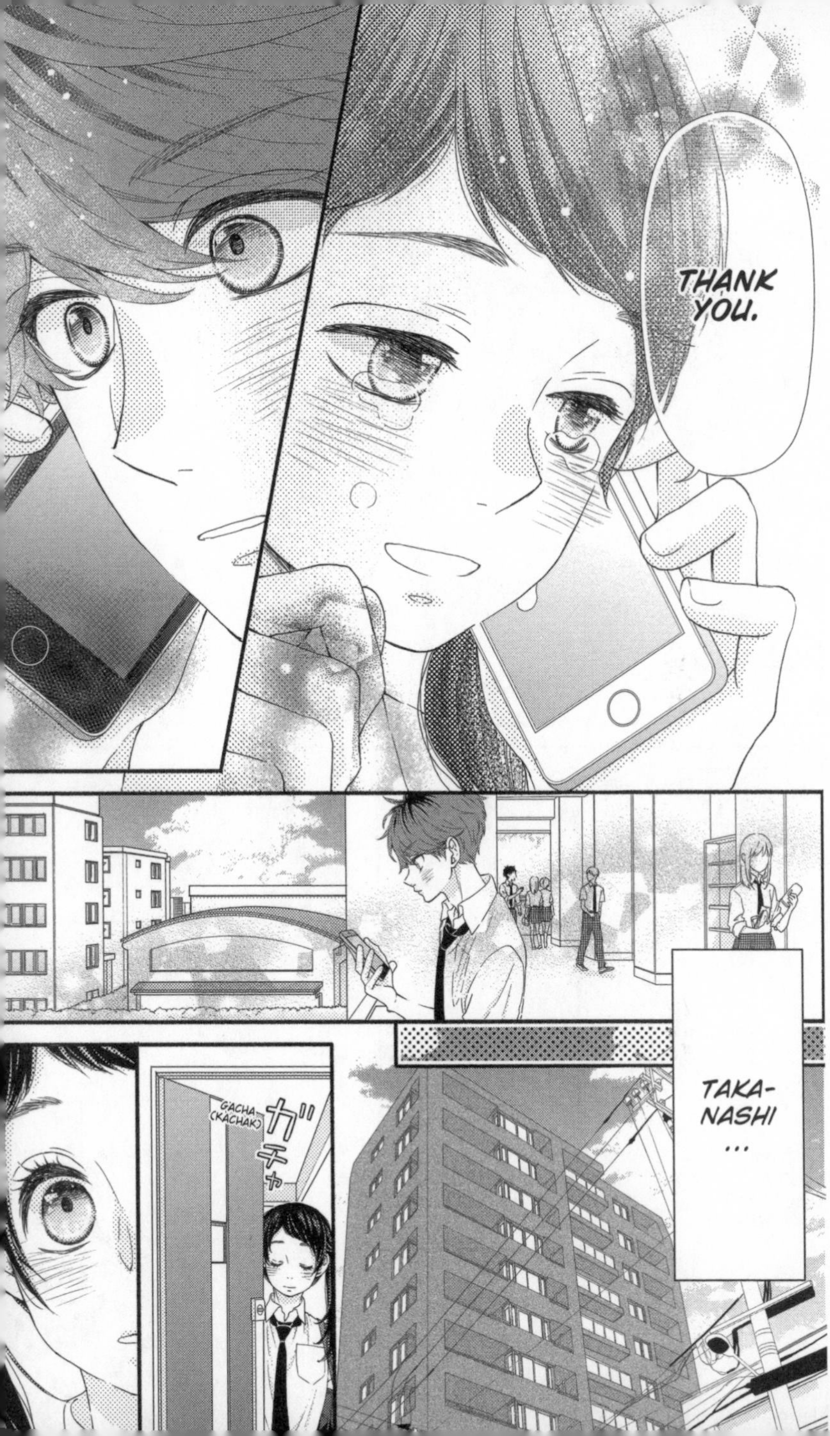
THANK YOU.
TAKA-NASHI...
GACHA (KACHAK)

....
......

....
......

...OH...

RIKO...

...D-DID YOU HAVE TESTS TODAY?

YOU'RE HOME EARLY.

...I HAVE TO GO ON A BUSINESS TRIP.

I'LL BE GONE OVERNIGHT.

I WAS GOING TO LET YOU KNOW—

WHAT ABOUT YOU, MOM? WHAT ARE YOU DOING HOME AT THIS HOUR?

WHAT'S THE BAG FOR?

!?

WHAT !?

I SKIPPED SCHOOL.

AND HEY.

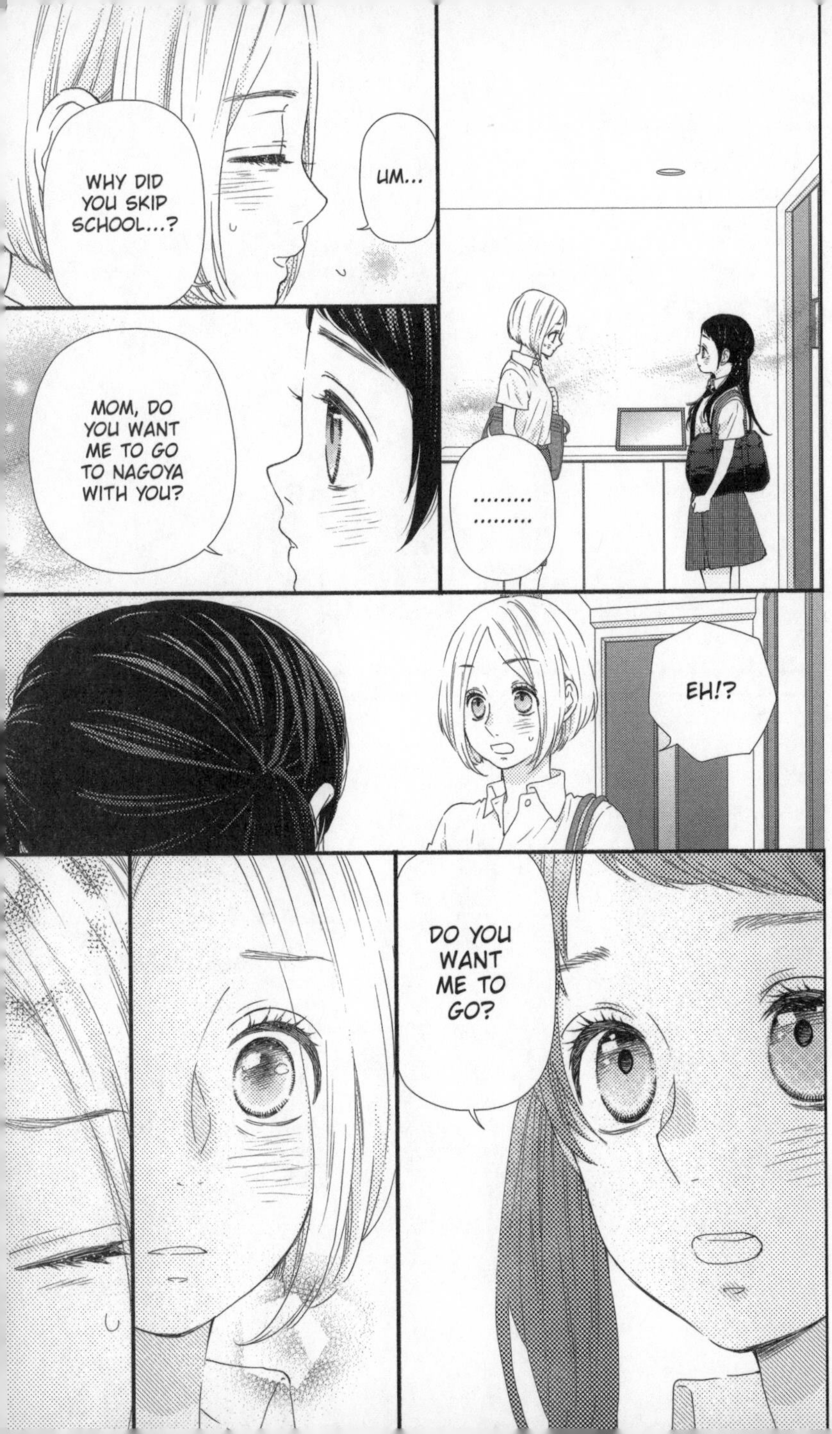
....
....
UM...
WHY DID YOU SKIP SCHOOL...?
MOM, DO YOU WANT ME TO GO TO NAGOYA WITH YOU?
EH!?
DO YOU WANT ME TO GO?

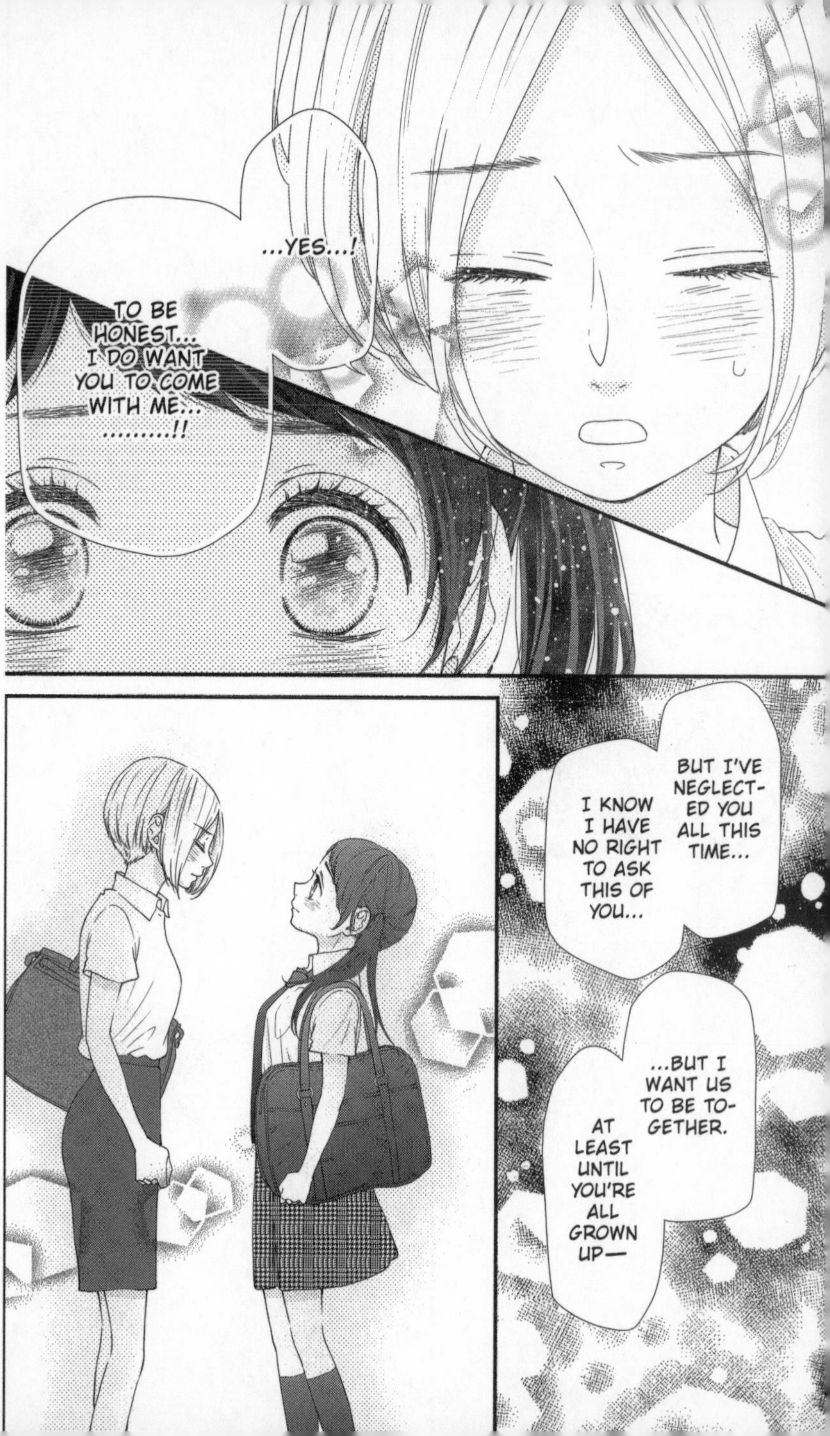
...YES...!
TO BE HONEST... I DO WANT YOU TO COME WITH ME... ....!!
BUT I'VE NEGLECTED YOU ALL THIS TIME...
I KNOW I HAVE NO RIGHT TO ASK THIS OF YOU...
...BUT I WANT US TO BE TOGETHER.
AT LEAST UNTIL YOU'RE ALL GROWN UP—

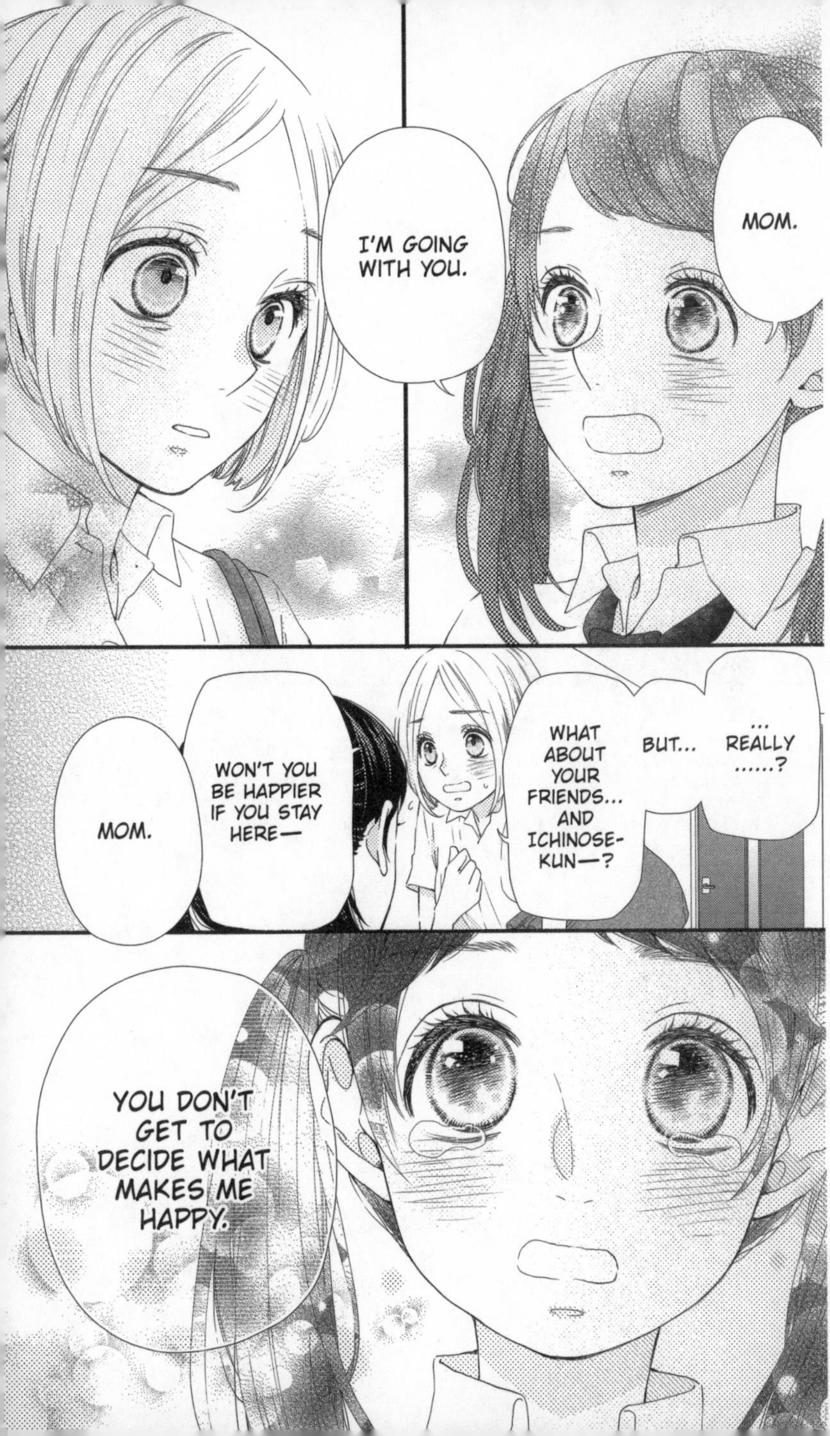
MOM.
I'M GOING WITH YOU.
... REALLY ......?
BUT...
WHAT ABOUT YOUR FRIENDS... AND ICHINOSE-KUN—?
WON'T YOU BE HAPPIER IF YOU STAY HERE—
MOM.
YOU DON'T GET TO DECIDE WHAT MAKES ME HAPPY.

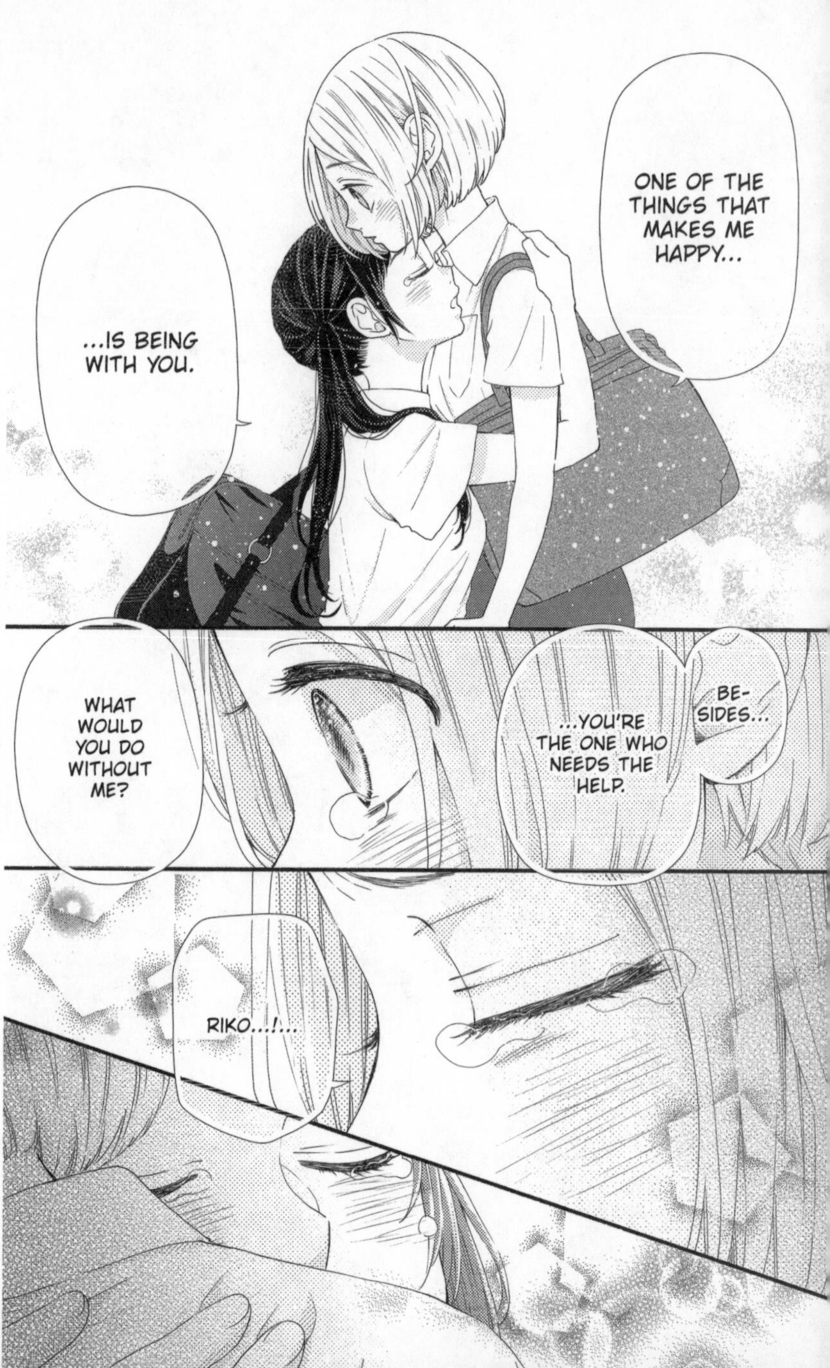
ONE OF THE THINGS THAT MAKES ME HAPPY...
...IS BEING WITH YOU.
BE-SIDES...
...YOU'RE THE ONE WHO NEEDS THE HELP.
WHAT WOULD YOU DO WITHOUT ME?
RIKO...!...

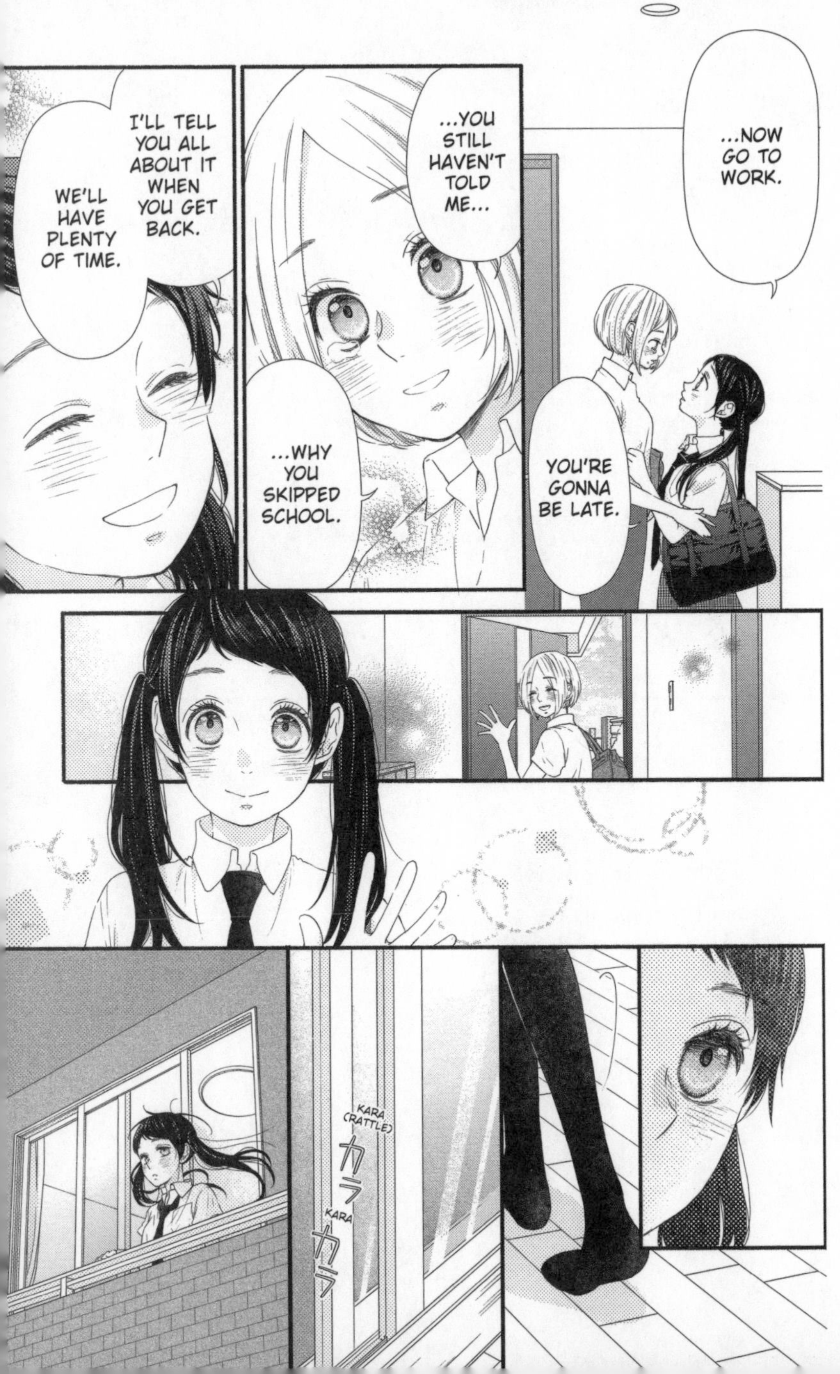
...NOW GO TO WORK.
YOU'RE GONNA BE LATE.
...YOU STILL HAVEN'T TOLD ME...
...WHY YOU SKIPPED SCHOOL.
I'LL TELL YOU ALL ABOUT IT WHEN YOU GET BACK.
WE'LL HAVE PLENTY OF TIME.
KARA (RATTLE)
カラ
KARA
カラ

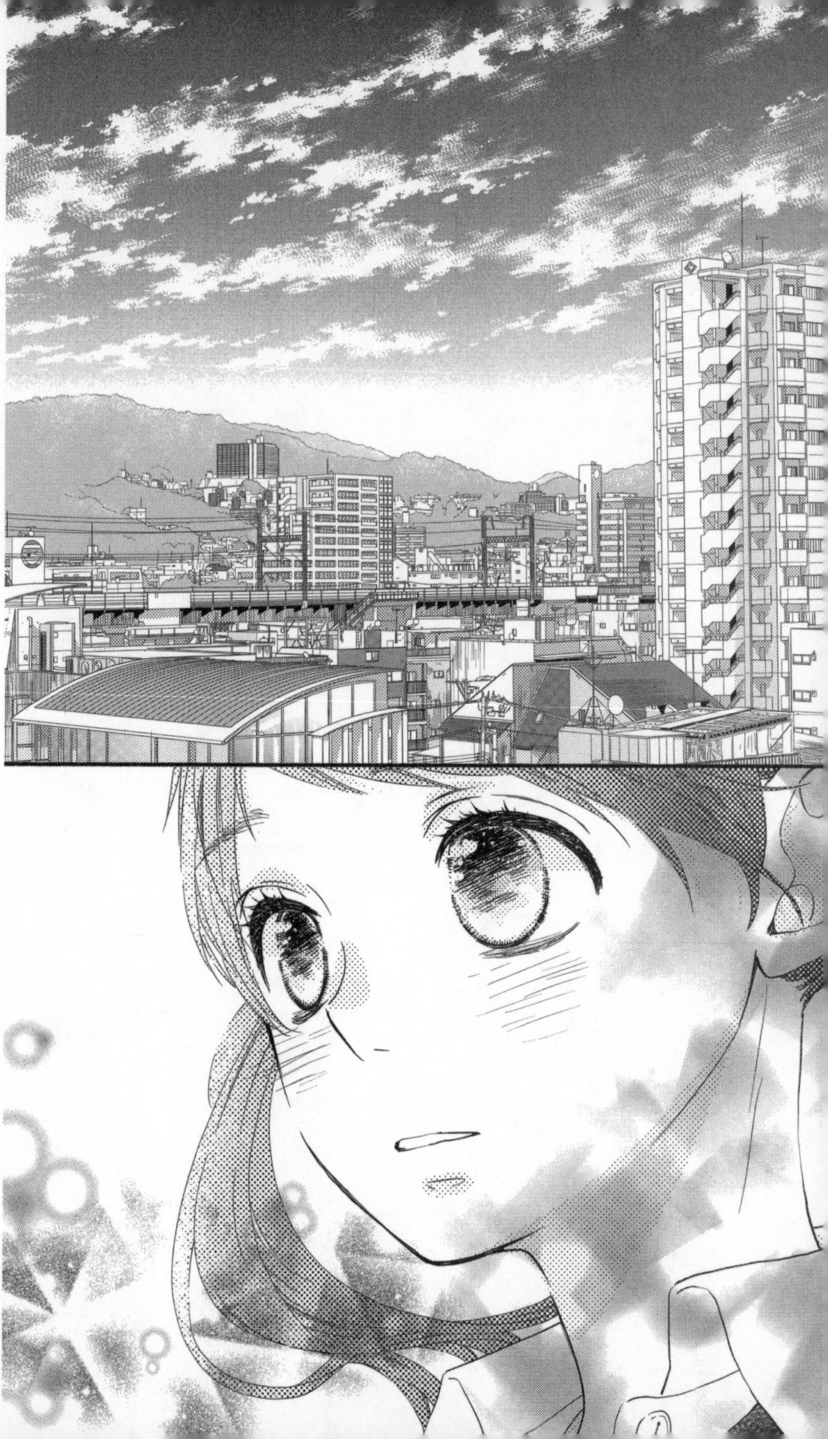

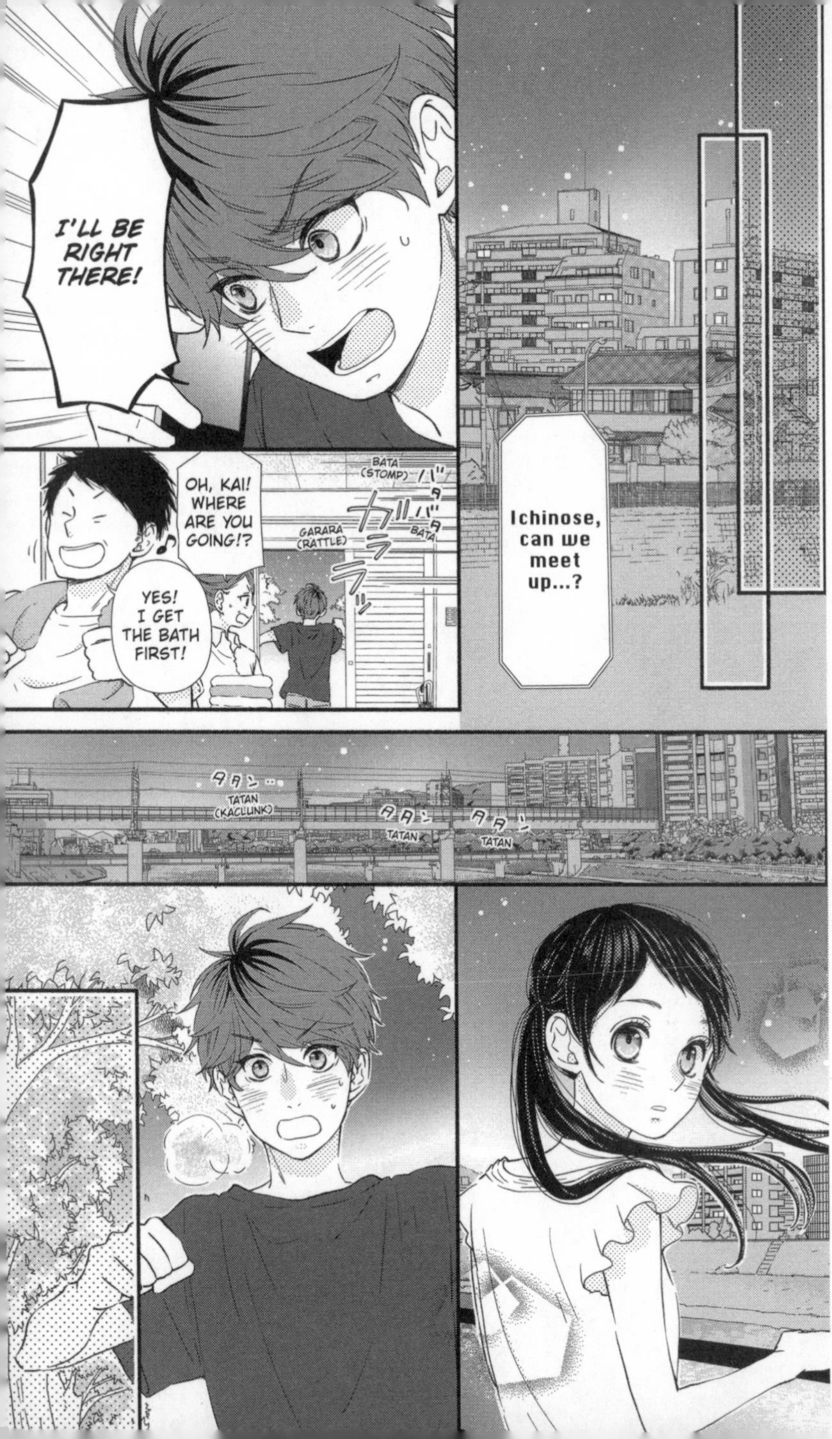
Ichinose, can we meet up...?
I'LL BE RIGHT THERE!
BATA (STOMP)
BATA
GARARA (RATTLE)
OH, KAI! WHERE ARE YOU GOING!?
YES! I GET THE BATH FIRST!
TATAN
TATAN
TATAN (KACLUNK)

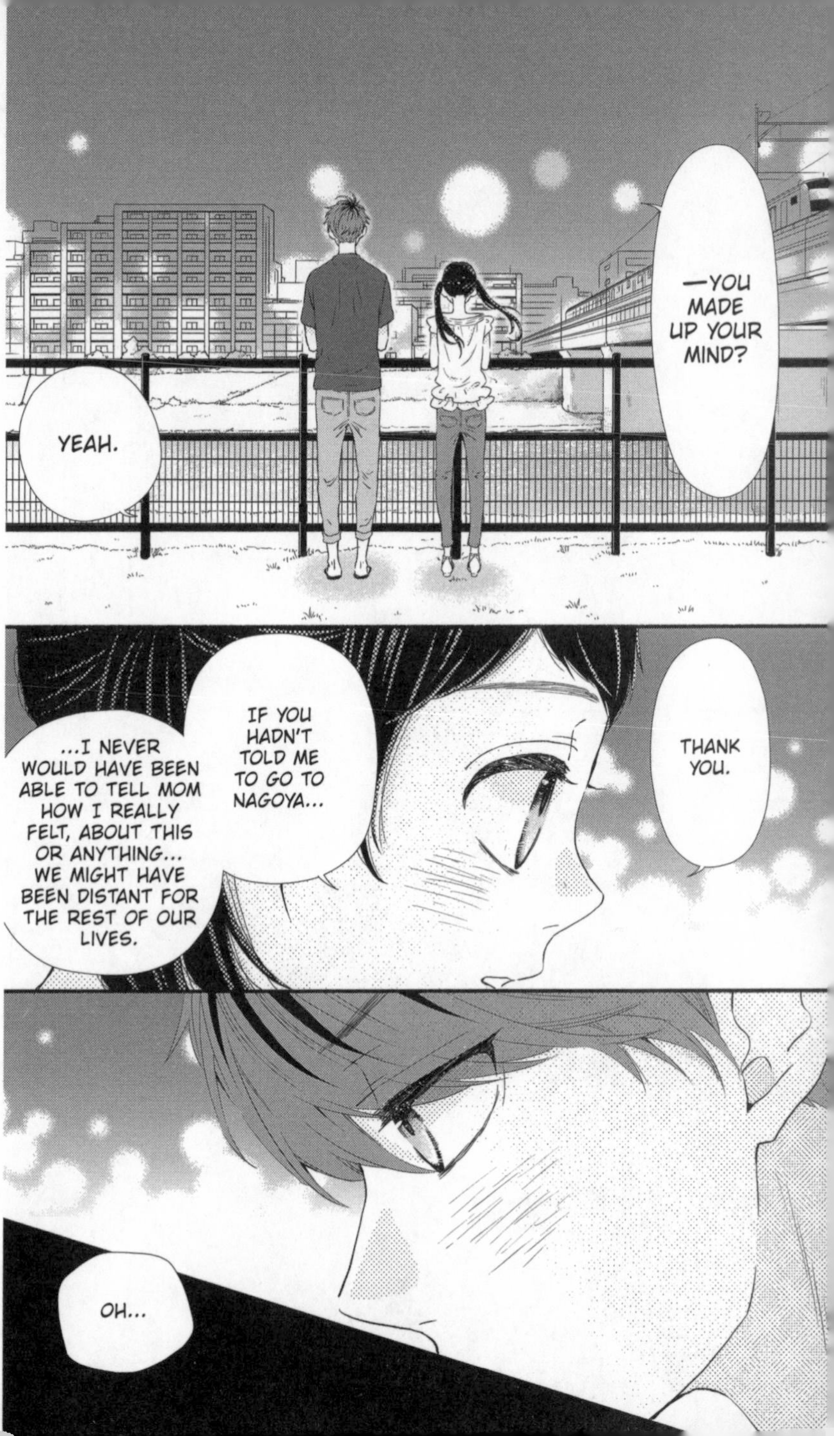
—YOU MADE UP YOUR MIND?
YEAH.
THANK YOU.
IF YOU HADN'T TOLD ME TO GO TO NAGOYA...
...I NEVER WOULD HAVE BEEN ABLE TO TELL MOM HOW I REALLY FELT, ABOUT THIS OR ANYTHING... WE MIGHT HAVE BEEN DISTANT FOR THE REST OF OUR LIVES.
OH...

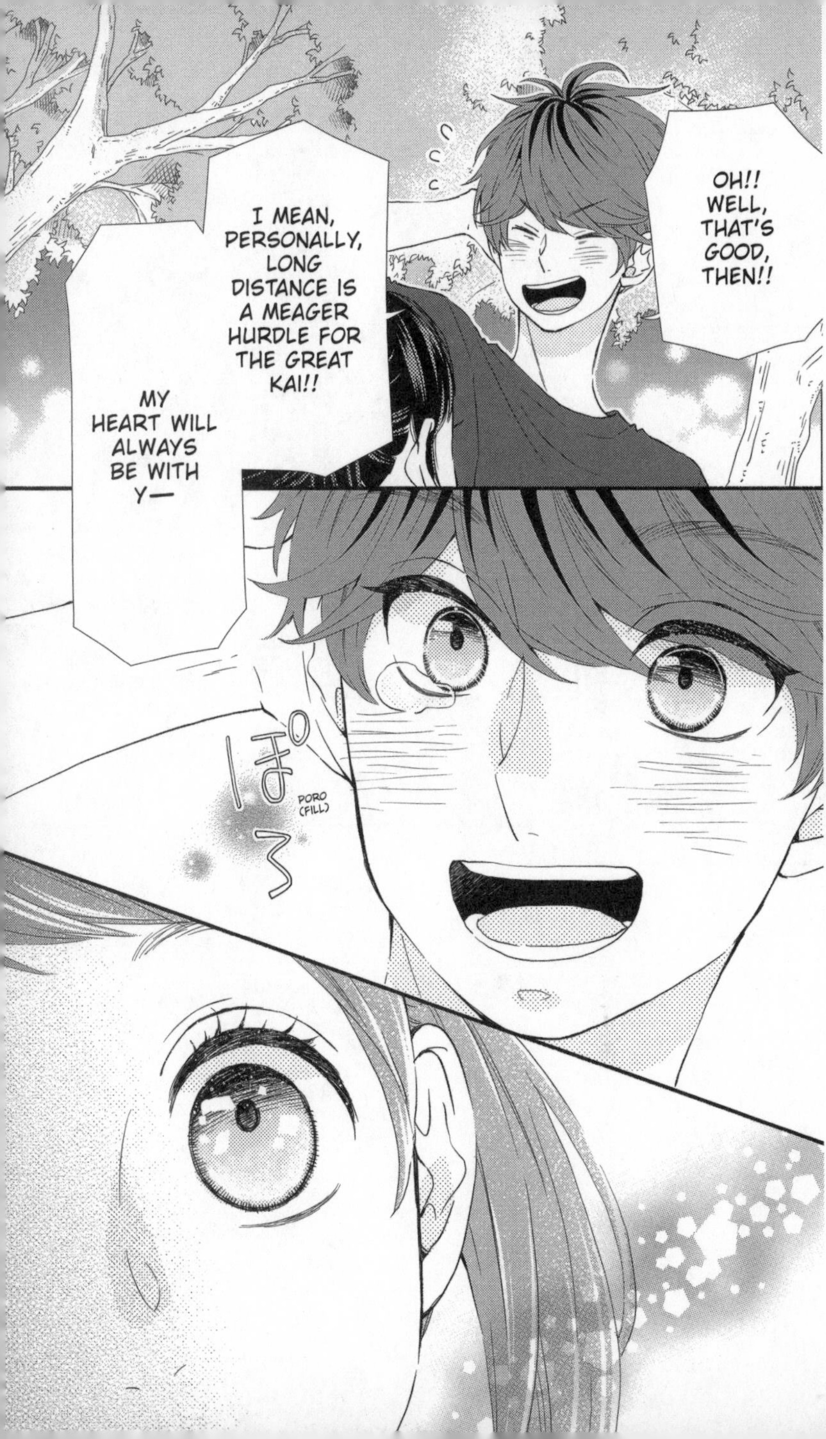
OH!! WELL, THAT'S GOOD, THEN!!
I MEAN, PERSONALLY, LONG DISTANCE IS A MEAGER HURDLE FOR THE GREAT KAI!!
MY HEART WILL ALWAYS BE WITH Y—
ぽろ
PORO (FILL)

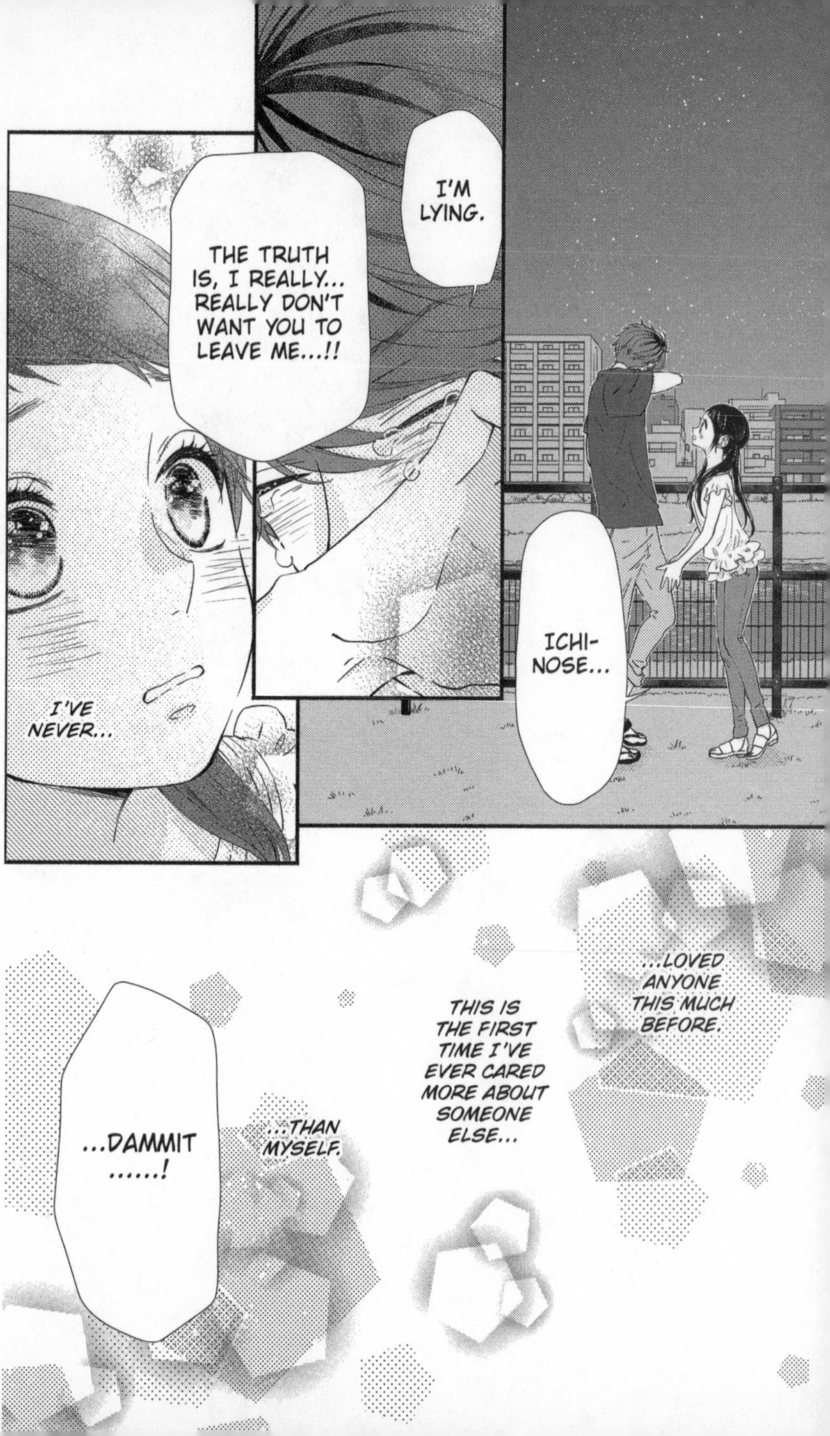
ICHI-NOSE...
I'M LYING.
THE TRUTH IS, I REALLY... REALLY DON'T WANT YOU TO LEAVE ME...!!
I'VE NEVER...
...LOVED ANYONE THIS MUCH BEFORE.
THIS IS THE FIRST TIME I'VE EVER CARED MORE ABOUT SOMEONE ELSE...
...THAN MYSELF.
...DAMMIT ......!

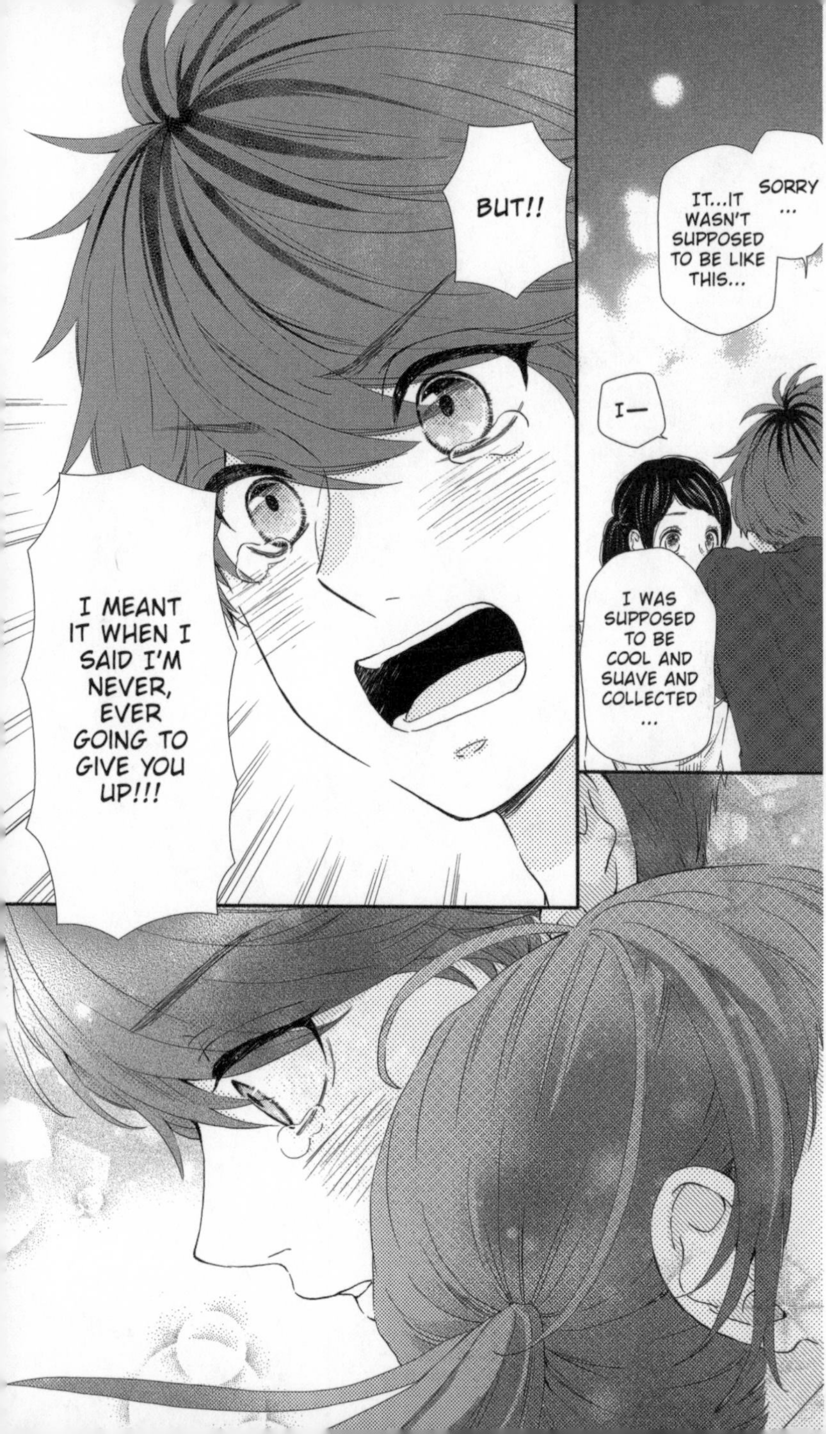
SORRY … IT…IT WASN'T SUPPOSED TO BE LIKE THIS…
I—
I WAS SUPPOSED TO BE COOL AND SUAVE AND COLLECTED …
BUT!!
I MEANT IT WHEN I SAID I'M NEVER, EVER GOING TO GIVE YOU UP!!!

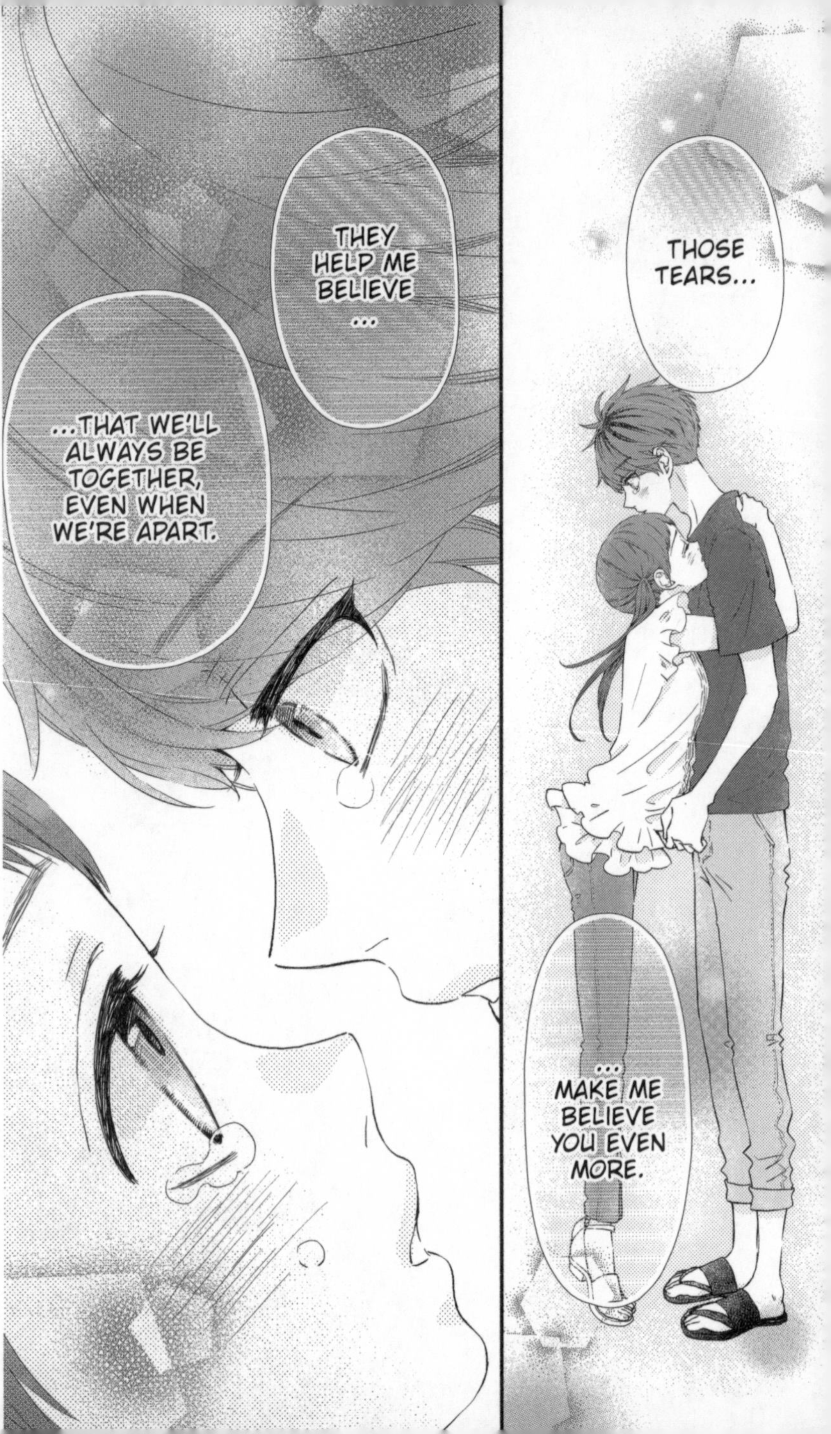
THOSE TEARS...
...MAKE ME BELIEVE YOU EVEN MORE.
THEY HELP ME BELIEVE ...
...THAT WE'LL ALWAYS BE TOGETHER, EVEN WHEN WE'RE APART.

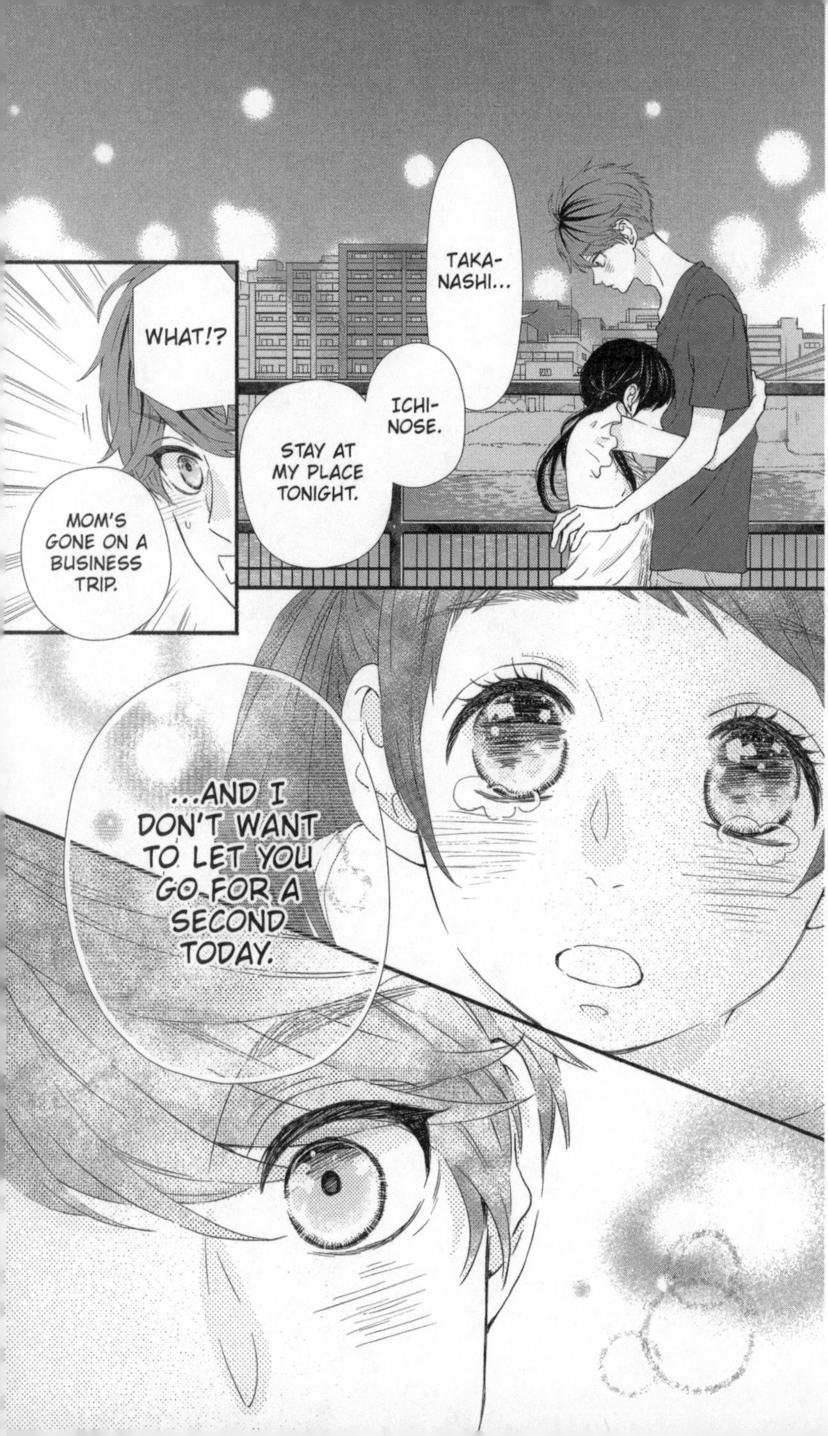
TAKA-NASHI...
ICHI-NOSE.
STAY AT MY PLACE TONIGHT.
WHAT!?
MOM'S GONE ON A BUSINESS TRIP.
...AND I DON'T WANT TO LET YOU GO FOR A SECOND TODAY.

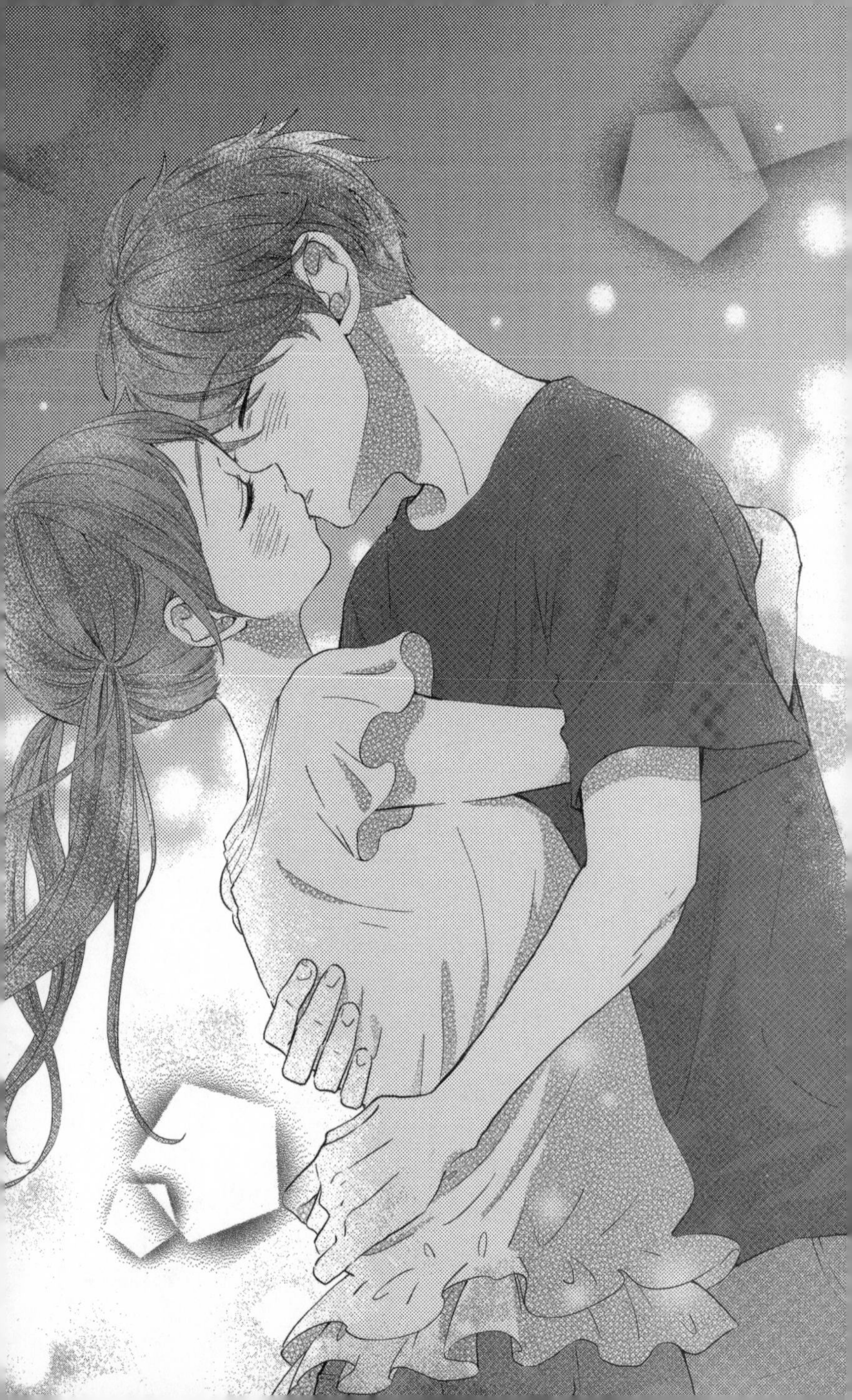

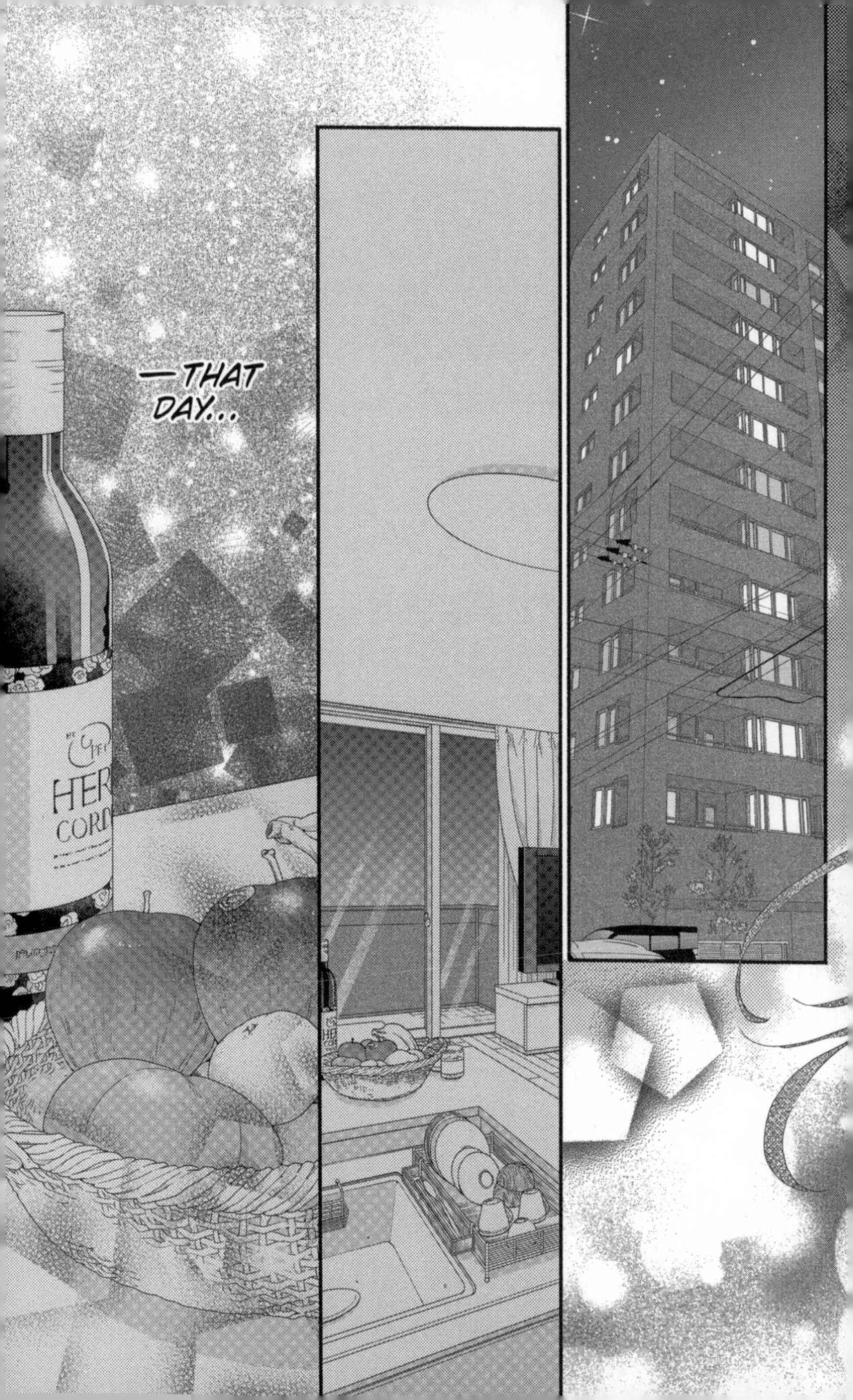
—THAT DAY...

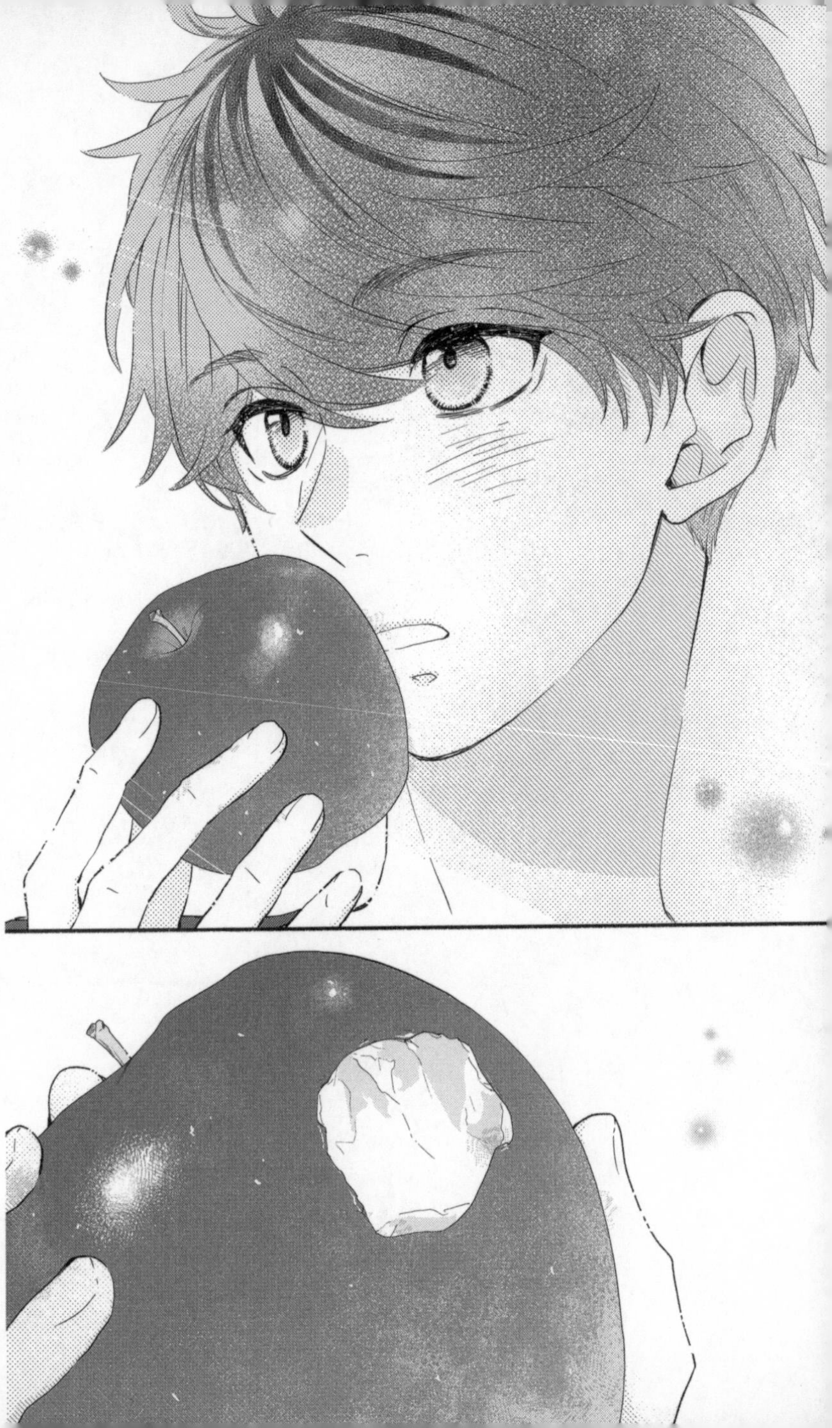

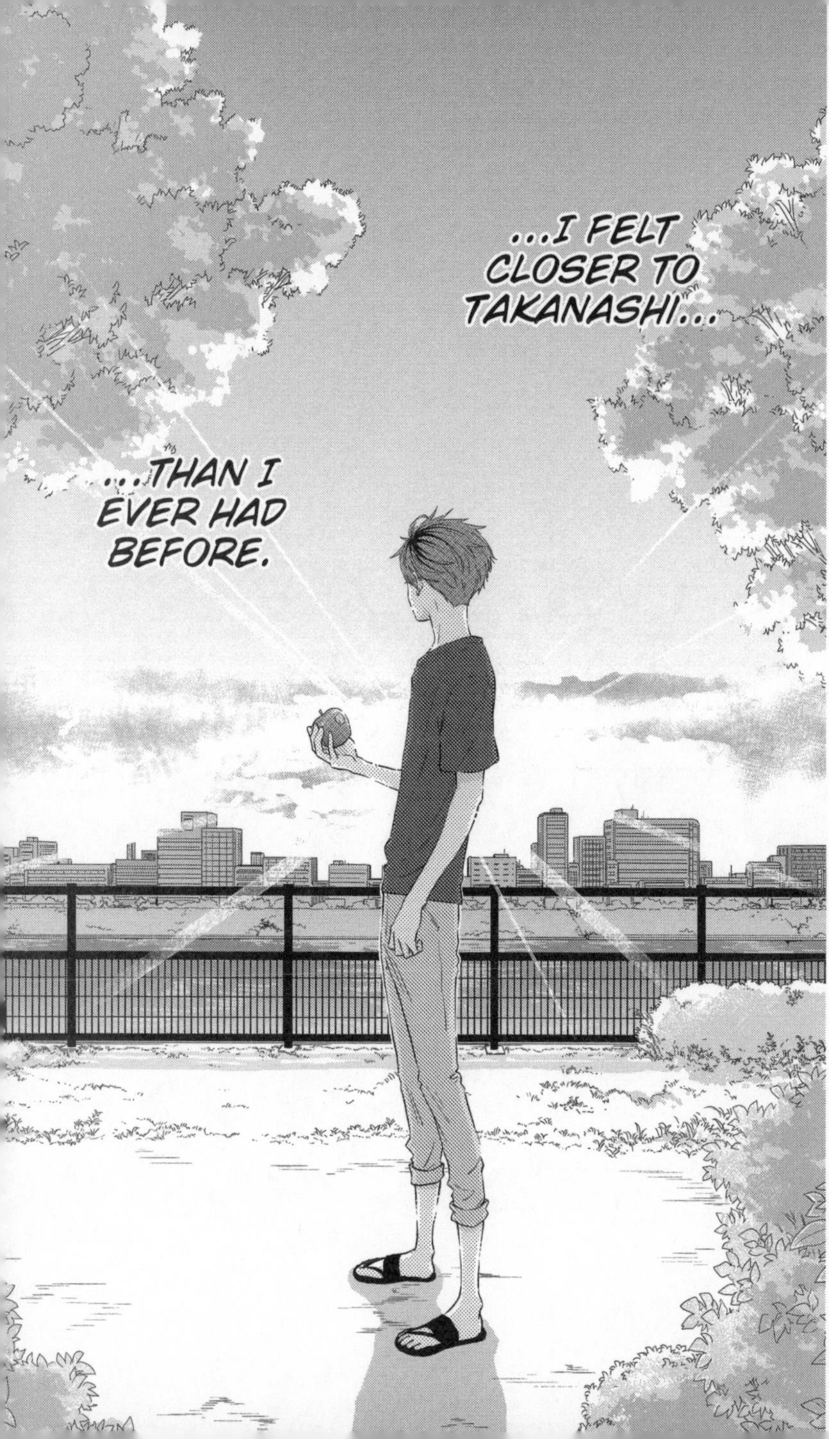
...I FELT CLOSER TO TAKANASHI...
...THAN I EVER HAD BEFORE.

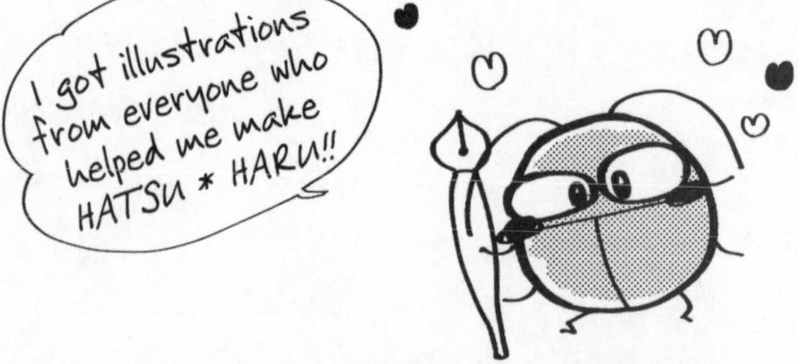
I got illustrations from everyone who helped me make HATSU * HARU!!

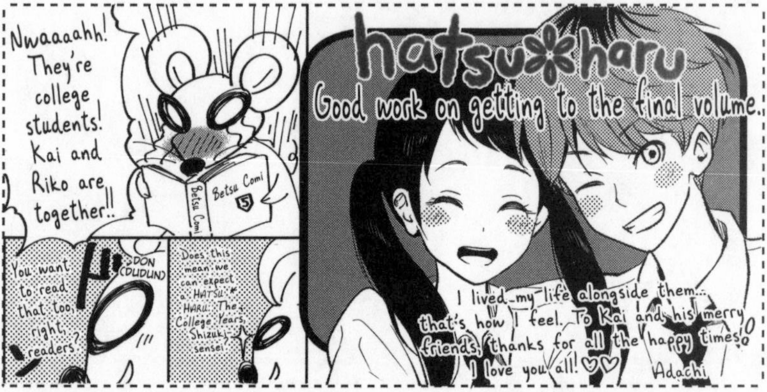
hatsu haru
Good work on getting to the final volume.
I lived my life alongside them... that's how I feel. To Kai and his merry friends, thanks for all the happy times! I love you all!
Adachi
Nwaaaahh! They're college students! Kai and Riko are together!!
Betsu Comi
5
Does this mean we can expect a HATSU * HARU: The College Years, Shizuki-sensei!
DON (DUDUN)
You want to read that too, right, readers?

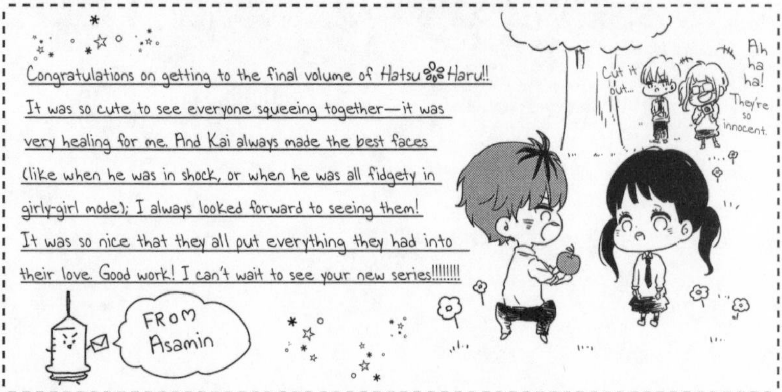
Congratulations on getting to the final volume of Hatsu Haru!! It was so cute to see everyone squeeing together—it was very healing for me. And Kai always made the best faces (like when he was in shock, or when he was all fidgety in girly-girl mode); I always looked forward to seeing them! It was so nice that they all put everything they had into their love. Good work! I can't wait to see your new series!!!!!!!!
FROM Asamin
Cut it out...
Ah ha ha! They're so innocent.

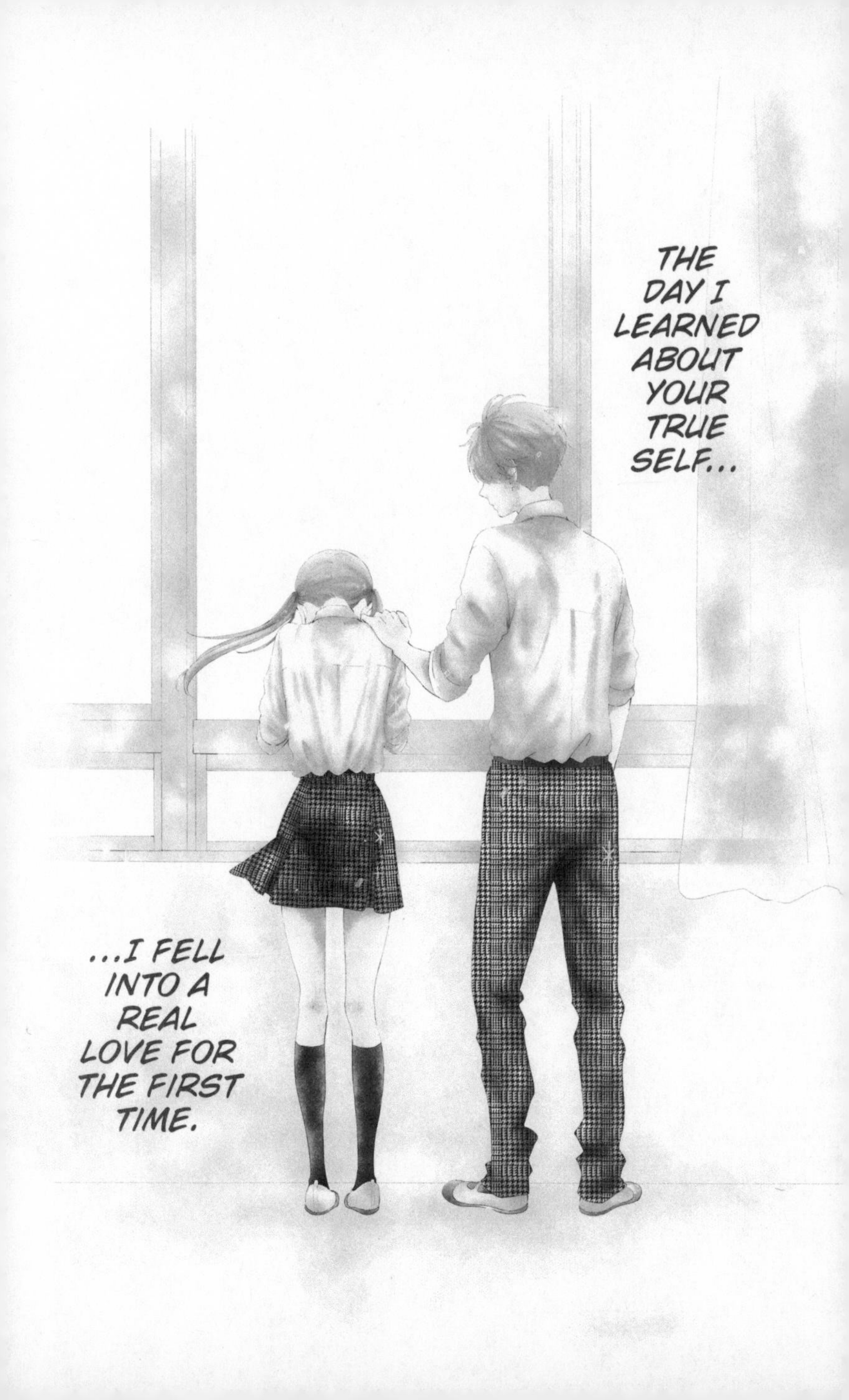
THE DAY I LEARNED ABOUT YOUR TRUE SELF...
...I FELL INTO A REAL LOVE FOR THE FIRST TIME.

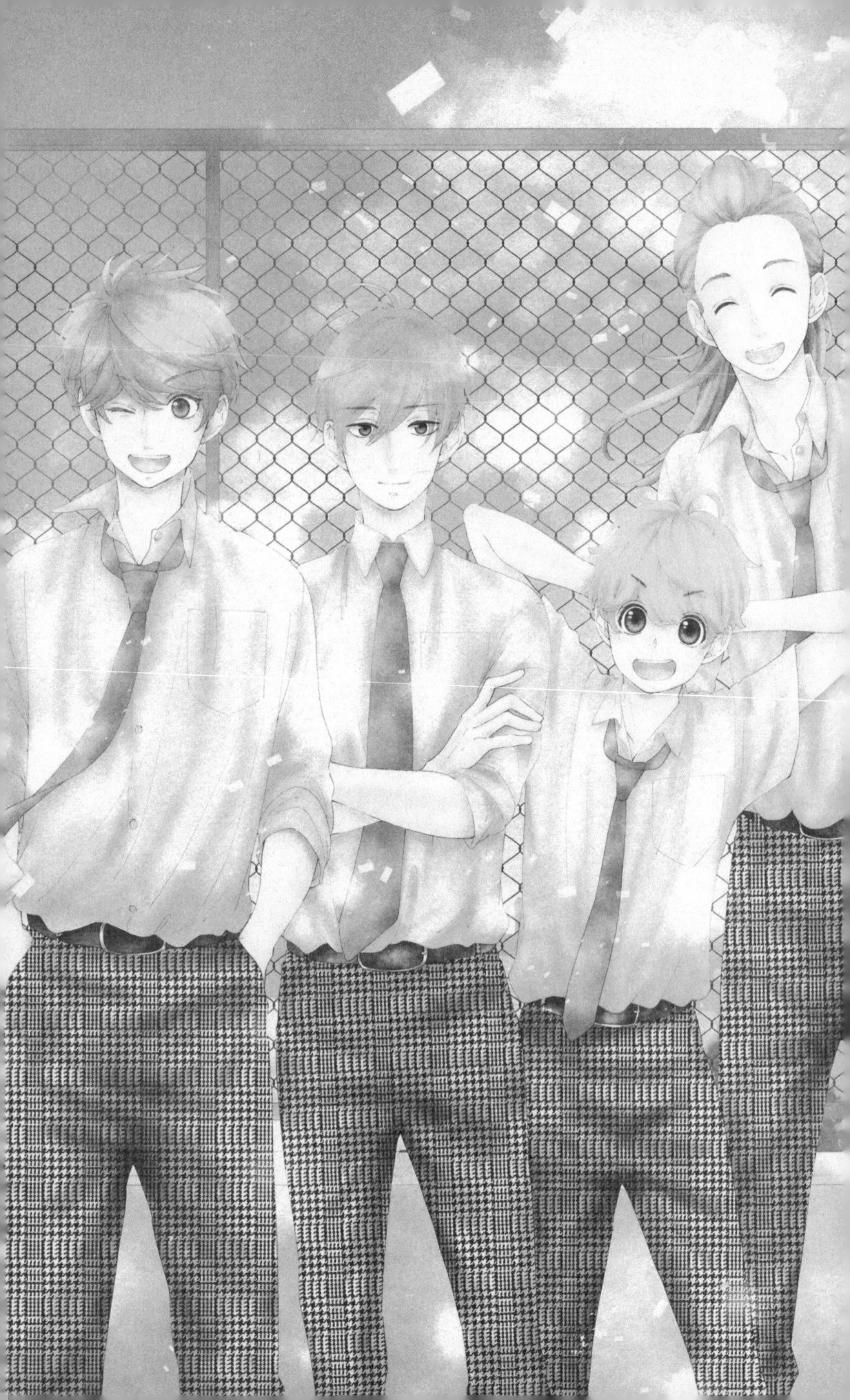

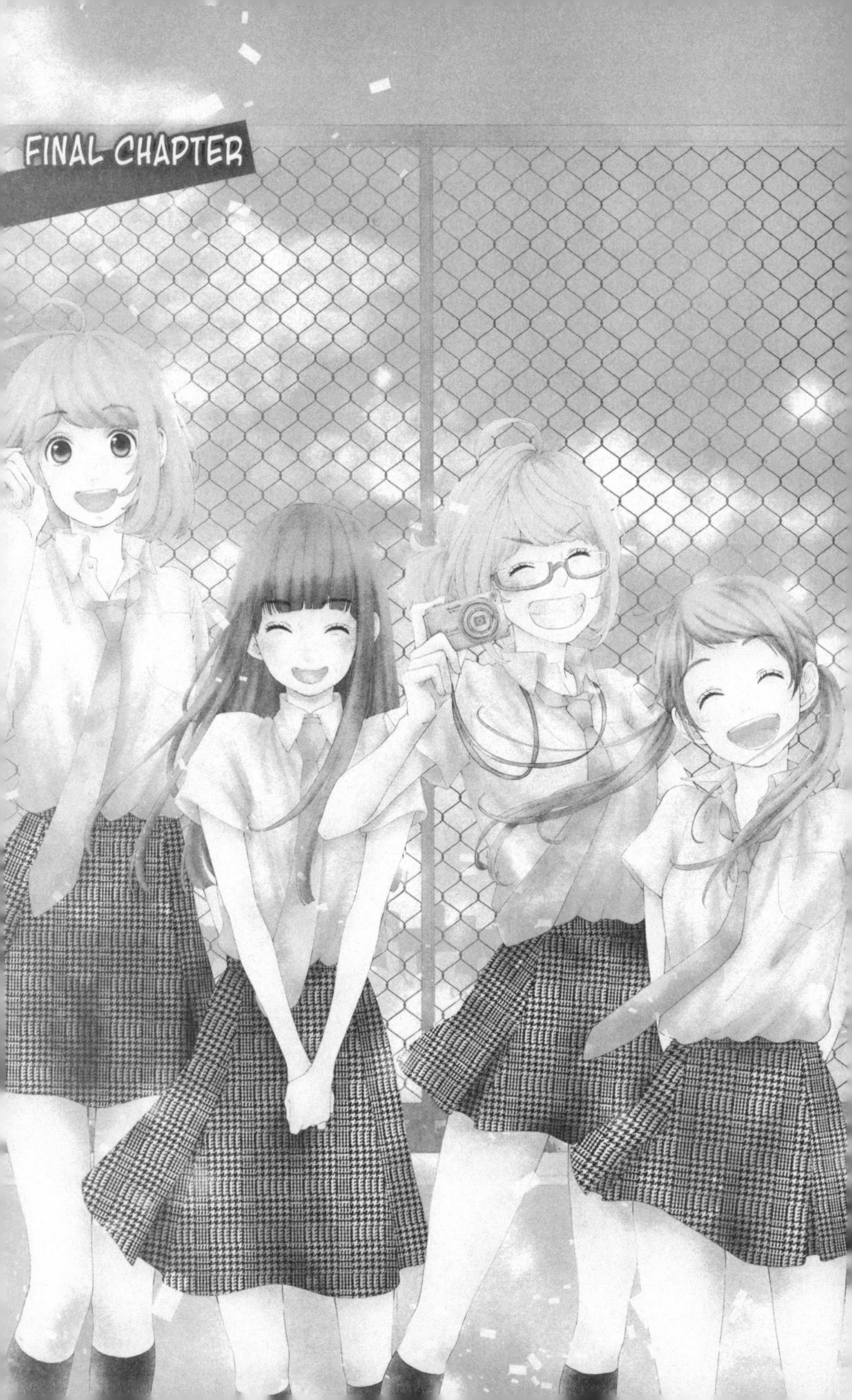
FINAL CHAPTER

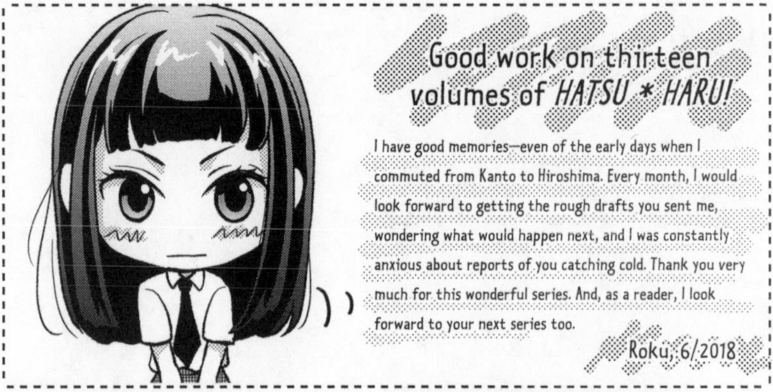
Good work on thirteen volumes of HATSU * HARU!
I have good memories—even of the early days when I commuted from Kanto to Hiroshima. Every month, I would look forward to getting the rough drafts you sent me, wondering what would happen next, and I was constantly anxious about reports of you catching cold. Thank you very much for this wonderful series. And, as a reader, I look forward to your next series too.
Roku, 6/2018

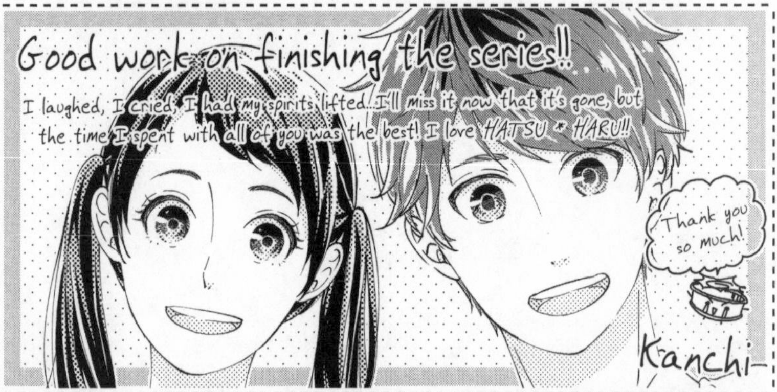
Good work on finishing the series!!
I laughed, I cried, I had my spirits lifted...I'll miss it now that it's gone, but the time I spent with all of you was the best! I love HATSU * HARU!!
Thank you so much!
Kanchi

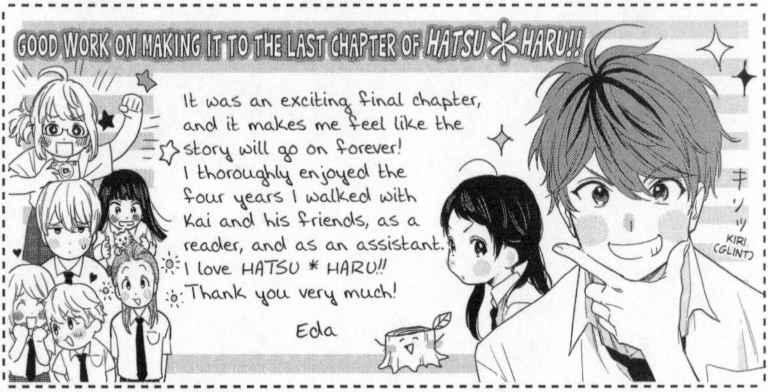
GOOD WORK ON MAKING IT TO THE LAST CHAPTER OF HATSU * HARU!!
It was an exciting final chapter, and it makes me feel like the story will go on forever!
I thoroughly enjoyed the four years I walked with Kai and his friends, as a reader, and as an assistant.
I love HATSU * HARU!!
Thank you very much!
Eda
キリ
KIRI (GLINT)

Thank you!!

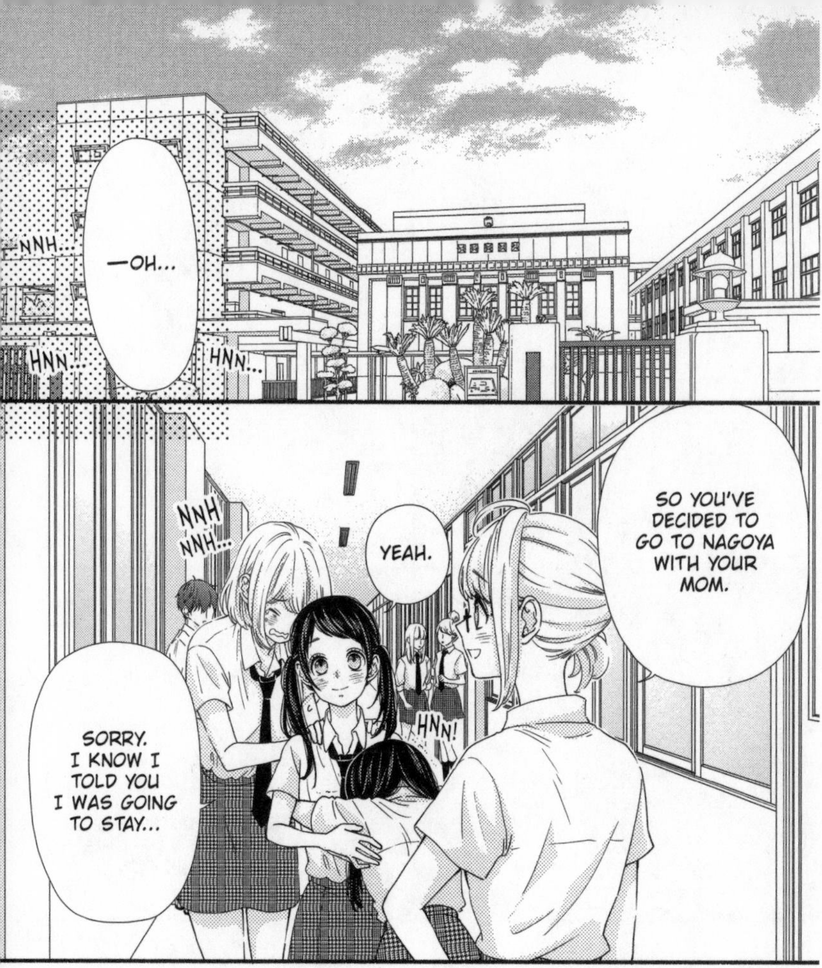
HNN...
—OH...
NNH...
HNN...
SO YOU'VE DECIDED TO GO TO NAGOYA WITH YOUR MOM.
YEAH.
HNN!
NNH NNH...
SORRY. I KNOW I TOLD YOU I WAS GOING TO STAY...

hatsu haru

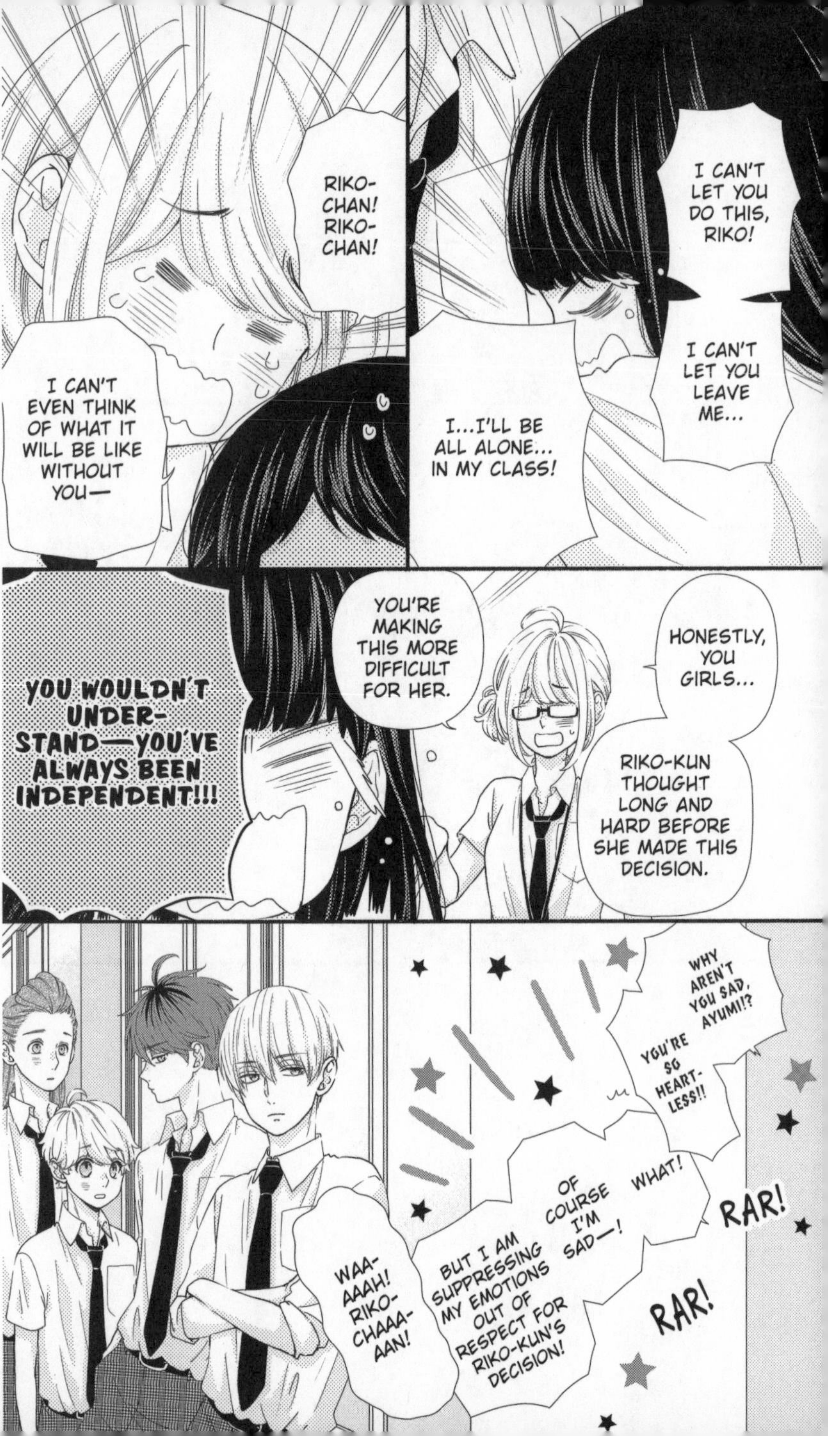

I CAN'T LET YOU DO THIS, RIKO!
I CAN'T LET YOU LEAVE ME...
I...I'LL BE ALL ALONE... IN MY CLASS!
RIKO-CHAN! RIKO-CHAN!
I CAN'T EVEN THINK OF WHAT IT WILL BE LIKE WITHOUT YOU—
HONESTLY, YOU GIRLS...
RIKO-KUN THOUGHT LONG AND HARD BEFORE SHE MADE THIS DECISION.
YOU'RE MAKING THIS MORE DIFFICULT FOR HER.
YOU WOULDN'T UNDER-STAND—YOU'VE ALWAYS BEEN INDEPENDENT!!!
WHY AREN'T YOU SAD, AYUMI!?
YOU'RE SO HEART-LESS!!
RAR!
WHAT!
OF COURSE I'M SAD—!
BUT I AM SUPPRESSING MY EMOTIONS OUT OF RESPECT FOR RIKO-KUN'S DECISION!
RAR!
WAA-AAAH! RIKO-CHAAA-AAN!

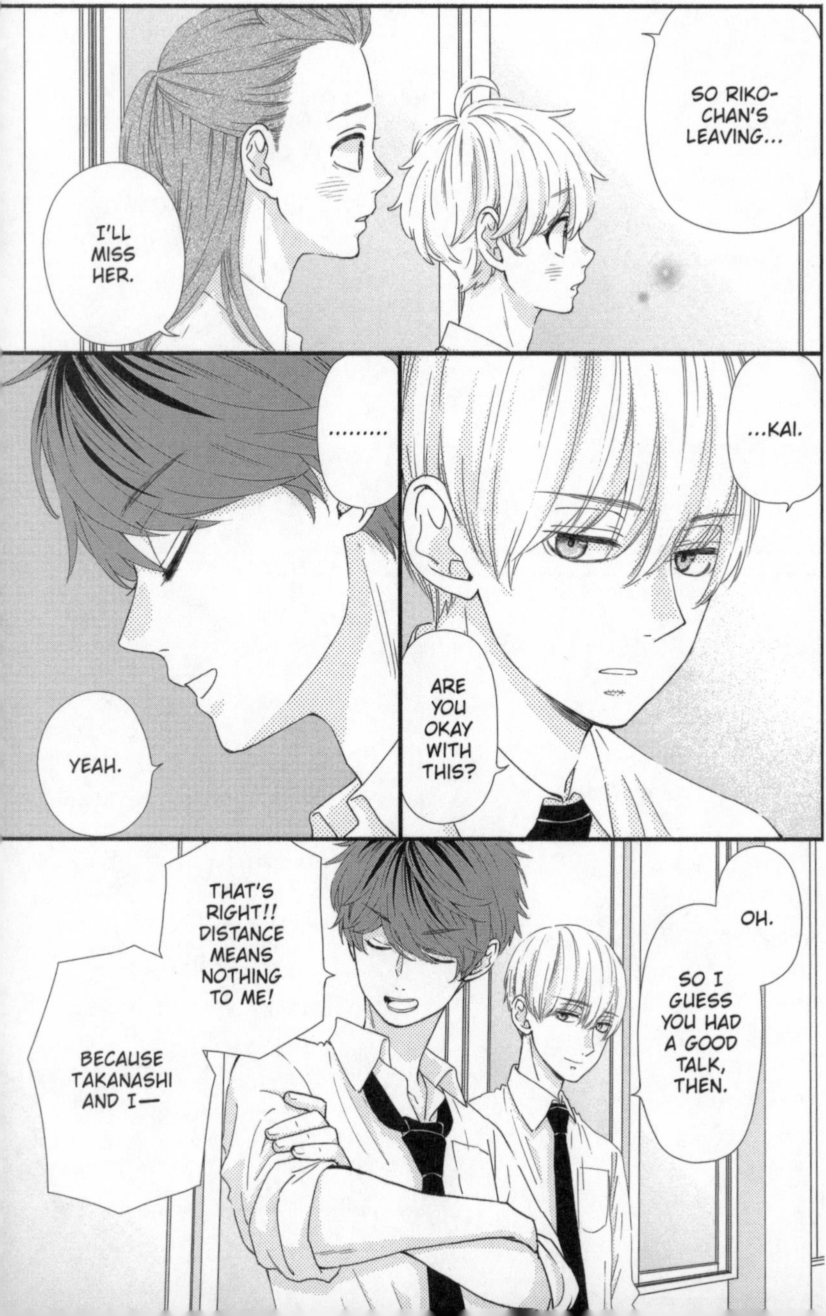
SO RIKO-CHAN'S LEAVING...
I'LL MISS HER.
...KAI.
ARE YOU OKAY WITH THIS?
....
YEAH.
OH.
SO I GUESS YOU HAD A GOOD TALK, THEN.
THAT'S RIGHT!! DISTANCE MEANS NOTHING TO ME!
BECAUSE TAKANASHI AND I—

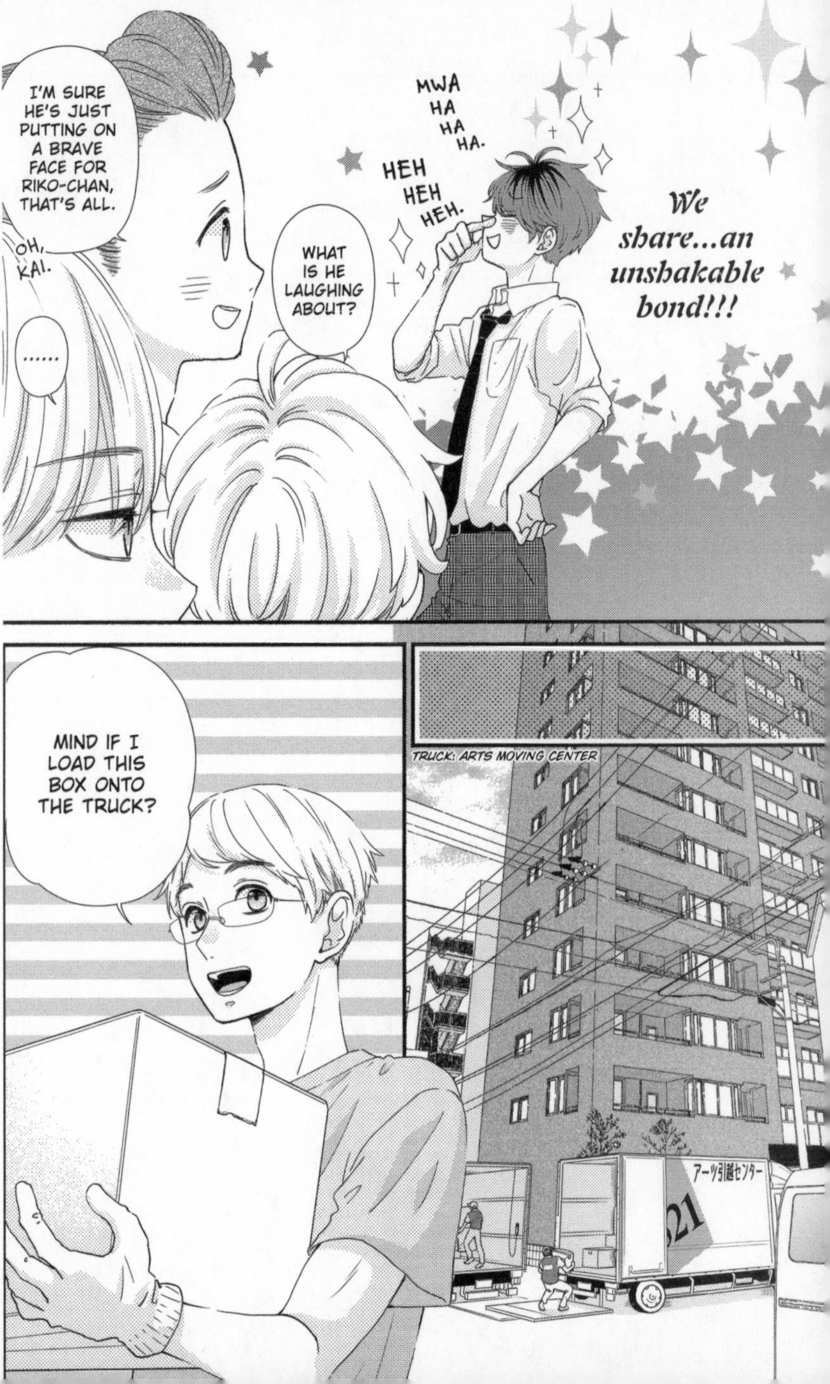
We share...an unshakable bond!!!
MWA HA HA HA.
HEH HEH HEH.
WHAT IS HE LAUGHING ABOUT?
I'M SURE HE'S JUST PUTTING ON A BRAVE FACE FOR RIKO-CHAN, THAT'S ALL.
OH, KAI.
......
TRUCK: ARTS MOVING CENTER
アーツ引越センター
MIND IF I LOAD THIS BOX ONTO THE TRUCK?

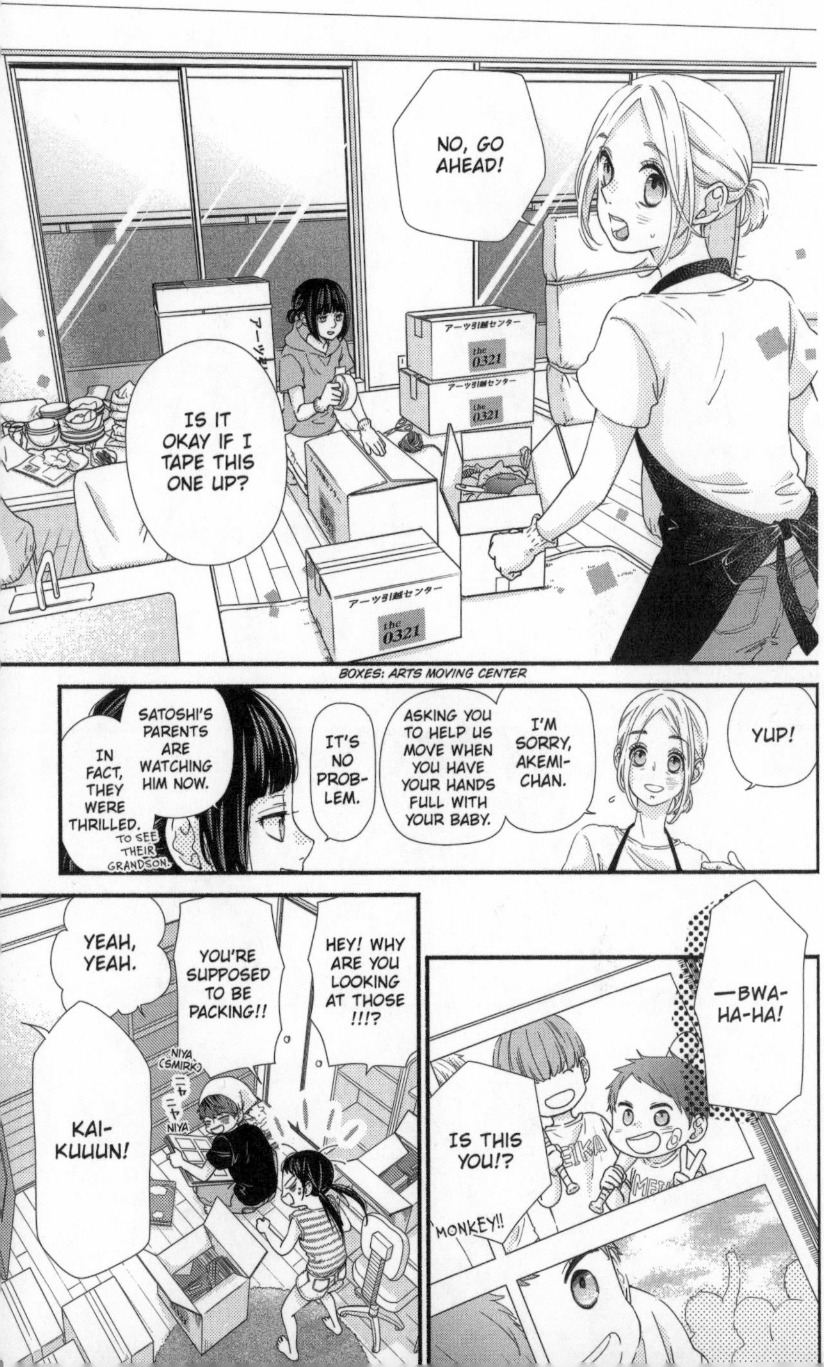
NO, GO AHEAD!
IS IT OKAY IF I TAPE THIS ONE UP?
アーツ引越センター
BOXES: ARTS MOVING CENTER
YUP!
I'M SORRY, AKEMI-CHAN.
ASKING YOU TO HELP US MOVE WHEN YOU HAVE YOUR HANDS FULL WITH YOUR BABY.
IT'S NO PROBLEM.
SATOSHI'S PARENTS ARE WATCHING HIM NOW.
IN FACT, THEY WERE THRILLED.
TO SEE THEIR GRANDSON.
—BWA-HA-HA!
IS THIS YOU!?
MONKEY!!
HEY! WHY ARE YOU LOOKING AT THOSE!!!?
YOU'RE SUPPOSED TO BE PACKING!!
YEAH, YEAH.
NIYA (SMIRK)
ニヤ ニヤ
NIYA
KAI-KUUUN!

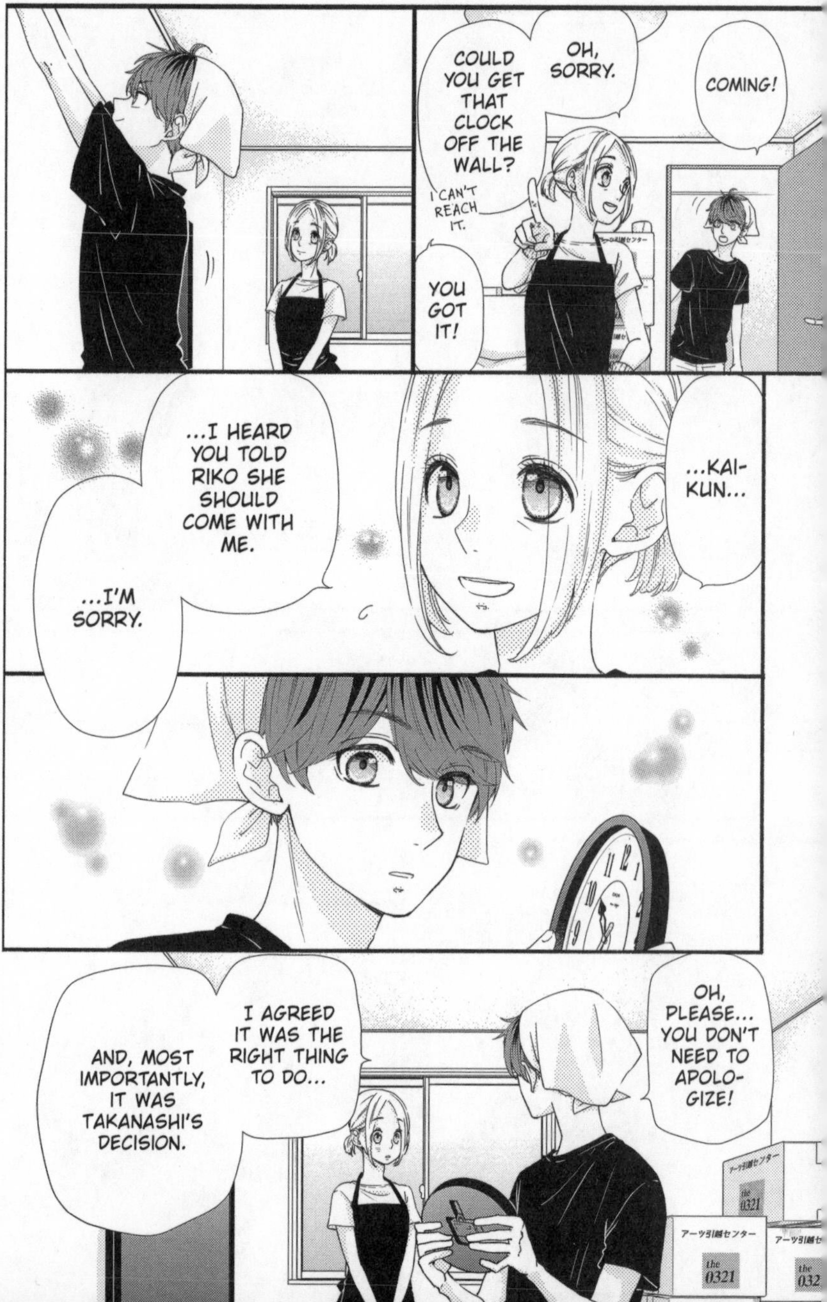
COMING!
OH, SORRY.
COULD YOU GET THAT CLOCK OFF THE WALL?
I CAN'T REACH IT.
YOU GOT IT!
...KAI-KUN...
...I HEARD YOU TOLD RIKO SHE SHOULD COME WITH ME.
...I'M SORRY.
OH, PLEASE... YOU DON'T NEED TO APOLO-GIZE!
I AGREED IT WAS THE RIGHT THING TO DO...
AND, MOST IMPORTANTLY, IT WAS TAKANASHI'S DECISION.

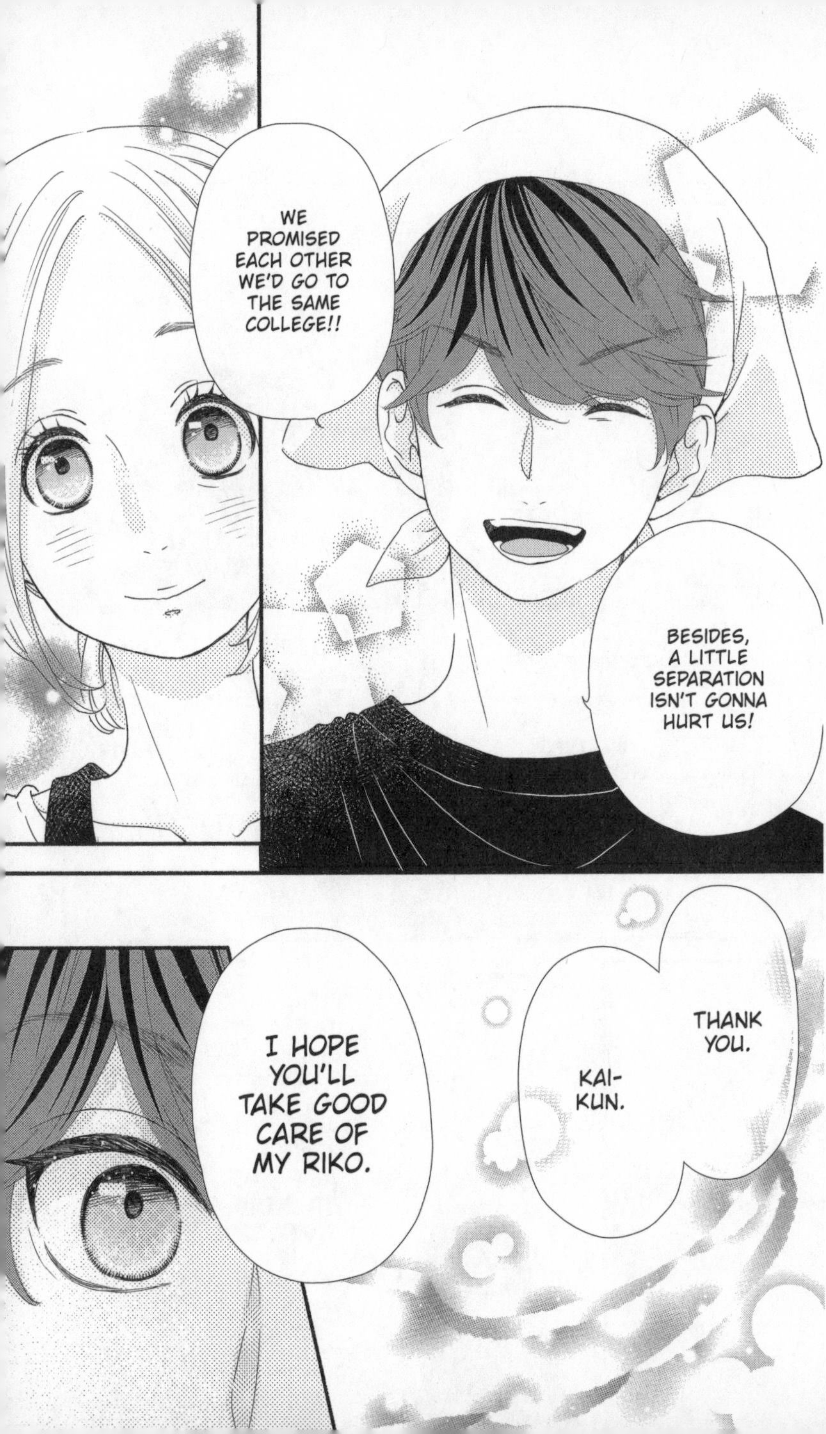
WE PROMISED EACH OTHER WE'D GO TO THE SAME COLLEGE!!
BESIDES, A LITTLE SEPARATION ISN'T GONNA HURT US!
THANK YOU.
KAI-KUN.
I HOPE YOU'LL TAKE GOOD CARE OF MY RIKO.

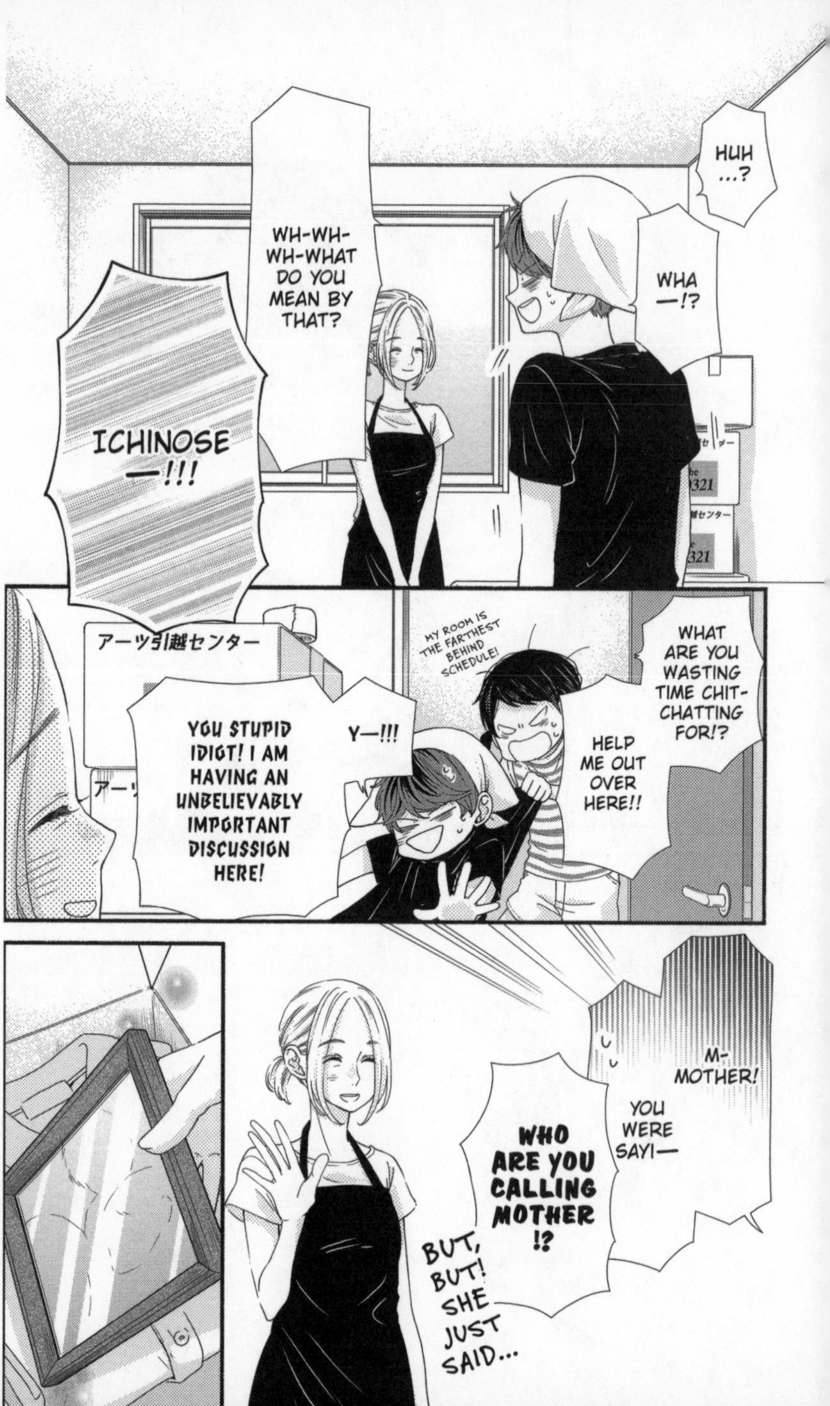
HUH ...?
WHA—!?
WH-WH-WH-WHAT DO YOU MEAN BY THAT?
ICHINOSE—!!!
アーツ引越センター
WHAT ARE YOU WASTING TIME CHIT-CHATTING FOR!?
MY ROOM IS THE FARTHEST BEHIND SCHEDULE!
HELP ME OUT OVER HERE!!
Y—!!!
YOU STUPID IDIOT! I AM HAVING AN UNBELIEVABLY IMPORTANT DISCUSSION HERE!
M-MOTHER!
YOU WERE SAYI—
WHO ARE YOU CALLING MOTHER!?
BUT, BUT! SHE JUST SAID...

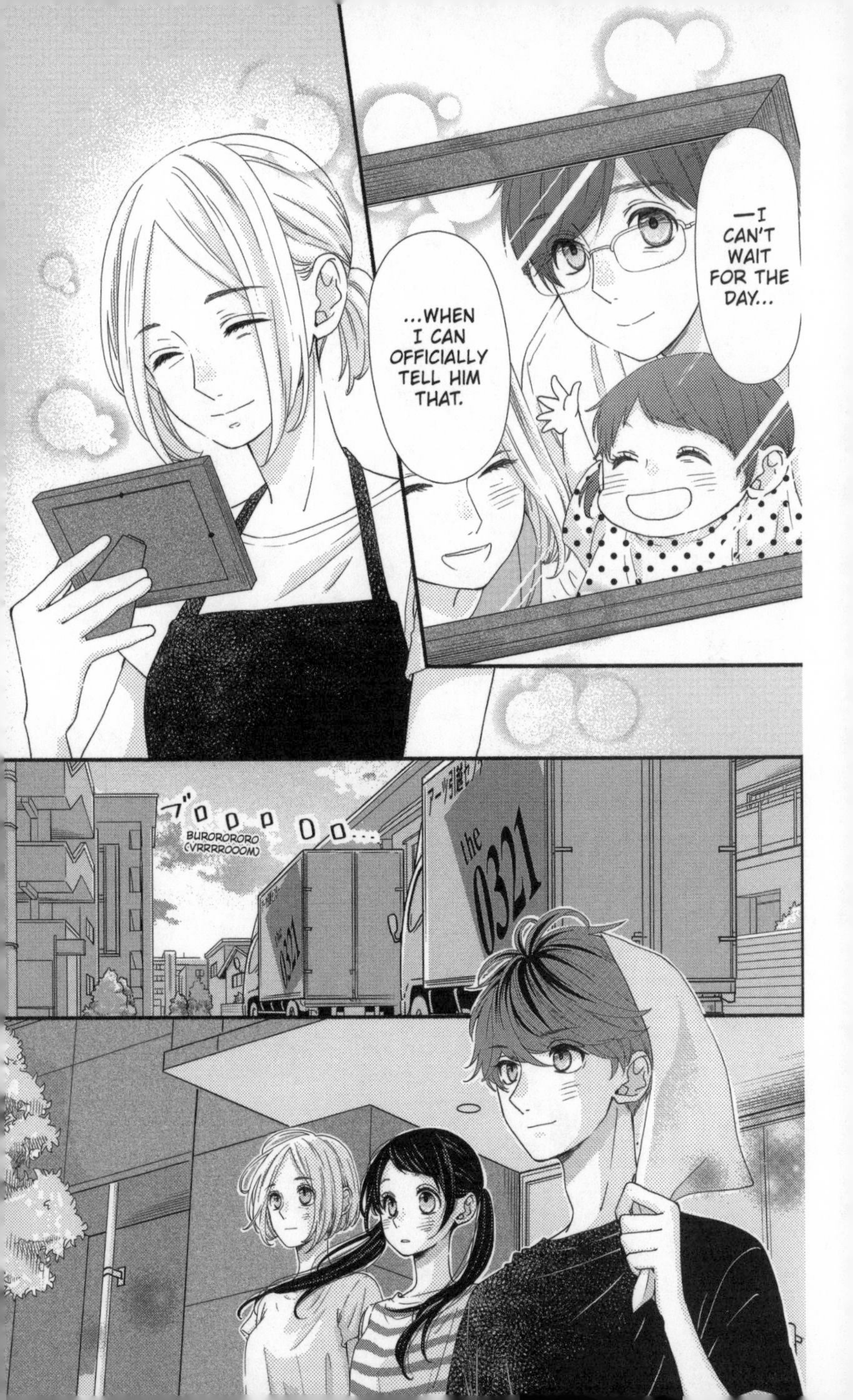
—I CAN'T WAIT FOR THE DAY...
...WHEN I CAN OFFICIALLY TELL HIM THAT.
ブロロロロロ…
BURORORORO (VRRRROOOM)
the 0321

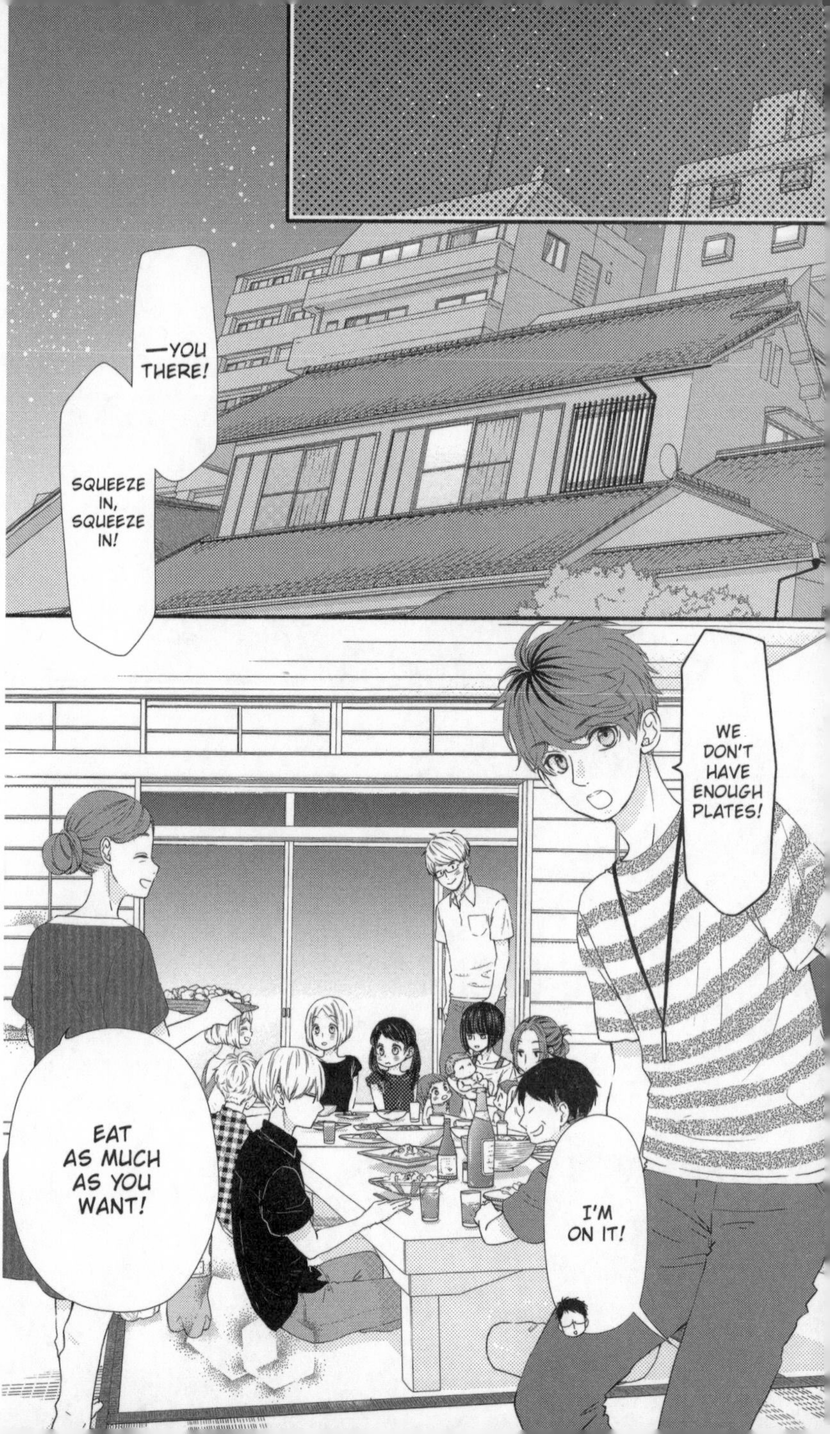
—YOU THERE!
SQUEEZE IN, SQUEEZE IN!
WE DON'T HAVE ENOUGH PLATES!
I'M ON IT!
EAT AS MUCH AS YOU WANT!

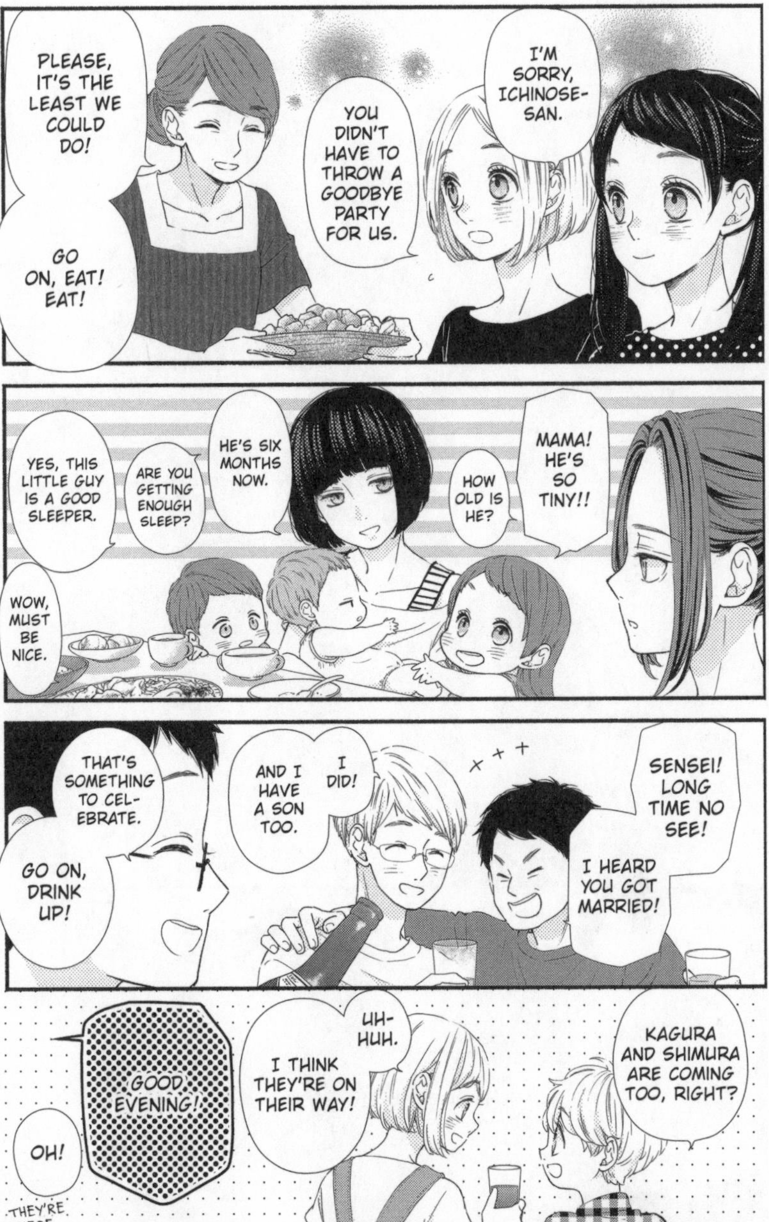
I'M SORRY, ICHINOSE-SAN.
YOU DIDN'T HAVE TO THROW A GOODBYE PARTY FOR US.
PLEASE, IT'S THE LEAST WE COULD DO!
GO ON, EAT! EAT!
MAMA! HE'S SO TINY!!
HOW OLD IS HE?
HE'S SIX MONTHS NOW.
ARE YOU GETTING ENOUGH SLEEP?
YES, THIS LITTLE GUY IS A GOOD SLEEPER.
WOW, MUST BE NICE.
SENSEI! LONG TIME NO SEE!
I HEARD YOU GOT MARRIED!
I DID!
AND I HAVE A SON TOO.
THAT'S SOMETHING TO CEL-EBRATE.
GO ON, DRINK UP!
KAGURA AND SHIMURA ARE COMING TOO, RIGHT?
UH-HUH.
I THINK THEY'RE ON THEIR WAY!
GOOD EVENING!
OH!
THEY'RE HERE.

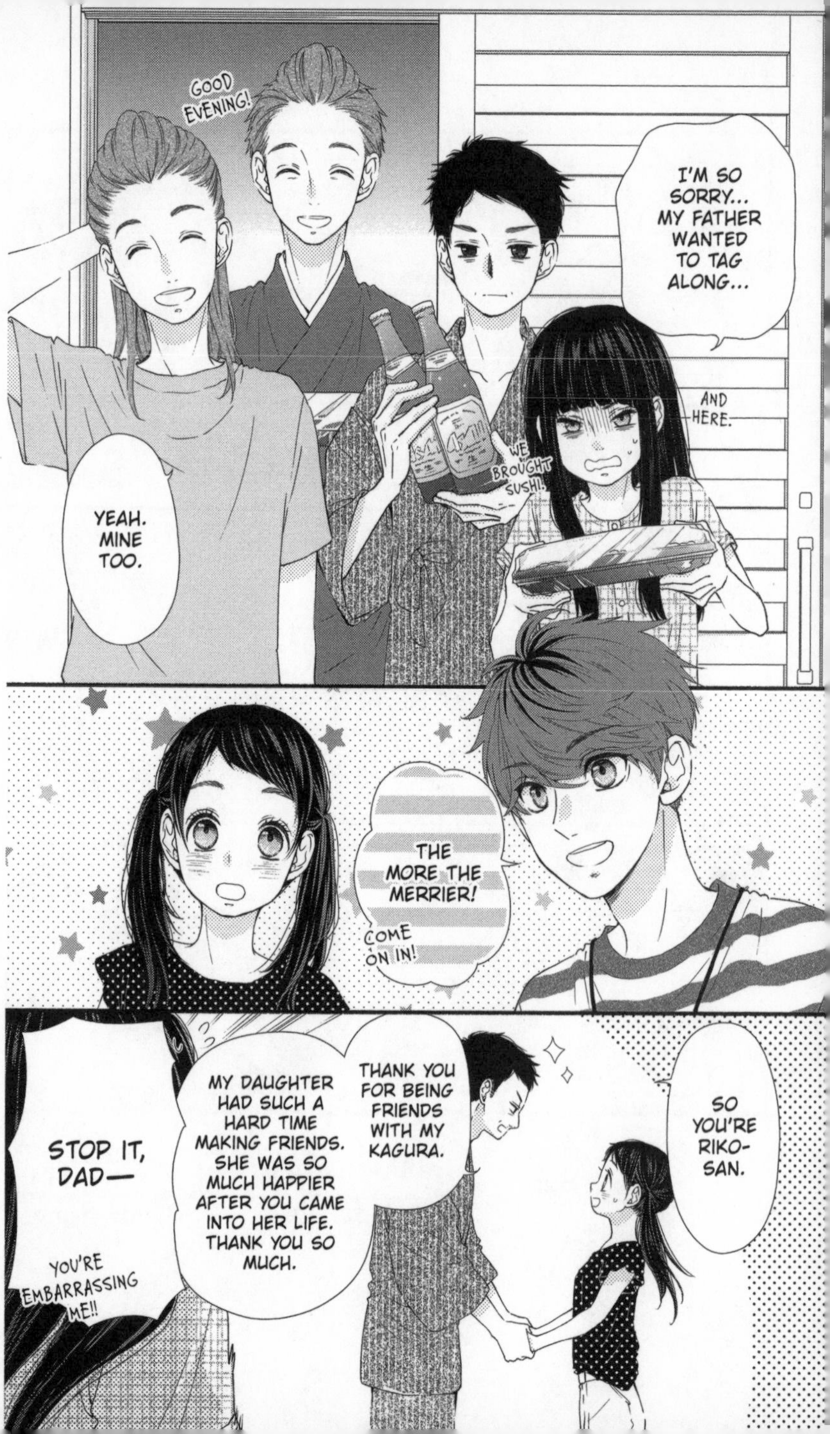
I'M SO SORRY... MY FATHER WANTED TO TAG ALONG...
GOOD EVENING!
YEAH. MINE TOO.
WE BROUGHT SUSHI!
AND HERE.
THE MORE THE MERRIER!
COME ON IN!
SO YOU'RE RIKO-SAN.
THANK YOU FOR BEING FRIENDS WITH MY KAGURA.
MY DAUGHTER HAD SUCH A HARD TIME MAKING FRIENDS. SHE WAS SO MUCH HAPPIER AFTER YOU CAME INTO HER LIFE. THANK YOU SO MUCH.
STOP IT, DAD—
YOU'RE EMBARRASSING ME!!

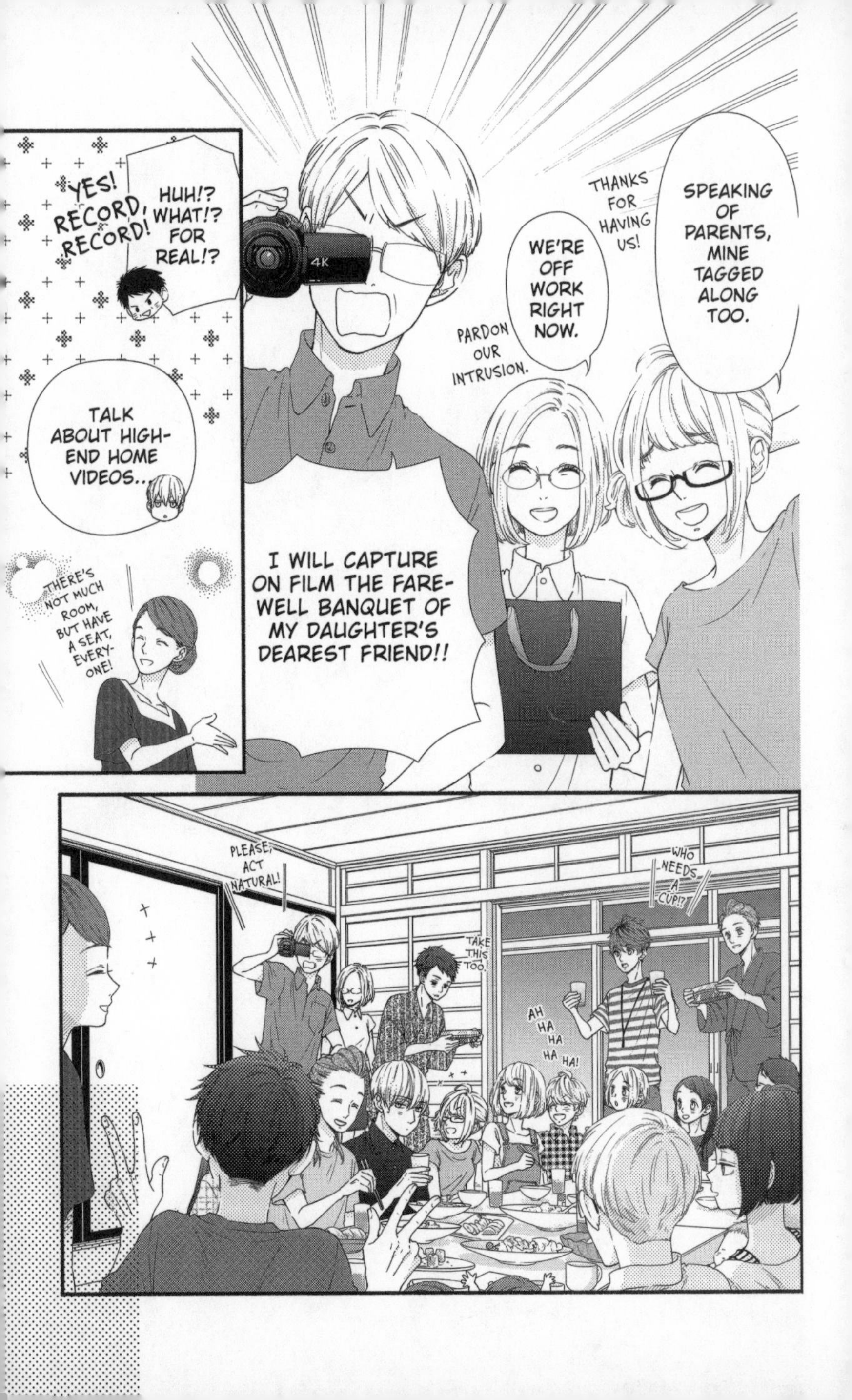
SPEAKING OF PARENTS, MINE TAGGED ALONG TOO.
THANKS FOR HAVING US!
WE'RE OFF WORK RIGHT NOW.
PARDON OUR INTRUSION.
I WILL CAPTURE ON FILM THE FARE-WELL BANQUET OF MY DAUGHTER'S DEAREST FRIEND!!
HUH!? WHAT!? FOR REAL!?
YES! RECORD, RECORD!
TALK ABOUT HIGH-END HOME VIDEOS...
THERE'S NOT MUCH ROOM, BUT HAVE A SEAT, EVERY-ONE!
WHO NEEDS A CUP!?
TAKE THIS TOO!
PLEASE, ACT NATURAL!
AH HA HA HA HA!

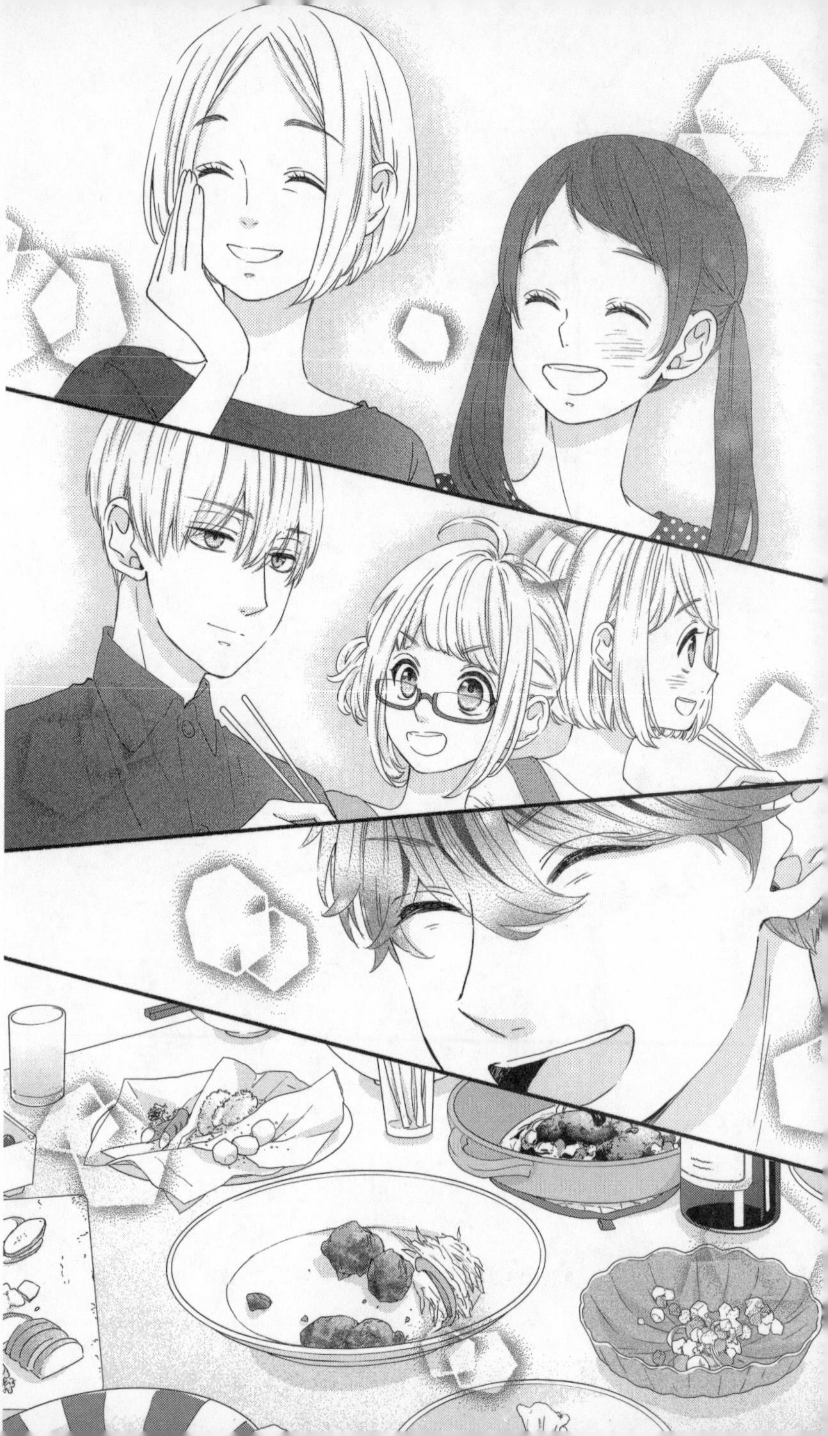

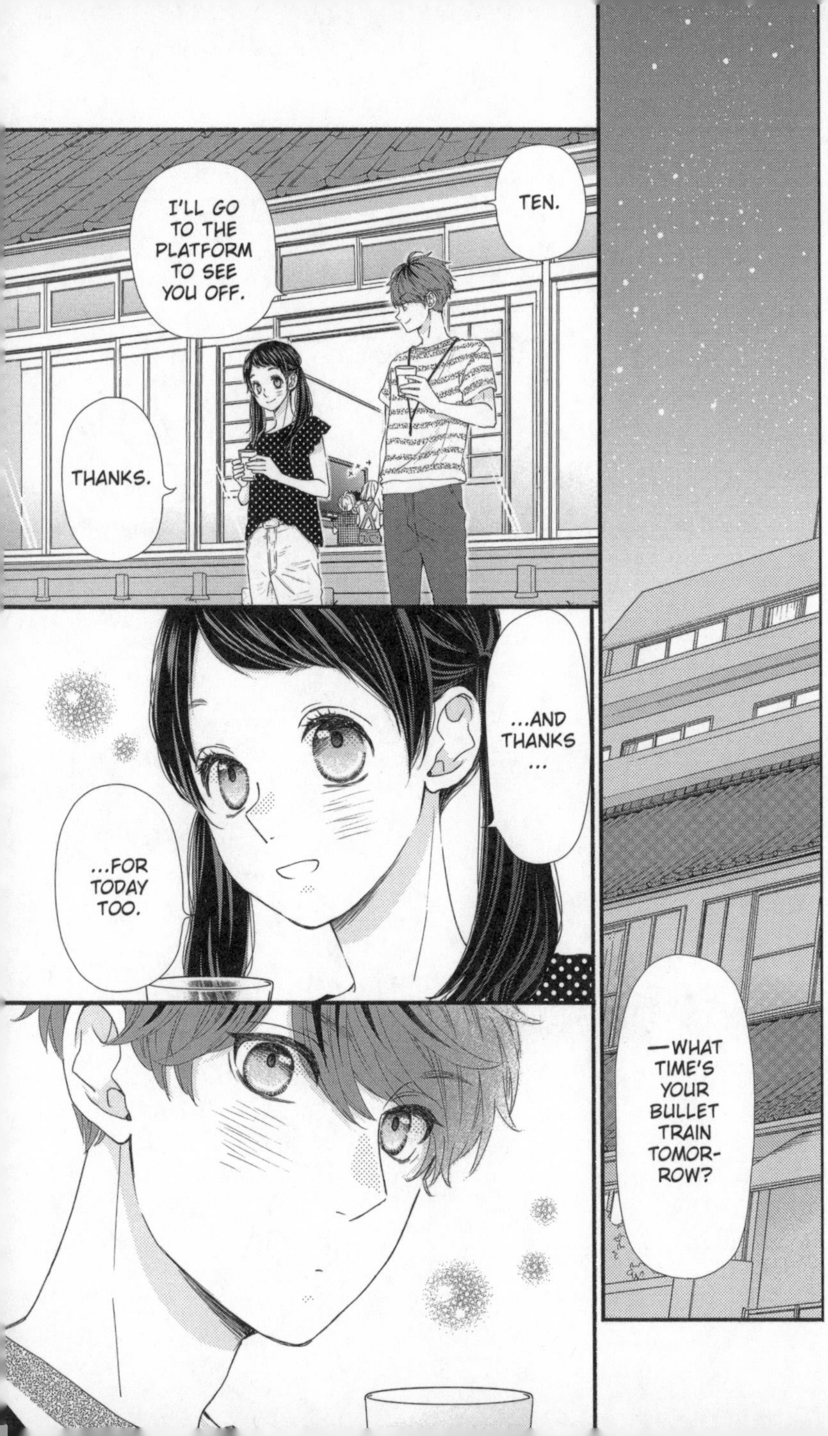
—WHAT TIME'S YOUR BULLET TRAIN TOMORROW?
TEN.
I'LL GO TO THE PLATFORM TO SEE YOU OFF.
THANKS.
...AND THANKS...
...FOR TODAY TOO.

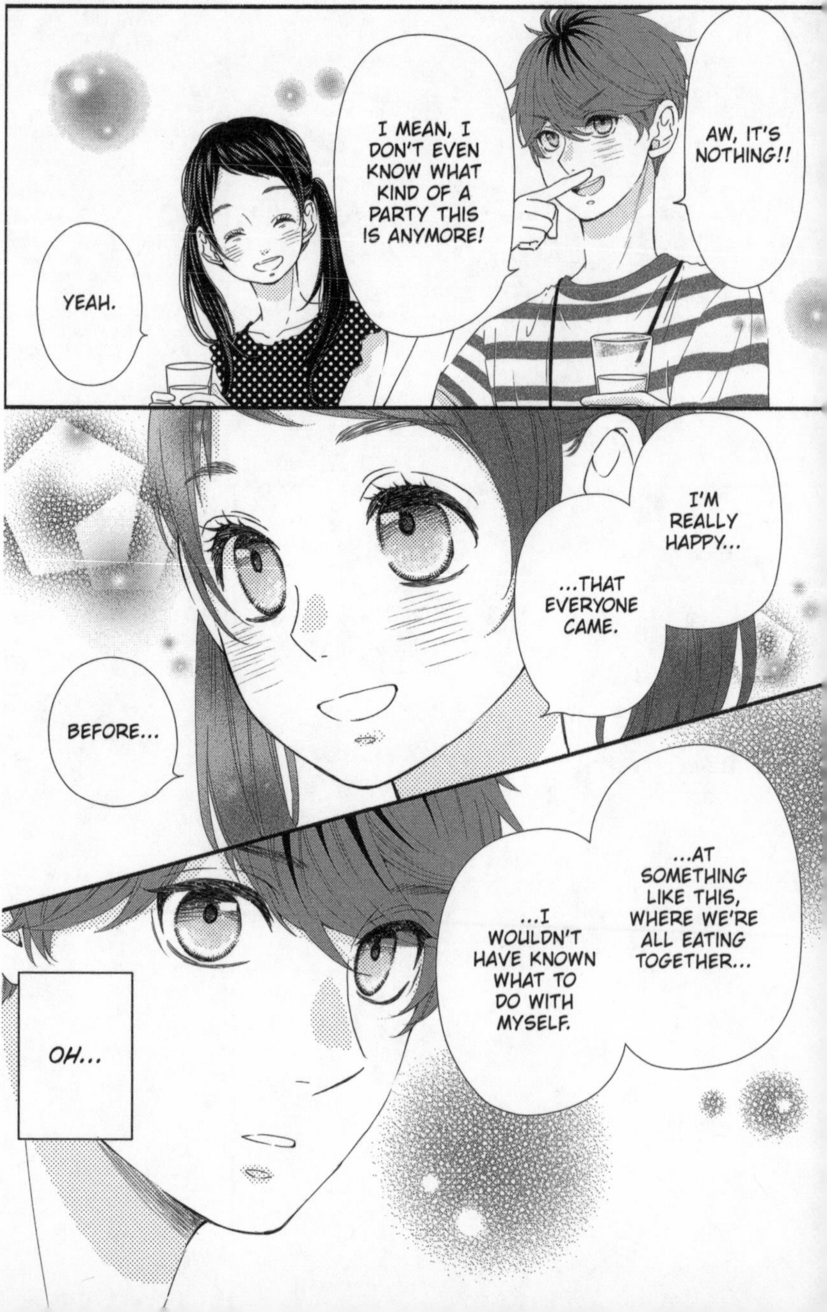
AW, IT'S NOTHING!!
I MEAN, I DON'T EVEN KNOW WHAT KIND OF A PARTY THIS IS ANYMORE!
YEAH.
I'M REALLY HAPPY...
...THAT EVERYONE CAME.
BEFORE...
...AT SOMETHING LIKE THIS, WHERE WE'RE ALL EATING TOGETHER...
...I WOULDN'T HAVE KNOWN WHAT TO DO WITH MYSELF.
OH...

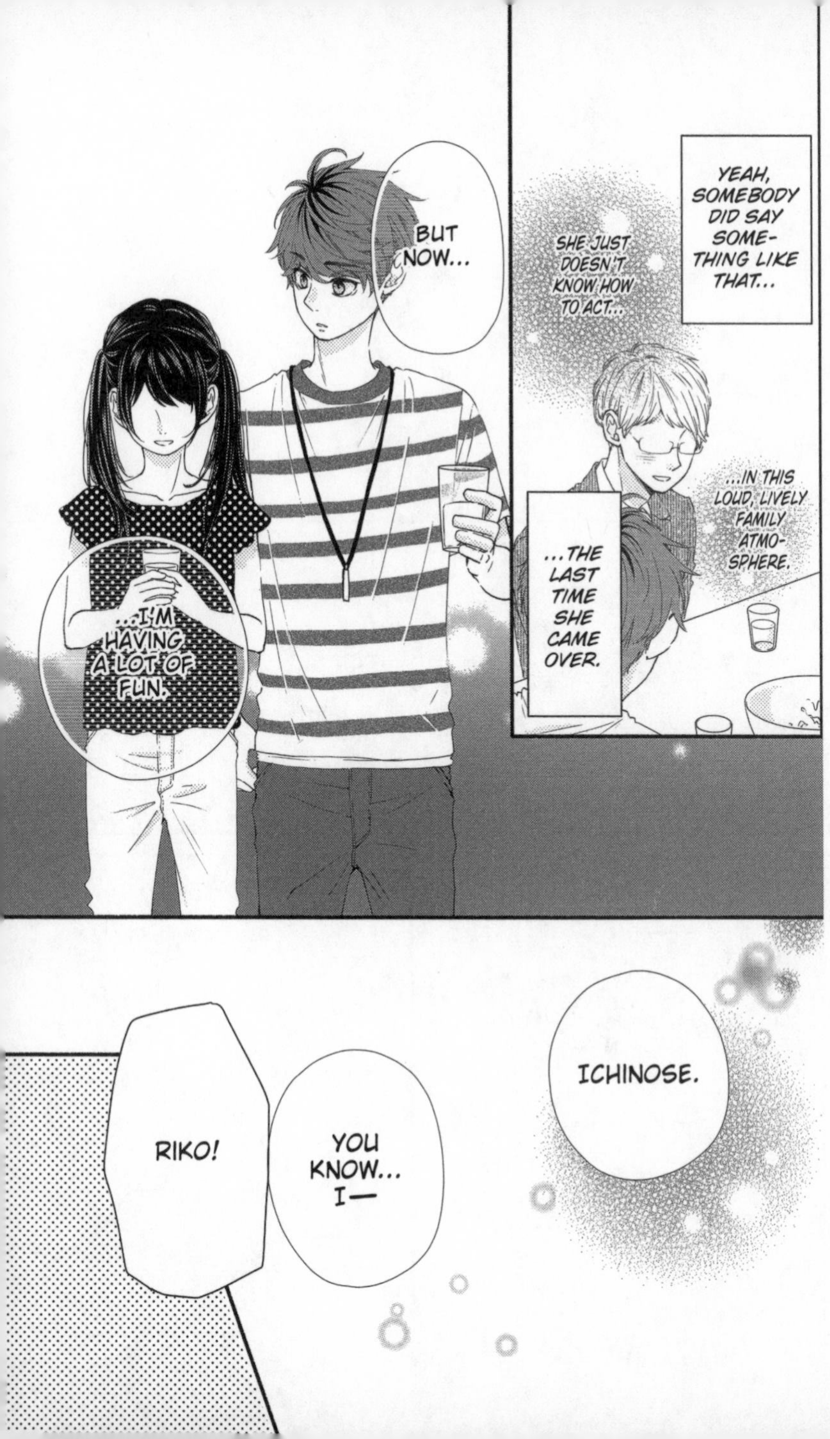
YEAH, SOMEBODY DID SAY SOME-THING LIKE THAT...
SHE JUST DOESN'T KNOW HOW TO ACT...
...IN THIS LOUD, LIVELY FAMILY ATMO-SPHERE.
...THE LAST TIME SHE CAME OVER.
BUT NOW...
...I'M HAVING A LOT OF FUN.
ICHINOSE.
YOU KNOW... I—
RIKO!

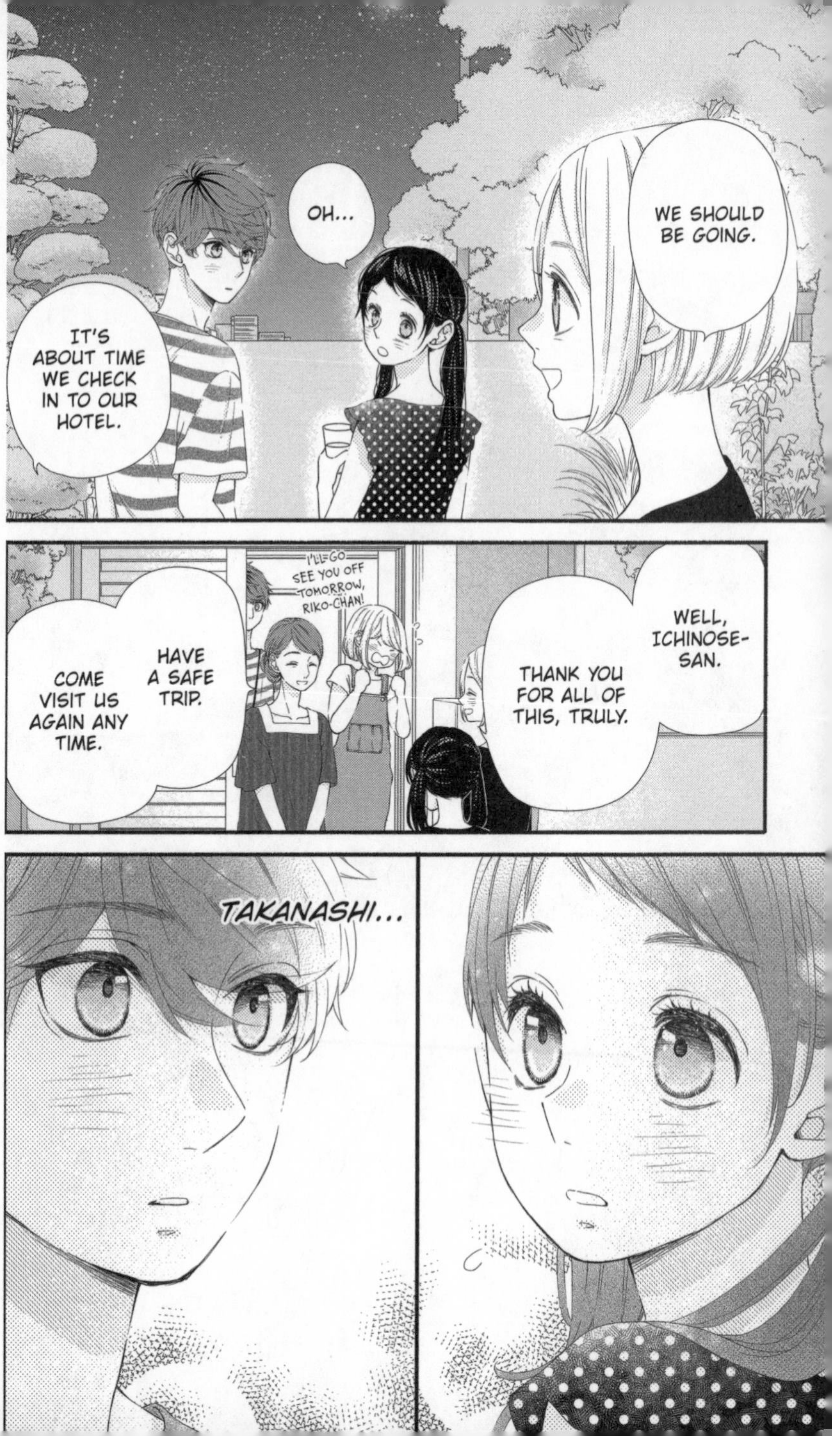
WE SHOULD BE GOING.
OH...
IT'S ABOUT TIME WE CHECK IN TO OUR HOTEL.
WELL, ICHINOSE-SAN.
THANK YOU FOR ALL OF THIS, TRULY.
I'LL GO SEE YOU OFF TOMORROW, RIKO-CHAN!
HAVE A SAFE TRIP.
COME VISIT US AGAIN ANY TIME.
TAKANASHI...

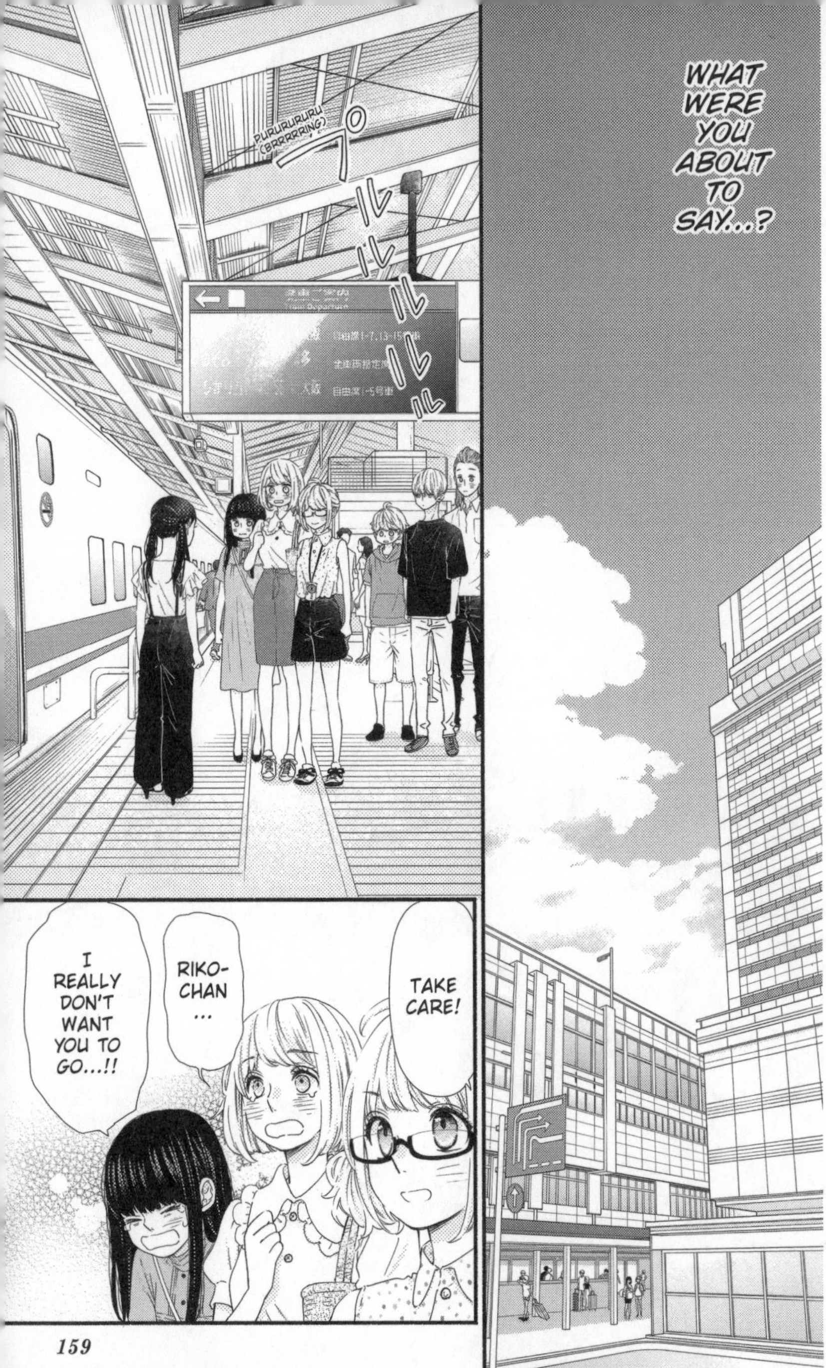
WHAT WERE YOU ABOUT TO SAY...?
PURURURURU (BRRRRRING)
プルルルルル
TAKE CARE!
RIKO-CHAN...
I REALLY DON'T WANT YOU TO GO...!!

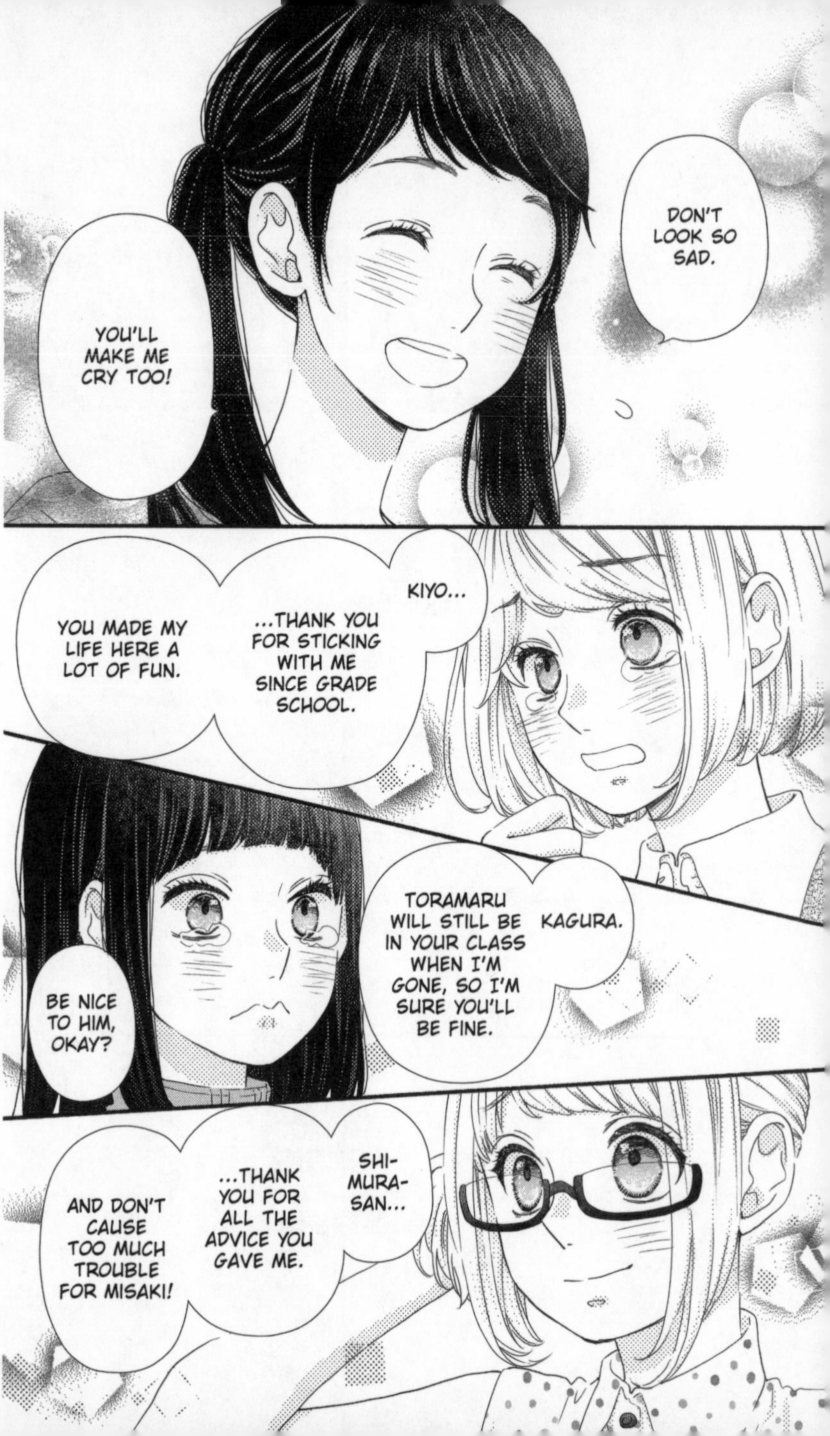
DON'T LOOK SO SAD.
YOU'LL MAKE ME CRY TOO!
KIYO...
...THANK YOU FOR STICKING WITH ME SINCE GRADE SCHOOL.
YOU MADE MY LIFE HERE A LOT OF FUN.
KAGURA.
TORAMARU WILL STILL BE IN YOUR CLASS WHEN I'M GONE, SO I'M SURE YOU'LL BE FINE.
BE NICE TO HIM, OKAY?
SHI-MURA-SAN...
...THANK YOU FOR ALL THE ADVICE YOU GAVE ME.
AND DON'T CAUSE TOO MUCH TROUBLE FOR MISAKI!

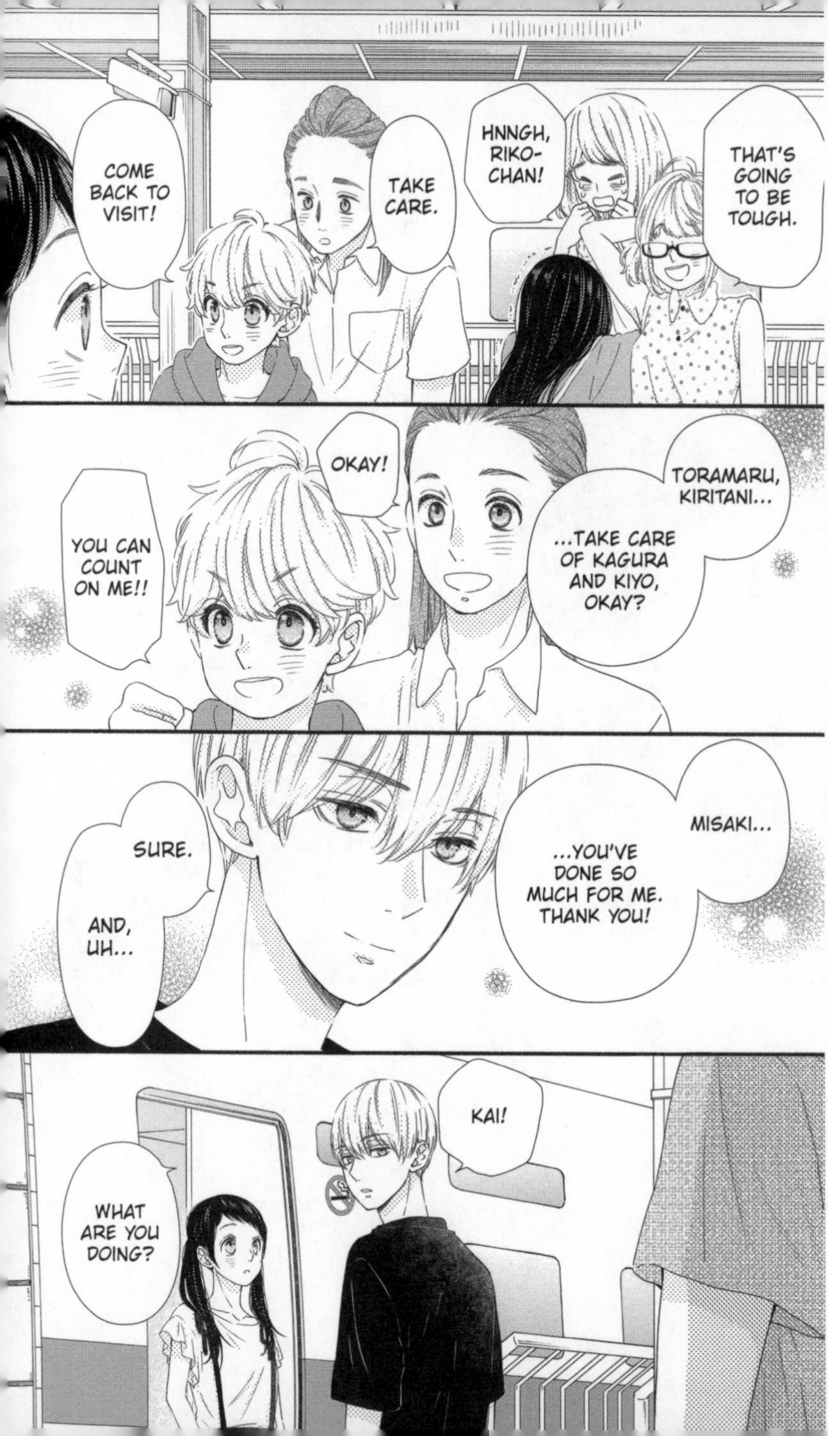
THAT'S GOING TO BE TOUGH.
HNNGH, RIKO-CHAN!
TAKE CARE.
COME BACK TO VISIT!
TORAMARU, KIRITANI...
...TAKE CARE OF KAGURA AND KIYO, OKAY?
OKAY!
YOU CAN COUNT ON ME!!
MISAKI...
...YOU'VE DONE SO MUCH FOR ME. THANK YOU!
SURE.
AND, UH...
KAI!
WHAT ARE YOU DOING?

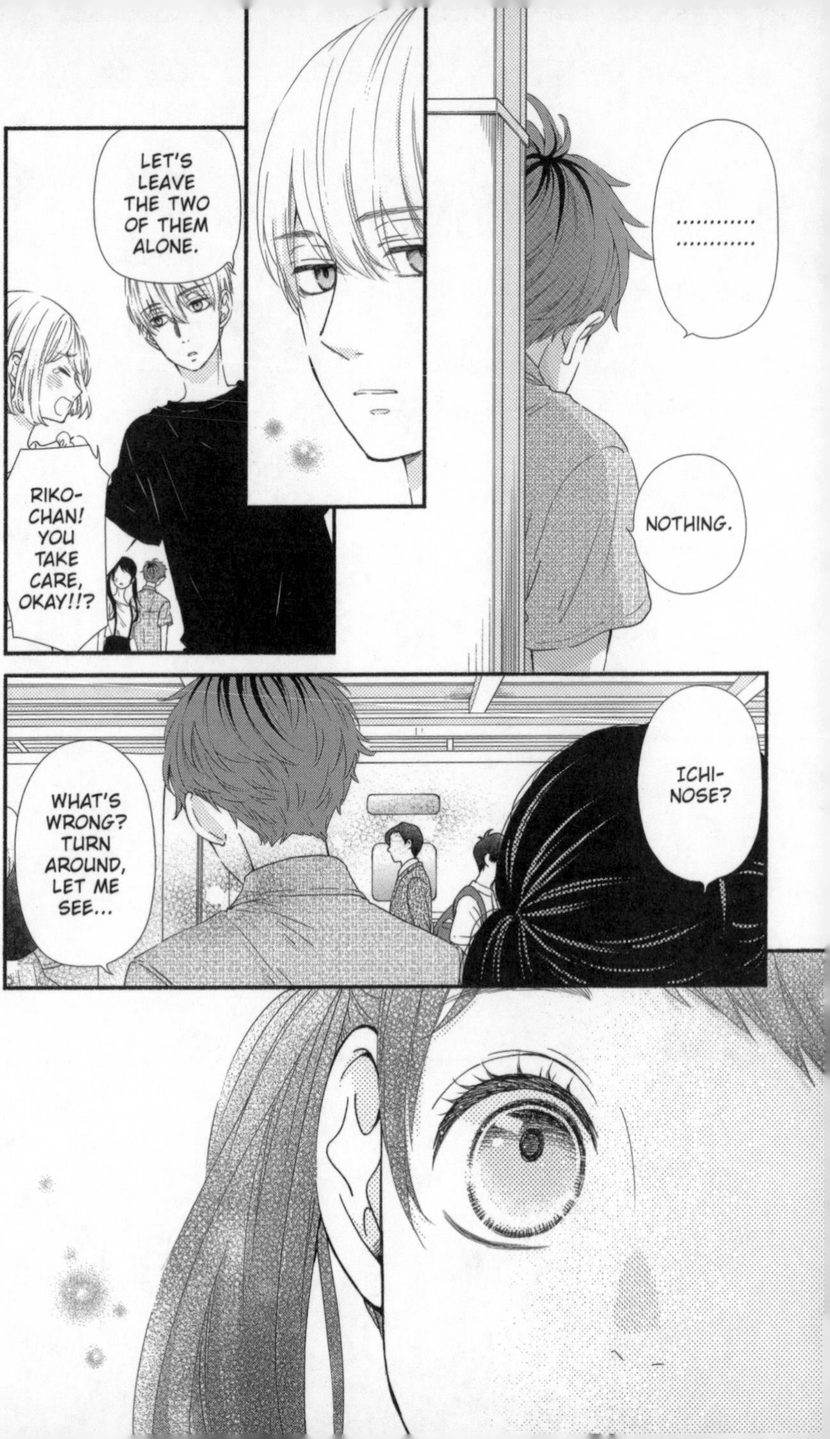
....
NOTHING.
LET'S LEAVE THE TWO OF THEM ALONE.
RIKO-CHAN! YOU TAKE CARE, OKAY!!?
ICHI-NOSE?
WHAT'S WRONG? TURN AROUND, LET ME SEE...

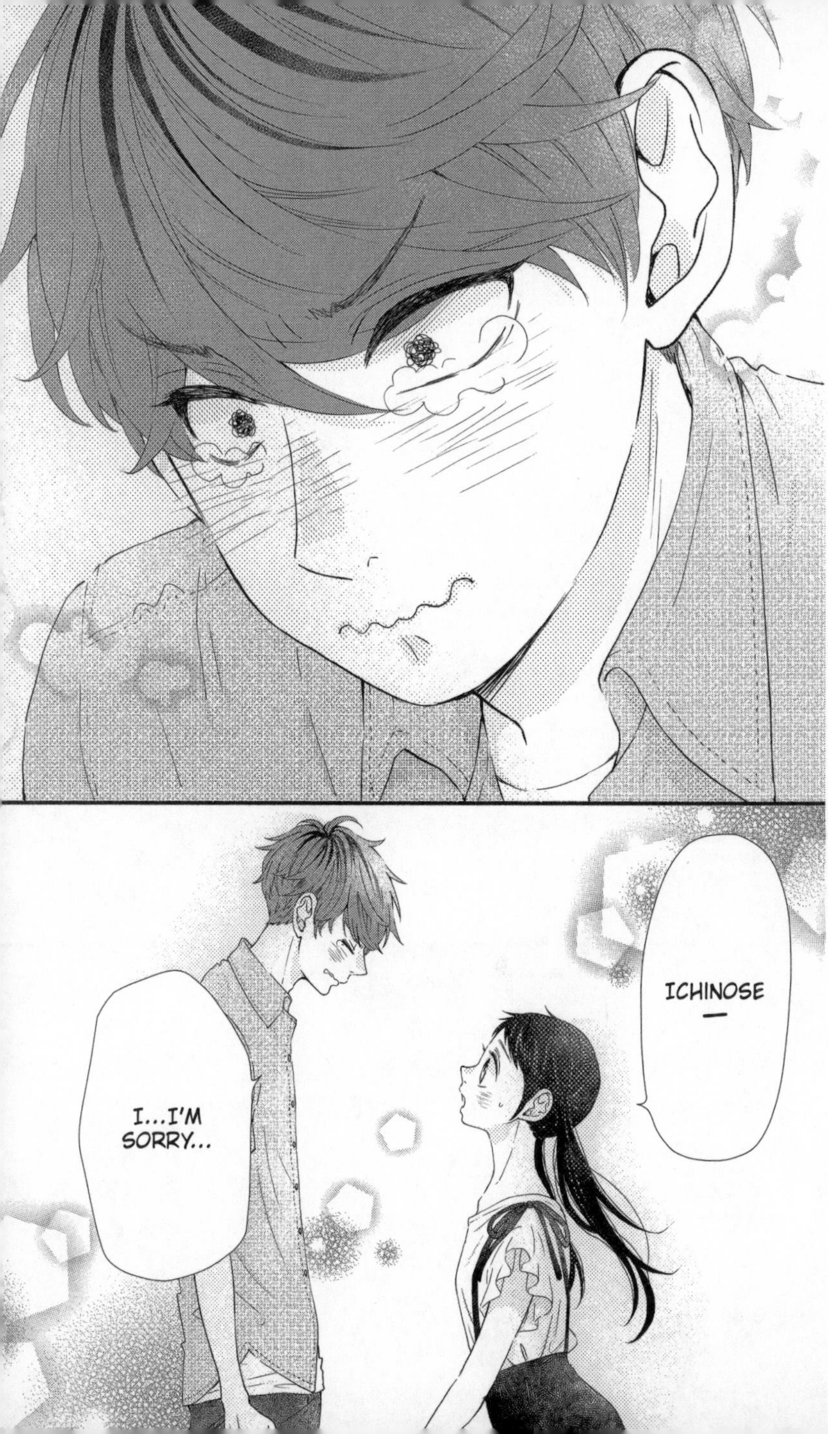
ICHINOSE —
I...I'M SORRY...

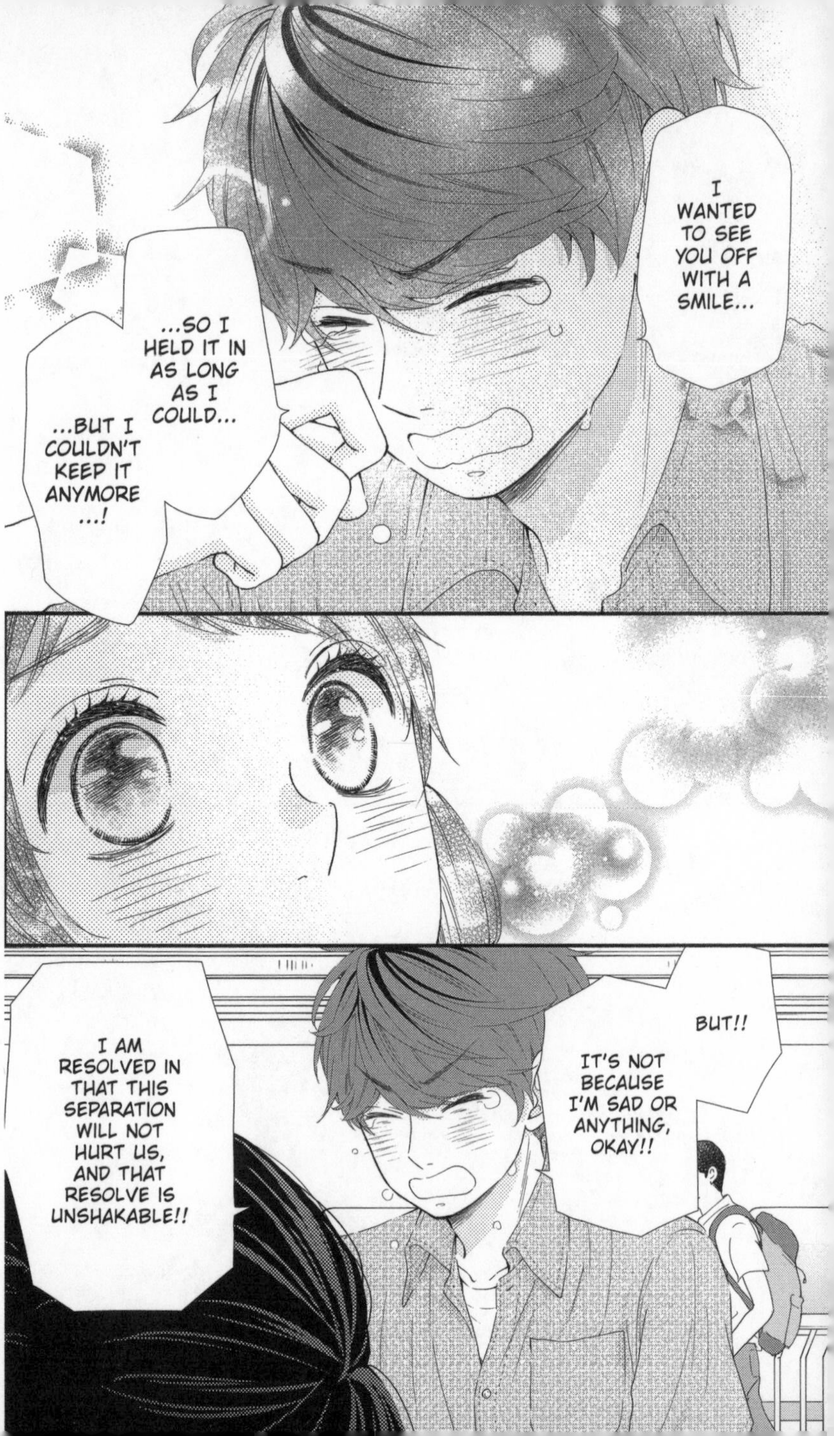
I WANTED TO SEE YOU OFF WITH A SMILE...
...SO I HELD IT IN AS LONG AS I COULD...
...BUT I COULDN'T KEEP IT ANYMORE...!
BUT!!
IT'S NOT BECAUSE I'M SAD OR ANYTHING, OKAY!!
I AM RESOLVED IN THAT THIS SEPARATION WILL NOT HURT US, AND THAT RESOLVE IS UNSHAKABLE!!

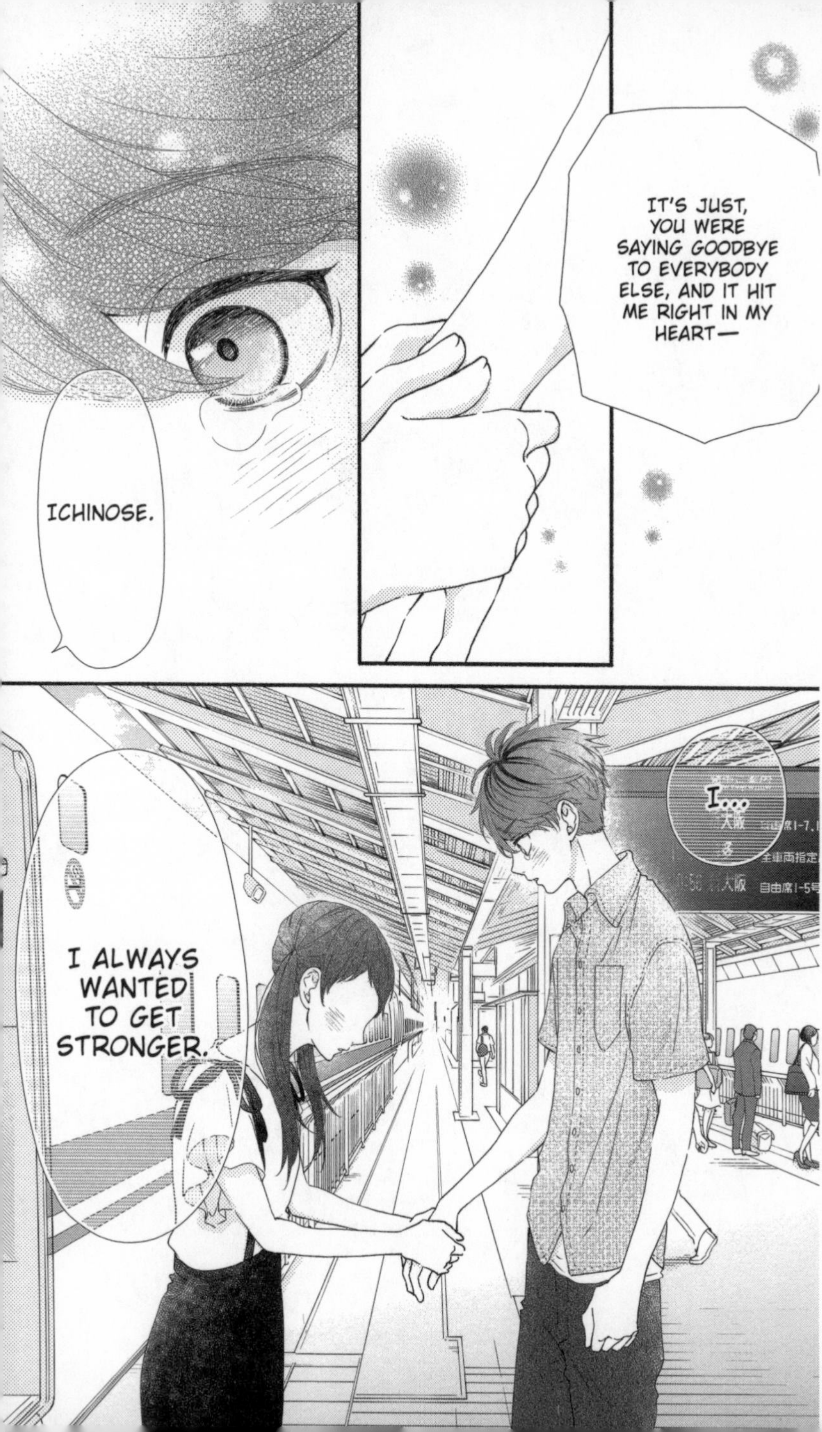
IT'S JUST, YOU WERE SAYING GOODBYE TO EVERYBODY ELSE, AND IT HIT ME RIGHT IN MY HEART—
ICHINOSE.
I...
I ALWAYS WANTED TO GET STRONGER.

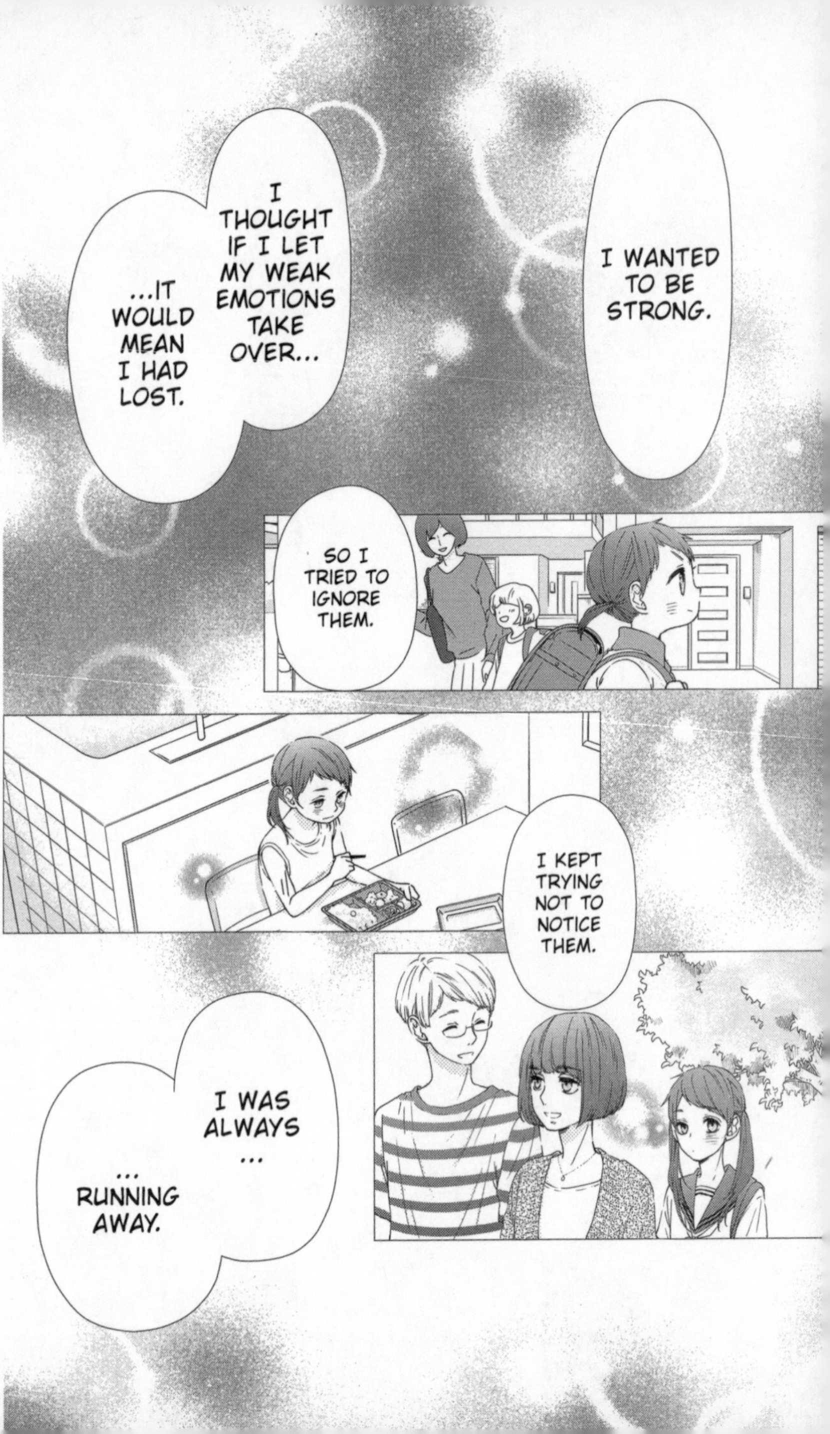
I WANTED TO BE STRONG.
I THOUGHT IF I LET MY WEAK EMOTIONS TAKE OVER...
...IT WOULD MEAN I HAD LOST.
SO I TRIED TO IGNORE THEM.
I KEPT TRYING NOT TO NOTICE THEM.
I WAS ALWAYS ...
... RUNNING AWAY.

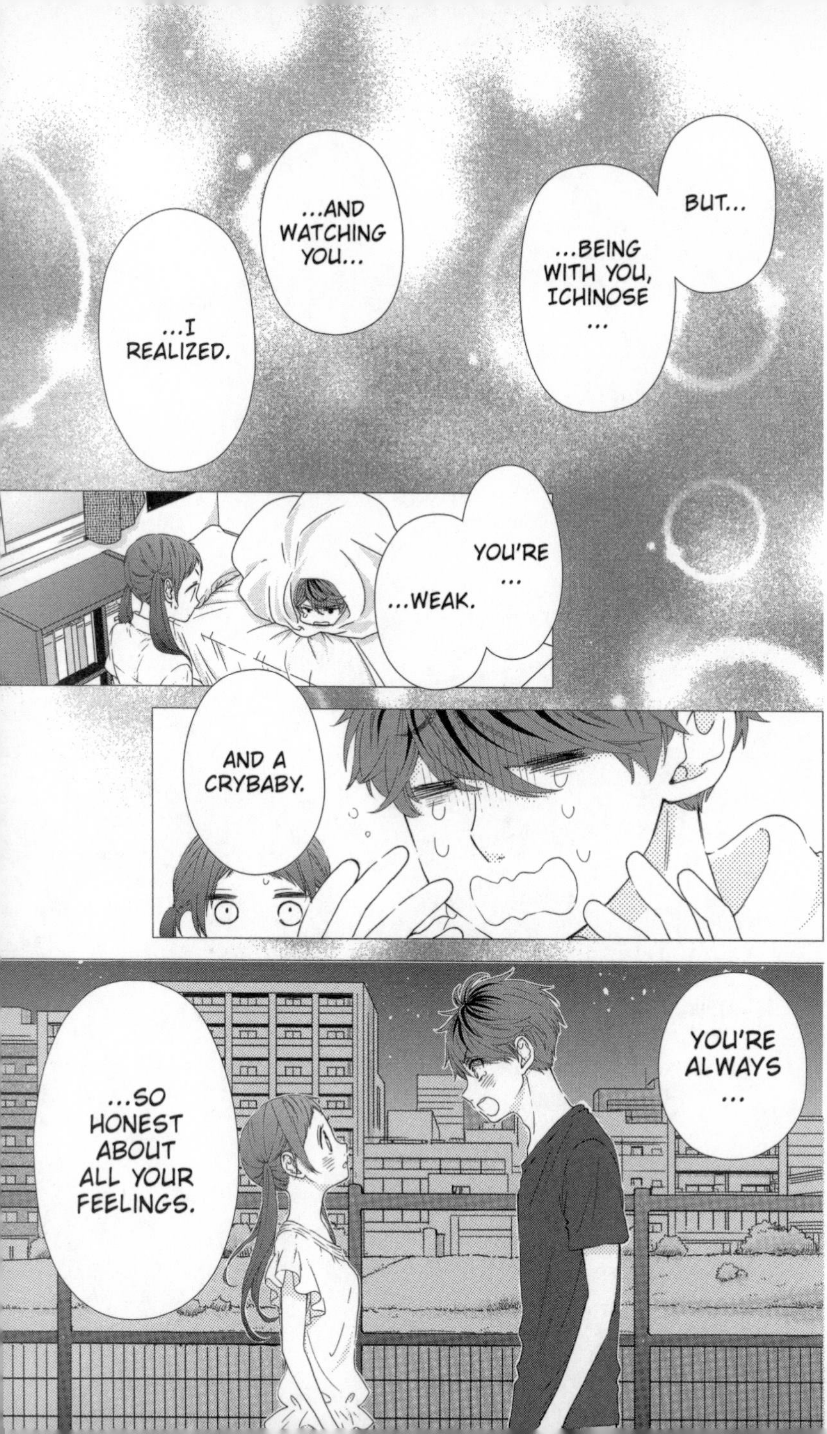
BUT...
...BEING WITH YOU, ICHINOSE ...
...AND WATCHING YOU...
...I REALIZED.
YOU'RE ...
...WEAK.
AND A CRYBABY.
YOU'RE ALWAYS ...
...SO HONEST ABOUT ALL YOUR FEELINGS.

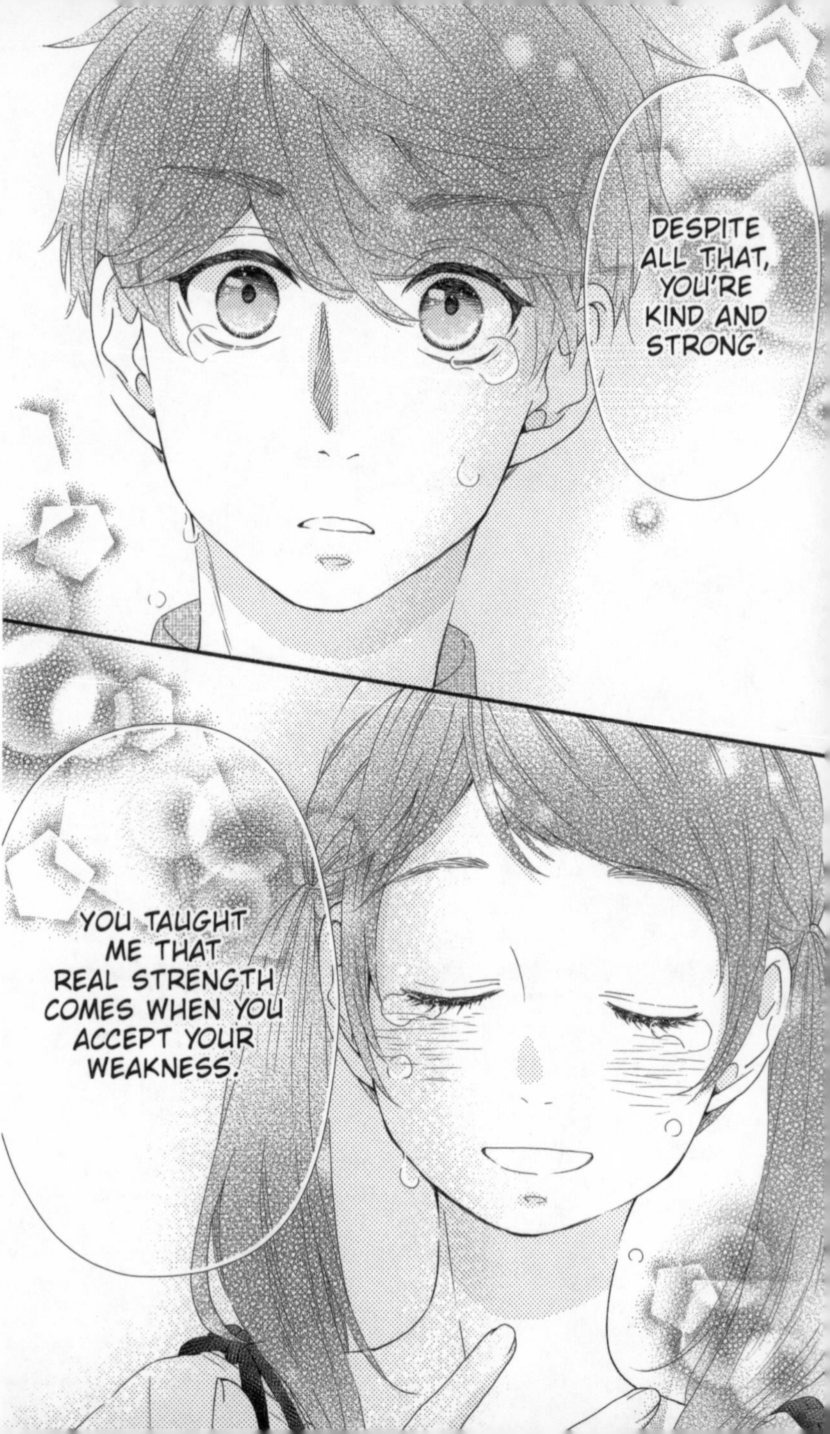
DESPITE ALL THAT, YOU'RE KIND AND STRONG.
YOU TAUGHT ME THAT REAL STRENGTH COMES WHEN YOU ACCEPT YOUR WEAKNESS.

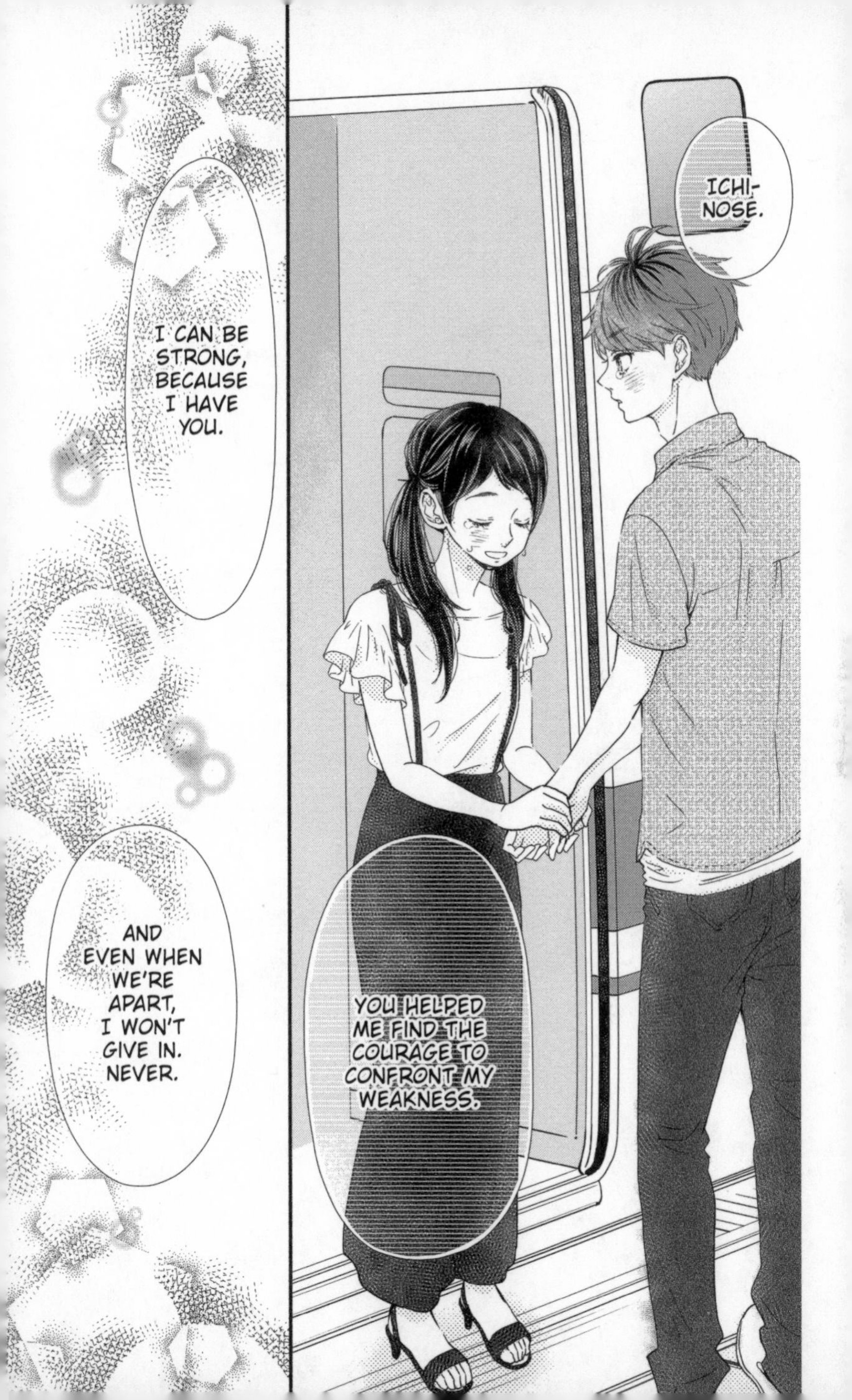
ICHI-NOSE.
YOU HELPED ME FIND THE COURAGE TO CONFRONT MY WEAKNESS.
I CAN BE STRONG, BECAUSE I HAVE YOU.
AND EVEN WHEN WE'RE APART, I WON'T GIVE IN. NEVER.

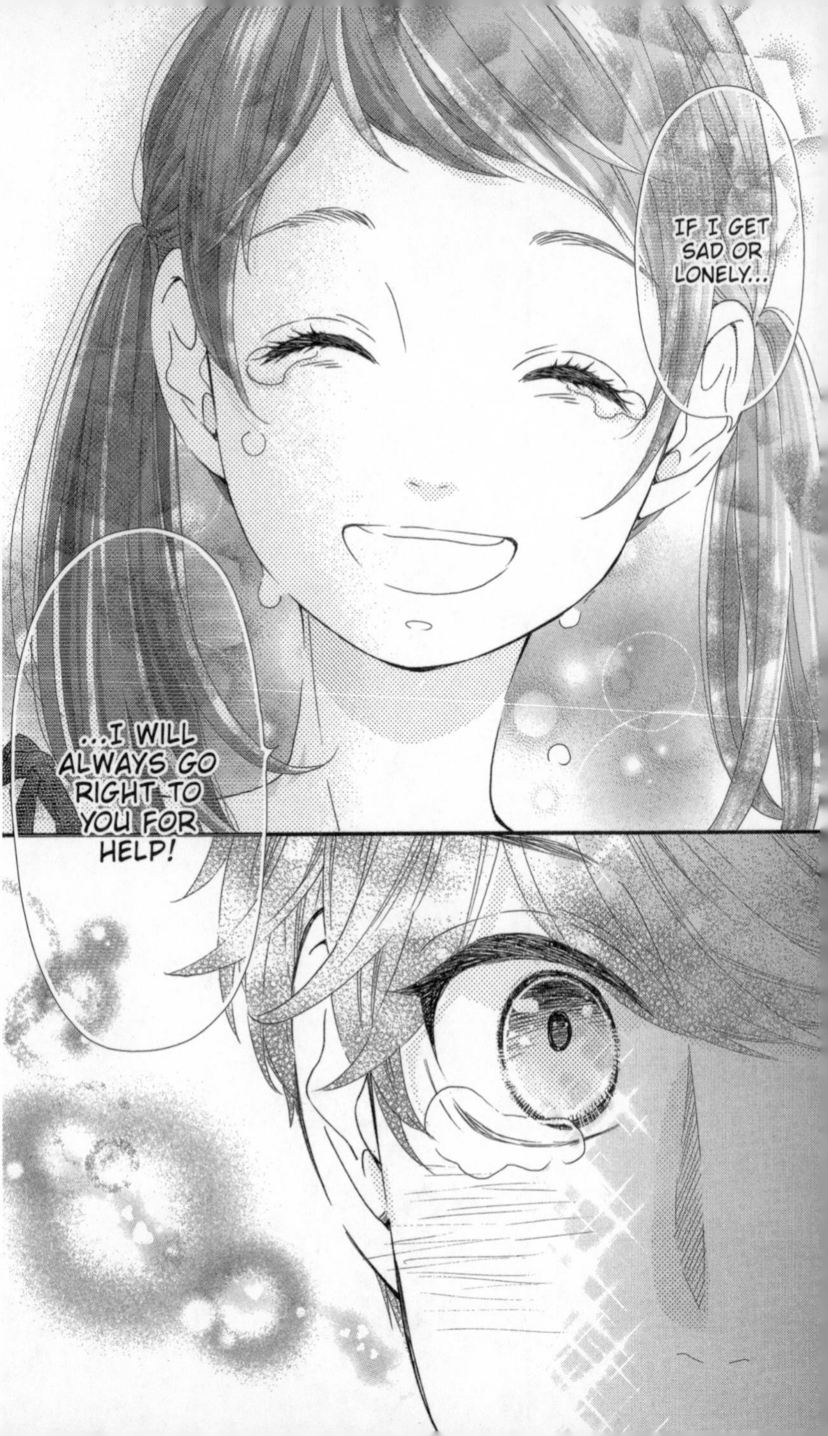
IF I GET SAD OR LONELY...
...I WILL ALWAYS GO RIGHT TO YOU FOR HELP!

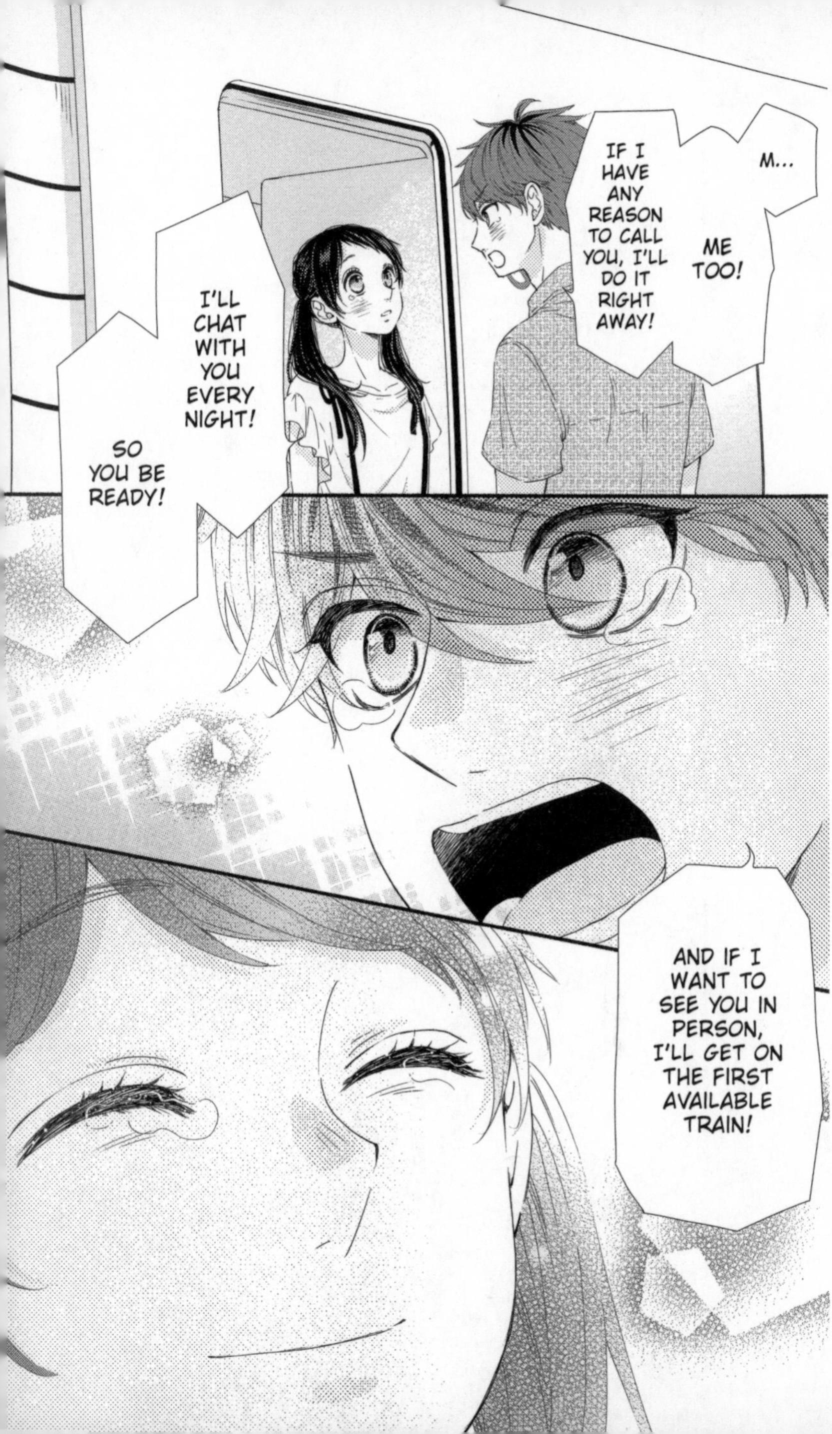
M... ME TOO!
IF I HAVE ANY REASON TO CALL YOU, I'LL DO IT RIGHT AWAY!
I'LL CHAT WITH YOU EVERY NIGHT! SO YOU BE READY!
AND IF I WANT TO SEE YOU IN PERSON, I'LL GET ON THE FIRST AVAILABLE TRAIN!

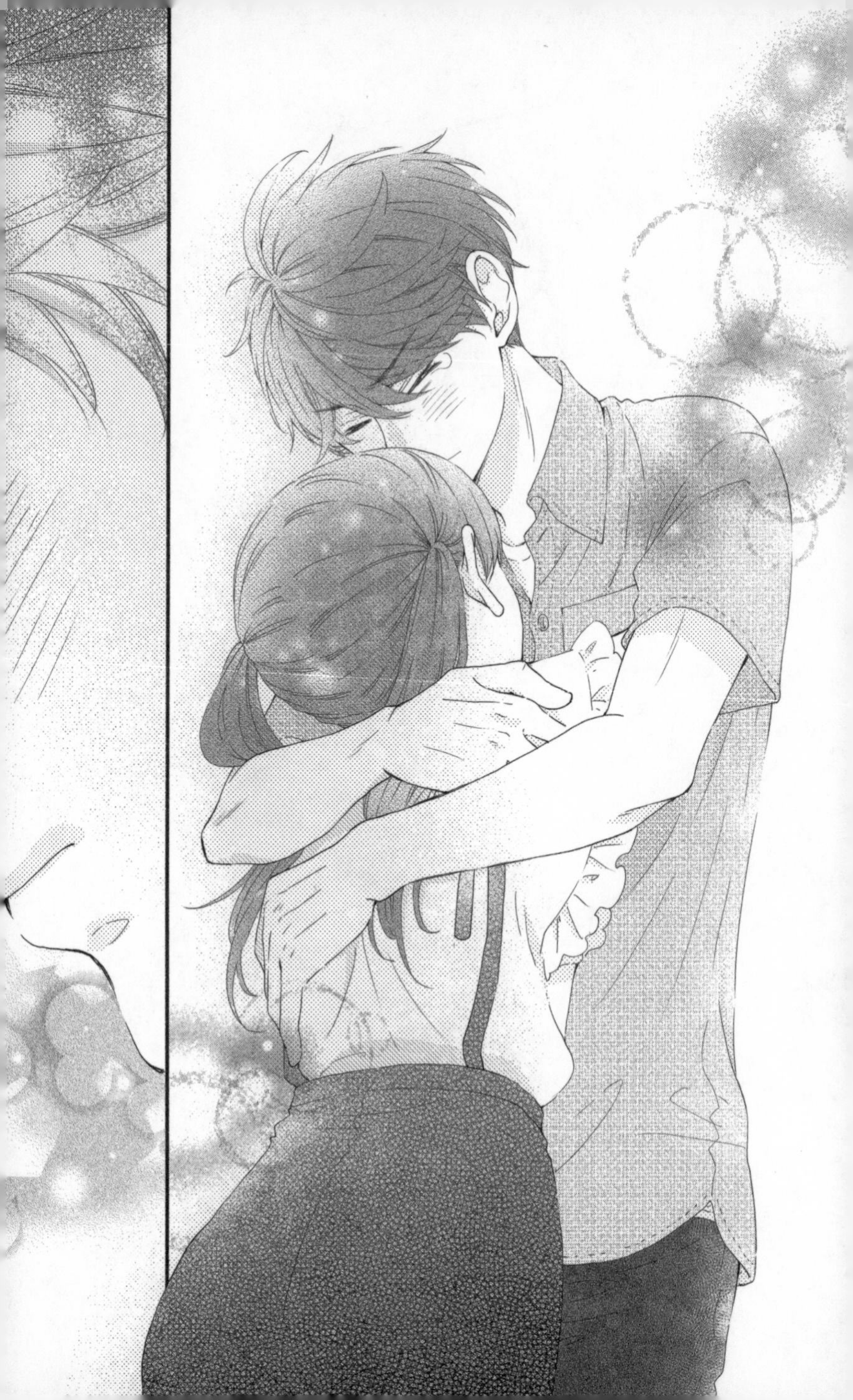

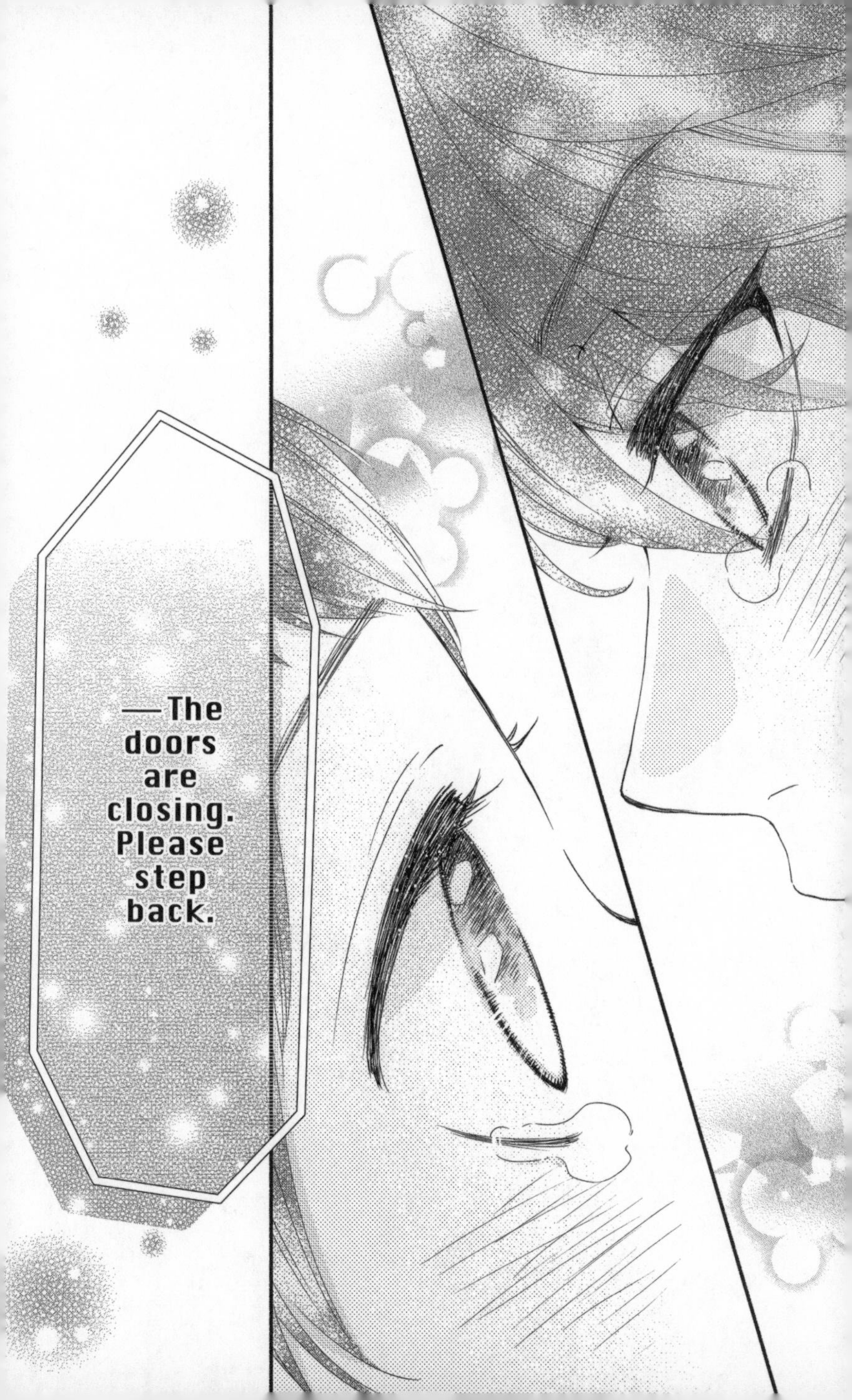
—The doors are closing. Please step back.

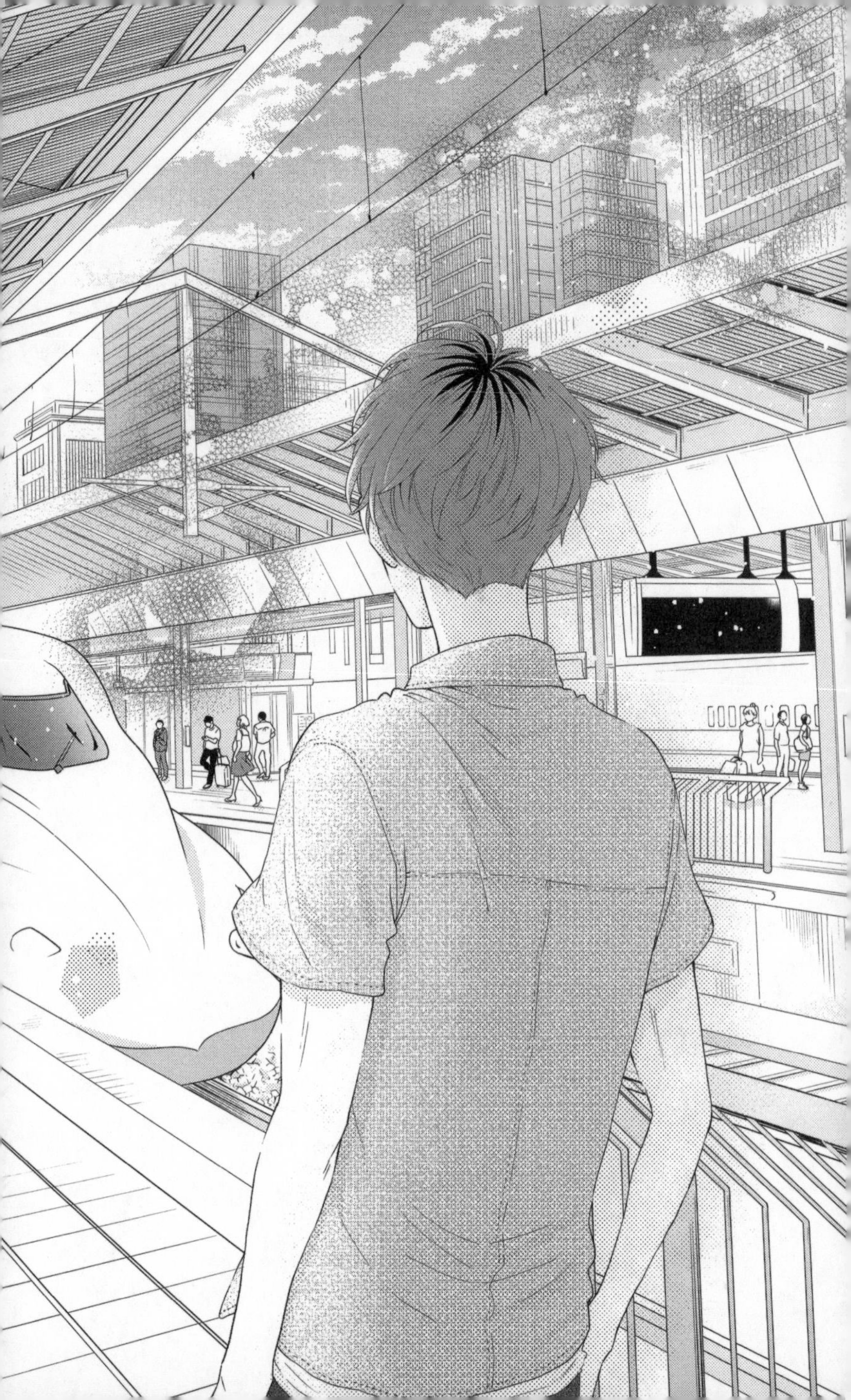

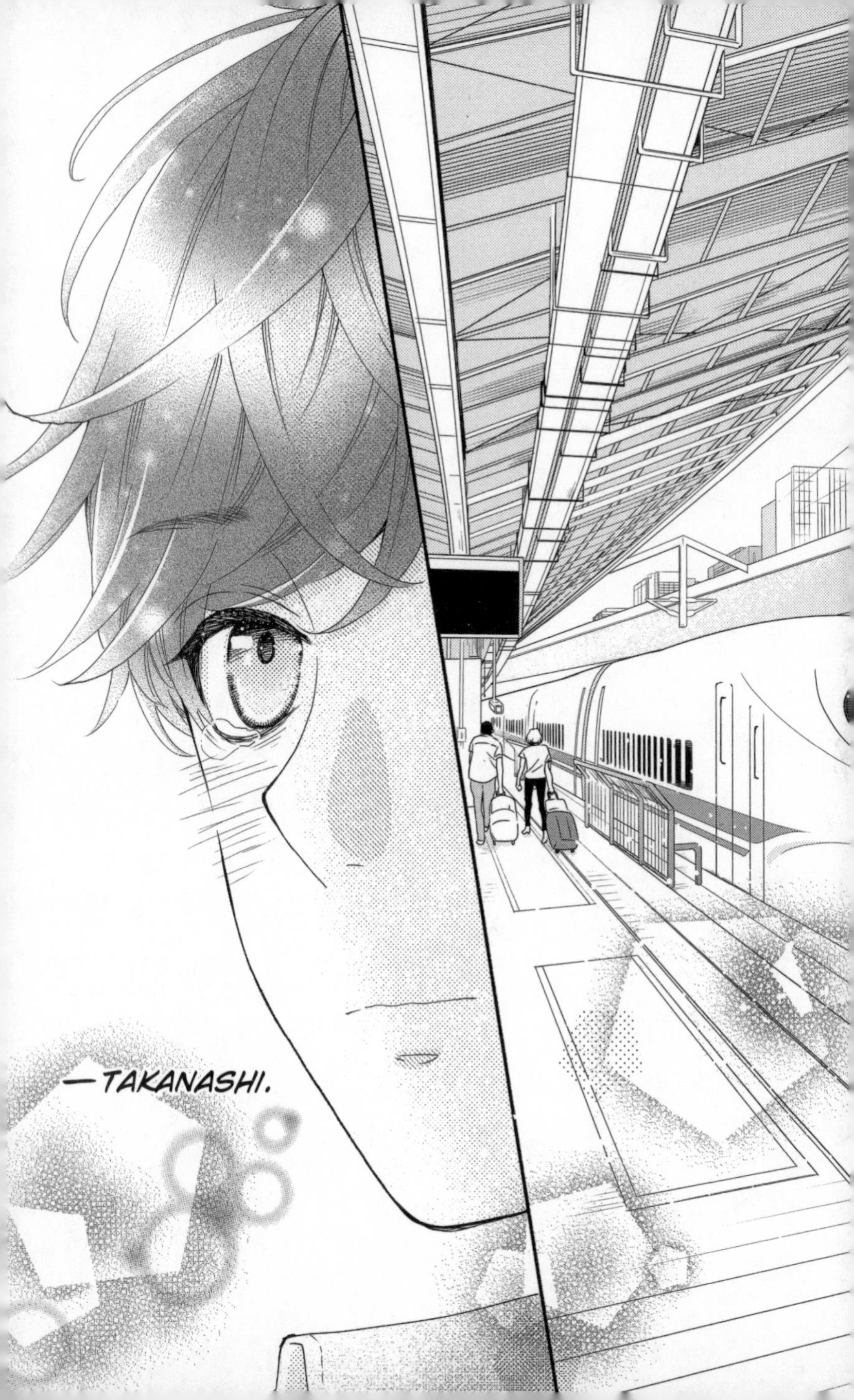
—TAKANASHI.

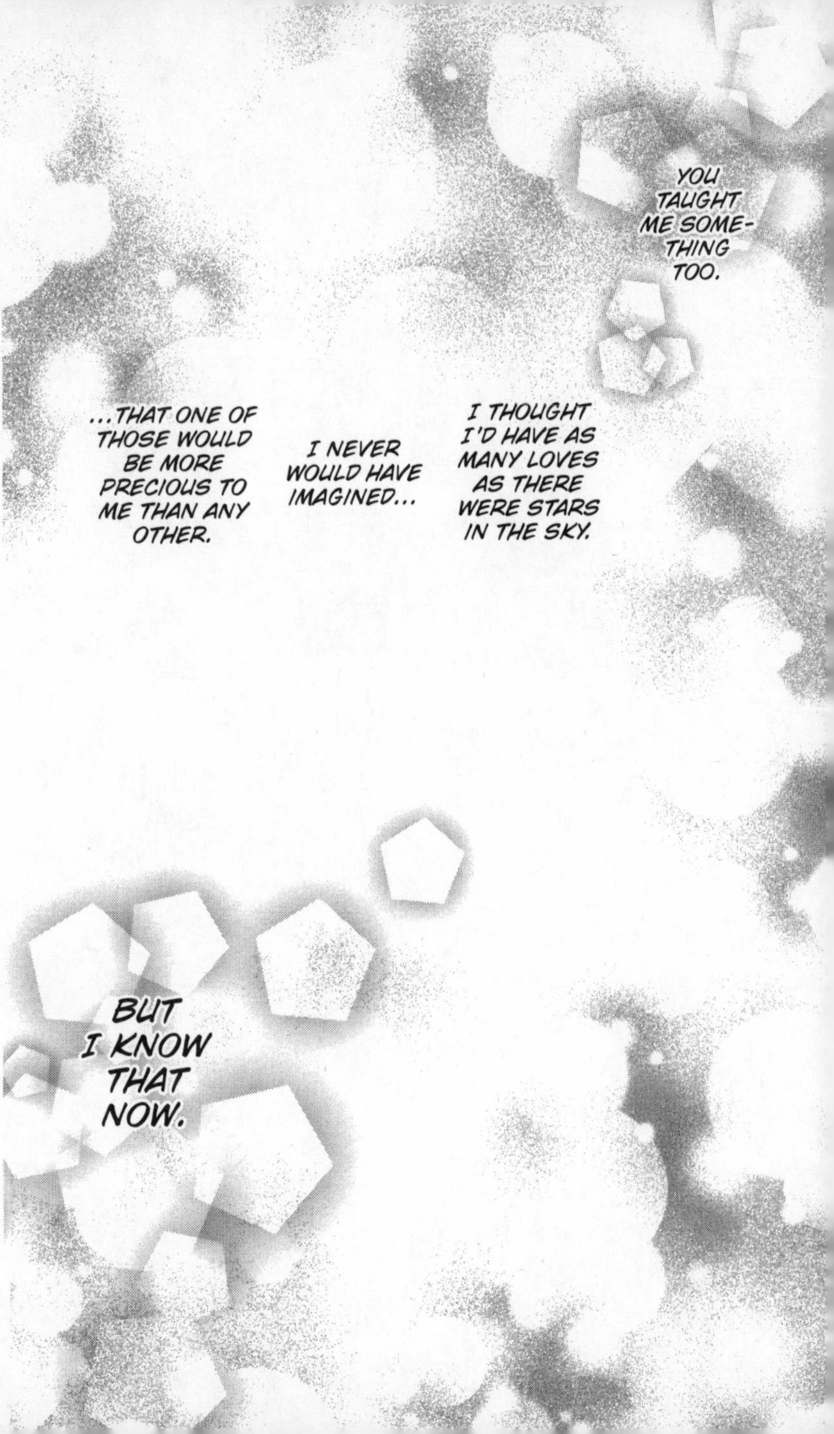
YOU TAUGHT ME SOME-THING TOO.
I THOUGHT I'D HAVE AS MANY LOVES AS THERE WERE STARS IN THE SKY.
I NEVER WOULD HAVE IMAGINED...
...THAT ONE OF THOSE WOULD BE MORE PRECIOUS TO ME THAN ANY OTHER.
BUT I KNOW THAT NOW.

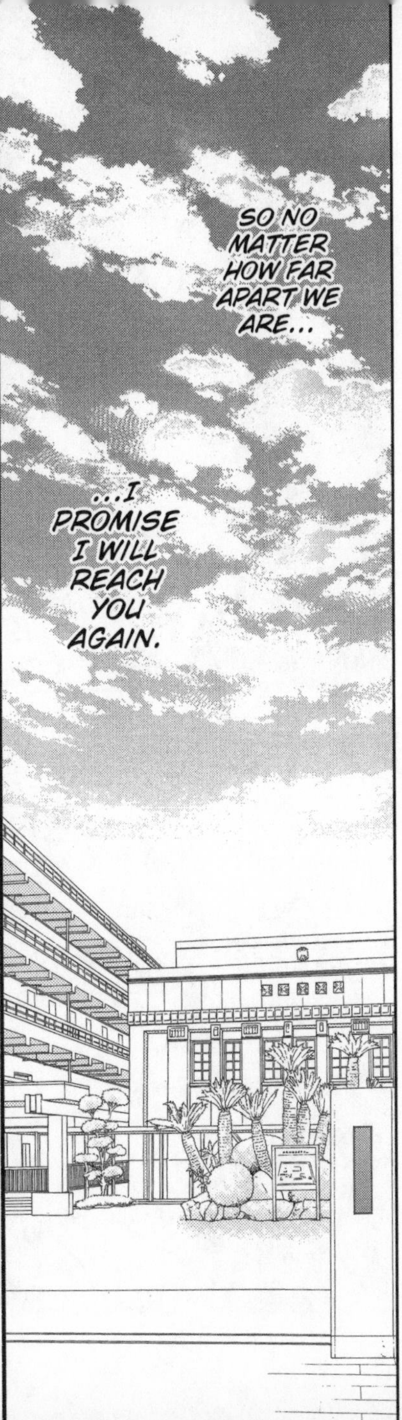
SO NO MATTER HOW FAR APART WE ARE...
...I PROMISE I WILL REACH YOU AGAIN.

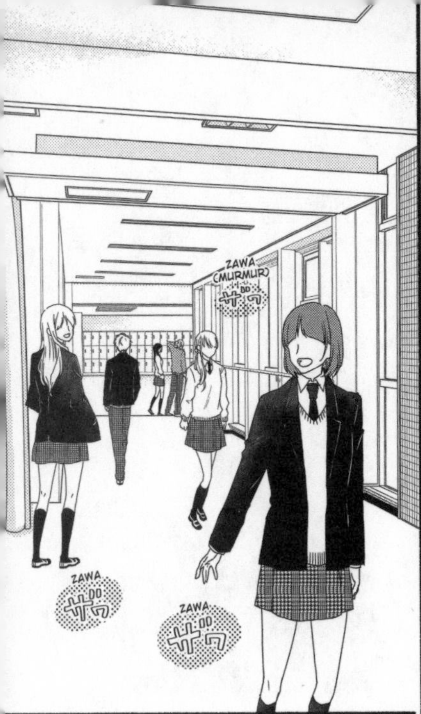
ZAWA (MURMUR)
ZAWA
ZAWA

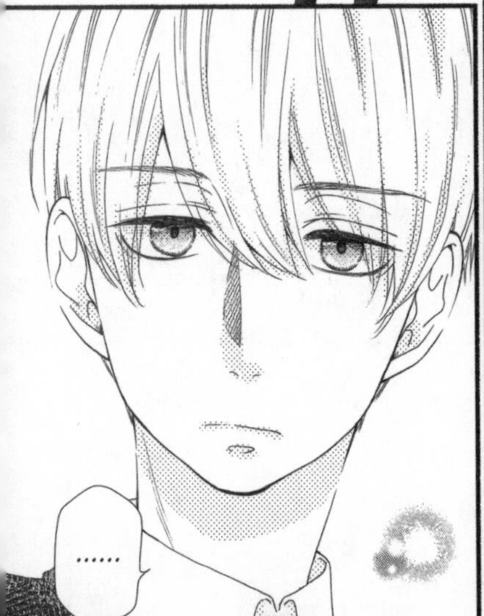
......

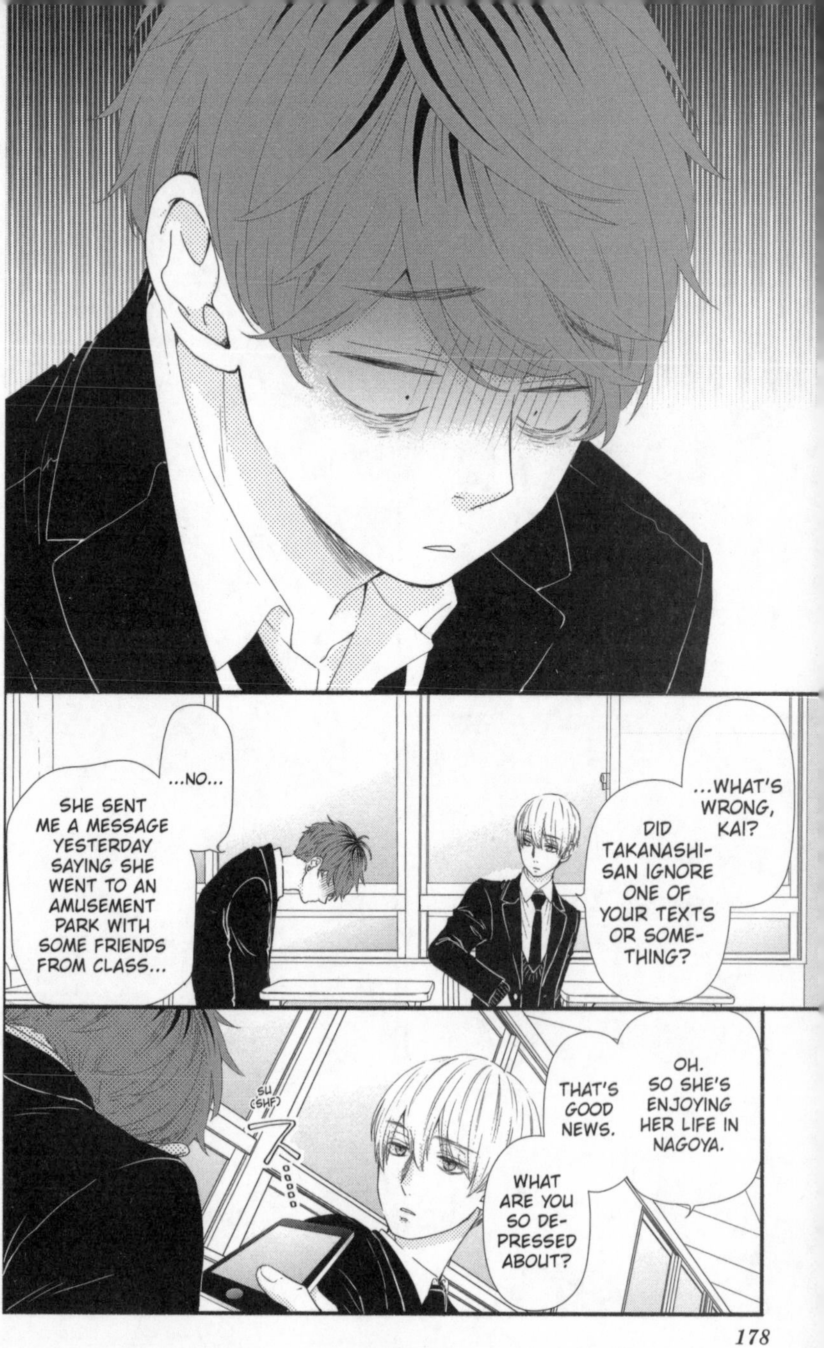
...WHAT'S WRONG, KAI?
DID TAKANASHI-SAN IGNORE ONE OF YOUR TEXTS OR SOME-THING?
...NO...
SHE SENT ME A MESSAGE YESTERDAY SAYING SHE WENT TO AN AMUSEMENT PARK WITH SOME FRIENDS FROM CLASS...
OH. SO SHE'S ENJOYING HER LIFE IN NAGOYA.
THAT'S GOOD NEWS.
WHAT ARE YOU SO DE-PRESSED ABOUT?
SU (SHF)

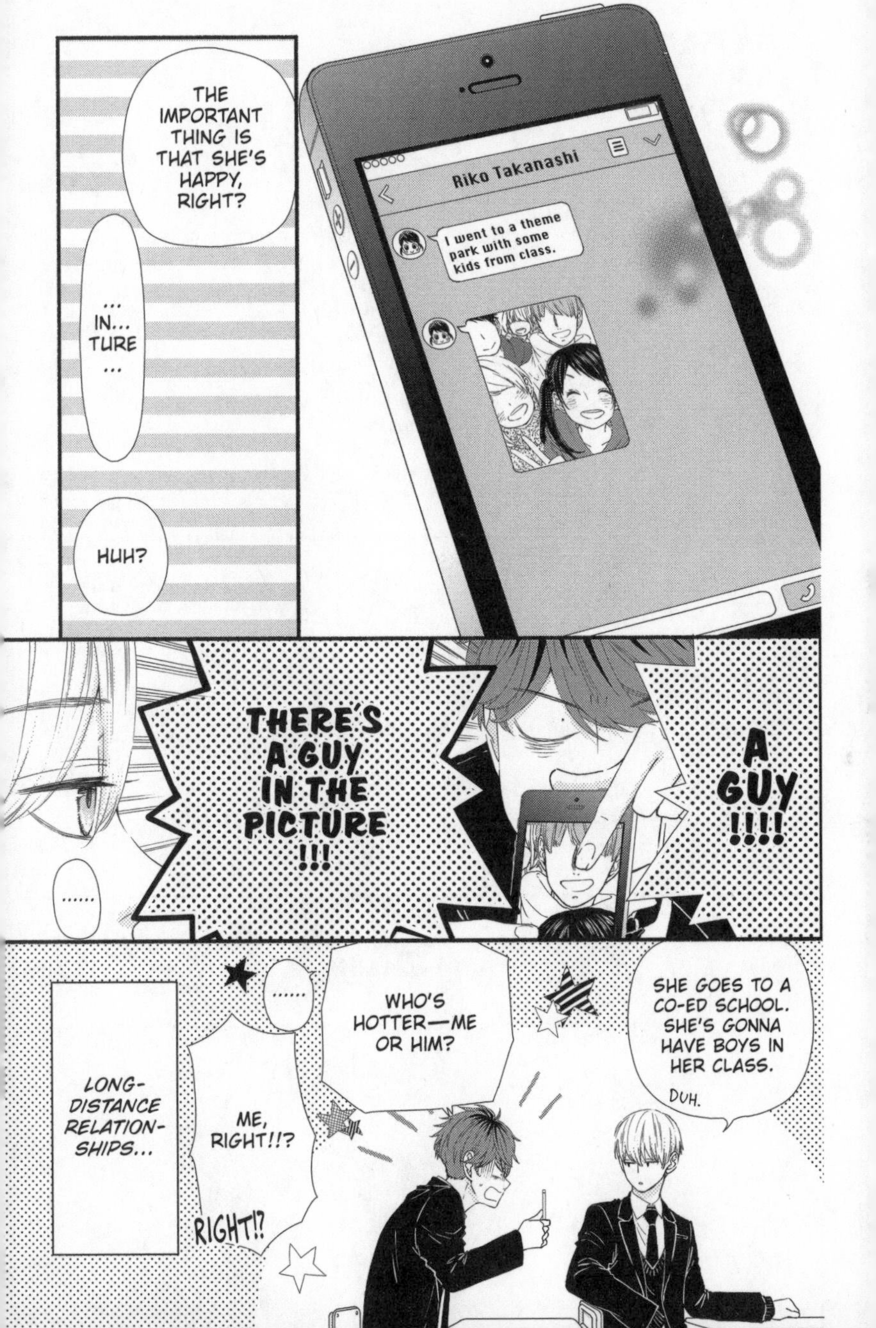
Riko Takanashi
I went to a theme park with some kids from class.
THE IMPORTANT THING IS THAT SHE'S HAPPY, RIGHT?
... IN... TURE ...
HUH?
A GUY!!!!
THERE'S A GUY IN THE PICTURE!!!
......
SHE GOES TO A CO-ED SCHOOL. SHE'S GONNA HAVE BOYS IN HER CLASS.
DUH.
WHO'S HOTTER—ME OR HIM?
......
ME, RIGHT!!?
RIGHT!?
LONG-DISTANCE RELATION-SHIPS...

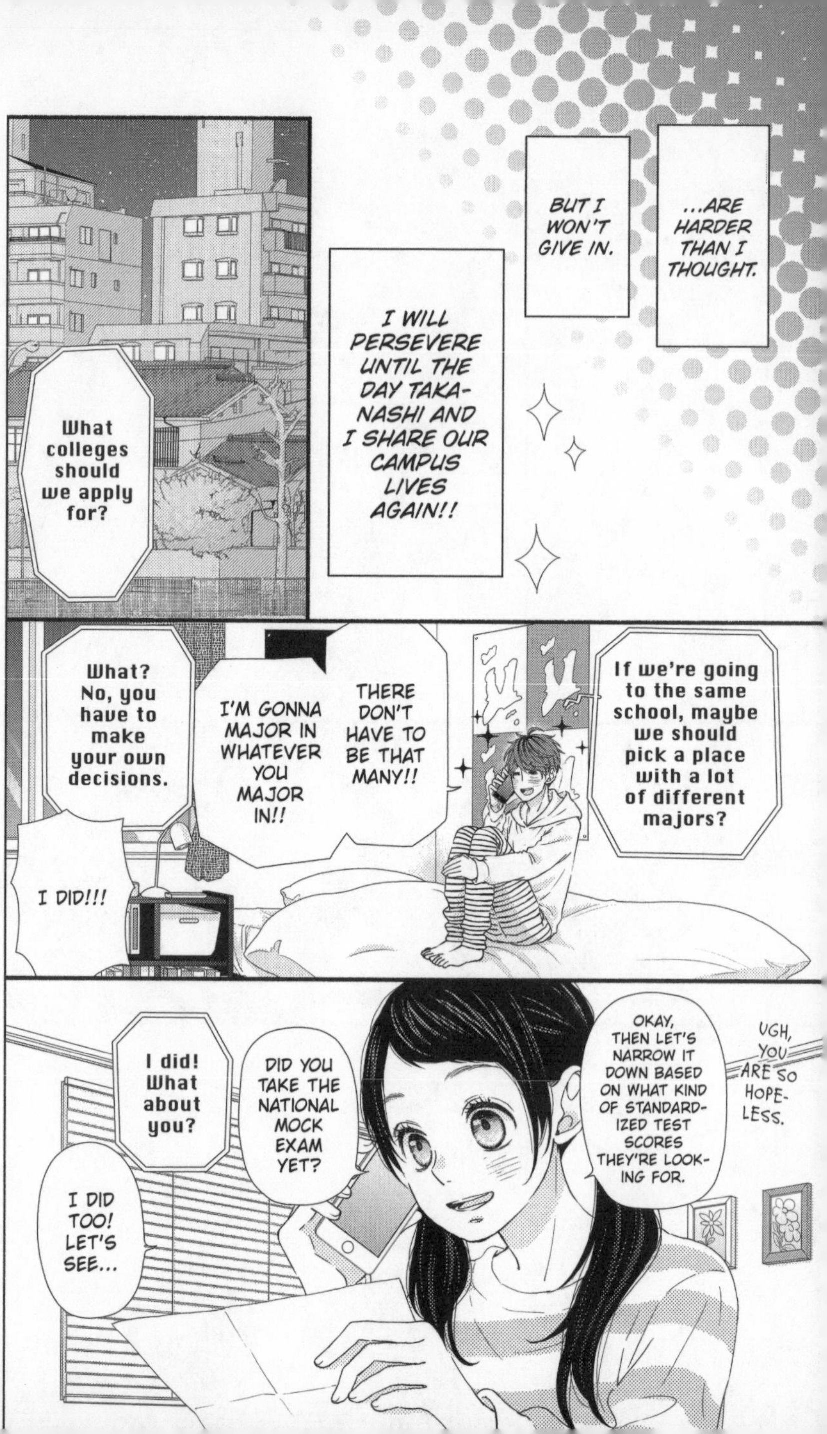
...ARE HARDER THAN I THOUGHT.
BUT I WON'T GIVE IN.
I WILL PERSEVERE UNTIL THE DAY TAKA-NASHI AND I SHARE OUR CAMPUS LIVES AGAIN!!
What colleges should we apply for?
If we're going to the same school, maybe we should pick a place with a lot of different majors?
THERE DON'T HAVE TO BE THAT MANY!!
I'M GONNA MAJOR IN WHATEVER YOU MAJOR IN!!
What? No, you have to make your own decisions.
I DID!!!
UGH, YOU ARE SO HOPE-LESS.
OKAY, THEN LET'S NARROW IT DOWN BASED ON WHAT KIND OF STANDARD-IZED TEST SCORES THEY'RE LOOK-ING FOR.
DID YOU TAKE THE NATIONAL MOCK EXAM YET?
I did! What about you?
I DID TOO! LET'S SEE...

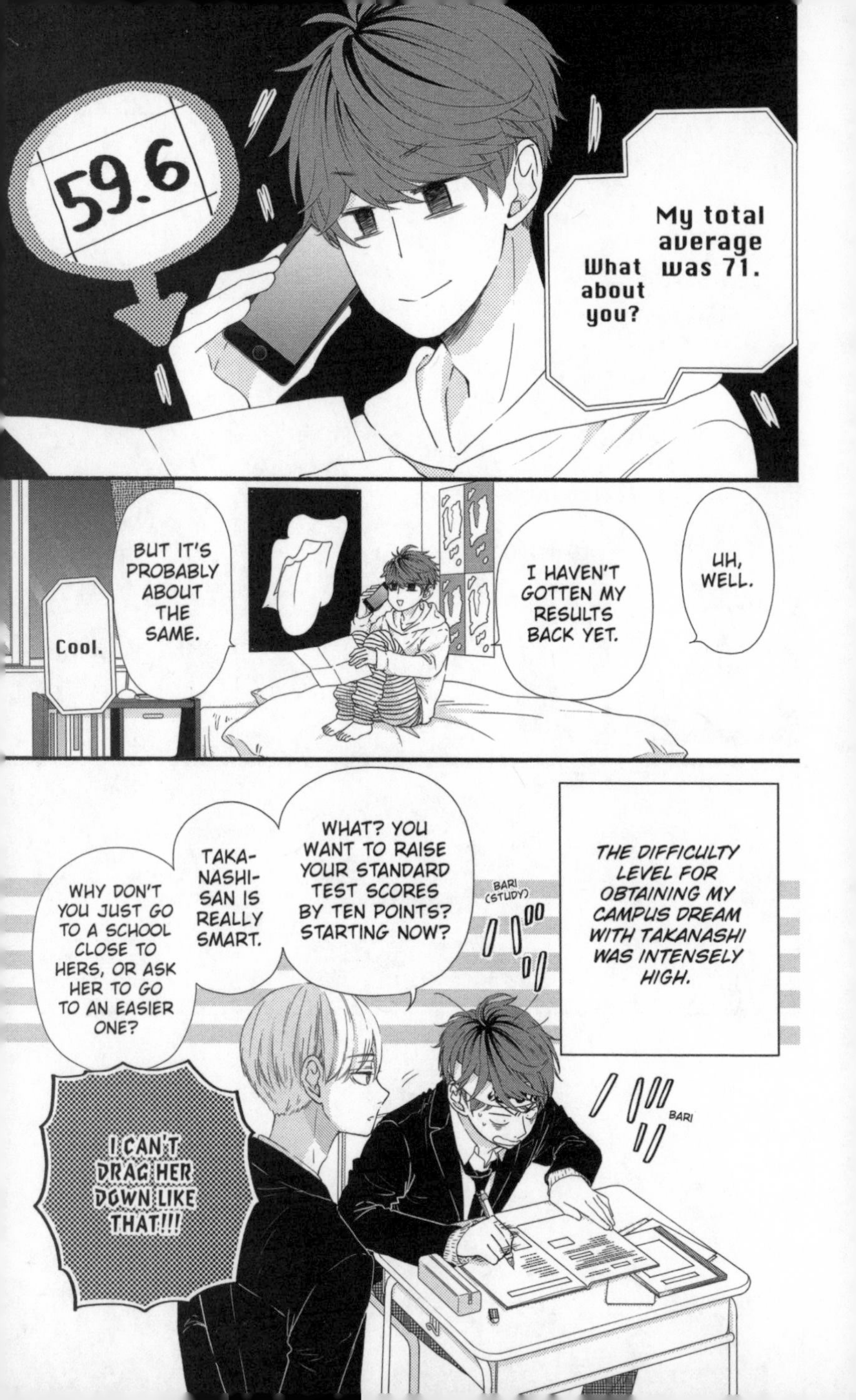
My total average was 71. What about you?
59.6
UH, WELL.
I HAVEN'T GOTTEN MY RESULTS BACK YET.
BUT IT'S PROBABLY ABOUT THE SAME.
Cool.
THE DIFFICULTY LEVEL FOR OBTAINING MY CAMPUS DREAM WITH TAKANASHI WAS INTENSELY HIGH.
BARI (STUDY)
WHAT? YOU WANT TO RAISE YOUR STANDARD TEST SCORES BY TEN POINTS? STARTING NOW?
TAKA-NASHI-SAN IS REALLY SMART.
WHY DON'T YOU JUST GO TO A SCHOOL CLOSE TO HERS, OR ASK HER TO GO TO AN EASIER ONE?
BARI
I CAN'T DRAG HER DOWN LIKE THAT!!!

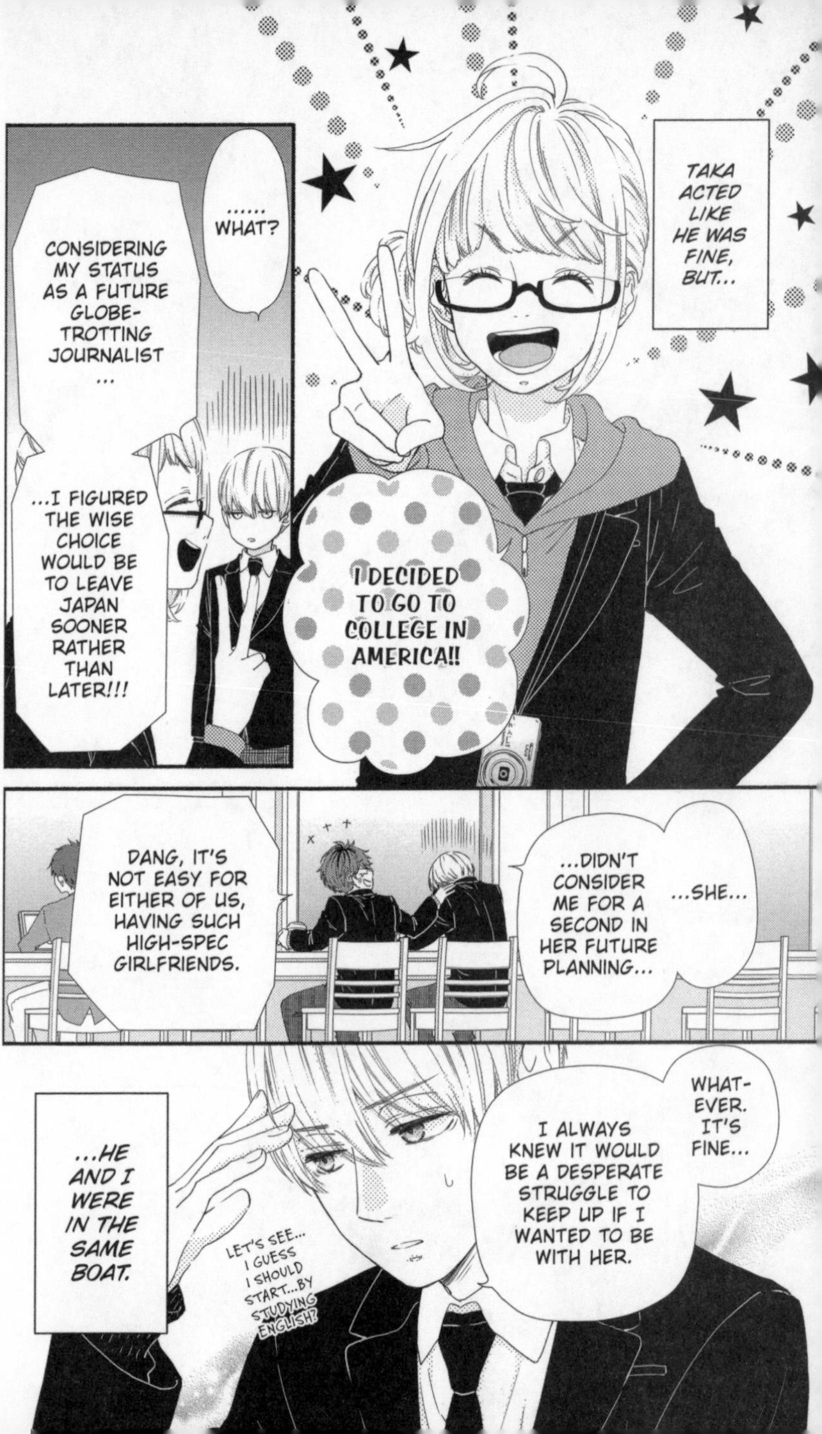
TAKA ACTED LIKE HE WAS FINE, BUT...
I DECIDED TO GO TO COLLEGE IN AMERICA!!
......WHAT?
CONSIDERING MY STATUS AS A FUTURE GLOBE-TROTTING JOURNALIST...
...I FIGURED THE WISE CHOICE WOULD BE TO LEAVE JAPAN SOONER RATHER THAN LATER!!!
...SHE...
...DIDN'T CONSIDER ME FOR A SECOND IN HER FUTURE PLANNING...
DANG, IT'S NOT EASY FOR EITHER OF US, HAVING SUCH HIGH-SPEC GIRLFRIENDS.
WHAT-EVER. IT'S FINE...
I ALWAYS KNEW IT WOULD BE A DESPERATE STRUGGLE TO KEEP UP IF I WANTED TO BE WITH HER.
LET'S SEE... I GUESS I SHOULD START...BY STUDYING ENGLISH?
...HE AND I WERE IN THE SAME BOAT.

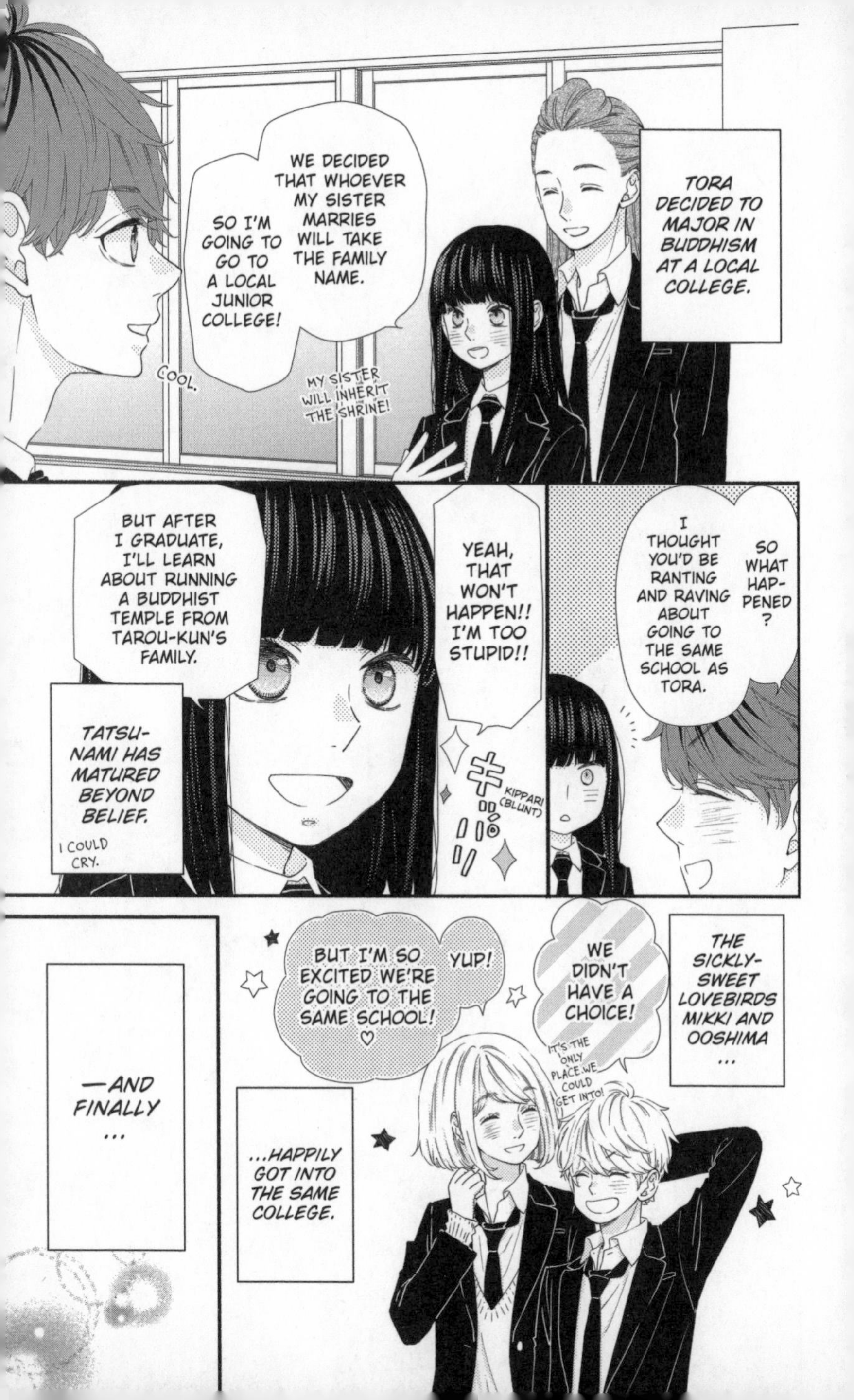
TORA DECIDED TO MAJOR IN BUDDHISM AT A LOCAL COLLEGE.
WE DECIDED THAT WHOEVER MY SISTER MARRIES WILL TAKE THE FAMILY NAME.
SO I'M GOING TO GO TO A LOCAL JUNIOR COLLEGE!
MY SISTER WILL INHERIT THE SHRINE!
COOL.
SO WHAT HAP-PENED?
I THOUGHT YOU'D BE RANTING AND RAVING ABOUT GOING TO THE SAME SCHOOL AS TORA.
YEAH, THAT WON'T HAPPEN!! I'M TOO STUPID!!
KIPPARI (BLUNT)
BUT AFTER I GRADUATE, I'LL LEARN ABOUT RUNNING A BUDDHIST TEMPLE FROM TAROU-KUN'S FAMILY.
TATSU-NAMI HAS MATURED BEYOND BELIEF.
I COULD CRY.
THE SICKLY-SWEET LOVEBIRDS MIKKI AND OOSHIMA ...
WE DIDN'T HAVE A CHOICE!
IT'S THE ONLY PLACE WE COULD GET INTO!
YUP!
BUT I'M SO EXCITED WE'RE GOING TO THE SAME SCHOOL! ♡
...HAPPILY GOT INTO THE SAME COLLEGE.
—AND FINALLY ...

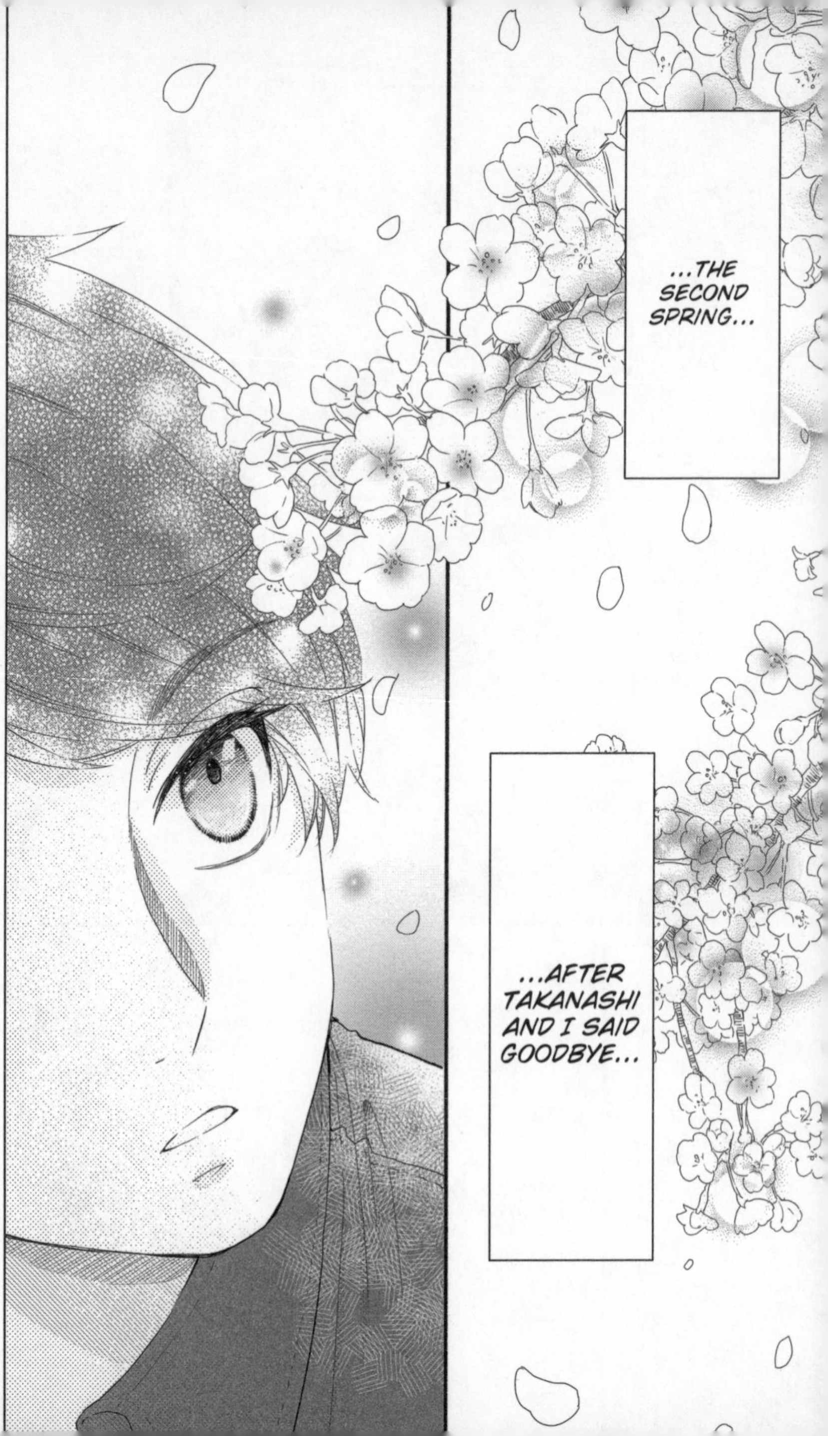
...THE SECOND SPRING...
...AFTER TAKANASHI AND I SAID GOODBYE...

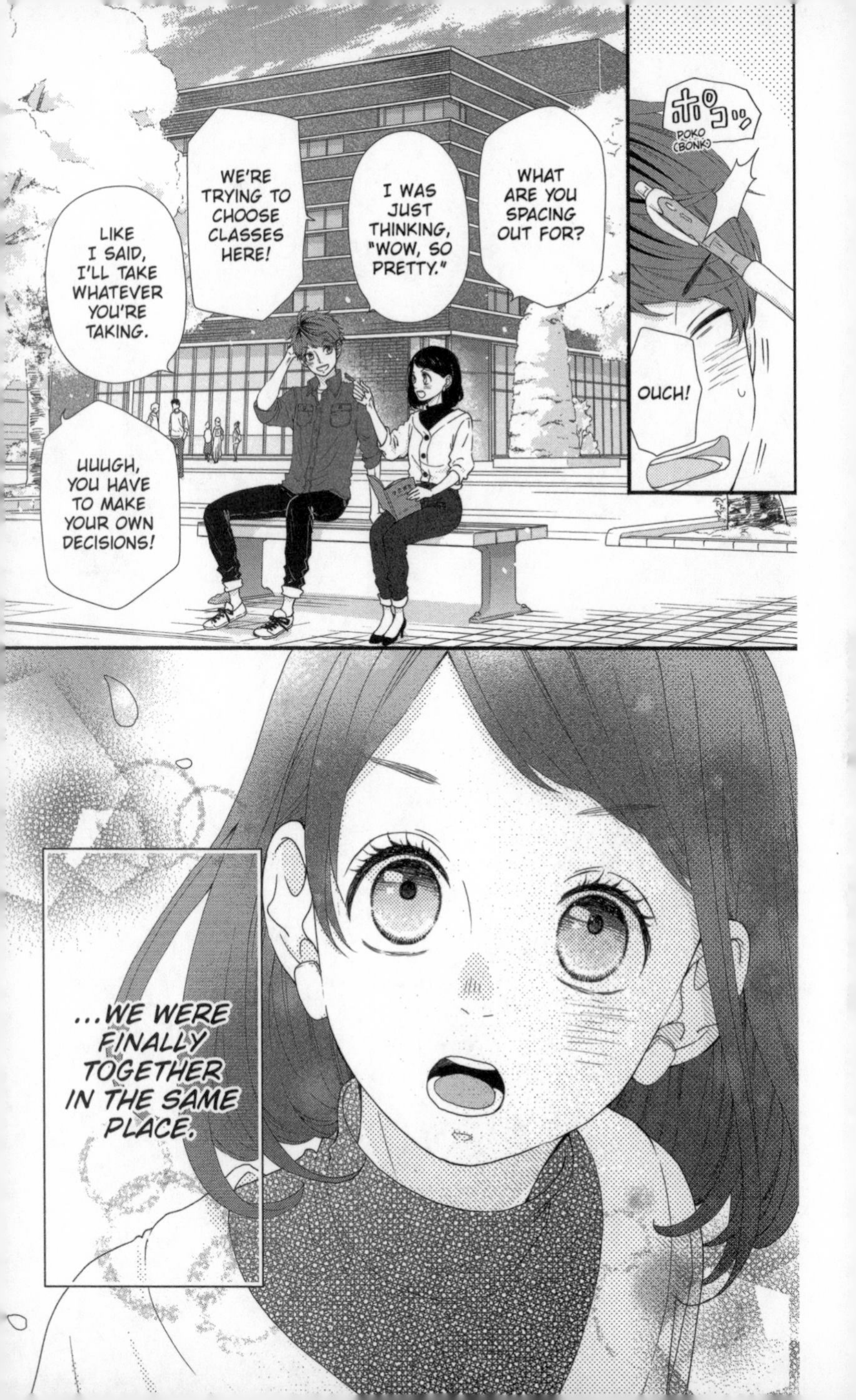
ポコッ
POKO (BONK)
OUCH!
WHAT ARE YOU SPACING OUT FOR?
I WAS JUST THINKING, "WOW, SO PRETTY."
WE'RE TRYING TO CHOOSE CLASSES HERE!
LIKE I SAID, I'LL TAKE WHATEVER YOU'RE TAKING.
UUUGH, YOU HAVE TO MAKE YOUR OWN DECISIONS!
...WE WERE FINALLY TOGETHER IN THE SAME PLACE.

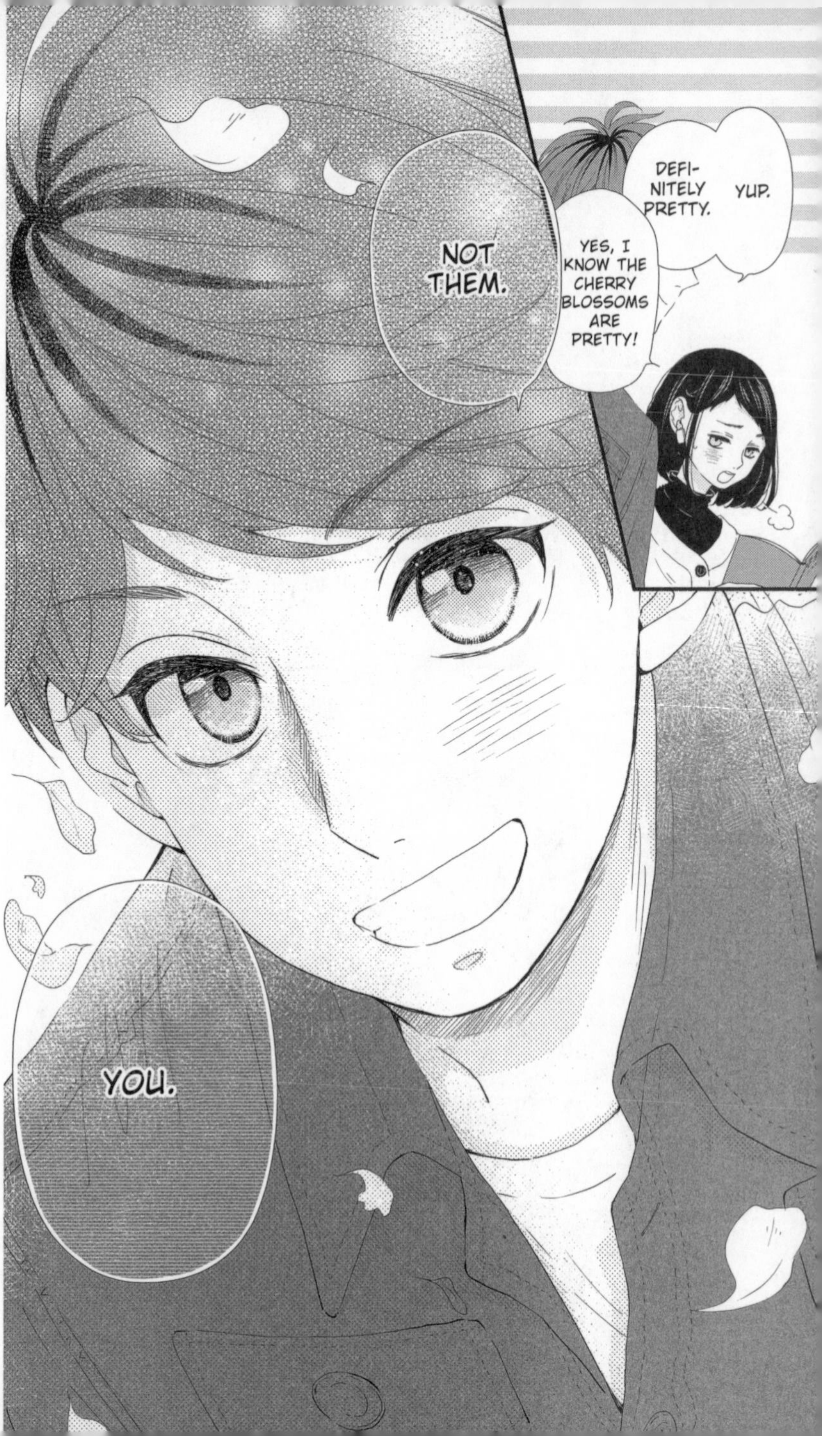
YUP.
DEFI-NITELY PRETTY.
YES, I KNOW THE CHERRY BLOSSOMS ARE PRETTY!
NOT THEM.
YOU.

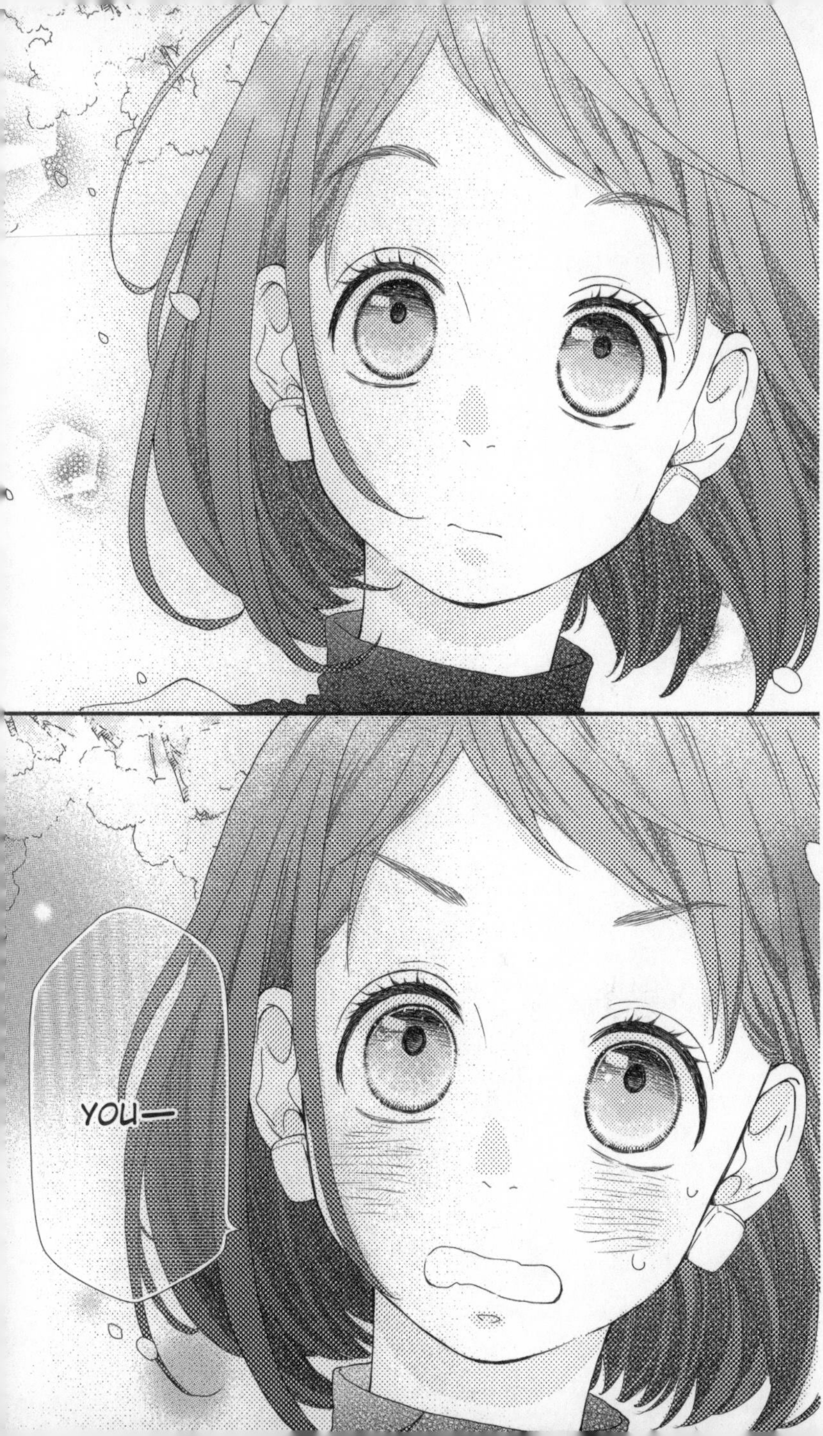
YOU—

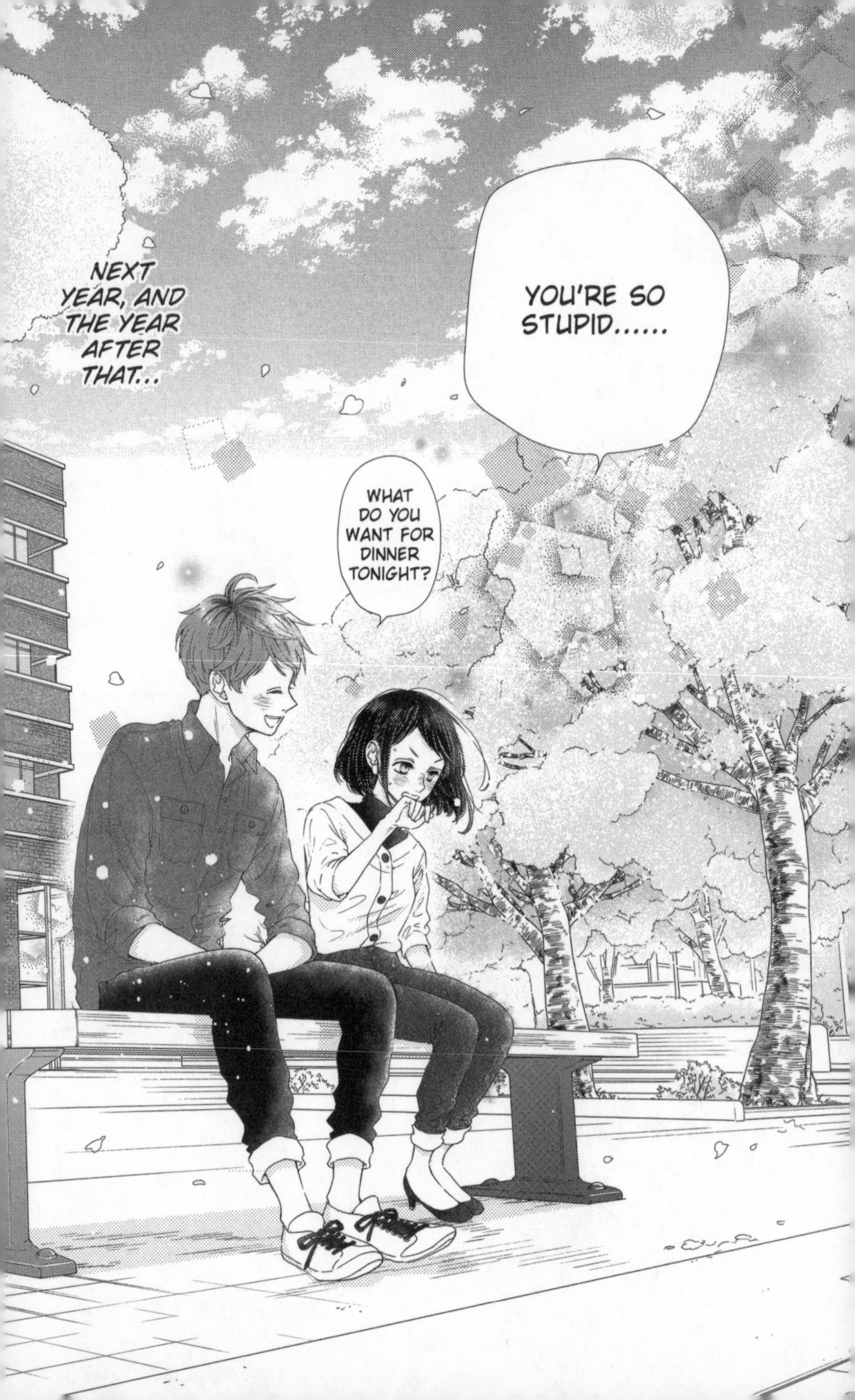
YOU'RE SO STUPID......
WHAT DO YOU WANT FOR DINNER TONIGHT?
NEXT YEAR, AND THE YEAR AFTER THAT...

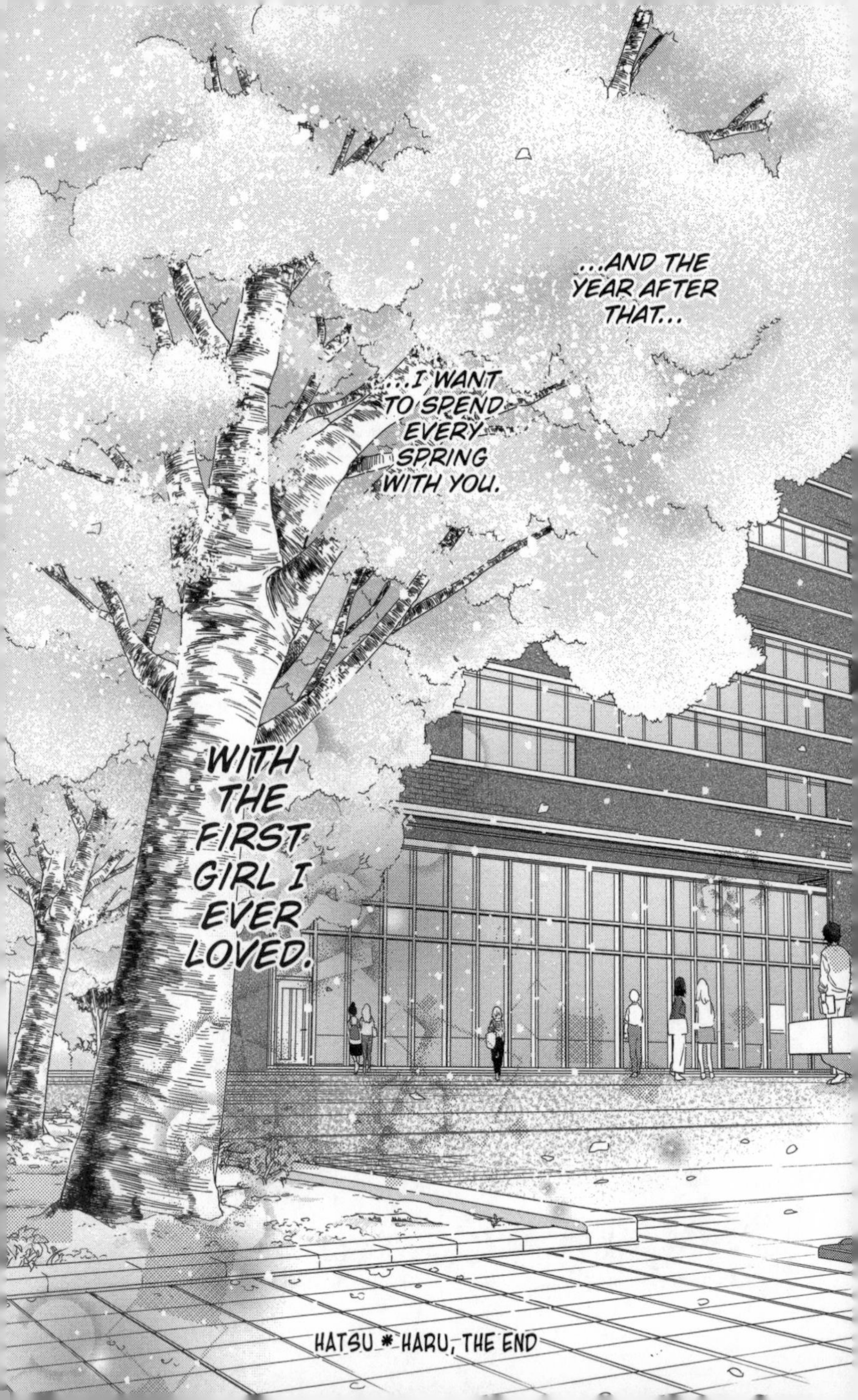
...AND THE YEAR AFTER THAT...
...I WANT TO SPEND EVERY SPRING WITH YOU.
WITH THE FIRST GIRL I EVER LOVED.
HATSU * HARU, THE END

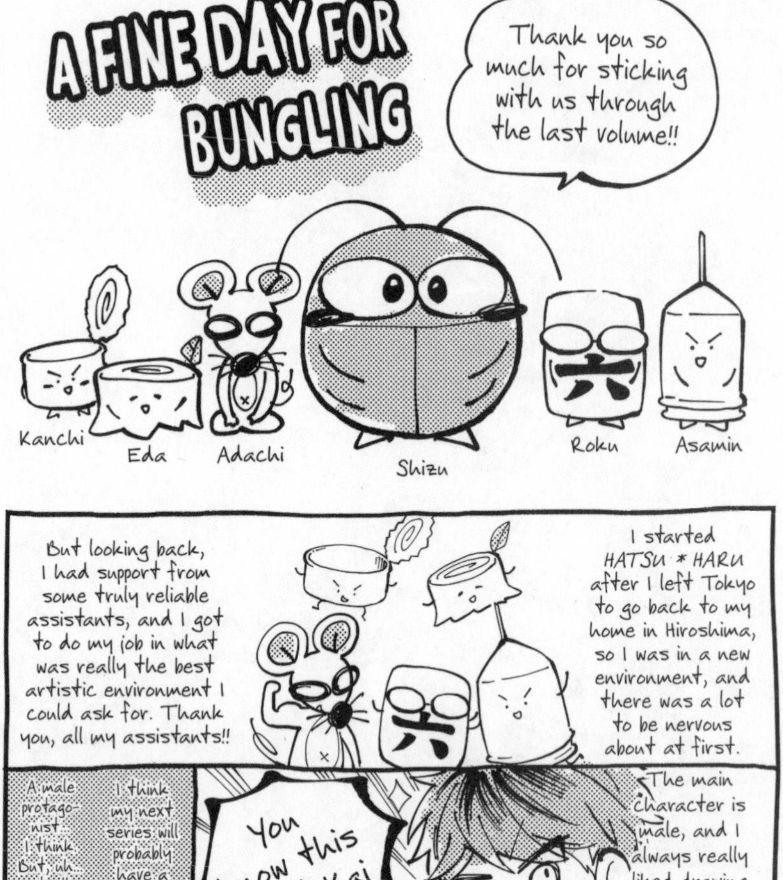
A FINE DAY FOR BUNGLING
Thank you so much for sticking with us through the last volume!!
Asamin
Roku
Shizu
Adachi
Eda
Kanchi
I started HATSU * HARU after I left Tokyo to go back to my home in Hiroshima, so I was in a new environment, and there was a lot to be nervous about at first.
But looking back, I had support from some truly reliable assistants, and I got to do my job in what was really the best artistic environment I could ask for. Thank you, all my assistants!!
The main character is male, and I always really liked drawing cute girls, so I wasn't sure if this was going to work, but I was surprised at how easy it was to draw Kai!
You know this great Kai rocks!!!
What!?
It really is easy to draw idiots, isn't it?
I think my next series will probably have a male protagonist too.
A male protagonist... I think. But, uh... actually, very little is set in stone at the time of this writing.

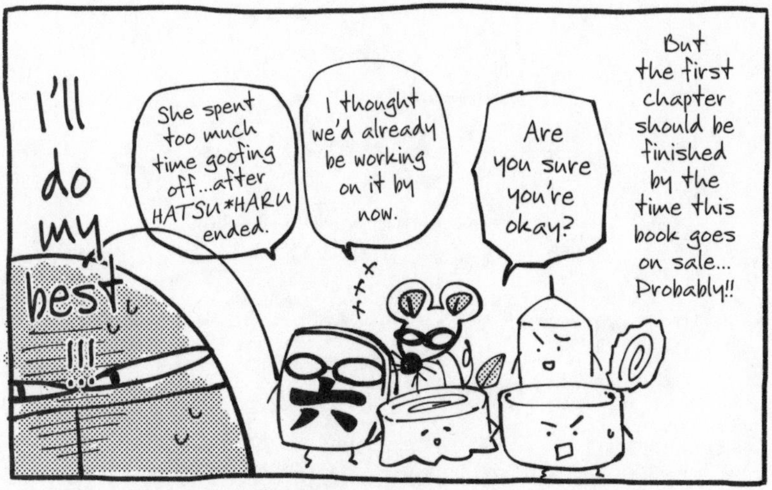
But the first chapter should be finished by the time this book goes on sale... Probably!!
Are you sure you're okay?
I thought we'd already be working on it by now.
She spent too much time goofing off...after HATSU*HARU ended.
I'll do my best!!!

Thank you for sticking with *HATSU * HARU* these four-plus years!! I always wanted to draw a manga with a lot of characters, and I had a lot of fun doing it. It was really hard too, though (ha-ha). Kai and his friends' everyday life will continue on and on, so if the chance comes up, I do hope we get to meet them again.

I'm going to work hard on my new series, so please check it out. I think I want to try a lot of things I haven't tried before!! Well, I hope we meet again. Thank you very much!

Shizuki Fujisawa

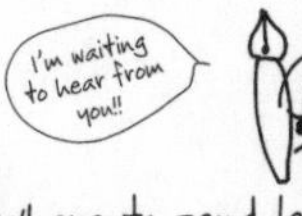
I'm waiting to hear from you!!

Where to send letters:

Yen Press, LLC
150 West 30th Street
19th Floor
New York, NY 10001

web → http://shizukifujisawa.amebaownd.com/

twitter & instagram → shizukifujisawa

hatsu✽haru 13

Shizuki Fujisawa

Translation/Adaptation: **Alethea and Athena Nibley**

Lettering: **Lys Blakeslee**

This book is a work of fiction. Names, characters, places, and incidents are the product of the author's imagination or are used fictitiously. Any resemblance to actual events, locales, or persons, living or dead, is coincidental.

HATSU * HARU Vol. 13 by Shizuki FUJISAWA
© 2014 Shizuki FUJISAWA
All rights reserved.
Original Japanese edition published by SHOGAKUKAN.
English translation rights in the United States of America, Canada, the United Kingdom, Ireland, Australia and New Zealand arranged with SHOGAKUKAN through Tuttle-Mori Agency, Inc.

English translation © 2020 by Yen Press, LLC

Yen Press
150 West 30th Street, 19th Floor
New York, NY 10001

Visit us at yenpress.com ✽ facebook.com/yenpress ✽ twitter.com/yenpress
yenpress.tumblr.com ✽ instagram.com/yenpress

First Yen Press Edition: November 2020

Yen Press is an imprint of Yen Press, LLC.
The Yen Press name and logo are trademarks of Yen Press, LLC.

The publisher is not responsible for websites (or their content) that are not owned by the publisher.

Library of Congress Control Number:
2018935618

ISBNs: 978-1-9753-1744-7 (paperback)
978-1-9753-2257-1 (ebook)

10 9 8 7 6 5 4 3 2 1

WOR

Printed in the United States of America

CITY OF KAWARTHA LAKES